PART I

IN THE BEGINNING

Louis F. Hemsey

The Legend of Justice and Diamonds

XULON PRESS

www.xulonpress.com

TO
TOM + ANGELA,
ENJOY THE READ!
SPREAD THE WORD!
GOD BLESS.

5/2014

The Legend of
Justice and Diamonds

HE Publishing a division of HEntertainment Inc.

Dedicated In Memory

In memory of my beloved sister Annette, who stared cancer squarely in the face and spit on it, battling her illness for six unrelenting years with the strength of ten men, until her death.

In memory of my dearest mother Mary, who after Annette's untimely death, she too died six weeks later, most assuredly mainly of a broken heart.

PROLOGUE

*S*uddenly, *I became aware; aware that I existed. In a flash I had cognition. Before me in majestic splendor, my eyes beheld the Creator. How I knew this, I did not know. I was humbled before him. His presence lit the emptiness around me; I could see the void. A sense of grandeur and perfection engulfed me, yet seemingly, we were alone in a glowing space.*

I looked out into the nothingness and turned to my maker confused. Then, in an instant, I saw it all. . . Creation! I stood in awe.

"You are the first," I heard him say in my mind. "Write what you see."

I turned from my Creator and looked out again across the void. There on the other side, I saw the sphere, a second realm—Earth. But this globe had been created before the Earth to come. . . This was where future had begun. . . The time before time. . . before the second beginning yet to be. How I knew this, again, I did not know; yet of my certainty— of that I was sure.

My name is Acellus, I am the Creator's scribe.

1.

THE SINS

I fixed my gaze and beheld a band of soldiers dressed in strange looking uniforms bearing the words KING OF CLUBS written across the chest. Each soldier wore an ideogram on his shoulder; marking either a 4, 7, 8, 9 or 10. Some of the soldiers rode on horseback while others were on foot. The 4's and 7's carried swords. The 8's and 10's held guns of unexampled shape.

The soldiers forcibly took money and tribute from village farmers; they were a simple people—defenseless. No one would stop them...As I looked throughout this realm, it seemed as though no one could.

After the soldiers left, the stronger of the village people took that which was not theirs from the weaker. They did to their own as the soldiers did to them. Despair ruled the air...It was all around.

Just beyond the parish, looming in the distance, I saw the fortress, The King OF CLUBS' CASTLE: an opulent edifice majestically built, stately and powerful; adorned with riches of every origin inside and out.

As I took in the citadel, I heard the sound of voices—human voices; coming from within the castle's walls. My eyes followed this particular timbre to a secret room hidden deep below the ground. I could see them clearly now — The King of Clubs and The Queen of Spades. . .

"I will have you forever, and you shall be my queen," proclaimed the powerful King of Clubs.

He stood next to his rumpled bed. Fire torches lit the room; their soft light flickering off the walls.

The defiant Queen of Spades shot back, emphatically, "No my King! Either I will have all of you. . . or you shall have no more of me!"

She was captivatingly beautiful, dressed in the finest of silks; her hair black as pure onyx. She turned to The King teasing him with her stance, her body radiating its sensuality.

"You must choose between your wife, the virtuous Queen of Diamonds. . . or me!" continued The Queen.

The King could not take his eyes off of her. With the cunning of a snake, she continued to tease him.

"Very well!" The King burst out, uncontrollably. "I will order her death! It shall be an accident, a tragic accident."

The Queen of Spades purposely turned her back to The King, then slowly looked back over her shoulder. He took in the beauty of her form.

"What of her child. . . your only legitimate heir?" she pressed, ever so carefully.

"What nonsense is this?! He shall be raised here in my castle; he is first in line for the throne!" The King vigorously replied.

"And our son?" she asked, now with the lightness of a dove.

"He will share equally with my first born in all that I possess, once we are married," decreed a somewhat disarmed King.

The Queen of Spades turned and walked toward her King. She stood directly in front of him, her dark eyes pierced into his. . .

"I will be your Queen!"

Possessed by her allure, The King forcibly took his prize into his arms.

The vision before me faded. For but a brief moment; I saw nothing. Then again my eyes did see her, in yet another room, somewhere deep inside the castle.

The Queen of Spades sat at an iron legged wooden table. Across from her, The King's 9 of Clubs sat silently. In the corner, I saw a baby lying in a bassinet. On the table laid a cloth bag, a pitcher, and two gold chalices; one filled with wine, the other empty.

Coyly, she inquired, "Tell me 9. . . do you love money?"

"Don't we all my Queen," the diplomatic 9 replied.

"Not at all 9. . . some crave power rather than wealth," she said, staring hard at him. "And then there are those who hunger for both!"

The 9 gestured with his eyes in silent agreement.

"9. . . you know that I am to be the new queen?" she asked, arching her eyebrows.

The 9 remained stoic. The Queen, impressed by The 9's deftness, coyly smiled.

"Very good 9! However, I know that King has chosen you to kill The Queen of Diamonds!" she said, emphatically.

The Queen slowly walked alongside of him. Her demeanor softened.

"An accident of course" she said.

The 9's eyes again signaled agreement.

"What is to become of her child?" she demanded.

"He is to be brought back here to the castle," answered The 9.

The Queen carefully considered her forthcoming reply, "No 9. . . He too will die!" She picked up the cloth bag from the table. "When you return to me with news of both their deaths. . . the gold in this bag will more than serve as sufficient payment for services rendered." The Queen of Spades looked directly into his eyes, warning, "And your silence!"

The 9 looked at the large bag of gold. His eyes slowly raised to The Queen as he took the bag of gold from her hand, feeling its weight. Calmly, he replied, "The King will never know."

Again, as before, the visions before me began to slowly disappear. My eyes grew heavy, closing for but a moment, or so I thought: for when I reopened them, I saw leagues of rocky hills and beautiful mountains overlooking a desert-like valley below; the air arid and dry. I could feel the heat. I still looked upon the Earth; but in another part of The King's Land. . . known as, "No Man's Land Land—Outlaw Territory."

As I looked harder, I saw him again, The King's 9, riding on horseback, approaching upon a lone deserted dirt road that wound its way up a small peak. In his arms, The 9 held an infant child. Draped across his horse lay two swollen saddlebags. From high up in the hills looking down, a man peered into a spyglass, his face rugged, his countenance savvy. He wore leather gloves that marked the figure 3; the number curiously branded into the hide.

The 3 mounted his horse, skillfully guiding the painted chestnut down the rocky path to the waiting 9. As The 3 neared the bottom, he carefully surveyed The King's 9: taking full notice of his hand resting calmly on his holstered gun. Satisfied, he gestured to the saddlebags. . .

"Lets see the money," The 3 demanded.

The 9 grabbed the double bag from his horse; throwing it to The 3. The outlaw looked in; there were coins made from precious metals. . . Gold and Silver. The 3 nodded his approval and then looked to the child; his eyes lit up as he saw around the infant's neck a leather necklace, holding a great red diamond.

"That stays with him!" snapped The 9. "It's not part of your payment!"

The 3 reluctantly nodded his acceptance.

"Remember, no one is to know he is alive," reaffirmed The 9. "Only I will be back to check on him from time to time!"

The 9 handed the child to The 3 who looked down at the infant's face; the child smiled back up at him. The hardened outlaw softened and couldn't help but smile back.

"What's his name?" the bandit asked.

The King's 9 stood straight in his saddle, preparing his response.

"He is The Jack. . . The Jack OF DIAMONDS!" he proudly proclaimed.

The 3's eyes widened for now he understood. The outlaw silently saluted The 9, acknowledging the gravity of what he had just heard. But I knew what The 3 did not. For The 9's motives, like all those of the ruthless King, lie in his greed. . . not in his honor.

Without a word, the two men turned from each other. The 9 spurred his horse; galloping back across No Man's Land. The 3 slowly guided his horse up the rocky trail, holding the royal child close.

I could see the valley below fill with dust as The 9's mount raced in the distance. The rising earth obscured my eyes. I strained to see clearly but could not; now only hearing voices. I listened attentively, and as I did, I recognized her voice. . . dark and cunning, the voice of The Queen. . . The Queen Of Spades. The dust cleared and I saw them once again in her room, in further conspiracy. . .

"Both The Queen of Diamonds AND The Jack?" scowled The Queen.

"Yes, they are BOTH dead!" replied The 9, teeming with certainty.

The Queen softened, subtly teasing him. . .

"And what did you tell The King?" she eagerly asked.

"That after I had disposed of The Queen of Diamonds, we were attacked on the road back to the castle by a band

17

of outlaws who killed the child and two of my men!" said
The 9.

"And The King did not suspect?" she asked, firmly.

"No my Queen, not after he saw the bodies of the two
dead soldiers I shot; draped over their horses," answered
The 9.

The Queen smiled, a sardonic smile, as if tasting a delicacy. She walked to her infant son lying in his crib and
smiled down to him, intently staring at him. . .

"The Ace of Spades is now the SOLE heir to the throne,"
proclaimed The deceptive 9, seemingly speaking her innermost thoughts.

"You've done very well, 9," she said.

The soldier's chest puffed, as he silently thought his
shrewdness the better. I watched as The Queen of Spades
handed him the empty chalice from the table. As The 9 took
it, his covetous eyes looked to the bag of gold. With the
cunning of a viper, she reached for the pitcher and filled his
chalice. The Queen picked up her chalice, already filled, and
raised her glass to him, saluting.

They both drank; it happened in an instant. The King's
9 frantically grabbed his throat, dropping his chalice to the
floor; the wine flowed red over the stone. The 9 fell dead; the
poison quickly doing its work.

I watched as this woman of beauty slowly extended her
right arm out over the lifeless body of her conspirator. She
seemed to savor the moment in her mind, recalling her sexual
prowess that beguiled The King. And now, the culmination
of her ruthlessness completed, looked down sardonically
smiling, as she poured out her nectar onto the body of The 9.

The dark Queen picked up her child and held him out in
front of her.

"It is done my son. You are my Ace of Spades. . . now
sole heir to the throne! Have no concerns my child. . . Mother
will school you well."

The moment passed and the visions before me disappeared. I stood there recalling all the events that I had observed, wondering as to their meaning or purpose. I turned to my maker silently questioning. . . He smiled back and in that very moment, the entire universe glowed bright white, and then, quickly darkened. Now alone in the void, I took up my quill and opened the first scroll. I began to write, faithfully recording all that I had seen and heard.

With the last vision entered, I waited in the darkness, closing my eyes, knowing there would be more.

2.

THE BOX AND THE POND

As I slept, new visions appeared in my mind. I saw a vast expanse, desolate, covered with layers of snow. Beneath the white powder lay ice: hard shimmering crystal, clear as glass. I could feel the cold, yet I was not there, but I was. My eyes opened. . .

He stood tall, wearing a monk's robe; his face obscured by the cloth. A furious wind blew from every cardinal point, relentlessly pounding him, nearly knocking him to the ground. In his right hand he held a long wooden stick, seemingly defying the elements, using the staff to steady himself. There behind him, I could see a long trail of footprints quickly being covered by the swirling snow. The man seemed to come out of nowhere, purposely heading to a small mountain that stood alone in the middle of this frozen expanse.

I looked again to the vision of the man before my eyes, this time seeing with unconscious understanding. For these beings were called Keepers, and his name—Augustanian. Of that I was certain.

The Keeper reached the base of the mountain, moving directly to an obscure small opening in the rock. Curiously, he turned back for but a moment, cautiously surveying the desolate terrain. Satisfied, Augustanian continued onward, walking through the tiny breach in the rock, entering into the mountain.

Augustanian stood inside a narrow ice tunnel whose frozen walls were more circular than flat. As he walked on the tiny footpath, he bent his head: dodging clusters of hanging ice crystals. After fifty paces, the tunnel opened wide; there before him laid an open precipice revealing a magnificent underground cavern, a secret world hidden within a world. He looked out and downward, his eyes tracing the narrow footpath that wound its way down, deeper and deeper to the cavern floor below; ending at a small structure, almost hidden within the rock below.

The Keeper began his descent. No noise from the outside elements could be heard, save that of his light footsteps and the rhythmic digs of the staff that reflected off the cavern walls. As Augustanian's descent deepened, he came upon two pools of still water, one on each side of the way. The shimmering liquid quietly emitted beautiful refractive light whose source seemed to be the river's bottom. Just around the bend, the pools joined forming a waterfall. The liquid now glowed purple in color as it cascaded down the fitted rock. The sounds of the falling water fused with The Keeper's footsteps and staff: the three becoming one.

Upon reaching the end of the footpath, Augustanian spied a large old wooden door. The hinges were forged of heavy black iron. A yellowed parchment scroll had been nailed to the door. The Keeper walked up to it, spread out the roll and read. . .

Only the hands of a Keeper may open this door. . . Only one of that order may enter this room. All other who happen here either by choice or by chance, turn about your steps now. . . For this room is not yours to enter!

*All those who dare. . . **Fair warning and Farewell.***

Augustanian grabbed the iron handle with both hands and turned it slightly. A gust of air followed by dust laden dirt crept out from the door's frame. The Keeper opened the portal and entered. I watched the door close purposely behind him, its sound echoed off the cavern rock walls; seemingly bearing witness to the event.

Augustanian took only a few steps inside and surveyed the cryptic room. My eyes beheld a domed room of unusual geometric shape with walls formed by large blocks of stone, precisely fit together. Fragmented rays of dim light radiated down from the ceiling center-stone, focusing on a lone wooden table and high backed chair. Resting on the edge of the table, lay a small box ornately covered with precious stones embedded into the lid. The rays from the light sparkled off the jewel laden box into the open space.

To the right of Augustanian, a closed book laid on a waist high burnt iron stand. Attached to the stand on its right, sat a vessel of ink housed in small flat iron bands. From inside the well, jutted out a single writing quill.

The Keeper approached the book and opened it. As he did so, I read its title—

THE KEEPERS OF THE TAROT.

Augustanian opened the book to the last entry. He took the quill and carefully dipped it into the ink and wrote:

The Keeper Augustanian—During the sixth year's reign of the first KING OF CLUBS.

Augustanian walked to the table and sat. Ever so carefully, he reached for the enigmatic box and slid it across the table, stopping in front of him. The granite walls of the empty room amplified the sound of the wooded box as it moved across the table.

The Keeper lifted the jewel laden lid and I saw a silken sachet purse with tiny drawstrings. Augustanian reached in and held the purse carefully in his hands. He loosened the strings, reached in, and removed a deck of cards ornate with pictures and symbols.

The Keeper took the first card from the deck and placed it on the table. I saw an Angelic being with wings, yet with the likeness of a man, dressed in a white robe, holding two chalices in hand pouring water from one to the other. Written along the bottom, the card's name: TEMPERANCE. Augustanian placed that card in the center of the table. The card bore the numeral XIV.

The next two cards were similar to each other in that they were like that of a King and Queen, regally dressed, each sitting on a throne. Written on the card of The Queen, the name: THE EMPRESS. . . it bore the figure III. The name on The King's card: THE EMPEROR, its number—IV. The Keeper placed the royal couple directly under the Temperance card.

Augustanian stared at the three-card formation for a brief moment; then took the next card from the deck and placed it on the table. I saw the likeness of the Sun glowing brightly, its name and image the same; the card's number—XIX. The Keeper placed this card, the card of THE SUN, below the Empress and Emperor.

Carefully, Augustanian dealt the next card; it was completely blank. He placed this faceless card below that of The Sun and then leaned back, looking down at the card formation on the table.

The Keeper's fingers barely touched the back of the next card in the deck. He mindfully dealt this card face down, strategically placing it next to the blank card.

Augustanian again took the next card from the deck, keeping it face down, and reached out over the center of the table. Skillfully, he slowly let this card slip out of his fingers, falling to the table face up. There, right above the TEMPERANCE card, I saw the card of THE HERMIT. The picture was that of an old man in a monk-like robe holding a staff in his hand: the image struck a similar resemblance to The Keeper, yet different. The Hermit's number—IX.

Augustanian looked kindly to the formation, very subtly shaking his head in approval and understanding.

Then. . . I saw him! Not the image. . . but The Hermit himself!

#

He sat upon a large rock intently staring into a small pond. The Hermit stirred the waters with his staff which had the same number IX carved at the top. He wore a robe, long and frayed; his face bore the marks of years of forethought. . .

I looked around and saw flourishing greenery abound. There were beautiful trees, flowers, plants and little creatures of all types. A sweet fragrance filled the air: warm and inviting. I marveled at the magnificence of my Creator. . . My eyes began to tear, but I did not feel sadness. To the contrary. . . wonder filled me.

I began to feel many new qualities and attributes all around me, yet all my eyes beheld in front of me—The Hermit. His traits were strong, radiating outward. I could feel his prudence, good judgment, his forethought; I felt his wisdom. But yet, I still sensed other qualities not ascribed to The Hermit. I seemed to be in another realm different from that of The Keeper. Then it became clear. . . I had found the place where human attributes, qualities, and virtues existed, the third realm—<u>The Forest Of Cards</u>.

I quickly wrote all that I saw.

As I paused from my record, again I heard their voices! They were coming out from The Hermit's pond. I looked in to see, just as The Hermit had done, and there in the center of the water, I saw the image of The King of Clubs' castle.

I watched The Hermit again stir the waters: staring more determined than before. I could see clearly now, just as before. . . The King of Clubs and The Queen of Spades!

As their voices grew louder, disdain and contempt crossed The Hermit's face. At first I did not understand and then I began to feel. I soon realized what The Hermit had reacted to. . . EVIL!

I knew he was preparing to do battle with it! Quickly and faithfully, I wrote all that I saw as well as what I now felt.

The Pond's images faded and then disappeared; the waters now reflecting back only the pensive face of Prudence. The Hermit turned suddenly, seemingly knowing someone was approaching; I too could sense it. Nothing seemed to move, as if The Forest had died. Then I saw him coming into the clearing—DEATH.

He sat on a magnificent pale white horse, wearing black armor covering his entire body. In his hand, Death held a banner which bore the image of a red and white mystic rose. In the upper corner of the banner, his number—XIII.

Death lifted the eyepiece of his helmet, his cold empty eyes were barely visible. The Hermit looked up to him, boldly. . .

"Your master, the Prince of Darkness, has grown very strong. . . and by what I've seen," The Hermit gestured to The Pond. "You serve him well," said Wisdom.

"This is only the beginning, Hermit. Soon, ALL who live in The King's Land on the Earth will serve us or DIE. . . We have won!" boasted Evil.

The Hermit stood steadfast, not giving an inch.

"Death, All darkness, no matter how strong, is always overcome by the light! Take these words to your master," instructed The Hermit, with unwavering affirmation.

"How can one who possesses wisdom, now speak so foolishly? There is no card of Light in The Forest!" Death joyously proclaimed.

"All in good time Death. . . All in good time," portended The Hermit.

I could tell Death had been caught off guard by The Hermit's cryptic response.

"Then, we shall see, Hermit, if this Light of yours can overcome the powers of DARKNESS!" Death challenged, arrogantly.

The Hermit stood firmly.

"Indeed we shall. . . for this is but the first of many encounters yet to come," The Hermit said, with certainty.

Death stared down at a steadfast Hermit. Then he turned and flipped his visor back down over his eyes, slowly riding off back into the dense forest.

As I watched all unfold, a bitter cold had come over me; a freeze I had not been aware of—until Death had gone. I faithfully recorded all that I had observed.

#

Augustanian sat in his underground chamber room staring at the card formation on the table. Somehow I felt that he and The Hermit were one, yet they existed in different realms; but how they were connected, I did not know.

I watched as The Keeper placed his left hand on the card of THE EMPEROR and his right hand on the card of THE EMPRESS. He carefully slid the two toward each other till they just touched.

Then his slid the card of TEMPERANCE down until it touched both THE EMPEROR and THE EMPRESS cards equally. I carefully observed him slide the card of THE SUN up till it barely touched the bottom of THE EMPEROR and THE EMPRESS.

With a sense of purpose, The Keeper raised his right hand, his fist clenched. He held it still in the air for a moment and then brought it down to the table, holding his fist over the

Blank Card. I watched him extend his index finger, pointing it straight at the card with no face. Slowly, he touched this card with the tip of his finger. As he did so, I now saw a ring, formed of gold, molded around a beautiful purple stone. The Keeper touched the jewel ring to the blank card for but a moment. Then—it happened.

I marveled as the faceless card transformed into a new card, the card of Justice, THE LADY JUSTICE: its image that of a young beautiful female, bearing the number XI.

I don't know why, but I became keenly aware of feelings that were pleasing to my being—I felt pure. I dutifully wrote what I saw.

3.

THE JOURNEY

The Hermit walked alone in The Forest holding a small iron lantern suspended on a black chain. The lamp had been fashioned with five small panes of glass that housed a tiny lit candle. It seemed odd to me, but I felt The Hermit regarded the object as one would an old friend. . .

"There is much to be done. . . now we must seek out Temperance," he said.

#

The young man dressed oddly, yet elegant. On his head, he wore a three-pointed cap bearing the number 0. He seemed perplexed, not knowing where he was going, as he mindlessly sauntered up and down the low rise hills along The Forest of Cards' inner pathway; tall picturesque trees lined his way. The youthful gentleman feverishly looked over his shoulders as if he had lost something. His hands, out of sync with his head, patted his front pockets, repeatedly. His name—THE FOOL.

"My wallet! Where is my wallet? I know I put it somewhere. . . or did I?" he spoke into the air, his gaze now captured by the cloud formations in the sky. "Oh what a lovely day," The Fool mused. Again, he looked over his shoulders, more confused than before. "Now where is my. . ."

While still in mid word, the young man mindlessly skipped off an eight foot precipice. The Fool fell to the ground rolling head over heels, screaming a high pitch yelp as he tumbled down the embankment. His fall came to a stop directly in front of The Hermit's feet. Somewhat shaken, he looked up. . .

"Oh Hermit! I'm so glad it's you!" he said, purposefully. The Hermit extended his hand to him, helping him up. "Did you see him?! Did you see who pushed me?!" The Fool demanded. "Where was he? How did he do it?!"

The Hermit calmly ignored his questions.

"I trust you are alright?" The Hermit inquired.

The Fool dusted himself off.

"Well then, who was it? Tell me! Tell me, Hermit!" The Fool demanded, paying no mind to The Hermit, as he continued to haphazardly fuss about. Then the young man straightened up and looked straight into The Hermit's eyes demanding yet again, "Hermit, I beg you, you must tell me!"

"I have known you for many years, yet in all that time. . . you still have not learned," The Hermit said, with kindness.

The young man held The Hermit's gaze.

"Learned what?" The Fool said, momentarily contemplating his words. Then he burst out as before, "Where was he hiding? Did you see him jump from a tree!?"

The Hermit ignored his outbursts, again trying to instruct him.

"You still have not learned to look where your life is going, but instead. . . choose to dwell on where it has been," Prudence said, softly. The Hermit carefully measured his forthcoming words. "Mindlessness and folly will always lead one to a fall," he humbly decreed.

The Fool's eyes widened, reflecting on The Hermit's wisdom. Then again, as before. . .

"I beg you Hermit, did you see him!? Tell me his name! Who was it that pushed me!?" ranted The Fool.

"He is known as The Fool," the resigned Hermit replied.

The capricious Fool belly laughed, doubling over, holding his stomach.

"No matter. . . I'm sure I shall meet up with him down the road. So long Hermit!" The Fool replied, oblivious to the insight.

The carefree lad scampered off again looking over his shoulders while he continually patted his pockets. The Hermit stood by watching.

"I'm sure you will," replied The Hermit, shaking his head in disbelief.

#

The sky grew dim in The Forest of Cards. The wooded realm now radiated light from both the setting Sun and the rising Moon, each bisecting the other on their celestial paths; I felt at peace.

He came out from a nearby cluster of dense trees: tall, angelic, dressed in a white robe; wearing two golden chalices hanging from his waist cinch. I knew his name, I had seen it on The Keeper's cards: TEMPERANCE—his number, XIV. For the first time, I saw The Hermit smile.

I wrote as my Creator had instructed; ever mindful to vigilantly record all that I had seen. With each passing moment my curiosity deepened. I felt humanity more.

The younger Temperance hurried to The Hermit.

"It is good to see you my old friend, very good indeed!" Temperance said, as he wrapped his arms around him.

After a brief moment, Temperance oddly pulled back from the embrace.

"Your spirit weighs heavy with concern."

"There is much I must tell you," said a grave Hermit.

Temperance gestured to a fallen tree and the two friends walked over and sat; his gaze now locked on The Hermit. . .

"The evil one grows more powerful each day. The Pond now reflects the terrible wickedness of The King of Clubs' rule of the Earth," said Foresight.

"The King has fully embraced the ways of death?" asked Temperance.

"Yes, but not just The King. . . All of his soldiers and many of his subjects now too follow the ways of darkness. With each new cycle, more and more are deceived," The Hermit grimly replied.

Temperance removed the two gold chalices from his waistband. He held them out in front of him and then looked to the sky in fervent meditation. He raised one chalice high up over the other, and then poured. Out of nowhere, clear water flowed from the higher cup into the lower. The Hermit watched intently as Temperance repeated the pour three times, alternating one to the other.

"There is no harmony. . . the balance has gone!" exclaimed Temperance. "This cannot be!" The Hermit mindfully nodded his agreement. "Tell me Hermit, what must be done?!" Temperance implored.

"You and I shall help bring about Justice and Light. This new light will restore the balance," The Hermit assuredly replied.

"A new CARD in The Forest?" asked a bewildered Temperance.

"Yes Temperance, It will be the card of JUSTICE. . . THE LADY JUSTICE," proclaimed The Hermit.

"What qualities will she reflect?" asked Temperance.

"She will *possess* moral strength, integrity. . . pureness of heart and. . ."

A confused Temperance cut off The Hermit.

"You said *possess* not reflect. . . How can this be?" he demanded.

The Hermit affectionately smiled.

"I will tell you all as we journey," said The Hermit.

I saw a queried look cross Temperance's face. The Hermit knew what his trusted friend was thinking; I did as well.

Then, with the boldness of a seasoned warrior, The Hermit dramatically extended his arm outward, pointing to a faint location way off on the distant horizon, in the direction of the setting Sun.

"There!," he shouted. "To the other side of The Forest where Jupiter and Juno dwell."

"The Emperor and Empress?" exclaimed a shocked Temperance.

"Yes. First you must bring about their union of LOVE under THE SUN," The Hermit paused so Temperance could fully comprehend. "Then. . ."

An understanding Temperance smiled in silent amazement at his old friend. He put the two chalices back on his waist cinch and nodded his approval.

I watched as the two Virtues now walked as one in purpose; journeying to the far side of The Forest. I wrote all that I saw. . . All that I felt.

PART II

BLOODLINES

4.

TWENTY FIVE YEARS LATER

As I completed recording the visions, I pulled my gaze off of the Earth. In my mind's ear I heard the voice of my Creator. His words filled my being with love. He knew all that I wanted to ask: there were so many questions. The firmament glowed brighter, my uneasiness lessened.

When I turned back to see, all had changed! In an instant, The King's Land waxed full. There were more villages, more people; there were new things all around. I now realized that in the flash of an eye, time had gone by. Years. . . twenty five Earth years to be exact! How I knew this, I could not say. But I dutifully marked the passage of this time in the scroll.

#

I saw a young man riding on horseback in No Man's Land; his face bruised and cut. The skies above him ripped streaks of red clouds across the horizon. I watched as he crossed into outlaw territory; its majestic hills rising in front of him. The young man nervously looked right and left as he approached the base of the mountain canyon path.

With a sense of trepidation, he started the dangerous climb up the rocky mountain trail. The air cooled; it felt good on his face, soothing his bruises. I felt as he did, a growing apprehension.

As the stranger reached the halfway point in his ascent, he turned to look back out over the valley. There looming off in the distance, he saw The King of Clubs' castle. It stood defiantly on the horizon; its mere existence threatening to behold, dominating the being of all who dared to hold its gaze. The resolute young man reached deep within himself, determined to overcome his fears as he urged his horse onward, spurring him gently.

In an instant, the stranger's horse flinched, startled by The 3 who rode out from behind a large boulder, blocking his way. The outlaw carried a rifle pointed at the lad. The 3 looked different, he had aged. His face bore the reflection of a man in his fifth decade. The 3 still wore the leather gloves branded with the number 3.

"You have 10 seconds to give me a good reason why I should let you live!" The 3 demanded.

"Don't shoot! I have money!" The lad quickly blurted out, then taking in a breath. "My name is Kellin. I came to see The Jack, The Jack of Diamonds!" shaking as he answered.

The 3 carefully surveyed Kellin, and seeing that he had come unarmed, put down his rifle.

"Who sent you and what business do you have for The Jack?" The 3 pressed.

"No one sent me. I came on my own. I come seeking justice which I cannot get from The King," explained Kellin.

The 3 sarcastically laughed as he shook his head. . .

"Well you're right about The King. . . there's no justice to be found there," The 3 said, with a smirk. The 3's tone encouraged Kellin.

"However, The Jack does not *give* justice. The Jack doesn't even *care* about justice. But if the price is right, The Jack will *right* any wrong you may have suffered, or if you like—*wrong* any one who is right!" mused The 3.

Young Kellin's countenance fell, his anger stirred.

"I *told* you, I brought *money*. . . lots of money!" Kellin lashed back.

The 3 hardened, his eyes ripped into Kellin.

"For your sake, I hope you have," warned The 3, as he pointed to an obscure path behind the boulder. "This way." The outlaw kicked his horse leading Kellin deeper into the hills. I watched them both until they disappeared from my sight.

#

A small share of time had passed that I could not account for; I knew this as the rays of the burnt orange Sun had moved further to their set. Without warning, nature railed harsh, swirling dust in every direction. Her wind blew raw, smashing the flying dirt into the eyes of both men. Kellin and The 3 fought hard to maintain their mounts as they shielded their eyes from the blinding sand.

Then nature relented, as fast as it had begun. The men stopped to clear their vision. . .

"How much further?" asked Kellin.

"We're here," said The 3.

Kellin looked around and saw no one: only hills and rock that surrounded a clearing. Oddly, standing in the middle of the open space, Kellin saw a lone wooden post sticking six cubits up out of the ground. He could not help but notice the many bloodstains scattered about the wood. The 3 jumped off his horse and tied it to nearby sagebrush.

"Well!?" demanded The 3.

Kellin shrugged his shoulders, grabbed the saddlebags and jumped from his horse. He tied his horse and followed The 3 as he walked toward a huge rock edifice some fifty cubits in front of them.

"Remember, don't speak a word til' you're spoken to!' warned The 3.

Then before my eyes, an opening appeared within the side of the mountain. I saw a huge door, cut from the mountain rock, revealing a tunnel. The two men passed through the door into the tunnel, entering the hideout of The Jack of Diamonds.

As soon as they were inside, the door closed, seemingly on its own. Their eyes had to adjust to the dark. At first, the men could not stand fully upright, then the tunnel widened as it descended.

Kellin saw someone approaching from below carrying a torch. The firelight revealed the face of a woman, an exotic woman, young and well shaped: she moved with nature. The woman looked to The 3, and then guardedly at Kellin.

"Lena, where is he?" said The 3. "This is business."

"Follow me," replied Lena.

Lena turned and walked back down the dark corridor heading to a lower level of the hideout. She stopped in front of a door and then motioned to the entry with her head. The resolute 3 opened the door and went in first, followed by Kellin. Once the men were inside, Lena shut the door and left.

The outlaw led Kellin to a round stone table surrounded by five wooden chairs. Standing at the head of the table facing the two men—The Jack of Diamonds. He stood tall, his hair dark, his face chiseled to perfection: Diamonds wore black: his age, two decades and seven. Still circled around his neck, lay the leather necklace holding the large red diamond.

Young Kellin, uneasy, had been unnerved by Diamonds' gaze. He looked away and took notice of the many strange weapons hanging on the walls. There were swords and guns of various sizes, most of which were unusual in shape. Then Kellin looked back to The Jack, as if compelled by an unseen force; the young man stood silent.

Diamonds turned quizzically to The 3 who skeptically smiled back. . .

"He comes seeking justice," stated The 3.

The Jack looked hard at Kellin.

"What's your name?" The Jack demanded.

Grasping for courage, Kellin replied, "My name is Kellin."

"Well Kellin. . . you've made it this far," Jack mused. "Now state your business," continued the cynical Jack.

"As The 3 said, I come seeking justice! The King's soldiers come to our village every three months demanding more tribute than we can pay, we are poor!" Kellin explained, pausing to gain his courage.

"Go on," said The Jack.

"Now after paying tribute only two weeks past, they have come back yet again and taken what little money we had left!"

"So The King is greedy, we're all greedy," said an unsympathetic Jack.

Kellin, upon hearing The Jack's indifferent response, stiffened.

"After the soldiers took all of our money, one of the thugs, he is called TULL, came into our hut and took the last of our food!" pressed young Kellin.

I could see, as The 3 did, The Jack's growing impatience.

"My brother and I fought with him, but we are not strong. The King's soldiers stood by and did nothing. They watched in amusement as Tull killed my brother in front of his wife and infant child; they cheered the ogre on!" Kellin slammed his fist on the table.

The Jack carefully took in Kellin's sudden outburst.

"I want JUSTICE!" a righteous Kellin demanded.

The Jack snapped back, "No Kellin, you seek REVENGE! But make no mistake," said The Jack, firmly pointing his finger at Kellin. "It doesn't matter to me, as long as there's money to be made!"

Undeterred, Kellin quickly opened his saddlebags and emptied twenty gold coins on the table. He looked boldly up to The Jack.

"How much justice will this buy?" Kellin said, sarcastically.

The Jack smirked. "Only enough to kill this Tull, as for The King's men, it will cost ten times as much," replied an unimpressed Jack.

Kellin's countenance fell. The 3 stood by somewhat perplexed, as he stared at the gold coins on the table.

"Kellin, you told me The King's men took ALL of your money?" asked The 3.

"Yes!" Kellin answered.

"If that's true, then where did you get all this gold?" The 3 challenged.

"I stole it from the same soldiers who let my brother die! That night after they drank themselves into a stupor, I lifted this saddlebag right from their hands," Kellin said.

The 3 smiled at The Jack.

"Well Kellin, just for that, I'll kill this thug of yours and two of The King's men to boot!" said an impressed Jack.

"When?" asked Kellin, anxiously.

"All in good time Kellin. . . The 3 will escort you back," said the dismissive Jack.

The 3, seeing that Kellin was about to question The Jack further, quickly grabbed Kellin's shoulder.

"We must leave now, before Sundown."

An understanding Kellin turned and followed The 3. On their way out, Lena entered and looked to The 3.

"We're done," said The 3, answering her unspoken question.

Lena watched as Kellin and The 3 walked back up the dark corridor. Now alone, she turned and stared at The Jack sitting in his chair. Like a cat, she seductively moved toward him, stopping right in front of him. The Jack took her form in, undressing her with his eyes.

This was a new feeling for me, one I was not sure I should even feel. Again, I wrote all that I had seen as well as what I felt.

5.

HER PURPOSE

W hen I looked up from my scroll, I saw a great opulent room; in the center stood a long rectangular table. Hundreds of books of different sizes were strewn about; some opened with their pages carefully marked by leather bookmarks sticking out of the books. On the far end of the table lay many parchment manuscripts, yellowed from age, one on top of another. All four walls had wooden shelves, top to bottom, holding even more vessels of understanding. I soon realized what my eyes beheld—The Hall of Knowledge.

Hermit and Temperance were there sitting on one side of the table instructing a young woman some two decades and five in age. She too possessed much beauty, but yet, somehow different from that of the woman Lena. I was at a loss to explain the difference. She wore a long robe cinched at the waist which accentuated her female form. Her hair shone reddish brown in color; her countenance certain. I sensed her inner strength and resolve. She seemed formidable, yet respectful of her teachers.

Then I realized. . . this was the card, the new card to be. Before my eyes I beheld Justice, THE LADY JUSTICE. She was different from the other virtues in The Forest; but how, I did not know.

"Justice, you have worked hard for many Earth years. . . your formal instruction is now complete!" proclaimed The Hermit.

"Then, my time has come?" replied an accepting Justice.

"Yes Justice," answered The Hermit.

"Child, your destiny awaits you," declared Temperance.

Without any outward sign of emotion, Justice closed her books.

"I must bid farewell to my parents."

"Of course," said The Hermit. "Temperance and I shall go with you."

"You have done well Justice, very well indeed," Temperance said, with great admiration.

Justice looked to The Hermit for confirmation of Temperance's words; The Hermit nodded his head in silent affirmation.

#

My eyes momentarily blinded from the reflection of their two gold crowns. When my sight returned, I saw Jupiter, The Emperor; and Juno, The Empress. Each wore a majestic headpiece: The King's bore the IV, his Queen the III. They were seated upon lavish red velvet thrones, one next to the other; both adorned in long heavy bright colored robes. I could not help but notice The King wore a crown somewhat larger than that of his wife. Before them stood Justice and her two teachers. . .

"Father, my teachers tell me it is my time," spoke Justice, respectfully.

Jupiter turned to the two men. . .

"Her instruction is now complete?" he asked.

"Yes Jupiter, Justice has learned all that she can from the books. . . the remainder cannot be taught nor found in The Hall Of Knowledge," affirmed The Hermit.

"She will learn the rest of what needs to be as we travel back through The Forest, back to The Hermit's pond," Temperance confirmed.

"Then she will be ready to cross over," declared The Hermit.

"Will you both cross with her?" asked a concerned Jupiter.

"No, only I will cross with her," The Hermit replied.

"Hermit will lead Justice through the void to Earth, to the land of The King of Clubs," Temperance continued.

"That is where her destiny lies!" confirmed The Hermit.

"And when will you bring her back to us?" her mother asked, with concern.

Justice could no longer contain herself. She cut off The Hermit's forthcoming reply.

"Why do you all speak as if I am not here?!" she implored.

Justice quickly gathered herself and looked softly to her parents.

"When my destiny is fulfilled, then I shall return to The Forest," she said.

Justice softly kissed the cheeks of her parents. I saw Jupiter wipe his eyes, fighting back his tears. Then Juno kissed her daughter's forehead. The Emperor quickly collected his emotions and sternly pointed at her two teachers.

"Take good care of her!" he decreed, both as father and King.

"Protect her," said Juno. For as you know, she is the only one in The Forest that is not. . ."

The Hermit purposely interrupted Juno, quickly interjecting, "It is time to go."

I could see Justice's curiosity peak, fashioned by The Hermit's uncharacteristic behavior. About to inquire further, Justice paused and then relented—exercising discretion. The threesome stepped back two paces, bowed, turned and took their leave. As they walked, Justice alone turned back to her parents who were standing holding each other's hand.

"Do not worry, I will be back," she reassured her parents.

Justice once again turned away, quickening to catch up with her teachers as they walked out the throne room door. Now alone, a concerned Juno looked hard to her husband, silently expressing her deep concern.

"Juno, it is better that she does not know," Jupiter proffered.

6.

KNOWLEDGE
BEYOND BOOKS

Now I could see it all, the entire Forest of Cards; its total length some 50 stadia. At the southern end, The Hermit's Pond; the elevation there, level with the ground. At the other end of The Forest, rising two stadia in height, the throne of Jupiter and Juno.

The Forest contained a series of small enclaves hidden all to themselves; each unique with their own foliage and terrain. It appeared to me that every virtue existed in its own section and for the most part, remained there until acted upon, either directly or indirectly. I counted 7 to be exact. Small dirt pathways connected one section to the other; and I could see how one could easily be lost as if in a maze.

As I looked North and South, I could see hundreds of tall rugged trees surrounded by unusually shaped rock formations, slate in color. The plants that lined the many low level thickets were spiny in shape; most or their leaves were dark green or yellow.

At times I saw wild animals roaming, and yet at others, there seemed to be no signs of life: save the virtues themselves. Light and dark continually ebbed and flowed, changing on their own phase; a cycle of light not consistent with that of the Earth's celestial circuit. Curiously, in the sky above, I did not see any Sun or Moon!

I could feel energy, both positive and negative; and the strong pull of each shifted with no obvious causation, or so it seemed to me.

#

Once again, time passed that I could not account for and then I saw them: Hermit, Temperance, and Justice, walking on the pathway in another part of The Forest. The elements around them were rapidly changing. The wind began to howl, blowing dirt and leaves about as the sky filled with fast moving dark clouds. A light rain fell.

Looming in the distance, I saw an imposing structure standing 100 cubits in height. The edifice had been built on top of a small hill. It had four equal sides, each 10 cubits in length, constructed of dark wood and mortared bricks. Near the top, carved into the stone, I could see the number XVI: the number of — THE TOWER.

"Justice, look to the horizon! What do you see?" exclaimed The Hermit.

"Some kind of overlook, a tower," said Justice, somewhat indifferent.

"No Justice, not *some kind* of tower, but *thee* Tower," said an excited Temperance.

"This is the House of Life! It is an ever changing reflection of the state of humanity!" explained The Hermit.

"Why do the forces of nature surround it?" Justice asked.

"Just a little farther, then all will be clear," answered Temperance.

Justice, still somewhat unclear, accepted the words of her teachers as they continued on. In a matter of minutes, they approached a small clearing. There in the center, Justice saw a wooden circle eight feet in diameter, mysteriously suspended in air with no visible means of support. The peculiar round levitated between two exact stone pillars, 12 cubits in height.

At the four cardinal points of the wheel, were letters carved. I saw a **T**, on the north point; an **A**, on the east; carved into the south point, an **R**; burned into the west, the letter **O**.

Attached to the round on the top of the north point, I saw a double-edged sword that pointed straight up to the sky. Engraved in the center of the wheel, the number—X.

"Justice, this is Fortune's Wheel!" exclaimed The Hermit.

Before a mesmerized Justice could respond, rain began to pour. The sky resounded with loud claps of thunder followed by blinding flashes of lightning. The threesome watched a series of charged bolts that struck the top of The Tower at its highest point! After the lightning, the rain softened its fall.

"Justice, now see Fortune's Wheel!" instructed The Hermit.

I saw Justice's eyes open wide in amazement as the wheel began to slowly turn upside down: the sword which had pointed north, now pointed straight to the ground.

"What does this mean?" Justice asked.

"It is both a reflection of the present, and a prediction of the future as it will be now," explained Temperance.

"I do not understand," she replied.

"The strikes against The Tower symbolize the present evil in The King's Land; an evil which grows stronger by the day." continued Temperance.

"But what of The Wheel's turning, its meaning?" said Justice, wanting to learn.

"It is a foreboding prediction of what is to come," said a stoic Hermit.

Temperance quickly reassured, interjecting, "Justice, if left unchecked. . . then the forces of darkness will rule completely!"

"Child, herein lies your destiny. You are the one destined to bring justice and light to the hearts of men!" said The Hermit.

"Only then will the balance be restored. In that way the people will be able to freely choose!" Temperance said.

"Between the Darkness and The Light!" concluded The Hermit.

Justice smiled at her teachers, she took their hands.

"You have taught me well," she said, with humility.

The two Virtues softly nodded to her. The threesome continued on, but now with a new found sense of heightened purpose.

#

I heard a voice yelping, a familiar voice; then I saw him running through an open field in The Forest: The Fool. Why I found the vision amusing, I do not know: for the young man awkwardly ran for his life being chased by a beast of creation called Lion; the powerful animal was the male of its species.

In the middle of the field stood a large willow tree; scattered about the field were many of its smaller siblings. The Fool reached the tree seconds before the Lion. He positioned himself behind its broad trunk, madly moving back and forth in a desperate effort to protect himself from the animal's swiping paws.

Then I saw Justice and her two teachers walking on The Forest pathway leading to the clearing; their attention caught by the continuing screams of The Fool. They ran in the direction of the desperate cries and, as they entered the open field, The Hermit abruptly held out his arm some fifty paces from The Fool.

"Stop here!" The Hermit demanded.

The threesome stopped, Justice bewildered.

"But that man, we must help him!" she said to The Hermit, pointing to The Fool.

"Justice, look over there!" Temperance interjected.

He pointed just to the left of The Fool; I looked there and saw a woman not far from the tree, walking calmly toward it.

"Do you see her?" Temperance asked.

"Yes, but who is she?" asked Justice.

"She is called STRENGTH," informed The Hermit.

"Can she overpower the lion?" asked a perplexed Justice.

"Watch and observe," The Hermit instructed.

I reasoned Strength's age to be some five decades plus. Her build sturdy and her feminine form not as well defined. She too wore a robe but of lesser status. Her sleeves were pushed up and a belt made of flowers curved round her full waist tied in a knot at her side. The ends of the belt continued on down the left side of her leg nearly touching her foot. Strength wore a flowered necklace bearing the number VIII.

As she neared the lion, Strength calmly held her hand in the air. Curiously, the lion's yelps ceased; his anger calmed. The Fool seized the opportunity and quickly shinnied up the tree. Once high enough, he comically teased the lion who instantly roared up at him in response.

As before, fear once again overcame The Fool. Now Strength confidently placed her hands on the top and bottom of the animal's mouth, gently closing it. The magnificent beast did not resist her: again becoming docile. She looked up to The Fool.

"You can come down now, there is nothing to fear," she said, assuredly.

The Fool looked down at the quiet animal then shook his head.

"But the lion, not until he leaves!" he fearfully replied.

Then I saw The Hermit and Temperance leading Justice to the tree. The obedient lion stood next to Strength looking up at her. The Virtue extended her arm outward pointing to The Forest thicket a ways off. I watched in amazement as the lion obeyed her command: slowly ambling its way back into The Forest.

As the threesome reached the tree, The Fool yet again burst out.

"Hermit, Hermit! Did you see what she did!? Did you see it!? How did she do that!?" demanded the excited Fool.

"Come down Fool. . . as you can see, the lion has gone," replied The Hermit.

The Fool quickly shinnied down the tree. Temperance placed his hand on Justice's shoulder, then gestured to Strength.

"Justice, this is Strength," said Temperance.

Strength softly took Justice's hands into hers.

"I have been looking forward to our meeting," Strength softly said. I could sense Justice feeling Strength's inner spirit as she held her hand.

"Your hands convey a spirit of gentleness, yet you are called Strength. The lion obeys you, but it is not from fear nor physical force," proffered Justice.

Strength smiled, nodding to Justice.

"Then, where does *this* strength come from?" continued Justice.

"My strength is derived from complete confidence in the Divine. If one's faith is absolute. . . ALL is possible," said Strength, without equivocation.

Temperance nodded in affirmation upon hearing the words of Strength.

"Take hold of *this* strength Justice, for you will need to draw upon it when you battle darkness," instructed The Hermit.

The Fool stood by silently, listening to the teaching.

"Excuse me, but I have been paying very close attention to what you have just said, and I think *you* might just be the one who would know," said The Fool.

"Know what my young friend?" Strength replied.

"Why who was it that stole my wallet?" answered The Fool, his speech getting faster. "You must have seen him!? Tell me, which way did he go!?" ranted The Fool.

Strength gestured to Justice.

"The answer you seek is already within you, if you will only look," Justice replied.

The Fool sighed as he put his hand on his chin in deliberation. He purposely looked up at the sky and then down to the ground. . .

"I got it! I finally got it!" exclaimed The Fool, now looking to The Hermit. "She's great, better than *you*! Just follow the lion! That's it! He will lead me to my wallet, and the *thief*! Gotta go, see ya!"

In an instant, The Fool dashed off in the same direction as the lion. The foursome looked at each other trying not to smile as they shook their heads in amazement.

#

Time had passed, dusk began its rule. The Sun sat low on the horizon; barely illuminating a part of The Forest I had not seen before. I could not help but be aware of sound; there was none! The animals did not stir, the wind blew not one leaf, and there were no winged creatures that flew across the sky.

There up ahead of my gaze, the three Virtues continued their journey. The voice of Temperance rang out in the eve.

My eyes followed the sound and I saw The Hermit leading the threesome.

"The Forest seems unusually quiet," said Temperance.

"I agree," answered The Hermit.

"Why do we not hear any forest sounds?" Justice inquired, of either teacher.

"Because Death is near!" The Hermit prophetically asserted.

At that same moment, Death rode out from the thicket onto The Forest path, his presence ominous and raw. He guided his horse onto the pathway, blocking the threesome. Menacingly, he pointed to Justice, then turned to The Hermit.

"And who is this?" he demanded.

Justice boldly stepped forward, interrupting The Hermit's forthcoming reply.

"I am Justice, The Lady Justice! Do not block our way," she challenged back.

Death dismissed her reply as he looked her up and down, taking in her form.

"All these years. . . and *this* is your answer, a *woman*!?" he said to The Hermit.

I watched as Death sat back in his saddle, laughing, mocking his nemesis. He scoffed at her seeming nothingness to him, snapped the reins of his horse, and rode off. Justice quickly stepped in front of his steed, forcefully blocking his way. Death pulled up, stopping his mount. He looked down to her; undaunted, she glared back up to him.

"You are of Darkness, but I am of the *Light*!," she boasted.

"As I once told The Hermit many years past. . . We shall soon see which power is the stronger! Now, out of my way, woman!"

Justice remained steadfast, not giving an inch.

Death turned his horse from Justice and rode off in the opposite direction. A triumphant Justice remained on the pathway, her hands on her hips.

"You see, Death has not made me move!" she proudly proclaimed to her teachers.

The Hermit's eyebrows furrowed.

"Justice, remember what you have been taught. Pride *always* goes before a fall!" chided The Hermit.

"Be strong Justice, be confident. . . but have no arrogance," Temperance added.

"Do not fall prey to Evil's trap!" Hermit counseled.

An admonished Justice freely accepted the reproach. Her bravado softened.

"I will remember," she humbly replied. "I will remember," she mused to herself.

#

A glorious morning light followed the night, the air crisp and alive. I now saw The Hermit's pond as before, its water swirling, but by what cause I did not know. Justice sat on a large rock near The Pond while The Hermit and Temperance stood away from her, talking. I sensed they wanted to keep her from their words—I perceived rightly.

"Surely you will not cross without telling her?" Temperance said.

"The time has come for her to know *one* my friend. . . but not the *other!*" replied a resolute Hermit.

Temperance reluctantly accepted The Hermit's decision. The two virtues broke off their conversation and approached Justice. However, I was certain that Justice knew all was not apparent. . .

"Justice, before we cross, there is something you must know," The Hermit said, carefully.

"Yes?" she replied, waiting.

"All of us here in The Forest exist, and have always been, just as you see us. . . we never change," explained The Hermit.

"Justice, we are immortal," Temperance proclaimed.

"But you, Justice, are different!" The Hermit added.

"In what way?" she asked.

"As long as you *remain* in The Forest, you too have immortality. However, once you cross over to the Earth, to The King's Land, you will *become human* like those of the Earth; You can be killed, you are mortal—you can die!" revealed The Hermit.

I watched as Justice took what she heard into her being. She showed no outward emotion. Temperance faced her.

"But, when your destiny is fulfilled in The King's Land and you cross back to The Forest. . ." Temperance said, reassuring her.

"I will again regain my immortality," Justice stated.

"Yes," confirmed The Hermit.

I could sense that The Lady Justice instinctively knew her teachers were not telling all of the matter.

"Is there more?"

I saw Temperance anxiously look to The Hermit. He felt sure she must know the other.

"There is one other quality which only you possess, but the time has not yet come for you to know," said a resolute Hermit.

Temperance as before, accepted The Hermit's decision. However, Justice's incense grew. This time she caught her rising negative emotion and slowly overcame it until it disappeared.

"It is time to cross over!" The Hermit firmly said.

Justice turned to Temperance, warmly embracing him.

"I wish you too were going with us," she said, somewhat apprehensively.

"And I as well Justice, but my place is here. Take what you have learned and bring *The Light* to those who now suffer under The King; for this is your purpose," Temperance reassuringly spoke.

"I will," she replied, faithfully.

Temperance looked to his old friend.

"When will you return?" he asked.

"After I safely guide Justice across, I will immediately return here to The Forest," The Hermit answered.

With a fatherly softness in his eyes, The Hermit extended his hand out to Justice. She softly put her hand into his and the two walked to the edge of The Pond. Justice paused for a brief moment, looking down into the water. Then she softly smiled at The Hermit indicating her readiness. I watched The Hermit tighten the hold of her hand, ever so slightly, as if protecting her.

"I am ready," Justice calmly said.

The Wisdom of The Hermit and the Moral Strength that is Justice, still hand in hand, stepped into The Pond. In an instant, a blinding white light flashed, illuminating their beings. Temperance shaded his eyes with his hands and watched as the two disappeared from his sight.

They had crossed over. . .

7.

THE LIGHT SHINES

I looked down at my scrolls and realized I had shed tears. The water drops fell from my eyes, unaware by my conscious self. I mused as to why, knowing full well she had been the cause. I felt a strong connection with Justice, keenly aware of the tremendous task ahead of her. I marveled at her unselfishness, her determination, her integrity.

I wiped my eyes, took the quill in hand and looked out; ever mindful not to let pass any vision or its meaning.

#

The Hermit and Justice were standing on the edge of a dirt road surrounded by throngs of villagers. Some of the mass walked, others were on horseback; still others rode in small open wagons pulled by various species of farm animals. I could feel excitement in the air; the mood, festive.

Most of the villagers seemed happy, yet a curious dichotomy existed: sadness coupled with an anticipation of upcoming pleasure. Once again my eyes found The King of Clubs' Castle off in the distance as before, but this time from the opposite cardinal point.

The Hermit pointed to the road; Justice surveyed the passing rush of people. . .

"Follow this road, Justice!" said The Hermit.

"To where does it lead?" she asked.

"To where you must be," declared The Hermit.

Justice pondered his words, still unsure, as scores of villagers continued to pass them by. The Hermit's eyes gently gestured to the road. Justice smiled, and the two began walking on the road's edge.

"Trust in all you have learned and remember that which you have seen. Most importantly, Justice, do not forget the words of Strength!" a reassuring Hermit counseled.

"That real strength comes from complete faith in the Divine," she affirmed.

"Yes, Justice."

The Hermit stopped and, as a father to his child, took Justice's hand into his. He lightly kissed her cheek and gestured for Justice to continue on. She forced a faint smile of courage and turned from her teacher, joining the crush of people traveling the road.

After walking less than twenty paces, she looked back and saw The Hermit standing firm with both hands on his staff. He smiled reassuringly to her. Encouraged, Justice resumed her walk; this time with more authority and lightness of being. I could tell that his smile filled her with courage. And then, like a schoolgirl, she turned yet once again, now smiling—The Hermit had gone.

Undaunted, and full of The Spirit, she continued on in confidence, meshing into the crowd. Justice did not know where she was going, only trusting in the Divine as she had been taught.

And then Justice observed a small bottle of water roll off the back of a passing open wagon. She picked up the bottle and hurried to catch up with the cart. She waved her arms trying to get the attention of a portly woman, some three decades plus, who sat in the back of the wagon holding an infant in her arms.

The woman yelled up to the driver, a young man seated in the front of the cart.

"Kellin, stop the wagon. . . stop it now!" she implored.

An irked Kellin pulled back hard on the reigns, guiding the wagon to the side of the road, stopping it.

"Why have we stopped!?" Kellin barked.

Justice reached the front of the wagon and held up the bottle of water to Kellin.

"I believe this is yours, it fell from your wagon," she said.

"Praise God, someone who is honest! Can you believe it Kellin, someone who is actually honest!?" said the woman, all amazed.

Kellin looked down to Justice guardedly, his face stern.

"No I can't! What do you want of us?" snapped a suspicious Kellin.

"I only want to give you that which is already yours," Justice calmly replied.

The woman looked to Kellin, jubilantly smiling. She turned to Justice eyes wide.

"Are you traveling alone?" she asked.

Justice quickly turned again, confirming The Hermit had gone.

"Yes," replied Justice.

"You are welcome to ride with us. The castle is still a long ways off and you don't want to be late for the start of Jubilee!" the woman said.

"Thank you, you are very kind," Justice said.

The woman motioned to a resigned Kellin who helped Justice into the wagon. She sat down in the back next to the kind woman and her child.

"I am Myra and this is my brother-in-law Kellin," Myra said.

Justice respectfully nodded.

"My name is Justice."

Myra's baby started to kick and fuss in her arms.

"Oh, I almost forgot. This is my son Kent. Kent, say hello to Justice... my Lady Justice," Myra said, formally.

Baby Kent smiled up to Justice. A waiting Kellin snapped the reigns and steered the wagon back onto the road as the two women played with the young infant. I continued to write, now starting yet another scroll.

#

I saw The King of Clubs' castle before me. It stood tall, powerful and formidable. I felt strangled by the image, as if gasping for air. I could see a massive crowd arrayed in the flat expanse directly in front of the fortress. Many of The King's soldiers were entwined in and around the gathering of villagers.

The mood was festive, but restrained; yet another dichotomy. I saw smoke coming from pits of fire that were burning around the grounds; there were pigs and cows being roasted on skewers of wood. Large black cauldrons filled with boiling water hung on chains suspended over the pits. Carts full of vegetables stood nearby. As the starving villagers looked to the massive amounts of food, I could feel their growing sense of anticipation and frustration.

The crowd stared up at the lone castle balcony, two tiers high. They could see the royal triangle sitting at a sumptuous table. The King of Clubs, now five decades in age, sat at the head of the table, dressed in excessive opulence. To his left sat his Queen, the dark Queen, The Queen of Spades. Her age now four decades and six, her beauty as intense as beforehand. She wore a gold crown slightly smaller than that of The King, her figure meticulously adorned in flowing black silk that obeyed every curve of her form. The Queen's eyes saw all, not missing a quiver.

Opposite The King and Queen sat their son and chief Warlord—The Ace of Spades. He stood tall, his age two decades and five, his countenance powerful. The Ace bore the same darkness of soul as that of his mother; their strong bond, undeniable. As compared to his father The King of Clubs, The Ace demonstrated more self-discipline and consideration: his position second only to King and Queen.

The King rose and walked to the balcony's edge. Once there, he could clearly hear the groans of frustration from the impoverished villagers below. The King looked down at the crowd, a hush quickly came over the assembly; a silence born from fear.

"Welcome loyal subjects, welcome to this year's Jubilee!" greeted The King.

The King breathed in deeply, taking in the pleasing aromas from the fire pits.

"As most of you know, each year during Jubilee, I grant seven days of grace at which time no taxes or tribute will be collected, and no one is allowed to take from another that which is not already his. But this year, in addition to the seven days of grace. . ." The King gestured to the vast array of food below. "I have prepared for you a week long feast. . . for ALL of you!" he pompously proclaimed.

The starving crowd became unruly, their self control waning; having been overcome by the hunger in their flesh.

"Let the feast begin," a voice shouted up to The King.

"Let us eat!" another joined in.

"Our children are starved'" yet a third shouted.

The powerful King, unaffected by their desperate needs, raised his hand in dominance. The crowd relented. The Ace smiled at his mother, pleased by the continued show of control his father had over his subjects. The King pointed down to the gathering.

"However, mark my words carefully. . . After festival's end, be prepared to pay even *more* tribute than before!" warned The King. "For my royal storehouse and treasury have insufficient reserves for my needs."

The crowd, now more like a mob, erupted in shouts of protest. The King responded swiftly.

"Resist, and you shall surely die! Obey, and you are free to do and to take. . . *anything* that is left over from those that are pitiful and weak!" said the condescending King.

I watched the bullies among the throng react wildly as they took in The Kings' words. Like jackals hunting prey, they immediately roamed about their weaker neighbors, intimidating them with things to come, once Jubilee past.

Then, it happened—Light spoke.

Justice, standing next to Myra and Kellin near the center of the mob, stepped forward a bit and boldly shouted up to The King. . .

"What kind of King are you that rules by force and punishes the weak?!" she demanded.

The stunned crowd quickly came to a hush by this bold rebuke. Myra clutched her child, and anxiously looked to Kellin. Justice now tried to force her way all the way through the crowd into the open grounds directly beneath The King's balcony, but the soldiers and hooligans blocked her course. The King shouted down to them.

"Do not stop her! Let her pass," he commanded.

The soldiers obediently cleared a path for her as she made her way to the front. She stood alone, separated form the crowd, standing directly below the balcony of The King. The ever observant Queen of Spades and The Ace quietly rose and flanked The King at the balcony's edge.

"You have picked a most fitting time for your insolence woman, as this is Jubilee. Please. . . do continue!" The King mocked.

Many in the crowd laughed uncontrollably. The Queen and The Ace smiled. The King raised his hand, the crowd came to a hush. He sarcastically gestured to Justice below seemingly enjoying the unexpected spectacle.

"A righteous King governs with fairness and justice for ALL. He is one who has respect for **Life** and **The Spirit!**" Justice boldly continued.

The arrogant King held his hand to his chin in a mock display of new found enlightenment.

"I see. . . What else do you wish to say?" queried The King.

"The strong should *help* those that are weak, not dominate them! *Love*, not hate, should live in one's heart!" Justice implored.

I observed that there were some who took in the words of Justice with meaning and understanding—a precious few. However, I also saw the ever vigilant Queen and her Ace take careful notice of the new converts as well. Moreover, I could feel the spiritual opposites. . . they were squaring off.

"What is your name woman?" said The King.

"My name is Justice!" she replied.

"How fitting a name. . . and since you are so concerned with the love found in one's hearts. . . from this time forward, you shall be known as," The King gestured royally to the crowd, as if introducing her. . . "THE QUEEN OF HEARTS!" mocked The King.

Upon hearing The King's insult, the soldiers and the hooligans laughed and berated her. However, I saw a noticeable few—who did not.

"My dear Queen of Hearts. . . you have seven days to enjoy your royal position. But after Jubilee's end. . ." The King leaned forward with the full force of Evil. "You will **pay me** my tribute, you will **worship me**. . . or you will **DIE!**" warned The King.

Justice stood strong. The two held each other's stare; neither giving in. Finally, The King, seemingly dismissing her, broke off his stare and looked to the crowd.

"Let the festival begin!" he shouted.

The crowd roared as the moment finally had come; the villagers rushed to the pits. Soldiers shot off their guns into the air in celebration as the poor villagers stuffed themselves; not knowing when they should ever eat like this again. Minstrels played music as they walked about the gathering. Soon, some began to scandalously dance and sing as the power of strong drink exerted its control.

The King and Queen returned to their chairs. Immediately, the servants appeared carrying immense platters of the finest foods, while others placed individual tables in front of them.

Curiously, The Ace of Spades remained at the balcony's edge watching Justice who still stood alone from the crowd. Then I saw, as The Ace did, Myra and Kellin quickly join her; followed by two older women and one young man soon after.

The Ace watched this group guardedly, observing their gestures of admiration for Justice. Now somewhat uneasy, he turned to his father. . .

"My King, there are a few who have joined your Queen of Hearts," warned The Ace.

"Do not concern yourself with her. . . Come and sit, enjoy this fine food," replied the blasé King.

The Ace sat. The servants quickly brought him his food.

"Father, where there is one, there will be more," pressed The Ace.

The King shrugged, then turned to his wife.

"Does my beautiful Queen of Spades agree with our young warlord?" queried The King, more concerned with the turkey leg in his mouth than the question at hand.

"I do!" she asserted.

The King unconsciously grabbed the large leg bone from his mouth and pointed it at his Queen.

"What can she do with her words? She is only a foolish woman. I am The King!" he said, shaking the bone for emphasis.

The King quickly reached for the pitcher of wine and filled his goblet, waving off his doting servants.

"This is what I think of our impudent Queen of Hearts," spit The King.

He extended his arm, goblet in hand, as he stared at The Queen and The Ace, and purposely poured out his wine onto the floor.

"Now, the matter is over. . . let us all enjoy this fine food!" he concluded. "More wine!" shouted The King to his servants.

The servants quickly hovered about, filling The King's goblet first, followed by The Queen and The Ace. I watched as The Queen of Spades slowly raised her chalice to her lips. I could feel her recalling a former memory in her mind, a remembrance similar to this one, called to her consciousness by the wine flowing red about the floor.

Then, The Queen smiled broadly, but not for what The King had just done, as he foolishly thought, but to herself, secretly satisfied: basking in the prowess of her former deception. . . impressed by her clever cunning.

I wrote like the wind not missing any vision or feeling.

8.

THEY MEET

I heard a child's yawn; the sound of which lead my eyes to the hut of Kellin and Myra. When I looked inside, I could see Myra sitting in a rocker holding Kent in her arms; the child seemed tired, blissfully content in the grasp of his mother. Kellin knelt in the corner fussing with the fire, Justice sat next to Myra.

I saw a maternal longing in Justice's eyes as she observed the special bond between mother and child. I knew Justice wanted to play with the infant yet the more, but acquiesced to the child's mother who knew best.

Justice dutifully brought over Kent's crib. Myra put Kent down and covered him, he quickly fell asleep. Not being able to contain herself, and willing to risk awakening the child, Justice leaned in and kissed Kent's forehead. The two women smiled at each other, their female bond growing.

"These are the last two pieces of wood! How are we to stay warm?" blurted an angry Kellin, poker in hand, rekindling the fire.

Myra smiled at her brother-in-law.

"Somehow, things will get better," reassured Myra.

Kellin threw down the poker.

"No matter how hard we work, The King's men come and take what they will... They always do!" Kellin snapped back.

He gestured to the fire.

"Look, they leave us with only a few pieces for ourselves!"

"Kellin, soon many will resist the evil ways of The King," assured Justice.

"Justice, you are strong in spirit, but only a fool would believe that by spirit alone, one is able to overcome evil," Kellin countered.

"These things take time Kellin," insisted Justice.

"I'm sorry Justice, but I believe you can only fight force with yet a stronger force!" he asserted.

Myra shook her head.

"Don't worry Justice, he will learn," Myra said, assuring Justice, as much as herself.

Suddenly, loud noises coming from the outside filled the hut. Kellin and Myra ran to the window and spied a garrison of soldiers mercilessly knocking down villagers' doors as they shouted out demands for taxes and tribute. Myra instinctively grabbed a sleeping Kent from his crib. She stood afraid in the corner of the hut.

"Myra, what's wrong?" asked Justice.

"The soldiers have come back again!" Myra frantically replied.

"Where's your spirit now Justice?" Kellin sarcastically snapped, as two soldiers barged into the hut. A 7 held a sword while an 8 brandished his gun!

"Time to pay your fair share, yet again!" mocked The 7.

Kellin stood in front of Justice and Myra.

"We have nothing! Look, there is no more to give!" pleaded Kellin.

The 7 looked around the hut. He spied two pieces of firewood in the fireplace which had not yet burned, as well as a few small ears of old corn on the table. He pointed to the corn.

"Well then, what is this?" said The 7.

"Please, that is all the food we have left, there is a child!" implored Kellin.

The 8 commanded The 7, "Take the food. . . AND the wood!"

As The 7 walked to the table, Justice stood in his way.

"Well now, look who we have here. . . I do believe it's The Queen of Hearts!" said The 7, scoffing.

"You will leave this hut at once!" Justice demanded.

The 8 dismissed her paltry show of force..

"Kill her, and be quick about it!" he commanded The 7.

The 7 raised his sword. Justice stood her ground. As The 7 readied to run her through, Myra screamed! Out of nowhere, The Jack of Diamonds burst into the hut, gun in hand, knocking the two soldiers and himself to the floor. Both The Jack and The 8 lost their guns upon impact; while The 7 hit the ground, momentarily stunned. The Jack began punching The 8 mercilessly, immediately getting the better of him; the battered soldier yelled to The 7.

"Kill her I said!" commanded The 8.

The Jack smashed his elbow into The 8's stomach, doubling him over. The 7 drew his sword back about to kill Justice. I watched in astonishment as The Jack finally floored The 8, and then leaped across the table intentionally knocking Justice to the floor!

I could clearly hear the sword thrust of The 7 cut the air with a whoosh as it passed by Justice's falling body, barely missing her. My face grimaced at the sight of The 7's flying blade as it found a new mark, piercing The Jack's shoulder. Ignoring his wound, The Jack dove to the floor and grabbed his gun. The 7 made another parry at The Jack, who quickly rolled over, causing the sword thrust to go astray, landing firmly into the wood floor less than a digit from his side.

The 7 feverishly tried to free his blade from the wood as The Jack, while still on his back, coldly looked up and fired his gun, killing The 7 instantly. The beleaguered 8 recovered his senses and went for his gun which lay only a few cubits from him. As The 8 neared his weapon, Kellin quickly ran over and kicked it away. Jack nodded and then smiled at young Kellin.

"I don't think I'll be needing this!" asserted The Jack.

Curiously, The Jack threw his gun to Kellin. The 8's eyes immediately lit up seeing the outlaw unarmed. He quickly got up and charged The Jack who welcomed the fight. As The Jack and The 8 beat each other, I heard a young girl's screams for help coming from the outside. Justice collected herself.

"Stay here with Myra and Kent," shouted Justice, as she ran out of the hut into the street.

My eyes followed Justice outside the hut; chaos and pandemonium consumed the village. In the square, a mixed assembly of soldiers and hooligans had gathered surrounded by stunned villagers. All had converged around Tull, the village thug who was molesting a young village girl; her years no more than one decade plus six. The ogre's features were profanely grotesque as compared to most men, his weight heavy as stone.

The soldiers and hooligans stood by laughing in amusement as the powerless young girl screamed for help; they cheered Tull on! The horrified villagers were defenseless against The King's men who stopped any one who dared end their fun.

Then Justice emerged from the crowd. Undaunted, and without fear, she propelled herself into the back of Tull's legs, causing the monster to fall to the ground!

I heard the soldiers now jeer the clumsy ogre as he awkwardly picked himself up. Embarrassed, he quickly grabbed Justice around her neck. It was then that I saw the deformity in his hand: only two fingers and a thumb on his left. Determined to avenge his humiliation, Tull squeezed Justice's neck while looking into her eyes ready to devour her. . .

"You want to save her?" his voice heavily rasped, as he gestured to the village girl. "Then I shall have you!" he said, savoring his carnal thoughts.

Instantly, Tull ripped off the shoulder portion of Justice's garment exposing her shoulders. She quickly grabbed the falling cloth before exposing her breasts; her hands covering her womanhood.

Sensing the impending rape, the wicked soldiers again cheered Tull on. As he began to pull her hands apart to expose her, The Jack of Diamonds came up from behind; pushing Tull's body forward while grabbing his hair. Instantly, Tull's head violently snapped back! He screamed out in pain letting go of his hold on Justice. The Jack, still holding onto Tull's hair, ripped his neck backward: now rendering the thug under The Jack's complete control!

The outlaw turned the ogre's body to face Kellin who had just emerged from the crowd. He purposely whispered in the troll's ear.

"Remember his brother?" said The Jack.

The Jack once again snapped Tull around. With the thug now facing him, he drew his sword and ran Tull through. The ogre gasped as he clutched the blade with both of his hands; his blood running red out onto the cold steel.

Jack lifted his boot while still holding his sword, and kicked Tull in his stomach. The troll stumbled backward and fell to the ground dead; Jack's sword still in his hand.

I could see the face of Kellin, his grievance now avenged. For him it was a righteous kill. Justice stood by in shock as to what her eyes had just witnessed. The Jack turned to Justice, her hands still holding up her tunic. . .

"First he would have had his way with you. . ." said The Jack, his voice stone cold. "Then, he would have cut your throat!" he said, emphatically. Justice stood silent, mesmerized by The Jack.

Then I heard the sound of thunder, but not from the sky. They were hoof beats pounding into the Earth. Immediately, The Kings' men retreated in fear as they saw the rest of Diamonds' men approaching on horseback: the hooligans hid among the village crowd.

The 3 led a band of outlaws up to The Jack, bringing his mount to him. He looked to the ground and spied the dead body. The 3 smiled admiringly to his leader. The Jack mounted his horse and looked down to Kellin. . .

"I believe I kept my part of our bargain," said a stoic Jack, as he pointed to Tull's dead body.

"The thug is dead, and there are two dead soldiers back at your hut!" he said, efficiently.

Then Jack took his sword and threw it to the ground, impaling the Earth right next to Kellin. The blade stood straight up; its ivory handle wavering back and forth only inches from Kellin's hand.

"A souvenir for you, Kellin" Jack said.

Diamonds now looked to Justice who still had not fully regained her composure. He stared at her bare shoulders, obviously drawn to her beauty: the look of a man desirous of a woman. Justice tried to look away from his sensual eyes, but could not.

"Do try to keep yourself from being killed. . ." he said, somewhat roguishly.

The Jack reached into his saddlebag and threw down a cloth poncho to Kellin, and then turned and purposefully looked back at Justice, concluding. . .

"As you are much too beautiful for that!" confessed The Jack.

With that, The Jack spurred his horse, and he and his men stormed out of the village. As the dust settled, Kellin took the poncho and covered Justice's bare shoulders. She did not even realize what Kellin had done; her gaze remained fixed on The Jack, as he disappeared from her sight.

A small group of villagers gathered around Justice. They were astounded by her stand against Tull and The King's soldiers. . .

"No one has ever stood up for us before!" said an elderly villager.

"You saved my life!" proclaimed the young village girl, who had been attacked.

"You really are The Queen of Hearts!" declared yet another villager.

"That she may be, but now she must rest," said an arriving Myra, taking charge of Justice.

Justice took Myra's outstretched arm. She leaned on her as Myra led her friend back to the hut. The stunned crowd follow behind them still talking amongst themselves about her courageous stand.

Kellin remained by Tull standing perfectly still, his mind reflecting on what had just occurred. He looked down at the sword's handle which still beckoned only inches from his right hand.

Justice and Myra reached the hut, and as they were about to enter, Justice regained her senses fully, and realized Kellin was not with them; she turned to look back.

Myra look!" exclaimed Justice.

Both women watched in dismay as Kellin grabbed the handle of the sword. He purposely pulled it out from the ground and defiantly raised it high in the air!

"Oh Kellin, that is not the way," said an alarmed Justice.

A tear ran down Myra's cheek.

"Maybe now that he has avenged his brother's death, he will finally be at peace," said a mournful Myra. "Come Justice, now you must rest."

The two women entered the hut. The crowd scattered.

I looked to the street and saw Kellin, standing alone, still holding The Jack's sword in his hand, staring down at Tull's dead body.

9.

THE TEST

Time had passed, and once again I saw the hills of No Man's Land. They seemed to stand watch, looking out at the panoramic view of the valley below and beyond. A ray of light flashed across my eyes drawing my vision to The 3. I caught sight of him lying down behind a large boulder, spyglass in hand, high atop the hills; I could see as he saw, rising dust way off in the distance. The 3 changed the lens on his glass and looked out—It was Kellin.

The 3 jumped up and mounted his horse; quickly riding down the mountain road and waited for young Kellin behind a clump of tall sagebrush. I watched as Kellin approached the bottom of the climb and then saw the astonished look on The 3's face as he noticed that this time, Kellin came armed; wearing The Jack's sword on a belt around his waist.

The 3 rode out from nearby brush, intentionally surprising the young man. Kellin awkwardly pulled up on the reigns of his horse. . .

"Our business is done! Why are you here?" said The 3, carefully watching Kellin's hands.

"Take me to The Jack!" Kellin snapped back.

The 3, taken back by Kellin's forceful response, stared long and hard at him in attempt to understand its meaning.

Kellin remained stoic. The 3 took another look at his sword. . .

"Stay close, the light is fading. We'll take a different route," said The 3.

With that, The 3 spurred his horse and began the climb; Kellin followed.

"We'll make camp at midnight, then continue on at first light," informed The 3.

I continued to watch the two men ride to the top until they disappeared into the canyon. The majestic setting Sun cast a reddish yellow tint across the sky. I could see a lone eagle flying high above, his piercing shrieks echoed off the canyon rocks below. Day bowed its head to night. The Moon now ruled. I marveled at my Creator's work.

#

The morning Sun rose and darkness gave way to the light; its warm rays shone brightly on The Jack's hideout. There inside, standing in the meeting room as before, stood Kellin facing The Jack, who sat leaning back in his chair, with both his boots resting on the table. The 3 stood close to Jack's side. . .

"Have you noticed that Kellin dares to see me *armed*?" said the surprised Jack, to The 3.

Kellin stood visibly nervous, yet holding his ground.

"In life, every man faces a moment like this. . . Jack, I think this is Kellin's," stated The 3.

The Jack's expression turned hard.

"Well Kellin?" Jack demanded.

Kellin drew his courage.

"I have decided to join up with you, if you'll have me," Kellin declared.

"Kellin. . . You do know what me and my men do?" Jack said, now more tolerant.

"You fight The King's soldiers," answered a puzzled Kellin.

Immediately, The Jack got up from his chair.

"Follow me!" commanded The Jack.

The Jack walked to the door. The 3 motioned for Kellin to follow. The men walked up the tunnel stopping at the main door. Before opening it. . .

"Take him to the post, we'll soon see about young Kellin," instructed The Jack, walking off.

The 3 led Kellin outside to The Prisoner's Post where one of The King's 8's had been lashed to it. The soldier's hands were tightly fastened behind his back and a cloth gag had been stuffed in his mouth. Oddly, warm Sunlight lit the open courtyard; it seemed out of place.

Kellin and The 3 stood next to The 8 listening to his muffled cries as a purposeful Jack approached. Upon reaching Kellin, The Jack coldly stared into his eyes. . .

"Draw your sword and kill him!" The Jack ordered.

Kellin withdrew his sword from its sheath. He positioned himself directly in front of The 8. I could see his hands tremble as he raised the blade. The terrified 8, now knowing he was about to die, shook violently against his restraints. The soldier's moans grew louder, forcing their way through the cloth in his mouth. Kellin tried to blot out his pleas as he prepared to strike. . .

"WAIT!" commanded The Jack.

The Jack went up to the quivering 8 and removed the gag from his mouth.

"Now kill him!" The Jack ordered.

The 8 immediately bust out, "Please, I beg of you, spare my life! I am just a soldier following orders, I have a family, have mercy, PLEASE HAVE MERCY!"

Kellin looked into the tearing eyes of the helpless 8 and then back to The Jack; his eyes—stone cold. He took in a deep breath and again raised his sword, holding it high in the air. . .

In that moment, I could feel the raging battle of conscious that warred in his being: good and evil, each pulling Kellin in opposite directions. . .

Kellin relented, lowering his weapon to his side, stepping back from the speechless 8.

"Go home Kellin, you're not a killer," Jack said.

Kellin hung his head, embarrassed; feeling that somehow he let The Jack down.

The 3 quickly interjected, "The matter is over. If we leave now, we can make the canyon road by nightfall."

Kellin awkwardly nodded, following The 3 to their waiting horses. As Kellin walked past The Jack, he could not summon up the courage to look at him directly. I watched as The Jack stood by silently, waiting for the two men to mount up and ride off.

The 3 led Kellin around the side of the hideout. Then I heard a shot ring out; its echo ricocheting off the rocks. I saw Kellin writhe in his saddle, as his mind's eye fully conceived the sight.

"Don't look back," said The 3.

10.

THE GOOD NEWS

"**S**ummon The Ace, The 8 returns!" shouted The King's lookout to the soldiers below.

I could see the sentinel positioned atop of the castle's main front wall. Below, a small band of soldiers were arrayed around the perimeter. A King's 4 quickly ran into the castle as instructed by the lookout.

The waiting soldiers now spied The 8 approaching, his horse galloping like the wind. I heard them call out to him and couldn't help but observe their sense of bewilderment at the awkwardness of his form in the saddle. The soldiers ran out to meet him and quickly grabbed hold of the runaway steed. Immediately, they realized he had been killed!

The 8's lifeless body sat propped up in the saddle. His legs were tied to the foot stirrups and his glove clad hands bound to the saddle's horn. The soldier's body had been held upright by two ropes that tied to his upper arms and then diagonally crossed over his shoulders, tying again to the saddle's back. His tightly clenched fist had been tied around a rolled up parchment that stuck up out of his glove.

The Ace of Spades came out of the castle and approached his soldiers. His face riled upon seeing his man strung up and humiliated. I could feel the warlord's anger; its center—his pride! Once again, The Jack of Diamonds had bested him.

One of The King's 4's took the parchment from The 8 and quickly gave it to his commander. As The Ace unfolded it, The King approached. . .

"What does it say?" demanded The King.

The Ace read aloud, "My Dear King, why bother?"

"And the signature?" raged The King, knowing full well. . .

"The Jack of Diamonds!" said The Ace, as he crushed the parchment in his hand, throwing it to the ground.

"One day we shall meet. . . Diamonds and Spades face to face, then we shall see!" The incensed Ace said to The King.

The King and his son walked back to the castle as the soldiers cut down The 8 from his horse, carrying the dead body past the two men who now paid it no mind.

"This insolent outlaw continues to be a thorn in my side!" said the frustrated King.

"I will soon have this Jack of Diamonds, and when I do. . . I will cut him to pieces!" promised The Ace.

It began to rain. I watched the life-giving liquid fall from the sky onto the crumpled parchment on the ground; the black ink now smearing the yellowed paper, The Jack's words staining the dirt.

#

Justice stood tall on the wooden platform, confident and bold. All in the village gathered around The Speaker's Square to hear her speak. Arrayed in front of her were women with children, men with their work tools, and many young couples who held each other's hands. Among them, the hooligans snuck about. Myra stood directly in front of The Square, Kent in her arms. Justice surveyed the gathering; every one eyes were riveted on Justice. . .

"My dear friends, this is the last time I will speak to you. Tomorrow, I travel to Saxon village to speak with your distant neighbors," began Justice.

Murmurings of disappointment rose from the crowd.

"No Justice, you must not go!" cried out a villager.

"There is more you must teach us," another said.

"Who will stand up for us!?" implored yet another villager.

Justice softly raised her hand. . .

"You do not have to live in fear," Justice said. Then she pointed at the hooligans.

"And YOU must end the ways of hate!" she firmly instructed.

Some of the weaker villagers now looked boldly to the strong.

"As I have told you many times past, the strong *must help* the weak. In that way love abounds and peace prevails. All then give *willingly* from their hearts, the fruits of their labor, to those who have not," taught Justice.

"But what of The King's soldiers!?" one shouted up to her.

"How can love fight them!?" shouted yet another.

"We are a simple people, we are not strong!" implored an elderly villager.

Then Kellin emerged from the crowd; he stood next to Myra before turning to the assembly. . .

"It is true we are a simple people, but if we stand together in unity and love, our fear will cease. We will then be *stronger* than The King!" reasoned an impassioned Kellin.

Justice smiled in response to Kellin's words. Myra's joyful eyes filled with tears. Kellin took her hand into his.

Justice continued, "Love casts out fear. And while it is true that you are not soldiers or killers. . ." Justice looked pointedly, yet softly to Kellin. "Remember, true strength comes from within, from the spirit."

Most of the villagers smiled in response to Justice's words. Kellin turned to the crowd. . .

"Once The King and his men see that we fear no more. . . that we will stand firm with only farm tools in our hands for a JUST cause, and that we are willing to die if necessary for that cause. . ." said and impassioned Kellin.

"You will have broken The King's hold over you. You shall be forever free!" proclaimed Justice.

The crowd erupted with cheers of joy. They were now one in purpose and spirit! Many of the hooligans were also positively affected by the words of Justice.

"Never underestimate the power of evil. And be assured, if you have complete trust in the Divine, and listen to your hearts. . . Evil will **always be defeated!**" concluded Justice.

She stepped down from The Square and went to Kellin and Myra. Immediately, groups of villagers mobbed her, expressing their gratitude and understanding.

As the crowd continued to swell around Justice, I saw two men dressed as villagers, depart from the throng. They ran to horses that were tied up nearby and quickly mounted; riding off hooves thundering, yet unnoticed by the crowd. I had seen them before; They were The Ace's spies.

#

Inside The Great Hall, The King sat on his throne. Rays of light reflected off the ornate gold and silver leaf that covered the walls and ceiling throughout The Hall. The Queen of Spades stood calmly next to The King as the anxious Ace of Spades repeatedly slapped his black leather gloves into his hand. The Great Hall echoed with each rip of the hide. . .

"My spies should have been here by now!" said the impatient Ace.

The rear doors burst open and the two spies hurried in, bowing to The King.

"Well then, out with it, give us your report!" barked The Ace.

"My Lord, the stories are true about the woman called Justice," said the lead spy.

"Justice? I know of no woman called Justice!?" The King interjected.

The Queen of Spades coolly turned to The King.

"My Lord, she is the woman. . . *The Foolish woman. . .* you named The Queen of Hearts during Jubilee past," said the cunning Queen.

"You mean my impudent Queen of Hearts is the same woman he calls Justice?!" asked The King.

"The very same your grace," confirmed The Ace as The King shook his head, stunned.

"Go on," said The King, to the spies.

"She speaks of love and kindness," the second spy said.

"She teaches the values of moral strength and integrity," continued the lead spy.

"She denounces your rule as evil," the second spy added.

"And how do the villagers respond to this nonsense?" demanded The Ace.

"Her numbers grow daily," answered the concerned lead spy.

The King burst out, looking to The Ace!

"Send five of your men back to this pitiful village. Collect more tribute! *Double* the amount! Send them now! I will make them pay dearly for this public embarrassment!" The King commanded.

"Only five your grace?" questioned The Queen, raising her eyebrows, subtly challenging. . .

"What more do we need for this woman and her peasants!" replied the arrogant King.

"Change back into your uniforms and take three 7's with you. Show no mercy!" ordered The Ace, to his spies.

"Wait 'till the dinner hour, then enter their huts and take what is mine!" salivated The King.

The spies obediently bowed before The King, turned, and took leave. The King and The Ace smiled broadly one to the other, their egos full with the plan; while the face of the measured Queen, reflected her guile and cunning.

11.

TAKING A STAND

Once again I saw the village hut of Kellin and Myra, now the new home of Justice. I could smell a sweet aroma and knew it to be the call for nourishment as those of the Earth partake.

Inside, a large pot suspended on a chain hung over a wood burning stove. I watched as Kellin poked the fire with a black iron, rekindling the flame: the element obeying the rules of its purpose, boiling the water.

Myra stood nearby cutting up three small vegetables, throwing each into the pot. A serene Justice played with Kent, lifting him high in the air. As she looked at the child, I could sense her mind wandering to other thoughts. Jus-tice put Kent down in his crib. Her demeanor changed, curi-ously. . .

"Kellin, where did you go the day Tull was killed?" asked Justice, broaching the subject, discreetly.

Myra interrupted his forthcoming answer.

"I'll tell you where. . . He went to that hired gun, that killer, The Jack of Diamonds!"

"That killer Myra, *saved* Justice's life, *twice in one day mind you*! Not to mention avenging John's death," Kellin forcefully countered.

"Kellin, Tull's death has not brought back your brother, nor Myra her husband," proffered Justice, softly.

"Yes, you are right Justice; when John was killed, I was full of hate and consumed with rage and revenge; I was confused," reflected Kellin. But, it was The Jack who showed me **who I am**, and **what I am not!**" he said, proudly.

Justice took in his words. . . Myra stood confused.

"I *will* stand firm in the face of death for what is *right*, but I now know I cannot kill for no just cause at all," Kellin explained.

"And you learned this from The Jack of Diamonds?" asked Justice, her tone somewhat proud.

"Yes," confirmed Kellin.

"Nevertheless, his ways are just as bad as The Kings," Myra countered.

She paused to reflect. . .

"But, if it was The Jack of Diamonds who sent you back to us, I suppose we owe him for that," Myra conceded.

"Kellin, what do you really know about this Jack of Diamonds," said Justice, somewhat cryptic as to intent.

"Only that his sword and gun are the best!" Kellin proudly proclaimed. "Although there are some that say The Ace is his only equal."

Curiously, I could sense Justice being filling with pride.

"What else?" Justice pressed, carefully.

"That The Jack cares not in the right or wrong of a thing, only on its agreed upon terms for completion," said Kellin.

"Then, even though The Jack is a hired gun, he has a strange sort of integrity," Justice said, almost excusing his disreputable actions.

"Oh sure, if you call keeping your word about robbing or *killing* someone, *Integrity!*" Myra sarcastically interjected.

Again, I saw Justice in curious thought, seemingly not taking in Myra's words.

"Does he have a wife?" mused Justice, as an afterthought.

Justice's question stunned both Myra and Kellin.

"There are *many* women Justice, but no wife. Although, there is a particular woman called Lena," Kellin forcefully answered.

"Lena—who is this Lena?!" Justice bitterly replied.

Then I heard loud pounding on the door! I could hear a villager yelling from the outside.

"Justice, Kellin, come quickly! The King's soldiers approach!" he cried.

Justice and Kellin ran out into the street. I saw the Sun low on the horizon, its tiny specks of yellow light glowed in the distance. The King's soldiers were on horseback advancing at an even gallop; they held fire torches in their hands. Many villagers had already gathered in the street. Confusion and disorder overcame the air.

"Kellin, round up everyone in the village!" ordered Justice.

Kellin and a few others ran to those huts whose doors were closed. I could hear Kellin's impassioned cries. . .

"You must not fear! If we stand together, we will turn them back!"

I watched the remaining doors open one by one, all were now in the street. The soldiers continued their advance on the settlement. From afar, they could see the villagers standing as one with various farm tools in their hands. . .

"We will ride at full gallop right into the middle of the crowd!" shouted the commanding 7 to his men. "Those peasants will run in fear long before we get there!"

The leader spurred his horse, the others followed suit; their horses now charged at full gallop.

As The King's men drew near, the villager's resolve weakened!

"You must trust!" Justice implored. "Raise your hands and run right at them, NOW!" she shouted.

Justice grabbed a torch from one of the villagers, turned and ran full speed toward the advancing soldiers! Kellin immediately followed her, shouting back to the crowd as he ran. . .

"Follow Justice!"

Overcome with inspiration, the crowd responded; they too ran toward the soldiers, shouting at the top of their lungs. They waved their fire torches, rakes, and hoes; lifting them high into the air as they charged.

The two groups were now very close and just before they converged, the soldier's horses became frightened from the strange sights and sounds closing in on them. One by one, the horses reared up on their hind legs, sending their riders tumbling to the ground.

The pumped up crowd quickly surrounded the dazed band of soldiers, circling them; making ready to pounce. Justice held up her hand and the crowd ceased; all watched to see what she would do. Justice looked to Kellin.

"We have paid our fair share of taxes and tribute ten times over!" Kellin shouted, to the soldiers. "We will pay no more!" he defiantly decreed.

The crowd quickly became caught up in the moment.

"Tell The King we no longer fear!" shouted one of the villagers.

"We will only pay that which is fair!" shouted another.

"Soon, the other villages will hear the words of Justice as we have, and they too will do the same!" said Kellin.

The impassioned crowd closed in on the soldiers, smothering them. Justice stopped them and pointed to their horses milling about.

"Get on your horses and ride back to The King. Report to him what you have seen and heard in this village!" she demanded. Justice turned to the crowd, "Step back, let them pass."

The crowd gave way and the beaten soldiers ran like cowards to their mounts. The villagers shouted out with victory, congratulating one another! Myra put her arms around Justice and Kellin.

Day gave way to night. . .

12.

THE TOWER

The Moon waxed full, its icy glow shimmered in the darkness. The castle of The King seemed to be one with the night, as if born of this lesser light. Then I heard the voices of darkness impale the stone walls of The King's Great Room. . .

"You call yourselves soldiers!?" The Ace raged. "How could you be defeated by peasant villagers armed with nothing but farm tools and torches. . . led by a *woman* no less!?" he demanded.

"My Lord, we never expected them to charge us!" said the commanding 7.

The Ace railed at the soldier as the doors of the hall opened. The King and Queen entered just as their son drew his sword; they watched him deftly cut the cheek of The 7. The berated soldier grabbed his face, cowering, as a thin trail of blood ran down the side of his cheek. The Ace defiantly sheathed his sword.

"Get out of my sight, before I run you through! All of you!"

The 7 and his men turned and left, awkwardly bowing as they passed the approaching King and Queen. The King glared at his son.

"Your men could not handle these peasants!?" he shouted.

"This Queen of Hearts of yours used an old military trick. . . who would have thought she would posses that kind of knowledge?" The Ace said, defensively.

"Do you think the mighty Ace of Spades might be able to kill this woman and say. . . maybe ten villagers. . ." The King said, purposely pausing for effect. . . "With a whole *garrison* of soldiers!?" he mocked.

The Ace would not be humiliated.

"Father, do not rebuke me! It was **you** who underestimated the cunning of this woman!" He slapped his gloves into his fist. "I will go myself. I need no help from *anyone!*" said the defiant Ace.

The King accepted his son's rebuke and now smiled.

"Justice and your ten villagers will be dead by Sunrise tomorrow!" declared The Ace.

"No son, do not kill them!" snapped The Queen of Spades.

Father and son both expressed confusion.

"If you kill their Queen of Hearts, you will make her a martyr. Justice will be *stronger* in death than she now is in *life!*" said The Queen.

"Then, what do you suggest we do?" The King asked.

The Queen's hypnotic eyes tightened, I could feel her dark thoughts.

"You must capture her *alive* and bring her here to the castle. We will lock her in the tower prison! There she will remain till the end of her days.

Father and son sneered in approval. The Queen looked directly to her son. . .

"Do not kill anyone who tries to save her. Let them all live to see her capture. For in this way, we will destroy their precious *spirit*, and crush this rebellion once and for all!" said The Queen, with the cunning of a serpent.

The King beamed with pride toward his wife.

"In addition to your unequalled beauty. . . my dear, you are skillfully ruthless!" praised The King.

The Queen of Spades slowly bowed to her husband, being careful to hide her expression of superiority that crossed her face.

"When will this be done?" snapped The King to his Ace.

"The Queen of Hearts will be in the tower prison by noon tomorrow!" replied The Ace.

"How many men will you need to hold off the villagers?" asked The King.

"As I said before, none!"

The Ace snapped his gloves in punctuation, turned and purposefully walked to the rear doors. The King looked to his Queen.

"We will soon have her my Queen," he gloated.

I heard the sound of the hall's great doors slamming shut, the noise echoing off the walls.

#

My eyes could no longer see The Land of Clubs, only the void. . . why—I do not know. Now alone with my thoughts, I marveled about the wonders of Creation, and how I was formed. Why did my maker fashion me and what purpose do I serve? These and other thoughts mused through my mind.

I looked down at the scrolls and considered the work; who would read them and would they understand? Had I written accurately all that I saw, and would my Creator be pleased?

As I considered my questions, the firmament filled with light; God had answered. In an instant they were back: images from The Earth. I took up my quill.

#

I saw The Ace on horseback leading a despondent Justice and Kellin who were bound and gagged. The two prisoners rocked on their mounts in rhythm with their horse's gate. I could see The King's palace but a short distance ahead and heard the lookout on the castle wall yell to the foot soldiers below. . .

"Report to The King, The Ace returns!" he said.

Without haste, a 4 ran into the castle.

"Open the gates!" commanded The Ace, as he approached the stronghold.

Two soldiers quickly opened the bared doors. The Ace and his prisoners rode through. As the mighty Ace passed by, the soldiers dutifully saluted him, swords held high; as much from fear as from rank!

Once inside, the soldiers closed the gates. The Ace dismounted. . .

"Take them down and tie a rope about the waist. Tie them one to the other, the woman first," instructed The Ace. The soldiers quickly followed their command. The Ace took the loose end of the rope and pulled it to him.

"Follow me, my Queen," said The Ace, mocking her.

The soldiers laughed as Justice and Kellin were awkwardly pulled forward; The Ace herding them into the castle.

My eyes had not seen this part of the castle before; it was dark and cold. The Ace led his capture to the front of a heavy iron door, smiled at his quarry, and opened the entranceway, salivating.

I looked in and saw a dingy narrow circular staircase made of steps cut from stone that spiraled upward. The Ace raised his hand, enjoying the moment, and pointed to the very top. Justice and Kellin looked up, their eyes squinted, squirming at the sight.

"Your destiny awaits," said The Ace.

The Ace promptly snapped the rope tighter, forcing his prisoners into the room. He began the climb up the stairs with Justice and Kellin helplessly in tow.

My eyes raced upward and at the top I saw The King of Clubs and The Queen of Spades standing anxious vigil in the tower prison alcove. Behind them were two empty cells, each with its iron bared doors open. On the wall near the first cell, a wooden peg stuck out from the mortar; it held an black key hanging on a ring.

Both the ceiling and walls of the Tower were made of solid grey stone. Only the rear walls of each cell had a small opening, the width of two eyes, revealing a glimpse of the outside world below.

The King and Queen heard the sound of footsteps approaching and earnestly looked to the open door at the top of the staircase.

"Finally!" The King sighed to his Queen.

The Queen shrewdly smiled upon seeing The Ace approach the top of the stairs. He led his captives into the alcove and stood before The King.

"Father, I bring you. . ." The Ace turned toward Justice, and in grandiose fashion, mockingly bowed. Then he rose up and extended his arm outward pointing to Justice and proclaimed, "The Queen of Hearts!"

The King walked up to Justice, ignoring Kellin as if he were not in the room. He looked her up and down. His eyes pierced hers.

"Woman, ever since Jubilee past, you have caused me nothing but trouble. You and your peasant friend. . ." he pointed to Kellin without looking at him. ". . . may have momentarily succeeded in turning the villagers against me. But now. . ." The King pointed his finger directly into Justice's face, his eyes seething. "You are *mine!*" he triumphantly declared, savoring his accomplishment.

The Queen gestured to the first cell on the left.

"You will remain here locked in this cell. . . till the end of your days," she said, with delight.

Justice turned her head slightly, looking at the cell.

"You will never be *heard from*, nor seen by *anyone*, **ever again!**" proffered The Queen.

I watched The Ace take his sword and cut the rope that tied Justice to Kellin. Next, he nimbly cut the leather cord that bound her wrists. Then The Ace grabbed her upper arm and forcibly dragged her to the front of the open cell.

He threw Justice in and she fell to the floor, her face pounding the dirt. The Ace stood over her and skillfully wedged his sword between Justice's cheek and her gag. He held the razor-sharp blade against her skin; now taunting Kellin while his eyes remained on her face.

"Such a beautiful face," he mused.

Kellin, still bound and gagged, charged The Ace.

"One more step and she will be scarred for life!" he warned.

Young Kellin froze in his tracks. All watched in amazement as The Ace turned the blade of his sword, ever so slowly. I saw the edge of the weapon cut the cloth gag without marking her skin. Justice spit the rag out of her mouth onto the floor.

The Ace walked out of the cell, slammed the door shut and took the key from the wall. He locked the cell door and placed the key on a leather necklace he wore under his shirt. Then he grabbed Kellin and placed his sword on his throat! Justice quickly rose and frantically shook the bars of her cell.

"Do not hurt him!" she demanded.

"Hurt him. . . not at all my Queen. No, quite the contrary, I want him very much alive. Who better to tell the villagers what fate has befallen their beloved Queen of Hearts!" the sarcastic Ace reassured.

The Queen of Spades smiled; first to her son, then to The King.

"You have done well my son," said The King, as he walked over to Kellin.

"And your worthless life has been spared!" scoffed The King.

"Go to your village and tell all what you have witnessed this day with your own eyes and ears," instructed The Queen.

"And remember, peasant, if *anyone* dares not obey, she will be killed instantly!" The Ace threatened.

The King turned to his son.

"Send this bumpkin on his way!"

The Ace grabbed Kellin by his shirt, forcibly leading him back down the spiral staircase. As he disappeared from Justice's sight, she shouted out to him, beseeching.

Have faith Kellin, do not lose your faith!"

The King and Queen laughed at Justice's pitiful plea as they walked to the staircase. The King went down, but the dark Queen stopped at the alcove door. She turned and stared at Justice who defiantly stared back at her, neither giving any ground.

I watched the silent battle of wills last seemingly forever. Then the ruthless Queen broke off her menacing gaze, turned and went down the stairs, slamming the alcove door shut behind her.

Justice stood defiant, her hands tightly gripping the bars of her cell, alone in the Tower Prison—in the dark. I could feel her reaching deep down inside, searching for strength, Divine Strength; a power she needed now more than ever.

13.

THE DEAL

The Hermit stood motionless, staring into the waters of his pond. Although the liquid rippled smartly, the images were surprisingly clear. As I looked in, I still could see Justice locked in her cell, alone.

Then I saw a shadow float over the water. The air chilled. I could feel him before I saw him; Death—seated upon his pale white horse. His icy laughter rang out into The Forest of Cards, mocking The Hermit. . .

"Your eyes do not deceive you Hermit. The Lady Justice has been captured. It is over, the powers of Darkness have won!" boasted Evil.

"Won. . ? What has the Darkness won!?" replied The Hermit. "The prison walls may now hold Justice captive, but can those same walls take back that which has already been given. . ? The villagers have already taken her words deep into their hearts!" countered The Hermit.

Death carefully considered The Hermit's offset.

"So it may be Hermit, but *none will dare act on it!*" proffered Death.

The Hermit stood strong, glaring up to Death.

"It is far from over, Death" said The Hermit, with a sense of foreboding. "Ride on!" he concluded, dismissing him.

The Hermit curtly turned his back and walked away. I could sense Death had been unnerved by Wisdom's cryptic prophecy. I watched as the Evil one stared at The Hermit, waiting for him to turn back around and face him: he did not. Then, in frustration, Death spurred his horse, bolting off.

The Hermit sat back down on the rock near The Pond, reflecting on all that had happened. His thoughts were interrupted by Temperance, who quickly ran out from The Forest thicket into the clearing. . .

"Hermit, what has happened!? Death has just passed me by, he rides like the wind!" said Temperance, catching his breath.

"The forces of good and evil are again out of balance!" The Hermit stated, looking hard at his friend.

"Justice! What fate has befallen her?" said Temperance, somehow knowing.

"She has been captured by The Ace of Spades, and is now locked in a cell, a captive for life, alone in The King's Tower Prison," stated The Hermit, without any emotion.

"This cannot be! Only Justice can restore the balance. She must be free to bring about the Light!" Temperance implored.

The Hermit nodded his agreement. . .

"Friend, you must go to Jupiter and Juno and tell them what has happened. Bring them back here to The Pond!" instructed The Hermit.

Temperance's concern deepened. His countenance beseeching. . .

"Hermit, you know Justice can be killed if she remains in The King's Land. How will you free her, and protect her, and. . ?"

"If you hurry," interrupted The Hermit. "You will find CHARIOT nearby. Enlist his aide. He will take you to their palace and swiftly bring all of you back here to The Pond; there is none in The Forest mightier than he!"

"I have heard great accounts of his courage and skill, but how will I know him? For his reflection I have never seen," said Temperance.

The Hermit took his staff and drew in the ground the number VII.

"He bears the seven," Hermit replied.

Then he pointed to a lesser known spot in The Forest.

"He can be found there!" The Hermit declared.

"I will find Chariot, and we will bring back Jupiter and Juno," Temperance affirmed, his countenance expressing great concern. "Hermit, you must save Justice!"

The Hermit put his hands on the Virtue's shoulders.

"There is not much time friend. If we are to save her, you must hurry," concluded The Hermit.

Temperance nodded and ran off into The Forest. The Hermit looked to the sky, and as he did so, I could clearly see the expression on his face; one that bore much more concern than before.

#

I heard a great commotion and then I saw him—young Kellin. The overwrought villagers had surrounded him, all shouting questions at once.

"Kellin, what has happened?!" shouted the first.

"Where is Justice?!" came another.

"Is it true you were both taken prisoner by The Ace?!" yet another exclaimed.

"My friends, The Ace came while we were asleep, he made not a sound. He put his sword to Justice's throat. There was nothing I could do!" implored a distraught Kellin.

"Where is Justice, Kellin?!" another shouted.

Kellin's face hung low.

"She is locked in The King's Tower Prison," he reluctantly replied.

"In prison, how then were you able to escape?" questioned the first.

"I did not escape. The Ace set me free so I could come back here to tell you all that I have seen and heard," explained Kellin.

"Then, we will go to the castle and free our Queen, we must!" exclaimed one of the men.

The entire crowd shouted out in agreement.

"No!" said Myra. "We will do nothing! We cannot."

The villagers were all stunned by Myra's words. They looked to Kellin for an explanation. . .

"If we do not obey The King, and still refuse to pay his taxes, he will kill Justice!" said Kellin.

"As long as we submit to him, Justice will live. We have no other choice," said a resigned Myra.

"Is there no one that can defeat The King and his Ace?" asked one from the crowd.

"Yes, there is—The Jack of Diamonds," answered Kellin.

Myra's eyes bugged, caught off guard by Kellin's response.

"But we do not have any gold or silver to pay him," Kellin said, with frustration.

"But surely he will help if we explain our just cause," another villager reasoned.

"The Jack is a hired gun, he is not a man of conscience," Myra interjected.

"Then, we have lost our Queen and we are forever bound to The King," said the resigned villager.

With that, the crowd silenced; no one spoke but a word. The dejected group broke up into small groups, aimlessly walking back to their huts. Myra embraced Kellin with tears running down her cheek.

"Kellin, will we ever see Justice again?" she asked.

"I don't know, Myra," Kellin softly replied.

#

Temperance ran at full stride on The Forest pathway; his attention caught by someone calling out to him. . .

"Temperance, is that you, wait a moment!? What's your hurry? Did you too lose your wallet?" The Fool asked.

Temperance stopped for The Fool.

"I have no time for foolishness now. I must find Chariot. This is an urgent matter, Fool!" he explained.

"Chariot!? I know where he can be found," said The Fool, proudly.

"You do!? Take me to him now! There is no time to lose," implored Temperance. "I must get to the dwelling of Jupiter and Juno!" he explained.

"I will lead you to Chariot, but only if you let me come with you. Maybe they will know where my wallet is!?" spoke The Fool.

"Very well Fool, now take me to Chariot!" said an impatient Temperance.

Temperance followed the scampering Fool down the pathway.

#

I could see The Hermit as before, still sitting on the rock staring into The Pond. His concentration stiffened as he tried to look deeper into the still water. Curiously, he bent his neck, as if to see around an invisible force. Then I was back. . . back in The Keeper's underground chamber room, seeing the card formation resting on his table.

I could see THE LADY JUSTICE'S card in the center of table, flanked by the card of THE DEVIL on her right and the card of DEATH on her left. I watched as The Keeper drew the next card from the deck. He placed it sideways across and on top of THE LADY JUSTICE; then I saw its face, the card of Diamonds—THE JACK OF DIAMONDS! The images in The Pond held for a moment and then disappeared.

The Hermit quickly got up from the rock, grabbed his staff and walked over to his lantern resting nearby on the ground. He picked it up and returned to the edge of The Pond. Without hesitation, The Hermit stepped in.

As before, my eyes became blind from the glow of the white light that exploded before them; then they cleared, returning my sight. . .

The Hermit was gone. He had crossed back over. . .

#

I heard the cry of coyotes, there were many for sure. I could see the front door of The Jack of Diamonds' stronghold, illuminated by the light of the night, which revealed The Hermit, staff in hand, standing outside.

He knocked on the door with the point of his staff, and seemingly from nowhere, outlaws with guns drawn, quickly surrounded him. The Hermit paid them no mind, standing resolute as he waited. The door opened revealing The 3, who quickly scowled at his men at the presence of a stranger in the camp.

"How did this man get into our camp?!" he demanded.

"Do not bother with them, take me to The Jack. I bring untold riches," said The Hermit.

"Riches? Who are you?" replied the taken aback 3.

"I am The Hermit. We haven't much time," The Hermit concluded.

The 3 looked him up and down checking for any weapons. Satisfied that the stranger bore no arms, he looked to his men.

"I'll shoot the next man who fails to do his job," warned The 3.

"This way Hermit," said The 3.

The two men went inside and down the passageway stopping outside the door of The Jack's inner room. Inside, I saw The Jack of Diamonds sitting in his chair. The woman Lena sat on his lap, her lips pressing on his: their intimacy abruptly interrupted as the door opened. The 3 escorted The Hermit into The Jack's den. Lena got up, annoyed by the intrusion; she stared quizzically at The Hermit as she exited the room. The 3 waited for Lena to leave. . .

"Jack, he says he brings us untold riches, yet he carries no bags; but I think we should listen to what he has to say."

The Jack studied The Hermit carefully.

"There is a legend of men who dress and look like you. . . they are called Keepers. It is said they keep track of the good and bad in man. Is that who and what you really are?" said The Jack.

"I am The Hermit. That is who and what I am," The Hermit stoically replied.

The Jack smiled at The steady Hermit; approving of his vagueness. Then The Jack hardened somewhat. . .

"Very well Hermit, state your business."

"There is a woman called Justice, you may know her as The Queen of Hearts. She has been taken captive by The King's Ace of Spades and is now being held in the castle, in the Tower Prison."

The Jack looked to The 3.

"Isn't she that beautiful woman, the one with Kellin, the courageous one?" Jack paused to reflect, then smiled. "The one who brought Tull to his knees?"

"Yes Jack, the very same," confirmed The 3.

"Can you overcome the forces of The King and the power of his Ace, and free her?" asked The Hermit.

Before The Jack could answer, an indignant 3 interjected. . .

"Strong enough!? Do you know who he is?!" The 3 said, pointing hard at The Jack. "He is The Jack of Diamonds! There is no one better than The Jack!"

"Your loyalty is admirable," The Hermit said to The 3. "But I inquire of him," said The Hermit, looking to The Jack. "I humbly ask again. . . can The Jack of Diamonds defeat The Ace and free Justice?"

"I should think a better question might be, *will* I, not can I!" Jack countered. "Then, there's always. . . Why *should* I?!" Jack continued, somewhat arrogantly.

"If you can free Justice and bring her back here to me, I will give you wealth beyond your wildest dreams," declared The Hermit.

The Hermit reached into his robe and retrieved two coins, one gold the other silver. He placed them on the table.

"A trunk full of each," said The Hermit. Without hesitation, he reached in again, and this time he brought forth two large precious diamonds which he placed onto the table next to the coins. "And a third filled with these," The Hermit said, pointing to the precious gems.

The 3 stared at the bounty on the table, his eyes grinning broadly at the sight.

"Very well Hermit, our bargain is sealed. Now go and leave the rest to me," The Jack said.

The Hermit nodded his head, silently acknowledging their bargain.

"Escort him out," said The Jack to The 3.

The Hermit turned and followed The 3 out of the room.

"Lena!" Jack called.

I watched as the woman Lena appeared in the doorway. She stood there, alluringly, tempting The Jack with her female form.

14.

THE PLANS

Chariot drove his carriage along the narrow pathway that followed the outer edge of the mile high hill, yet deeper in The Forest of Cards. The chiseled muscles on his arms flexed solid as he pulled hard on the reigns, controlling his four thundering horses that raced like the wind. His years, three decades and some; he carried himself as one of the military. Chariot wore a medallion of gold on a chain around his neck: the insignia's number—VII.

Traveling with him were Temperance, Jupiter, Juno, and a panicked stricken Fool! Chariot skillfully guided his carriage perilously close to the road's edge. The deafening sound of the horse's pounding hooves blared out into The Forest.

"Slow down Chariot—slow down! You're gonna kill us all!" screamed The Fool.

"Do not pay him any mind, we must get to The Pond!" Temperance countered.

Up ahead, I could see a gorge in the road; its rift some 30 meters in length! In between the two sides, the Earth dropped some 200 meters below with large jagged rocks that laced the chasm bottom.

"Hold on, we're approaching the pit!" Chariot exclaimed.

I watched as the others looked out, resigned, but trusting; all except The Fool!

"We'll never make it!" cried out The terrified Fool.

Jupiter and Juno looked to Chariot for reassurance.

"Hold on tight, it will be a hard landing!" he said, confidently.

"Please stop, Chariot, there's still time to stop!" pleaded The screaming Fool.

Enjoying The Fool's display, Chariot chided playfully, "But what of your wallet Fool? It may be on the other side of the pit!"

The Fool took the fodder, quickly forgetting about the impending danger.

"Of course! The other side of the pit. That's where it is!" said The now eager Fool. "Faster, Chariot! Faster!"

As the carriage approached the breach, The Fool let go of his hold on the rails. Chariot snapped the reigns and the horses leapt across the divide. The chariot flew into the air. As the carriage soared, The Fool lost his balance and fell halfway out; his body now balanced perilously on the rail while his head helplessly looked to the rocks below. The Fool let out a long high-pitched yelp.

At the apex of the jump, The Fool's equilibrium failed and he tumbled out. Chariot quickly grabbed him with his right arm and pulled him back in!

The horses and the flying carriage just cleared the rift; the back wheels just reaching the rim's edge. The carriage landed fiercely on the other side, and with one hand still holding The screaming Fool, Chariot pulled up hard on the reigns. The horse's hooves dug in and the chariot swerved hard as its wheels burrowed deep into the loose dirt.

The Fool continued his incessant yelping all though the turbulent landing; the carriage finally came to a stop. Now safe, The Fool went limp! Chariot let go of his hold on the young lad and he fell amusingly into Jupiter arms.

"The horses need to rest, and I believe our friend has fainted," said a nonchalant Chariot.

"Finally, he is silent!" exclaimed Jupiter.

Juno, Temperance, and Chariot could not help but smile.

I carefully wrote all that I saw, filling the second scroll.

#

Inside The Jack's stronghold in his inner room, The 3 sat at the table putting crushed tobacco leaves into a cylindrical roll made up of thin white paper. Across from him, The Jack sat quietly, methodically cleaning his weapon. . .

"How many men do you think we'll need?" said The 3, without looking up.

"Five. . . you and me, plus three more," Jack replied.

The 3 put the tobacco roll into his mouth.

"Who should I get?" asked The 3.

The Jack grabbed a small candle burning on the table and held it to the paper, lighting it. The 3 drew in his breath and then exhaled smoke into the air; He seemed comforted by this experience.

"Hire Snake The 6. Get The 5, and one more man," The Jack said.

The 3 leaned back in his chair, savoring the taste of the tobacco, and exhaled more smoke into the air.

"What about The 2, the one they call Little Deuce?" posed The 3.

"If you like him, hire him," Jack said. "Go to The Shack, they'll all be there drinking or gambling. Bring them back here. . . I'll lay out the plan tonight."

The 3 stood, tobacco roll in hand.

"I'll be back in a couple of hours!" declared The 3.

I could sense an aura of anticipation that had come over The 3. . . so could The Jack.

"And if I were you. . . I wouldn't be messing around with those young beautiful women, they're gonna kill ya," said The Jack, coyly smiling at The 3.

"Listen Jack, if raising you since you were a baby hasn't killed me. . . those delightful young women sure won't," mused The 3, tipping his hat in jest, leaving the room. The Jack shook his head, smiling, as he continued to clean his gun.

I began writing the third scroll.

#

I heard their voices, the sounds of Virtues in discussion. Then I saw them; Hermit, Temperance, Jupiter, and Juno, all standing near The Hermit's dwelling a little ways from The Pond.

Curiously, The Fool stood away from the group, mulling about at the edge of The Pond. His eyes lit up upon seeing an image in The Pond and not understanding, attempted to go into The Pond to pick up that which he saw. The Hermit caught him from the corner of his eye. . .

"Get back Fool! Do not go into The Pond!" exclaimed The Hermit.

The startled Fool straightened, jumping back from The Pond.

"But I saw pictures. . . pictures in the water!" explained The Fool.

"Never mind what you saw, stay away from The Pond!" demanded The Hermit.

"The rebuked Fool sauntered away from The Pond. He ambled toward the meeting in progress, stood still, quietly listening. . .

"Who is this Jack of Diamonds?" Jupiter asked of The Hermit.

"His is an outlaw, a hired gun. He is reputed to be a man with no conscience. . ." The Hermit deliberately paused. "But The Jack is the only one that can save Justice," explained The Hermit.

"Maybe so, but can he be trusted?" asked Temperance.

"Trust is of no concern. That he will fulfill our bargain is all that is required," The Hermit answered.

"And will he. . ?" asked a suspicious Jupiter.

"I believe so," replied The Hermit.

"That may be, but I sense a more serious problem," Juno interjected. "Hermit, have you told Justice what will happen to her if she gives herself physically in love?" queried Juno.

"She knows that while she is out of The Forest, she is no longer immortal and can be killed. . . However, Justice does not know that she will also lose her immortality if she gives herself in human love, when two become one.

Juno's eyebrows furrowed.

"And you did not think to tell her this?" said an amazed Juno.

"I saw no need," replied The Hermit.

"Hermit, Justice is a young, vibrant, and beautiful woman. . . Did you not think she could fall in Love!?" said Juno, quite firmly.

Jupiter threw his hands in the air.

"Stop! Enough talk of love. Let us concentrate on keeping Justice alive and how we can free her to fulfill her destiny, and how we can get her back here in The Forest where she belongs!" Jupiter declared.

"Does The Jack of Diamonds know of her special qualities?" offered Temperance.

"No. He only knows that she is both beautiful and courageous, for he has already saved her life twice."

"And was he paid for this. . ?" Juno immediately asked.

"No." said The Hermit.

The group all looked to each other with a silent knowing. The Hermit sensed their concern with his judgment. He breathed deeply, rethinking his judgment. . .

"Nevertheless. . . Her destiny now lies in his hands," said The Hermit, without reservation.

With each passing day, I began to feel more and more emotion—human emotion. I was careful not to confuse my ever growing feelings with an accurate recording of all that I saw.

#

Night ruled, the Moon had quartered. Very little light shed upon No Man's Land; I barely could see The Jack's hideout. Finally my vision sharpened, and I saw inside the inner room.

The outlaws were there, those that Jack had requested. I saw Little Deuce, The 2, The 5, and Snake, The 6; all sitting at the table across from The Jack and The 3. The outlaws were in intense conversation. . .

". . . and at Sunrise we storm the castle. We'll have the element of surprise and should have no trouble getting past the posted sentries," The Jack said.

"Yeah, at that hour they'll all be sleeping, which is where we should be," interjected The 6.

The outlaws laughed.

"Once inside, we'll have our hands full. Remember, The Ace and his men will be everywhere, we have to move fast," The Jack said. His face hardened. "Very fast! I'll climb the stairs to the Tower Prison and free Justice," Jack continued. The men were confused. "The Queen of Hearts," he explained.

"Where do you want us?" asked The 2.

"The 3 will cover the door to the staircase; he's got my back till I come down with Justice. Snake, you and The

5 will back him up, it's gonna get rough. Little Deuce, I want you outside the main door," The Jack ordered. He stared hard at The 2, "Make sure no one gets in behind us!" warned The Jack.

"When do we get paid?" asked The 5.

"As soon as I deliver The Queen of Hearts to our benefactor, I'll send The 3 over to The Shack with equal shares for all. . . More money than you've ever made before." The hired guns smiled, savoring their forthcoming bounty. "Now get some sleep, you'll need it," The Jack concluded.

Little Deuce, The 5, and Snake got up and left the room. I could sense slight apprehension from The Jack. . .

"What do you think of The 2?" The Jack asked.

"Little Deuce, he's okay, Jack," replied The 3.

15.

BETRAYALS ABOUND

The torch in The Keeper's underground chamber flickered, its oil almost spent. The yellow bursts of firelight striped Augustanian's hooded face. I looked to the table and all I could see was The Jack of Diamonds' card; its face staring up at The Keeper. Carefully, Augustanian dealt the next card from the deck. I saw the card of The Juggler; his number—I. The Keeper placed it next to The Jack. I continued to write, being careful to accurately portray the formation.

\#

The 2 knelt in the darkness behind a clump of thick sagebrush: some 50 cubits away from The Prisoner's Post. The Little Deuce looked around the campgrounds making sure he was alone. . . one with the night. I watched as he changed his clothes, putting on the garments of a trickster. The 2 quickly put his outlaw clothes into a small saddlebag, carefully hiding it under a nearby rock. Once again, the outlaw looked around the camp, and seeing no one, quickly mounted his horse.

As I watched The 2 ride off, I could see The 3, inside the stronghold, still talking with a perplexed Jack. . .

"What's bothering you?" The Jack asked.

"It's this job, it's the most dangerous one we've ever taken. . . and. . ." said The 3.

"And what?" Jack countered. "Didn't I hear you say I'm the best?!"

"And you are, but. . . could you kill your father if you had to?" blurted out The 3, with great difficulty.

"Kill you!? What have you been drinking!?" exclaimed The Jack. "Why would I kill you, the only man that I trust with my life?!"

The 3 searched for courage.

"Jack, I've raised you since you were an infant, I taught you everything I know. . . But. . ." said The 3, taking another determined pause for courage. Finally, revealing, "I'm not your father!"

"What are you saying?" The Jack said, confused.

With the revelation now out in the open, The 3's spoke more freely.

"We loved you from the moment we saw you, and no one could have loved you more than my Cassie! She wanted to tell you when you were but a boy, but I thought it best not to. After she died, I decided to leave things as they were. . . but now. . ." The 3 said, again pausing.

"What are you trying to tell me? Just say it!" exclaimed The Jack.

"Your *real* father is *The King of Clubs* and your mother was *The Queen of Diamonds!*" exclaimed The 3.

For the first time I saw The Jack of Diamonds dumbfounded! I could feel his desperation as he tried to comprehend.

"When you were just an infant, The King ordered the death of your mother so he could marry The Queen of Spades," explained The 3. "You were not to be harmed, or so your father thought. However, it was The Queen of Spades who secretly conspired with one of The King's trusted 9's to have you killed as well!" The 3 clarified.

"Is this true!?" Jack implored.

"Yes!" The 3 said, now with more purpose.

"But why?" The Jack asked.

"So her son would be sole heir to the throne," explained The 3.

"The Ace of Spades?"

"Yes Jack! The Ace *of Spades* is your half brother!" said The 3. "I will tell you exactly how your life was spared and how Cassie and I became your mother and father. I guess Cassie was right; I should have told you years ago," said a remorseful 3.

The image before me changed of its own. I now saw Augustanian as he took the top card from the deck and placed it sideways across both The Jack of Diamonds and the card of The Juggler. I looked closely, as did The Keeper, and saw the card of The Moon! Its number—XVIII. The vision quickly crossed back to the inside of The Jack's hideout where The Jack sat attentively, listening to the explanations of The 3. . .

"And so The King, your father, thinks you are dead, believing what The 9 had falsely told him when you were a baby!" said The 3. "Everyone does!"

"The Jack clutched the red diamond around his neck.

"And that diamond you now hold in your hand. . . belonged to The Queen of Diamonds, your real mother. She put it on you at birth." continued The 3.

"Go on," said The Jack.

"The Queen of Diamonds was a beautiful woman, but your mother was also a moral and righteous woman. She would not condone the evil ways of your father, nor tolerate his indiscretions!" said The 3.

The Jack clutched the diamond hard, as if trying to touch the mother he never knew. For a brief instant, I felt him search for her spirit, a deep hidden longing. Then. . .

"You are my father and Cassie was the only mother I have ever known. As far as The King and The Ace are concerned, if they get in my way, they are as good as dead!" concluded The Jack.

The sound of a lone coyote howling caught my ear, then my sight. I saw the animal wandering alone in the hills of No Man's Land, its neck arching upward as it called to the Moon.

Not far away, The 2 rode back to the stronghold. He jumped from his horse, snuck to the Post, and retrieved the saddlebag containing his outlaw garb. He quickly took off the Juggler's disguise and changed back in to the same clothes he wore just hours before.

I recorded the events that I had seen and heard, most importantly, the revelations of The 3. In my mind's eye, the image of The Jack of Diamonds clutching his mother's red diamond, flashed repeatedly. . . Why I did not know.

16.

THE LAWS OF RETRIBUTION

T he morning Sun had begun its rise, once again reclaiming the Earth. The Jack and his men were on horseback approaching the main castle gate. As they drew near, Diamonds pulled up on the reigns and dismounted; the others followed suit. The 3 took out his spyglass and surveyed the sentries; he smiled. . .

"You were right," said The 3 to The 6. "They're all sleeping."

The 3 handed the glass to The Jack. He looked through the lens and saw the sleeping sentries. Then The Jack surveyed the entire front wall, and seeing it left unguarded, apprehensively handed the scope back to The 3.

"I don't like it, it's too easy," said a concerned Jack.

"So we don't *earn* our money, who cares. . . let's get it done," said The 2.

I could tell that Snake and The 5 agreed with Little Deuce. The Jack again looked at the abandoned front wall and the sleeping sentries, clenched his lips, and relented. . .

"Alright, we'll sneak past the guards at the gate, and go in the main door." He looked to The 2. "Deuce! Once we're inside, it's your job to keep them out," Jack reminded The 2.

"No problem," Little Deuce assured.

Diamonds nodded. He and his men quietly approached the main gate, staying close to the front wall. The Sun brightened. The outlaws deftly slipped past the sleeping sentries at the gate and continued on, stopping just outside of the main door. The Jack motioned for The 2 to position himself by the side wall, a few feet from the door. As soon as The Little Deuce moved into position, The 3 lifted the door's handle and the rest of the men went in.

The outlaws quietly snuck into the main hall; the room was deserted. The polished marble floors coldly reflected back the images of the men who walked on them. With the skill of many a past endeavor, the outlaws broke off.

The 6 went to the left, The 5 to his right. The Jack approached the lower alcove Prison door, The 3 covering him from the rear. As Diamonds opened the Prison alcove door, the main doors of the hall burst open!

The King's soldiers came storming in from the outside, through the same door the outlaws had just entered! The ambushed hired guns took cover where they could and began shooting. Snake and The 5 turned over tables and fired mercilessly at the soldiers!

The Jack used the Prison alcove door for cover as he shot at the approaching soldiers, killing two instantly! The helpless 3 jumped to the open floor and laid flat, firing at will.

More soldiers came in from the outside and fired on The 6. The barrage of bullets hit his heart; he fell to the ground, dead. The overpowered 5 fired nonstop in an attempt to get deeper cover. His eyes bugged wide open, as a sword bade from a King's 9 ran him through from behind!

The Jack came out from behind the Prison door, both guns blazing, hitting soldiers with every shot. The Jack defiantly stood in the open, giving the pinned down 3 cover and a chance to make it to the alcove door. The 3 looked to The Jack.

"Forget me, get The Queen!" The 3 shouted.

The Jack ignored him and kept advancing toward him, killing more soldiers with every shot! The Jack threw over a table giving both men momentary cover.

"Where's The 2!" raged The Jack, as his guns emptied of their bullets.

Quickly, The 3 got up, standing as The Jack did, with both guns blazing. He held off The King's men, giving the outlaw time to reload! Then The Jack stood and the two men made a break back to the stairs; The Jack first and The 3 behind.

The Jack made it through the door, now inside the Prison alcove. He turned and fired relentlessly, giving cover to the approaching 3. Just as The 3 was but a few cubits from the door, he fell forward into The Jack's arms; struck in the back by a lone bullet fired by one of The 10's.

The Jack pulled The 3's body into the stairwell and quickly closed the heavy wooden door, bolting it from the inside. The King's soldiers stopped shooting as soon as The Jack locked the door.

Jack held the dying 3 in his arms. With his last breath, The 3 labored to speak.

"You were right about The 2, Jack, a *traitor!*" gasped The 3, as his eyes closed.

The Jack laid his lifeless body down onto the stone floor. I could hear the soldiers laughing out in the hall from behind the door. The commanding 10 walked up to the door and looked in through the peephole.

"Go on Diamonds. . . go get your Queen!" he scoffed. "There's no way out, you're finally trapped!"

Again, the soldiers laughed. A resigned Jack, as if in a trance, began to climb the circular staircase, leading up to the Tower Prison—in the dark.

For the first time The Jack was really alone. I could feel his overwhelming sense of loss. The 3 was the only person The Jack ever trusted; the only father he had ever known.

Now, because of the darkness, my eyes could not see him: Instead, only able to hear the echoes of his boots on the iron steps as he climbed the spiral stairs, as well as the shrieking sounds of squealing rats that crawled at his feet, unseen in the dark.

Upstairs, waiting in the middle of the Prison alcove, The King of Clubs and The Queen of Spades stood; their eyes continually glancing to the entranceway door. The Ace of Spades paced anxiously back and forth. Justice stood in her cell wondering what fate had in store. There were two of The King's 10's with guns in hand, as well as two 4's with their swords drawn. The soldiers stood at the ready near the door as The Queen walked over to Justice's cell.

"It seems you have a champion, and soon he will be arriving right through that door," she mused, cryptically.

The Queen pointed to the door and then sarcastically laughed at a perplexed Justice.

"Unfortunately, you will not be rescued. . . but do not fret my dear, for The Jack of Diamonds will be occupying the cell next to yours" continued The Queen.

Justice's eyes widened, her anxiety waxed full.

"The Jack of Diamonds?!" replied a surprised Justice.

"Yes my Queen," The King interjected. "Maybe you can capture <u>his</u> heart. After all, are you not The Queen of Hearts?!" he said, scoffing.

The King's remarks drew laughter from the soldiers. The Queen of Spades smiled to herself. The Ace remained stoic, his eyes fixed on the alcove door.

"Relax my son, you have finally caught our nemesis," said The King.

I saw the alcove door open slowly. The Jack of Diamonds entered with no weapons drawn. The King's soldiers rushed to surround him. The Ace shouted out to them. . .

"Stand away!" commanded The Ace.

The soldiers moved back, continuing to be at the ready. The Ace menacingly walked up to The Jack, as an assassin would to his prey, and stared into his eyes. The Jack showed no visible signs of emotion or distress.

"So you are the great Jack of Diamonds. The most infamous outlaw, afraid of nothing and no one," said The Ace.

"I see you've heard of me. . . that's good. And who might you be?" mused The Jack.

"I am The Ace of Spades!" declared the pompous Ace.

"The Ace of Spades. . ?" The Jack paused to ponder. "Sorry, never heard of you," dismissed The Jack.

The Ace railed!

"Do not be trite with me outlaw, there is no one better than I, and you know it well to be the truth!" exclaimed The Ace.

The Jack's gaze mused about the room. He looked to the soldiers, to The King and Queen, to a bewildered Justice, and then back to The Ace.

"Well, with your four soldiers and your father and mother. . . I could see how you might feel you are the better. But if you plan to challenge me. . . I'm afraid you're gonna need just a little more help than that," replied The Jack, trifling with him.

The humiliated Ace exploded in anger. He quickly stepped back and drew his sword on The Jack.

"Put away your blade, and throw him into the cell!" ordered the forceful King.

"There will be no need of a cell for him father! He shall soon see who is the best!" The Ace countered.

"Draw your sword outlaw," commanded The Ace. "For today you die."

The Jack smiled as he shrugged his shoulders, again mocking The Ace. He carefully took one small step back and put his hand on his sword. The King's soldiers immediately charged.

"Halt! Do not interfere!" commanded The Ace. "This is between him and me," he said, savoring the impending contest.

The soldiers backed off. The Jack's smile turned cold as stone. He drew his sword and advanced toward The Ace. I could feel The Queen's uneasiness growing as she looked to The King.

"Let him avenge his honor my Queen. There is none better than my son!" reassured The King.

The King motioned to his soldiers to move further back. The Queen stood close to The King. Justice grabbed the bars of her cell.

"Jack, do not risk your life for me!" implored Justice.

The Jack looked to Justice, while keeping one eye on the circling Ace.

"Oh, I have no intention of risking my life," replied The Jack.

The Ace immediately advanced on The Jack. The blades of their swords clashed at an unbelievable pace! The two stood face to face hands blazing, neither giving any ground. They slowly circled each other as sparks flew into the air from the gnashing of their flying steel.

The Ace charged, The Jack defended. Spades charged again, this time straight at The Jack, lunging for his heart. I watched as The Jack turned the advantage around with his skillful parries. Now it was The Ace who fought off his back leg, trying hard to keep up with expert hands of The Jack.

Suddenly, The Ace stepped back, fully raising his sword in the air. The Jack remained focused on his eyes.

"For a man of low birth. . . you handle a sword well. But now you die!" declared The Ace.

Immediately, and at the same time, the two men charged: each man's sword lunging at the other's heart! Their blades clashed together and then deflected. The Ace cut The Jack on his upper shoulder, while the steel from The Jack slashed The Ace's cheek!

Justice and The Queen of Spades both sighed in desperation.

"Enough! Stop them!" ordered The King.

The obedient guards moved in quickly between the two bleeding men. They forcibly rustled The Jack back, disarmed him, and threw his sword to the floor. As they did so, his shirt tore, revealing the red diamond around his neck.

The King stared at the jewel. His eyes opened wide in disbelief!

"Where did you steal that Diamond!?" shouted The King.

"Steal this!?" This is the one thing that I did not steal!" Jack said. "It belonged to my mother."

It was at that precise moment that The Queen of Spades realized who he really was!

"How dare you lie to me outlaw! I gave that stone to The Queen of Diamonds many years ago!" exclaimed the belligerent King.

I know, and as I said. . . It was my mother's. . . FATHER!" revealed The Jack.

The Queen of Spades shouted to her son.

"Kill him now!" she commanded.

The Ace charged the unarmed Jack. The outlaw dropped to the floor using his dead weight to break the hold of the guards. The King, now realizing who he really is, yelled to The Ace.

"Stop! He is your brother!"

The incensed Ace paid his father no mind, intent on running the defenseless Jack through while on the ground. As The Ace charged, The Jack rolled on the ground in the direction of his advance, while at the same time swinging his boot, hitting The Ace's ankles, tripping him. The Ace fell helplessly forward onto The Queen of Spades, sword in hand! He gasped in horror, his face but only inches from hers: For The Ace of Spades had just run his mother through! Justice put her hands to her face, blocking the dreadfulness of the sight. The Jack grabbed his sword from the floor and got up. The soldiers advanced, but The Jack quickly grabbed The King and held his blade against his Father's neck.

"One more step, and he dies!" said The Jack.

Immediately, the guards froze. The mortified Ace stood unaware, in shock, holding his dead mother in his arms. Jack turned to The 10.

"Open the cell!" he shouted.

"I don't have the key," replied The 10.

The Jack pressed the sword's blade harder into The King's neck, just barely breaking his flesh; The King's blood trickled.

"Where is it!?" warned The Jack, to The King.

"Around your brother's neck" replied The King.

"Get it, and open the cell, now! I won't ask again," Jack said, to The 10.

The 10 hurried over to the dazed Ace. He opened his shirt and ripped the key from the leather around his neck, and hurried over to Justice's cell, unlocking it.

"Justice, get behind me! Quickly!" The Jack demanded of Justice.

Justice hurried to The Jack, standing behind him, her hands touching his shoulders. The Ace started to regain his focus and now lunged toward The Jack. The soldiers quickly restrained him.

"We're leaving. . . and if anyone tries to follow, I'll slit his miserable throat!" warned The Jack.

The Ace and the soldiers stood by, helpless.

"Open the door and stay close. You go down first." Jack instructed Justice.

Justice opened the alcove door and began her decent. With the sword still resting on his father's throat, The Jack and The King slowly walked backwards to the stairs and descended.

The overwrought Ace went to his mother lying on the floor, his sword still impaled in her heart. He carefully pulled it out, the blade dripping with her blood. The Ace raised his fist into the air.

"I swear by my mother's life. . . I will hunt you down and bring you back. . . and when I do. . . you will die the most *horrible* and *painful* death—**Brother!**" vowed The Ace.

The images faded. It seemed to me that time stood still.

I wrote all that I saw and heard this day, a day like no other. . . but somehow—I felt it was not enough.

17.

A FOOL NO MORE

I watched as the The Land of The King entered into night. I could clearly see its position on the Earth had rotated past the rays of the Sun. Once again, the Moon ruled over The King's Land.

The Jack of Diamonds and The Lady Justice sat close to each other in front of a blazing campfire; they had made camp for the night. Off in the distance, I saw The King of Clubs seated on his horse, helpless. His hands were tied behind his back and his mouth still gagged. The King's horse trotted aimlessly, wandering further and further away from their camp.

"What will happen to him" asked Justice, softly.

"The horse will wander lost for a day or two; eventually it should make its way back to the castle," Jack replied.

"Is it because he is your father that you let him live?" asked Justice.

"The 3 was my father. . . and he died in my arms back at the castle. I came for <u>you</u>, not to kill The King," Jack replied, as his eyes devoured hers.

The Jack took her forcefully her into his arms: a force of born of passion, not of dominance. Justice willingly succumbed, breathless. As he was about to kiss her, Justice noticed blood dripping from his shoulder. Instantly, she pulled back from his embrace.

"Jack! You are bleeding badly, take off your shirt," said a concerned Justice.

The Jack took off his shirt, still staring into her eyes. Justice ripped off a piece of her garment.

"I need to hold this against your shoulder or you will bleed to death" she said, as she placed the cloth lightly on his skin, staring at his bare chest, instinctively moving closer to him.

"Jack, why did you rescue me?" Justice coyly asked.

"I was hired by The Hermit" he replied, stoically.

Justice unconsciously pressed harder on his wound, obviously disappointed by his answer. The Jack grimaced. He pulled her hand off his shoulder.

"That's enough Justice," said The Jack.

"But you're still bleeding," Justice said, somewhat confused.

"It will stop. . . It always does," replied The Jack.

I could sense Justice feeling powerful emotions raging inside of her that were new and strange; these were physical feelings of the body. . . the callings of the flesh; emotions and drives she had never experienced, and Justice wanted more. She was uncontrollably drawn to him, her heart racing, wanting to know his touch, bewildered by his behavior, yet willing to be led wherever he would take her—he did not.

As glowing embers rose from the fire into the star filled sky, neither spoke a word. Justice fell asleep in his arms.

As I reflected back, I became overwhelmed by the power of human love. This love was different than that which I have for my Creator. It had a pull, a longing. . . born of the human emotions. I could feel its powerful physical attraction, and sense its impending union, a union both in body as well as spirit. My thoughts were interrupted by sound of water—swirling water.

My eyes returned to The Forest of Cards and saw The Hermit standing over his pond, stirring the water with his staff. His eyebrows furrowed, as no image appeared. The Hermit churned the water more deliberately than before, waited for the ripples to subside, and looked in again, showing no outward emotion.

I turned my gaze and found Temperance, seated with Jupiter and Juno, a little ways off from The Pond. The Fool stood nearby The Hermit, milling about, still searching for his wallet. The Hermit stepped back from The Pond and approached Temperance; The Fool followed him, not far behind. . .

"Hermit, tell us what you've seen!" asked Temperance.

"Has The Jack of Diamonds rescued Justice?!" Jupiter quickly interjected.

"Is our daughter safe!?" implored a worried Juno.

With no outward display of emotion, The Hermit answered, "The Jack has been betrayed by one of his own men. He has fought with The Ace to a draw, and he has *freed* Justice. She is with him now."

The group rejoiced at the wonderful news.

"Although Justice is now free. . . she still is not safe. The Jack will have to protect her from The Ace and his men who are at this very moment in full pursuit not far behind," continued The Hermit. "However, there is another cause of greater concern," said The Hermit, pausing. The group's attention sharpened. "It seems as though love has entered Justice's heart. You were right Juno," explained The Hermit.

"It's the outlaw, The Jack of Diamonds?" Juno instinctively asserted.

"Yes," Hermit replied.

"Hermit, can he save her from The Ace?" Juno softly asked.

"What do you mean *save* her, Juno! If she *gives* herself to him, or if he *takes* her in passion, she will *die!*" exclaimed Jupiter.

"Not exactly Jupiter, she will become forever mortal — human." The Hermit clarified. "Justice will still live the many natural years allotted to those on the Earth," said The Hermit. However, she can never return here to The Forest, for then she would die within days.

"Hermit, does Justice now know what will happen to her if she gives her heart and body in love?" Temperance asked.

"Or if it is taken!" Jupiter interjected.

"No," said The Hermit.

"Then, she must be told. And if knowing what will happen, she still chooses to love as a woman does a man. . ." Temperance continued.

I saw The Fool listening attentively to the discussion. I watched as he sauntered over in the direction of The Pond, unnoticed by the rest.

"Why do all men think love is a matter of choice? You cannot control love, nor can you deny it!" explained a frustrated Juno.

"But Juno, if Justice knows of love's *consequences* to her. . . she might choose to *resist* it!" Jupiter reasoned.

I saw Juno's eyes tear as only a mothers' can.

"Our only concern should be whether The Jack of Diamonds *truly loves* Justice! For if he does, then he will *always* protect her and never do anything to hurt her!" Juno poured out.

"Somehow, they *both* must be told," reasoned Temperance.

The Fool, standing at The Pond's edge with his back to the water, firmly shook his head in silent agreement.

"Temperance is right Hermit!" The Fool boldly proclaimed.

The startled foursome turned in The Fool's direction. The Hermit's eyes widened.

"Quickly Fool, away from The Pond!" shouted The Hermit.

"I may be The Fool, Hermit, but even I can plainly see they <u>both</u> must be told," said an adamant Fool, folding his arms together in punctuation. As he did so, he took an unconscious step backward. "Now, what are we gonna do?!" he demanded.

"Not another step, Fool!" Hermit shouted.

The Fool paid no attention to The Hermit, shaking his head in disagreement with him. As he did so, he took yet another step backward, unaware, and fell into The Pond. A blinding white light flashed. In an instant, The Fool disappeared. The foursome looked to each other, their faces in shock.

#

My gaze followed The Fool through the void across dimensions to The Land of The King. There he laid on the ground next to the Speaker's Square in the village. I could see him clearly, the morning Sun shining on his face, dazed, and barely conscious from the fall.

Some villagers passed him by unnoticed, while others saw him but paid him no mind. As his consciousness slowly returned, a young woman, two decades and one in age, heard his groans and came to his aid. She was small in stature, slender with hair cropped ever so short and dressed in a way that seemed odd and out of place, yet curiously attractive. She stood over The Fool looking down, her hands on her hips. . .

"Well well, will you look here. You're a sorry sight. Too much to drink did ya? No matter, Phoebe 'il help ya" said Phoebe, her accent and vocal cadence — strange.

Phoebe knelt down. As The Fool's eyes cleared, he saw Phoebe smiling at him. Remarkably, she took his head into her hands and began shaking it rather briskly, as if she were clearing out the silks of a spider.

"Unhand me woman, you're making me woozy!" said The Fool.

Phoebe stopped shaking his head, and while still holding it off the ground, furrowed her brow as she released her hold. The Fool's head thumped hard to the earth. The Fool maintained his composure, still not knowing what had happened to him, as his hands rubbed his head. . .

"That's better, I didn't mean to offend, but you were making me dizzy," apologized The Fool, still lying flat on the ground.

I don't know why, but I could sense he was now somehow different than before, more self-assured, reasoned. Phoebe took her hand and impulsively ran it through her short hair.

"Most men say I have that effect on them," she said, unconsciously flirting. "Are you going to speak?"

"Speak. . ?" he replied, confused.

"Yes, speak here," she said, pointing up to The Square.

The Fool, still lying down with Phoebe hovering over him, turned his head to look.

"This is the Speaker's Square. I'm sure someone will listen to you. I know I will," Phoebe assured.

The Fool got up, with Phoebe's help, and brushed himself off. Kellin and Myra now passed by the twosome.

"Hello Phoebe, how good to see you," Myra said.

Instantly, Phoebe grabbed The Fool, locking her arms within his.

"Good morning Myra. . . Kellin. This is my good friend," Phoebe said, awkwardly, as she looked at The Fool, her eyes demanding an answer.

"I am The F-o-o. . ." replied The Fool, pausing before he completed his name. "I mean. . . I am Henry. Yes, my name is Henry," he confidently stated.

Kellin extended his hand in friendship. The two men shook. Myra winked approvingly at Phoebe who then smiled and finally loosened her grip on Henry, The Fool.

"What brings you to our village Henry?" asked Kellin.

"I am looking for a woman and a man who are traveling together. I *must* find them quickly, and speak to them on a *most urgent matter!*" said a concerned Henry.

"Well Henry, we know most everyone. Just tell us their names and I'm sure we can help you," said Myra.

"Do you know a woman called Justice and a man known as The Jack of Diamonds?" asked Henry, his hopes rising.

"Justice!" exclaimed Myra.

"The Jack of Diamonds!" exclaimed an astonished Kellin.

"They are together?!" Myra asked.

"Yes, but it is most urgent that I. . ." Henry said.

"That *we!*" interjected Phoebe.

"That *we* find them," Henry said, not knowing why he corrected himself.

"Please Henry, tell me all that you know!" Kellin implored.

"I know that The Jack of Diamonds has rescued Justice from The King's Tower Prison," said Henry.

Kellin and Myra could not believe what they were hearing.

"Henry, is this really true!?" asked Myra.

"Yes, but will you help me. . ?" implored Henry, who stopped talking as Phoebe squeezed his arm. "I mean help *us,*" Henry corrected. "Help us find them?"

I watched as Kellin's demeanor changed. I could feel his cautiousness growing. He looked hard at Henry.

"Are you friend or foe, Henry?" demanded Kellin.

Henry cowered back in fear at the question, seemingly a reflex of his former make-up. Then, he took in a deep breath, and then with a sense of righteous indignation, he confidently asserted. . .

"The Ace and his men are in pursuit of Justice and The Jack. Justice is my friend! I do not know The Jack. That is all I can tell *you* for now. Now, do you know where they can be found or not?!" Henry concluded, with an audacious and reasoned spirit.

Both Myra and Phoebe looked to Kellin with complete belief.

"Do you ride Henry?" Kellin asked, now reassured of Henry's integrity.

"I hope you do not mean in a chariot?" said Henry, anxiously.

"Horses, Henry, I mean do you ride horses?" clarified Kellin.

"Horses?" said Henry, apprehensively; recalling his ride with Chariot.

"Henry will ride with me on my horse," interjected Phoebe.

"Good. Myra, round up the villagers and tell them what has happened. I will lead our friends to where The Jack might be found," said Kellin, taking charge.

"Help them Kellin!" Myra implored.

Kellin nodded to Myra. Confidently, he turned to Phoebe and Henry.

"The horses are over here. . . Lets go!" said Kellin.

Kellin and Phoebe, still holding Henry's arm, practically dragging him, both ran to nearby horses.

"H-o-r-s-e-s!?" Henry cried.

"Don't worry my love, I know how to ride!" Phoebe said.

"M-y l-o-v-e?" said a very confused and apprehensive Henry.

Kellin and Phoebe quickly mounted. Phoebe extended her hand down and yanked a clumsy Henry up into the saddle, seating him in front of her. Then Phoebe put her arms around him, tightly.

Kellin spurred his horse, charging off. Phoebe grabbed the reigns of her horse and snapped them, making her mount rear up on its hind legs.

"You're so brave Henry!" said Phoebe.

"I a-m?" replied a perplexed but resigned Henry, as the horses front hooves landed back on the ground.

Phoebe skillfully dashed off following Kellin. I continued to watch them until they disappeared from my sight. My inner spirit could not help but smile: for I still could hear Henry's hysterical cries, and vividly pictured the image of him bouncing on Phoebe's horse, but now—*no longer The Fool.*

18.

HONOR AMONG THIEVES

I heard the sound of thunderous horses, their mighty hooves pounding the earth, and then I saw Chariot driving his carriage into the clearing nearby The Hermit's pond; he brought Strength with him.

The two virtues got out and joined Temperance, Jupiter, and Juno, who were in deep conversation, looking anxiously at The Hermit, who stared with pain-staking attention into The Pond. As soon as The Hermit lifted his eyes from The Pond, the Virtues approached. . .

"Hermit, Justice has fulfilled her destiny, her message of Light has been delivered. You must bring her back now!" demanded Jupiter.

"No Jupiter! Hermit must only tell Justice what will happen to her if she gives her heart; she must choose freely," countered Temperance.

"None of this will matter if The Jack is not warned of the approaching Ace and his men!" warned Chariot.

Strength could see the strain on Juno's face, a mother's concern. She took her hand into hers, comforting her.

"Hermit, tell us what more you have seen," said Strength.

The Hermit looked to Juno and Strength with grave concern. . .

"The Fool has crossed over, but to where, I could not see for the portal has closed," Hermit said.

"Closed! When will it reopen?!" exclaimed Jupiter.

"I do not know," replied The Hermit.

"Are we to stand here and do nothing?!" Jupiter demanded.

"There is nothing anyone can do until the portal reopens," stated The Hermit.

"What will happen to Justice?" Juno asked, solemnly.

Without any emotion, The Hermit replied, "Her fate lies in the hands of The Jack of Diamonds. . ." The Hermit paused, now showing apprehension, ". . . and The Fool."

Juno embraced Strength as Temperance reacted with acceptance.

"The Jack is strong," interjected a reassuring Chariot.

"Maybe so, but what of The Fool!?" countered Jupiter.

The sound of loud crackling twigs being crushed interrupted The Hermit's forthcoming answer. The group turned and faced Death mounted on his horse, approaching. He brought his steed to a halt right in front of The Hermit.

"Yes, Hermit, tell us. . . what of The Fool?" mocked Death.

Not waiting for the answer, Death laughed and snapped the reigns of his horse, riding back into The Forest. All looked to The Hermit. . .

"I do not know," The Hermit replied, accepting the uncertainty of the situation.

The images faded; I quickly wrote all that I saw and heard.

#

I felt my mouth parched, a burn in my eyes, and my throat coarse; it felt like I had been eating dust from the Earth. Then I saw them, a band of soldiers on patrol, galloping through the northern hills of No Man's Land; in their wake, a large plume of dust rose into the air. Not far off, Kellin, Phoebe, and Henry were riding. Kellin spotted the dust on the horizon. . .

"Look, soldiers coming this way!" exclaimed Kellin.

"Do you know which way to go, Kellin?" said a cool headed Henry.

"I'm pretty sure The Jack can be found. . ." Kellin turned his head, surveying the landscape, and then pointed, ". . . in the hills to the north, but. . ."

Henry quickly interrupted, "Kellin, just make sure you point them in the wrong direction when they ask you."

Henry quickly fell to the ground and then looked up to a confused Phoebe.

"Phoebe, rip my shirt and scratch my face!" implored Henry.

Phoebe stared down at him, still confused.

"Hurry Phoebe, do it before they see you!" he exclaimed.

Phoebe ripped Henry's shirt and reluctantly scratched his face. Henry grimaced, Phoebe jumped back, thinking she had hurt him, but Henry quickly shook his head in approval, reassuring her.

"Kellin, run toward them and yell for help. Tell them I was attacked by a man and a woman. When they ask you which way they went, send them South!" planned Henry.

Phoebe's eyes lit up.

"Oh my Henry, you are so smart!" Phoebe said, beaming with pride.

She leaned over and kissed him repeatedly; Henry did not know what to do. . .

"Don't kiss him Phoebe! Just pretend you are tending to his wounds!" Kellin scolded.

Phoebe finally stopped kissing Henry, whose face blushed red. Kellin shook his head and then darted off in the soldiers' direction, frantically waving his hands. The soldiers approached with guns drawn. They pulled up their horses in front of Kellin.

"Thank God you are here! My friend has been attacked by an outlaw!" said Kellin, as he gestured to Henry. "We were just riding and. . ."

The Captain of the patrol held up his hand to Kellin and turned to one of his men.

"Ride over and see if he is telling the truth!" ordered The Captain.

A King's 4 rode over to a hysterical Phoebe who was crying over an unconscious Henry. Phoebe shook him and Henry began moaning, pretending to be coming around.

"Oh Henry, thank God you're alive! I thought you were dead, I thought I lost you!" exclaimed Phoebe.

She turned to The 4.

"You must find him and arrest him!" Phoebe demanded.

"Arrest who? Who was it that did this!?" demanded The 4.

"I don't know, but the woman called him Jack!" she replied.

The 4's eyes lit up and he quickly rode back to The Captain.

"It's them Captain, Diamonds and the woman! They can't be far!" exclaimed The 4.

"Which way did they go?" demanded The Captain from Kellin.

"He said he would come back and kill us all if we told," said Kellin, apprehensively.

The Captain cocked his gun and stared menacingly as he pointed it right at Kellin, who then relented.

"South! They went South!" blurted Kellin, pointing to the Southern hills. "Right over those hills!" he exclaimed.

The Captain swiftly turned to his men.

"We must report this to The Ace at once!" he exclaimed.

The soldiers rode off in the direction from which they came. Kellin ran back to Phoebe and Henry.

"It worked Henry! Lets mount up! I know I can find them," exclaimed a confident Kellin.

The threesome mounted.

"Isn't he wonderful Kellin?" praised Phoebe, while gloating at Henry.

Kellin looked to a bashful Henry just as Phoebe wrapped her arms around him, kissing him yet one more time. Kellin smiled at the sight and quickly spurred his horse; Phoebe did the same. As they rode off to the north, I could still hear Phoebe...

"Oh Henry, I love you," she said.

"Y-o-u d-o?" replied a very surprised and confused Henry.

The visions faded.

#

Again, The Keeper's mountain flashed before my eyes, existing in a realm that I did not know. Of the realms I had seen, there were three, of that I was sure: The Firmament, where I observed; The Forest of Cards, where Virtues of man existed, seemingly as humans, but yet they were not; and The Land of The King of Clubs on the Earth, a realm of flesh and blood where human kind live.

I have been sorely troubled by The Keeper, Augustanian, not sure if he was of The Earth, or of The Forest; or yet had existed in a fourth realm? I also questioned his dealing of the cards. Did they simply reflect, in another form, events which had already happened, or did the cards somehow predict that which would soon be? Then I wondered if he alone actually made events happen that heretofore had not?

I put away my thoughts and looked to The Keeper. On his table, I saw the card of THE JUGGLER and the card of THE MOON lying next to each other. I watched Augustanian place his hand on the top card in the deck, holding it there for many a moment before picking it up and observing its face. His brows furrowed.

There in his hand, seemingly staring back up at him, I saw the card of DEATH. The Keeper placed this card sideways across the cards of JUGGLER and MOON. Now with the utmost care, he dealt one more card placing it face down on top of the other three.

Finally, Augustanian took his finger and flipped this last card over revealing the face of THE JACK OF DIAMONDS. He sat back in his chair, his hood obscuring his face, and pondered the formation in front of him.

I too considered my earlier reflections. I wrote all that I saw as well as that which I measured in my thoughts. I sat staring at the scroll reading my observations. As I did so, my mind filled with many questions and feelings. When I looked out again, the image had changed.

Now before my eyes I saw an old wooden structure nestled in a hidden valley in the northern hills of No Man's Land—The Shack. Justice and The Jack were on horseback riding toward it. The Jack's face was that of a man not to be deterred, his eyes. . . cold.

"Must you do this?" implored Justice.

Without even looking at her, The Jack reached over and grabbed the reigns of her horse. The outlaw forcefully yanked back; both horses pulled up to a stop.

"Jack, is it not enough that I am free?" asked a distraught Justice.

The Jack turned and looked at Justice, directly.

"No, Justice, it is not!" he harshly answered. "You wait outside, and no matter what you hear, don't come in. . . this won't take long."

The Jack gave Justice the reigns to her horse and lightly spurred his mount. Justice remained behind, watching The Jack ride on. Reluctantly, she relented and followed suit. Soon, they reached The Shack; The Jack pulled up. With their horses barely two cubits from each other, The Jack handed Justice the reigns of his horse; she refused to take them.

"Jack, please, don't!" begged Justice, passionately.

Without hesitation, The Jack dismounted and walked his horse up to the hitching post. As he tied his mount to the post and without looking at Justice, he said, "My hideout is over there to the north." The Jack looked up to Justice, her eyes still pleading. "The Hermit should be there waiting," he said, void of any emotion.

The Lady Justice stared hard at The Jack, confused as to what to do. I could feel her inner conflict between the virtues she represented and her powerful newfound feelings as a woman. She sighed in frustration and defiantly spurred her horse, riding off. With no outward reaction, Diamonds turned and opened the door.

Now inside The Shack, I saw a room packed with many outlaws and loose women sitting at small tables strewn about. Noise filed the room and the atmosphere was that of a party; yet I could feel a level of intimacy between the men and women that was only of the flesh—I felt no spirit.

Near the back wall, I saw a long narrow table that spanned the entire length of the room. On one side, many men and women sat on tall chairs drinking fermented wine, their glasses being continually filled by a man who stood on the other side of the table. It was the first time I had observed a bar.

At first, The Jack of Diamonds entered the room unnoticed by the crowd. Then one outlaw, seated at a far table with his woman, reacted with disbelief upon seeing him.

"I thought he was. . ." said the startled outlaw.

"I'm not!" replied an emphatic Jack.

The Jack continued to walk slowly, surveying the room and then eyeing the bar. His eyes stopped near its far end where three men stood together. One of the men had his back turned; the other two faced The Jack.

The Jack drew his weapon and pulled back its iron hammer while still advancing on the three men. As soon as the sound of the hammer clicked into place, the room quickly silenced: the hardened outlaw eyes all looked for the readied weapon, and to their disbelief, recognized The Jack—all were in shock.

"Get away from him!" commanded The Jack, to the two men facing him.

The two outlaws quickly moved away leaving the third man alone, still with his back to The Jack. The man started to turn to leave.

"Not another step Little Deuce!" ordered The Jack. The 2 froze in his tracks. "Stay where you are, and don't turn around."

The 2, not moving a finger, shouted to the other outlaws in the room, "The Ace and The King will pay dearly for him, dead or alive! Look!" he said.

I watched The 2 throw a small cloth pouch over his head; the purse landed on one of the small tables, opening. Gold and silver coins spilled out onto the table, rolling off, falling to the floor. All the outlaws' eyes widened, yet, no one made a move.

The Jack's eyes never left The 2 as he shouted to one of the outlaws sitting nearby.

"Pick a coin up, and throw it back to him!"

The outlaw picked up the coin and threw it to The 2 who caught it, still with his back to The Jack.

"Look at it Little Deuce!" Jack demanded. "All of you look at it!" Jack said, to the crowd. "This was his reward for betraying me and my men; it could have been one of you. Now I'm going to reward him," Jack declared.

The Jack of Diamonds coldly fired three shots into The 2's back.

"As a traitor deserves!" The Jack decreed.

The 2 fell dead to the ground. I could see his lifeless hand still clutching the gold coin. Calmly, The Jack turned to the crowd and holstered his gun. Seemingly, rendering himself at their mercy. . .

"Now, if you want gold like this for yourselves, take your business to The King. Or is there still honor among us thieves?" Jack concluded.

I saw the outlaws look to each other. One by one they each drew their guns and stared at The Jack. Nobody moved. Then one outlaw walked right up to The Jack with his weapon drawn, looked him right in the eye, and quickly turned and fired one shot into the back of the dead 2.

"Traitor!" exclaimed the outlaw, as he nodded his allegiance to The Jack.

Like a dam busting, each of the outlaws came up and did the same. Now satisfied, The Jack walked to the door and opened it; shots still ringing out. As he exited The Shack, The Jack saw Justice seated on her horse, waiting. Showing no outward emotion, he mounted up. . .

"I heard shots, I thought it was you," she said, tears running down her face.

"Not yet!" he replied, still void of any outward emotion.

The Jack kicked his horse, Justice quickly followed. They rode off next to each other—in silence.

19.

LOVE LIES BLEEDING

My morning Sun flashed brightly across my eyes. When my vision returned, I saw three open trunks resting near the edge of The Hermit's pond; each filled with precious gold, silver, and diamonds: the riches radiantly reflecting the light.

The Hermit stood over his pond, stirring the waters, while Temperance, Jupiter, and Chariot were gathered not far off in heated discourse. Near to them, a more serene Juno and Strength gave confidence to each other. The Hermit looked up from the water. . .

"The portal has reopened! We must place the trunks into The Pond, now" he said.

Everyone quickly hurried to The Pond.

"Finally, we're getting somewhere. I must warn The Jack!" said Chariot, eagerly.

"Just bring Justice back!" countered Jupiter.

Temperance was about to interject when Strength politely interrupted him; he respectfully gave way to her.

"Hermit, what will you do?" she asked.

"I will keep my word, Strength. . ." The Hermit pointed to the trunks, "and deliver this payment to The Jack."

A concerned Juno went to The Hermit who took hold of her hand in his.

"What Justice and The Jack of Diamonds will do, if they are still alive, I do not know," The Hermit said, softly. Then he turned to the men, "The trunks must be in The Pond before I step in."

The men placed the trunks into The Pond. Without a word, The Hermit stepped in. Once again, my sight was momentarily blinded by the magnitude of the exploding white light. When my vision returned, all I could see was The Pond's water rippling.

As before, The Hermit had crossed over. . . Back to The Land of The King of Clubs.

#

I saw Kellin, Phoebe, and Henry riding up a steep mountain trail in the northern hills of No Man's Land. As they neared the top, a single gunshot rang out, ricocheting off the rocks. Both Kellin and Phoebe's horses startled, rearing up on their hind legs. Henry fell off Phoebe's horse, plopping to the ground. He tumbled back down the hill, rolling over and over until a leather boot stepped on him, stopping his fall.

Phoebe quickly jumped off her steed and ran down the hill toward Henry. As Henry's eyes cleared, he looked up from the ground, staring into the barrel of a gun.

"Are you The Jack, The Jack of Diamonds?" asked an undaunted Henry.

"Yes," Jack replied.

Phoebe reached Henry and knelt down putting her arms around him. She boldly looked up to The Jack and his gun. . .

"Don't you dare hurt my Henry!" she charged.

At the same time, Justice came out from behind nearby brush, ecstatic.

"Fool, is that you!? I can't believe it! How did you get here!? It's so good to see you!"

The Jack holstered his gun and let Henry up. Justice embraced him; Phoebe's eyes bristled at her. Then Kellin approached Justice, her eyes tearing as she warmly embraced him.

"Kellin, I never thought I would ever see you. . . or The Fool," said Justice, being cut off by Phoebe as she grabbed Henry's arm tightly.

"His name is Henry!" said a defiant Phoebe.

Justice was puzzled by Phoebe's words, but did not challenge them.

"Excuse me, or *Henry*. . . ever again!" said Justice.

Kellin quickly interjected, "We don't have much time. Thanks to Henry's quick thinking, we've been able to lead The Ace's men to hills in the South. But soon they will figure it out and head back north!" Kellin looked directly at The Jack. "Jack, I will stand with you!"

Justice looked with great admiration to Kellin.

"Kellin, show me exactly where you led them," The Jack said.

Kellin took The Jack back to the top of the hill. Phoebe tugged on Henry's arm.

"Ah.. Justice, this is my good friend Phoebe," said Henry, somewhat awkwardly.

Justice warmly smiled.

"It is good to meet you Phoebe," said Justice, putting Phoebe more at ease.

At first Henry smiled, but then his countenance dropped.

"Justice, there is something of great importance that I must tell you. I hope that I am not too late," said Henry.

Henry paused. I could sense that he did not know where to begin.

"Go on F-o-o, I mean Henry," Justice encouraged.

"It's about love," said a somewhat bashful Henry.

"Well, I certainly could not help but notice that you and Phoebe. . ." said Justice, smiling.

"No Justice," Henry corrected, now very grave. **"This is about you."**

I looked up and saw The Jack and Kellin at the top of the bluff. The Jack pointed off on the horizon. "Our only chance is to get to my hideout. From there we will be able to hold them off," The Jack said. He looked Kellin straight in his eyes, "When we get there Kellin, no matter what I do. . . you must do *exactly as I say*, without question!"

"I will Jack," Kellin assured. "You can count on me."

"Good. Now lets get back down to the others and get off this bluff," The Jack concluded.

As the two men walked back, my eyes saw a great plume of smoke rising high into the air of the Southern hills. I followed the dust and saw The Ace and his soldiers thundering across the hills, heading to the north. The plume rose higher and higher until it blocked my vision, completely. I lost all sense of time. When the dust cloud finally cleared, I looked further North and saw The Jack leading the group to his hideout. As they approached, The Jack took careful notice that his compound had been left unguarded. He rode up to the front entrance and dismounted; the invisible door opened, revealing The Hermit standing in the doorway.

Justice quickly ran up to The Hermit and threw her arms around him. As he embraced Justice, The Jack walked right past The Hermit, their eyes momentarily meeting. I could feel each of their thoughts; silently acknowledging they both knew what the others did not. The Jack continued on inside, alone, leaving the others outside. . .

"Oh Hermit, I have done it! I have brought the message of love to the villagers. Many have understood! So much has happened, there is a great deal I must tell you!" said an overwhelmed and excited Justice.

145

"There is no need child," said The Hermit.

Justice, still very much excited, grabbed Kellin's arm. "This is my good friend Kellin. It was he and his sister-in-law Myra who took me in!" Justice declared.

The Hermit nodded and smiled to Kellin. Justice now grabbed Phoebe by the arm, practically yanking her off her feet.

"And this is Phoebe. She is my newest friend and *quite a horsewoman!*" said an admiring Justice.

Phoebe took hold of Henry's arm and smiled at The Hermit, half curtsying to him.

"But, if it wasn't for Henry's. . ." continued Justice.

"Henry's?" interrupted a confused Hermit.

"Oh, I mean The Fool's," Justice corrected.

Phoebe scowled.

"His name is Henry!" snapped Phoebe, correcting both Justice and The Hermit.

"I mean, *Henry's* courage and quick thinking," exclaimed Justice. The Hermit raised his eyebrow in curious amazement. "We never would have made it back here!" confirmed Justice.

Kellin cleared his throat.

"Justice, the three of us have helped, but, the only reason you are alive and free. . . is because of The Jack, The Jack of Diamonds!" exclaimed Kellin.

"Well of course Kellin," Justice replied. "Not only did The Jack *save* my life, he *is* my life!" proclaimed an overwhelmed Justice. "Hermit, I have found Love," she said, from the depth of her soul.

The concerned Hermit looked to Henry, hoping for silent confirmation. Henry understood his unspoken question, and subtly nodded *'yes'* back at him. In all her excitement, Justice realized The Jack was not with them.

"Where is Jack?" Justice asked the group.

Before anyone could answer, Lena came to the doorway. Justice was taken back by her presence.

"You must come inside now! The Ace and his men are not far off. The Jack is waiting downstairs; follow me, said Lena.

As the group followed Lena inside, Justice and Lena made brief but stinging eye contact. The center of the conflict—The Jack of Diamonds.

The three trunks of payment sat in The Jack's inner room. Oddly, The Jack ran his hands through the gold, silver, and diamonds, as if in a trance.

"Lena, come here woman and see what we have!" shouted The Jack, as the group entered the room.

Lena seductively walked over to The Jack. His eyes purposely looked her up and down. Then, he lifted her up from her waist, holding her high in the air. Lena held him tightly, pushing her ample breasts close to his face. Finally, like a prize, The Jack placed her on top of the trunk full of diamonds. Lena gloated back at a confused Justice who could not believe what she had just observed. . .

"Who is this woman!?" Justice demanded of Jack.

"I am Lena."

"I did not ask you, Justice scowled back. "I asked him!" she said to The Jack.

"She is my woman, Justice!" replied The Jack.

No one in the group moved or said anything.

"But, I thought that you. . ." Justice said.

"That I what?!" Jack interrupted. "That I Love you!? Don't be silly. You were a job, just like any other!" Jack scoffed to Justice.

In an instant, her spirit was crushed; her heart had been broken. Justice hung her head low, in pain and in shock. Despair, as well as embarrassment, poured out of her.

Kellin could not contain himself and took in a breath, about to speak. The Jack quickly shot him a stare that cut like a knife! Then Kellin remembered his promise to The Jack and relented, as an unaware Henry, Phoebe, and Kellin came over to Justice in an attempt to console her.

"Take her out of here now while there's still time," The Jack said, to The Hermit.

The Hermit softly took Justice by the hand, not showing any emotion.

"I will take you and The F-o-o. . . you and *Henry* back now, said The Hermit, to Justice, still in shock.

"No Hermit, I'm not going back. I'm staying here, with Phoebe," declared a cogent Henry.

Phoebe drew near to him. The Hermit stared at Henry, nodding his understanding and acceptance of the strange turn of events. With tears running down her cheeks, Justice embraced her new friends, Kellin and Phoebe, goodbye. Then she turned to Henry and hugged him, tightly.

"Take care of each other; I will miss you all, I shall never forget you," cried a mournful Justice.

I saw The Lady Justice look one more time at the man she loved. The Jack coldly turned his back to her, smiling at Lena while he ran his hands through the gold, as if Justice were not even in the room. My heart broke for her. . . A heart I did not even know I had.

"Henry," said The Hermit. "The portal will remain open for one more hour! If you change your mind, you must be at The Jack's front door within the hour. I do not know how long it will be till the portal will again reopen!" cautioned The Hermit.

Henry's eyes began to tear.

"Take care of her Hermit," he said.

"You have learned much and done well, Henry. . . Indeed, I am proud!" declared The Hermit, coming from the depths of his soul.

The Hermit took Justice by the hand and exited the room. Kellin, Phoebe, and Henry all walked into the tunnel and watched the two ascend to the top and go outside, closing the door behind them.

Instantly, a flash of bright light crept in from the outside, silhouetting the outline of the door's frame.

The Hermit and Justice had crossed over—Back to The Forest of Cards.

20.

BUYING TIME

They came quickly, yet quietly, hurrying into position. The soldiers of The Ace, his forward detachment, had arrayed themselves outside, all around The Jack's stronghold. . .

"Fire!" commanded The Ace.

A nonstop rainstorm of lead pellets erupted from their guns; all aimed at the front door of the hideout. Wood chips, rock, and clumps of dirt flew in every direction. I could smell the strong odor of burnt sulfur rising into air—gunpowder.

Inside the hideout, Diamonds ran out of his room into the tunnel.

"Kellin, get them all back in here now!" ordered The Jack.

Kellin, Phoebe, and Henry reentered the room. Jack turned to Lena who stood near the rear wall.

"Open the passageway!" he shouted.

I saw Lena pull a distinctly marked brick out of the back wall. As she did so, water poured in from the other side onto the floor. I watched as a portion of the rear wall began to rotate open, its driving force. . . the escaping water. The three outsiders were amazed by what they saw. The Jack turned to Kellin.

"This tunnel is the only escape route! Lena will lead you through. There are fresh horses waiting on the other side. I'll hold off The Ace. . . We'll meet up later," said The Jack.

The shots grew louder.

"No Jack, I stand with you!" implored Kellin.

Phoebe trembled, unconsciously digging her nails into Henry's arms.

"Kellin, if your friends are to live, you must leave with Lena now! I need you to lead them and protect them once you are through the tunnel. Now Go!" commanded The Jack.

Kellin nodded. The Jack grabbed one of his guns from the wall and threw it to Kellin. Lena took Phoebe's arm and led her into the escape tunnel; Henry followed close behind them. Kellin turned once more to The Jack, and in an unspoken declaration of loyalty and admiration, stood at attention, as if a soldier responding to his commander's order. The Jack tilted his head sideways, in proud acknowledgement of the show of respect. Their eyes locked for but a brief moment, yet in that instant, their bond had been sealed forever. Then Kellin turned and quickly followed the others into the tunnel.

The Jack of Diamonds closed the escape tunnel door, and then the front door to his room. Now alone, sealed in, he methodically collected all his guns from the wall and placed them on the table in a pile near to his right hand.

Calmly, as if knowing the impending outcome, and curiously at peace, The Jack sat down, put his feet up on the table, and then picked up the first gun. I watched in sheer amazement, as he mindlessly began to shoot at the walls as fast as he could. As soon as the weapon emptied, he threw it to the floor and grabbed the next one, repeating the process. I could see at least twenty different types of weapons arrayed on the table.

Inside the escape tunnel, Lena led the group, fire torch in hand. They walked as fast as they could, constantly ducking the jagged rock formations that seemed to pop out at will. As they went deeper into the damp and dark tunnel, I could feel their bodies chill.

"It's not much further," said Lena.

The passageway was getting smaller with every step. Suddenly, Lena stopped. They were now standing in near total darkness.

"From here, we will have to crawl on our hands and knees in the dark. But do not worry, I've done it many times before. After about fifty cubits, the tunnel widens again and we can continue on foot to the exit," she said.

"Oh my God!" said a claustrophobic Phoebe, her breathing increasing rapidly.

"Phoebe, you can make it, I'm right behind you," said Henry.

"Henry, I'm so afraid of small tight places," cried Phoebe.

"Now Phoebe, please do as I say, he said calmly. "I want you to close your eyes while we crawl. Let your hands touch the back of Lena's feet and my hands will touch the back of your shoes. . . Don't open them until I tell you, can you do that?" said Henry.

The group could still hear shots echoing in the passageway. Lena's torch went out.

"Henry, I don't think she can make it," said Kellin.

"Yes she can! My Phoebe can do anything," countered Henry.

"M-y P-h-o-e-b-e?" mused a rallying Phoebe, inspired by his claim of her. She took in a deep breath, "Lead on Lena."

Lena knelt down, her torch extinguished by the dirt. The group began their crawl—in the dark.

Inside the hideout, I watched as The Jack took his last two guns off the table, holding one in each hand, and fired at will into the air: their chambers quickly emptied. The Jack put the spent weapons down and took out some tobacco, rolling a cigarette exactly as I saw The 3 do, days before. I could not understand why he just sat there, calmly, blowing puffs of smoke into the air, seemingly unaffected by the shouts of The Ace's men who were now breaking into the front door of the stronghold.

#

Lena had just exited the escape tunnel, passing through an opening on the far side of the mountain that was perfectly hidden by natural rock and sagebrush. Not far behind her, Phoebe and Henry followed. Nearby, there were fresh horses tied to a hitching post. As Lena ran to the post, a shot rang out. Immediately, she grabbed her stomach and fell to the ground. In the nearby brush, I saw a lone soldier, a 10, lying down holding a riffle; smoke billowed up and out from the barrel of his weapon.

Phoebe and Henry ran toward Lena and as they did so, The 10 boldly got up and sighted them while they were now out in the open. Just as the soldier made ready to kill them, Kellin emerged from the cave, and without hesitation, fired three rounds at The 10—killing him instantly.

Henry and Phoebe made it to Lena. They quickly knelt down and placed their hands under her head. She was bleeding badly, her hands tightly grasping the wound in her stomach. Kellin joined them and also knelt down as Lena fought for her last ounce of being. . .

"I have loved him all my life, but I never had his heart," said a resigned Lena.

"Lena don't talk, save your strength," Kellin said.

"The Jack *truly loves Justice!* He knew that if he did not break her heart, she would not go. . . It was the *only way* he could save her life!" explained Lena.

She struggled to continue, now coughing up blood. Phoebe ripped off a piece of her shirt and dabbed Lena's mouth. Henry put his hand on top of Lena's hands, putting pressure on her wound. I could tell the touch of another comforted her.

"Lena please, you must save your strength," said Kellin, more resigned to her immanent death.

"Kellin, if you are truly his friend. . . you will help him! The Jack will not resist when The Ace comes. He will allow himself to be taken to the castle, tortured, and then killed!" said Lena, fighting to explain.

Now Lena was barely conscious, her spirit departing from her mortal body. She made one last attempt to speak, holding Henry's arm.

"He had to hurt her. . . to break her heart! It was the only way he could save her from certain torture and death—the only way. . . Henry, you must tell Justice, you must!" said Lena. Her grip on Henry's arm relaxed. Her body fell limp. Phoebe's tears fell onto Lena's face, washing the dirt that stained her skin. Phoebe gently wiped Lena's face clean and then softly closed her lifeless eyes.

"We must do something!" exclaimed Phoebe. "The Jack has not only saved Justice, but our lives as well!" said Phoebe, as she wiped her tears.

"I will ride to the village. By now Myra has rounded up most of the men from the nearby villages. We'll storm the castle. If we are lucky, one of us might get to him in time!" exclaimed Kellin, methodically.

"Kellin, without The Jack of Diamonds, we cannot fight The Ace. . . Don't do anything until I return!" implored Henry.

Kellin and Phoebe looked to each other, confused.

"I must go back and tell Justice of The Jack's love for her! And when I return, I will bring back Chariot. He will lead the village militia against The Ace!" Henry said.

"But Henry, there is barely enough time for you to cross back over! And even if you make it, the portal surely will close before you can get back!" countered Kellin.

"Yes, Henry, Kellin's right. You heard The Hermit say, 'He doesn't know when it will again reopen!'" pleaded Phoebe.

"It's a risk we have to take. We need Chariot. . . and Justice must know about The Jack's love for her!"

Kellin reluctantly shook his head, and then declared, "I'll only wait three days, Henry. If you're not back by then, I will lead the villagers against The Ace!"

"No Kellin, you must wait till I return! Without Chariot, you don't stand a chance!" Henry countered.

"Three days Henry. . . The Jack is my friend!" exclaimed Kellin, emphatically.

Henry paused and accepted Kellin's loyalty to The Jack. The two men briefly hugged. Henry looked reassuringly to a teary Phoebe.

"Don't worry Phoebe, I will be back," said a convictive Henry.

Phoebe threw her arms around him and kissed him. Henry blushed.

"I know you will my Henry," said Phoebe, with great admiration.

Henry turned and ran back to the escape tunnel.

"Phoebe, do you think Justice will return with Henry?" asked Kellin.

"Kellin, Justice loves The Jack, and once she knows the real truth, how could she not," said Phoebe.

Kellin smiled and then his face suddenly showed concern.

"What is it Kellin? asked Phoebe.

If Justice does return, and. . . if we are too late to save The Jack. . . The Ace will surely kill her as well!" offered Kellin.

"Kellin, how long do you think The Jack can hold out?"

"Three days at the most," answered Kellin, with grave concern all over his face.

I too considered, anxiously, the fate of The Jack. When I looked out again, the Sun neared the end of this day's cycle. The hills of No Man's Land were bathed in a burnt orange glow. There in the center of the courtyard, outside of the main door of the hideout, stood The Jack of Diamonds, a prisoner.

A company of The Ace's 5's riffled about, searching the near perimeter. A unit of 4's went inside the stronghold. The Jack of Diamonds stood silent. I could see a long rope some 20 cubits in length, tied about his waist. The other end lied loose on the ground. Two 10's stood only a few feet away from the infamous outlaw, their rifles trained on the prize.

The Ace emerged from the company soldiers and approached his brother; The Captain of The 4's at his side. Both men stood in front of The Jack.

"My Lord, we have searched everywhere. The hideout is deserted, The Queen of Hearts is nowhere to be found!" said The Captain.

The Jack smirked.

"My dear brother, you will just have to be satisfied with me. Justice is free, and you will never see her again!" The Jack declared.

"Yes, you may have managed to save her life. . ." replied The Ace. "Tie his hands behind him," commanded The Ace to The Captain.

As The Captain tied The Jack's hands behind his back, Diamonds watched another soldier pick up the loose end of the long rope that tied about his waist, quickly fastening that end to the saddle horn of one of the nearby horses.

The Ace pulled out his sword and placed it next to The Jack's throat.

". . . However, before I'm done with *you*. . . you will *beg me* to slit your throat, *Brother!*" The Ace ominously concluded.

The Ace turned from his brother and walked back to his horse. Then The Jack's eyes caught Henry's head peering out the hideout door from the inside. He realized Henry was going back to The Forest. . .

I could feel The Jack's worst fears coming to fruition: a fear that Henry would bring Justice back; and now a prisoner, he would not be able to save her from certain torture and death at the hands of The Ace!

"Drag him back to the castle!" commanded The Ace.

The soldiers spurred their horses. The rope snapped tight; Jack's body snapped forward, slamming into the dirt. As The Jack was being dragged across the ground, he saw a flash of light coming from the door.

"N-O!" screamed The Jack to Henry, his cries muffled by the hooves of the thundering horses.

Henry had crossed back over.

I watched in horror as galloping horse ripped The Jack's body across the terrain; his face and body being repeatedly smashed with each helpless strike with the ground.

I took up my quill and faithfully entered the accounts of this day.

21.

THE SALT OF THE EARTH

I heard a great clamor about, coming from The Forest near The Hermit's Pond. Jupiter and Juno, Temperance and Strength, as well as Chariot and the returning Henry, were all embroiled in feverish conversation with each other, and with Justice. I saw The Hermit standing apart from the group, next to The Pond. . .

"Justice, you are not going back and that is final!" shouted Jupiter.

The stunned group fell silent at Jupiter's stern outburst to his daughter. Justice softly took the hands of both her parents.

"I am going back with Henry and Chariot. . . to where I belong. . . to the man I love." said a resolute but respectful Justice.

"Justice!" countered Jupiter, not swayed.

"Father, The Jack gave up his life for me, and if need be, I would gladly give up mine for his," she declared.

Juno put her arms around her daughter. Strength came over and did likewise. Jupiter's eyes began to tear: now the tears of a loving father.

"If that outlaw ever hurts you I'll. . ." said a resigned Jupiter.

Justice cut him off, reassuring him, "Father, as you could never hurt mother. . . The Jack could never hurt me."

Jupiter opened his arms to his daughter. Justice came into his embrace and softly whispered into his ear.

"I love you father."

Jupiter hugged her even tighter, then pulled back, regaining his royal demeanor.

"Have you worked out a plan?" he inquired of Chariot.

"Yes, Jupiter. Once we cross over, I will. . ."

"The portal has closed!" interrupted The Hermit.

Justice ran over to The Pond, the others quickly followed, all looking to The Hermit.

"There is nothing we can do. . . but wait," he declared.

The vision faded and then I heard The Forest wind rustling through the treetops, catching my attention. Strangely, it felt cold, yet the Sun's rays radiated strongly. I followed the light and saw Death, camouflaged by dense forest, peering through a cache of trees behind The Pond.

He pulled back the foliage into place and turned to MAGUS, THE MAGICIAN. His age, two decades and eight. He stood tall, his frame slender. On his right side, he wore a pouch that attached to a belt around his waist. Magus dressed in a white tunic that bore the number I on the front; across his shoulders draped a bright red shawl.

"Magus, go deep into the western forest and seek out Pride, The Hanged Man. He will be suspended upside down, dangling from the Tree of Vanity! It is the only tree whose branches bear no leaves. Cut him down and bring him back here with you!" ordered Death, in a whisper, barely above life's breath.

"That will take days. . . What if the portal should reopen before I return?" reasoned Magus.

"YOU are The Magician! Cast an invisible cloud over the top of The Pond. If the portal should reopen before your return, they will never know," proffered Death.

Magus slyly smiled, amazed by Death's unending cunning. Then I watched as Magus opened his pouch and removed a tiny candle and small clear empty glass bottle. The Magician placed his finger on the candle's tip; it lit! Then, he placed the burning candle underneath the bottle, heating it.

Next, Magus dropped the candle to the ground, and carefully using both hands, raised the bottle up to his lips, lightly blowing on it. I could see his face smile in approval, although I could not discern why.

"It is done, the cloud hovers above the water, invisible. . . they will never know," declared a pompous Magus.

"Excellent! When you return with Pride, you will lift the cloud. After Justice and Chariot cross, then you and The Hanged Man will secretly cross behind them," said Death, peering through the trees at Justice and The Hermit. "The Light will not triumph over the powers of Darkness!" prophesied Death, salivating over their impending destruction.

#

My eyes shuttered at the sight of his brutalized body. There in the open courtyard of the castle, in the center of The Ace's Ring of Torture; The Jack of Diamonds hung from a beam with his hands tied to a short rope that suspended him in the air. His boots sadistically dangled but less than a half a cubit from the ground. Arrayed around him inside the ring, were various devices of human torture.

Two soldiers holding black whips flanked him, one standing in front, the other directly behind. For a brief moment, I could feel the stings from their lashes as the two soldiers ripped the leather tails of the flogs across his bare chest and back. The Jack hung there delirious, his skin ripped to shreds and bleeding badly; his blood running onto the ground. The Ace approached. . .

"Stop!" commanded The Ace.

The soldiers quickly obeyed, yet were confused. The Ace slowly and methodically circled around his brother, carefully examining his torn up body.

"Now that his wounds are sufficiently raw. . . get the salt. The noon day Sun should burn it in quite nicely!" said the sadistic Ace.

The two soldiers smiled, agreeing with their lord. They picked up nearby buckets of salt that were nestled in among the torture devices.

"My dear brother, if you can. . . do look around you," said The Ace. He gestured to the array of grotesque torture devices; The Jack's eyes followed his hands. "For this is but the first of what I have in store for you!" The Ace turned to the two soldiers, commanding, "BURN HIM!"

The soldiers each threw their bucket of salt on him; one onto his chest, the other pelting his back! The Jack screamed out in unbearable pain as the salt burned into his raw open flesh!

"J-U-S-T-I-C-E!" screamed The Jack.

#

In an instant, two cycles of the Sun and Moon had passed. Time seemed to dissolve. I found him before Magus did. As I looked over a knoll in The Forest of Cards, I saw a clearing—the Valley of Vanity.

Scattered throughout the dell were many small trees of various sort. In the center of the hollow stood the tree with no life, no leaves: The Tree of Vanity. It stood fifteen cubits in height, and nature shaped its form liken to that of the letter T.

I saw Pride, The Hanged Man, suspended upside down, slowly swinging to and fro. His right ankle had been tied to the top of the tree, and the attribute's left leg folded ninety degrees, bent at the knee. Pride was dressed in a one piece shirt and shorts; his hands were folded behind his back. The Hanged Man wore moccasins on his feet. Etched into Pride's right shoe—the number XII.

Magus stood at the top of the knoll looking down to the valley below. I could feel his astonishment at the unusual sight of the upside down Hanged Man, swinging from the rope. The Magician quickly rushed down the embankment, heading to The Tree.

#

It was the morning of the third day since Henry's departure. A nervous Kellin looked down the road that led to the village; he saw no one coming. All the villagers were gathered nearby making preparations. As fast as they could, they constructed makeshift weapons from the simple materials that laid about.

Myra, holding Kent in her arms, and Phoebe stood with the villagers as Kellin addressed the crowd. . .

"My friends, we cannot wait any longer! If The Jack dies, The Ace will surely lead The King's soldiers against us. He will kill all who dared to follow our Queen of Hearts! We must ride now!" said an impassioned Kellin.

To a one, the villagers shouted out in agreement. They quickly assembled into marching ranks; those that had horses mounted up. Most carried farm tools now repurposed as weapons; only a precious few had guns.

Kellin walked his horse to the front of the militia taking to Phoebe and Myra.

"Phoebe, ride out to The Jack's hideout and wait for Henry and Chariot. If they should return, you lead. . ."

"He *will* return, Kellin!" interrupted a certain Phoebe.

"When they return, bring them to the staging area as fast as possible! Chariot will lead us against The Ace," Kellin instructed.

"I will Kellin!" replied Phoebe.

"If they do not return within four hours, we will have no choice but to fight as best we can; then I will lead them.

Kellin mounted his horse and turned to the rag tag contingent.

"For our Queen of Hearts, our Justice, who brought us The Light!; For The Jack of Diamonds, who defended us from certain death!; And for *our freedom!*" shouted an impassioned Kellin.

The inspired militia marched out, echoing Kellin's words. The remaining crowd dispersed leaving Phoebe and Myra standing by themselves in the middle of the street. Phoebe embraced Myra, then mounted her horse.

"Phoebe, do you think Henry will return in time with this Chariot?" asked a concerned Myra.

"He must Myra. Without Chariot or The Jack of Diamonds, our men don't stand a chance," she answered.

Myra reluctantly nodded her head, understanding full well the gravity of their situation. Phoebe kicked her heels and rode off. Myra stood quietly, holding Kent close to her heart.

As I watched Phoebe ride off, I wondered once again, the purpose of my existence? Who would read the accounting in my scrolls, and why did the Creator want this? As I considered these questions, I began to feel uneasy; worried that I may not be doing correctly that which my Creator had instructed. For now I had begun to feel human emotions — more and more with each passing Moon. Should I not write that which I felt, as well as all that I saw? These thoughts I further considered. I know I had taken great care, making certain that when I entered my feelings into the scrolls, I had been most diligent in declaring them as such!

My thoughts turned to Phoebe. Would she be able to make it back through the escape tunnel, alone in the dark, crawling on her hands and knees, not being able to stand? I let the mounting emotions fill my being. Then I put away my thoughts, picked up my quill and looked out across the void. . .

I could see Henry standing off from The Pond; he had wandered some forty paces to its rear. His eyes marveled as he spotted fresh hoof prints in the ground. Quietly, and without notice, Henry followed their trail, leading him directly behind The Pond to a thicket of trees and foliage.

Henry's eyes, now more keen, observed broken tree branches and then saw a burnt candle discarded onto The Forest floor; next to that, two sets of footprints, freshly made. Henry considered the totality of what he had observed, and quickly went back to The Hermit who still stood quietly, staring into The Pond. . .

"Hermit, I have seen fresh prints and have found a spent candle lying on the ground behind The Pond. I think Death has been here, spying on us!" said a well reasoned Henry.

Immediately, The Hermit looked back into The Pond, even more closely than before. He handed Henry his staff and then rolled up his sleeve. Carefully, he placed his hand into the water, moving it slowly back and forth, then stopping. His eyes astonished! He pulled his hand out from The Pond and looked with great favor to Henry.

"You are right Henry, and probably Magus as well, for the portal appears closed, the work of the Magician no doubt, but is in fact—Open!" The Hermit confirmed.

The Hermit turned to the nervous group pacing a little ways off.

"The portal is open!" The Hermit declared.

Justice grabbed Chariot's arm, dragging him over to Henry.

"Hurry, Henry, we must cross!" she implored.

As Justice began to embrace the group, The Hermit covertly spoke with Henry, pulling him away from the other virtues. Chariot noticed The Hermit's strange behavior but went along, saying nothing.

"Henry, you cannot cross with them now. You must once again act The Fool that you no longer are," instructed The Hermit.

Henry listened attentively, trying to understand, obviously somewhat confused. The wind now curiously blew strong.

"Death is once again near, I can feel him," warned The Hermit. We must delude him. Henry, you will cross, but only after we know what he is planning!" said The Hermit.

Henry smiled, now understanding fully.

"If you can convince Justice that you are once again The Fool, Death will drop his guard as far as *you* are concerned," reasoned The Hermit.

"Of course, Hermit, I'll do it!" said Henry.

Henry immediately broke away from The Hermit and ran to and fro ranting and raving as he once did before.

"My wallet! My wallet! Someone has stolen my wallet! I found footprints! Let me see your feet!" Henry demanded of Chariot.

"What are you saying, Fool?!" Chariot replied.

Henry ran over to Chariot and quickly bent down, trying to pick up his feet, alternating between his left and his right. In order to stop Henry's foolishness, Chariot put his hands around Henry's waist, about to lift him high into the air, but then caught a subtle look from The Hermit and relented. The mighty virtue played along, trusting The Hermit.

"Stop your foolishness this instant!" Chariot ordered.

Henry paid him no mind and then spied Temperance and Jupiter. He quickly ran over to them as well. . .

"Was it you Temperance!? You are supposed to be my friend!" scolded Henry. Then he turned knowingly to Jupiter.

"Or maybe it was his royal highness, to gain more wealth no doubt!?" accused Henry.

Henry kept running around trying to measure everyone's feet. Justice and the group were truly stunned at the sight.

"That is enough Fool! Quiet down and leave us!" scolded The Hermit.

Henry scampered off, mumbling and looking to the ground for his wallet. The wind continued to blow, strangely. I could see Death, now on foot, still spying, looking in through the trees, keenly observing The Fool's rants.

"I can't believe it Hermit! He is again The Fool. . ! What will I tell poor Phoebe?" said a dumbfounded Justice.

"I'm afraid Justice, once The Fool, always The Fool. Pay him no mind. I will take care of him as before. You and Chariot must leave now while there is still time," Hermit said.

Chariot hurried to The Pond's edge. Justice sadly looked back to where Henry stood, sighing at the sight of his foolishness. Then she turned to her friends, Temperance and Strength and warmly embraced them. Her parents held out their arms to her and Justice quickly went to them; they held her tightly as their eyes began to tear.

"Go on Justice. . . to your new friends, to your new life. Go to the man you love," urged Juno, softly.

Once more Justice looked to Henry, still off in the distance, mumbling to himself. Then I saw Magus and Pride, quietly sneaking in, joining Death; the three covertly watched in silence. Justice looked to Strength.

"Don't worry Justice, we will all watch over him," Strength reassured.

"You must go now Justice," said Temperance.

Justice hurried to The Pond's edge. She took Chariot's hand.

"I love you all," professed Justice.

Chariot led her in. . . the light flashed, they were gone.

22.

SLIGHT OF HAND

Phoebe stood over Lena's rock grave, her hands covered in dirt. She kept looking down at the grave and then back to the escape tunnel opening. I could feel her fear mounting as she considered the trek back through the narrow passageway that would eventually close in on her. Then, for no apparent reason, she smiled broadly; I felt certain, thoughts of Henry were the source of that emotion. Now with a new resolve, she entered the tunnel.

Shortly thereafter, as before, the passageway narrowed around her; forcing her onto to her hands and knees. With each movement forward, the tunnel's diameter continued contracting tightly around her until she stopped crawling. Now totally alone in the dark claustrophobic tunnel, her fears again raged; paralyzing her in place. I could no longer see her through the black pitch, instead only hearing her terrified sobs that filled the secret passageway.

I looked for light to illuminate my vision and now saw Justice and Chariot standing outside of The Jack of Diamonds' stronghold, the front door now visible and left open. As Chariot looked around, carefully surveying the empty compound, only The Jack's horse remained, still tied to the Prisoner's Post, left there by The Ace.

"Are there any weapons inside?" asked Chariot.

"Yes, in The Jack's room, I will show you," replied Justice, as she led him in and down the passageway.

Justice led Chariot to Jack's inner room and entered. Inside, they saw the door to the escape tunnel open, and the floor soaking wet. All four walls were pock-marked full of bullet holes as if an intense shootout had taken place. Justice looked befuddled. . .

"They were all there, on the walls, his guns. . . all kinds of guns, more than thirty; of that I'm sure!" said Justice, her voice growing in volume.

"This doesn't look good Justice!" said a concerned Chariot.

Inside the tunnel, Phoebe could hear muffled voices, her spirit rose.

"Henry! Is that you?!" she cried out, repeatedly.

Justice and Chariot heard the faint cries and followed the sounds to the door of the escape tunnel. Justice's eyes opened wide.

"Oh my God, it's Phoebe!" she said. "Phoebe, it's me, Justice! Are you alright?" Justice shouted into the tunnel.

"I can't move!" Phoebe replied.

"Something is wrong, Chariot! Her voice, I can tell by her voice!" exclaimed Justice.

"I'll go in and bring her out, you stay here" said Chariot, as he entered the tunnel.

"Phoebe, don't be afraid, Chariot is coming in to get you!" exclaimed Justice, standing at the tunnel's entrance.

I watched Chariot move with precision, using his hands to feel his way deep into the dark mountain.

"Phoebe?" Chariot called out, warmly. "I'm almost there, I can hear you breathing," he said.

In the dark, Chariot's hand gently touched Phoebe. Instantly, she let out a shrieking scream.

"Phoebe!" Justice cried out.

"It's alright Justice, I have her!" declared Chariot. "It's me Phoebe, Chariot. Just take my hand, I will lead you back," he said, softly.

"Oh thank God it's you!" said Phoebe, catching her breath.

Moments later, Chariot and Phoebe emerged from the escape tunnel back into The Jack's room. Phoebe ran into the room looking for Henry. She turned to Justice, confused. . .

"Justice, where is Henry!? He said he would come back! He said he would Justice!" exclaimed Phoebe.

Chariot gestured to Justice, who held back her forthcoming answer, not wanting to break Phoebe's heart.

"He is coming back, isn't he Justice!?" Phoebe questioned.

Justice put her arms around Phoebe, consoling her in silence. I could feel Phoebe's spirit fighting her outward assumption. . . desperately not willing to give up her faith and belief in Henry.

"I will explain what I can. . . but first you must tell Chariot where Kellin and the villagers are," said Justice.

Phoebe pointed up, somewhat disoriented.

"Go back out, follow the road that led to the hideout. By now they are about an hours ride away."

"Hurry, Chariot, you take Jack's horse, I will take care of her," said Justice.

Chariot nodded and quickly exited the room. He ran back up the tunnel and out of the hideout.

"Phoebe, are there any other horses around here? I must get to The Jack!" asked Justice.

"Yes, on the other side of the escape tunnel. I will show you," said Phoebe.

"Are you sure you can make it back through?" asked Justice.

"Yes," said Phoebe, as she purposely led Justice to the escape tunnel door. Then Phoebe stopped and turned around, defiantly. . .

"Henry will come back to me! He will come back Justice! I know he will!" said an impassioned Phoebe.

Justice fought back tears of compassion.

"I hope so, Phoebe, I really hope so," she softly replied.

I could feel Phoebe's complete faith in Henry and their love, filling her with newfound strength, winning the battle of spirit in her mind; she would not be deterred.

"Justice, when we get to the middle of the tunnel, we will have to crawl on our hands and knees in the dark. Don't be afraid, just hold on to my feet; I'll get us through," said Phoebe, with a new found sense of purpose. "And Justice, I know you think Henry is not coming back, but he will!" Phoebe declared. "Watch your head."

Phoebe went into the escape tunnel, Justice followed closely behind her.

#

I could see bottles of water, fifty of them by my estimate. They were all spread out on tables that had been arrayed around the Speaker's Square. Near the well, Magus and Pride, The Hanged Man were filling the last of the bottles with an elixir of some sort.

Also laid out on the tables were three piles of colored powder: blue, red, and green; a large bucket filled with the mixture, a mixing bowl, as well as the wand of Magus. The Magician threw one of the filled bottles to The Hanged Man and gestured for him to get up on The Square and speak. Pride effortlessly hopped up onto the square.

"My friends, my friends, my very good friends indeed. My name is Pride, and today is your *lucky* day! For we have brought you a wondrous elixir that will give one the strength of *ten men!*" exclaimed Pride, proudly.

Myra and the other wives of the militia, as well as the older villagers, now gathered round The Square. One of the older men eagerly tried to grab the elixir from Magus who stood holding two bottles of the tonic, one in each hand. Magus teased the man by pulling his hands away and shaking his head. Then Pride called out to the elderly villager. . .

"Not so fast my good man. I'm afraid this elixir is only for younger men, it is far too strong for one of such noble years. If you or any of the fair women of this village were to drink of this. . . I'm afraid your hearts would give out!" proclaimed Pride.

"How do we know it works!?" shouted one of the villagers.

"Ah. . . Pride will show you," he said, tempting with his eyes.

Pride opened his bottle and drank a few sips. He then put the bottle down and placed one hand on the floor of The Square, and effortlessly leaned over, performing a one-arm handstand. He held his upside down position and then bent his left leg down ninety degrees, smiling at the crowd. Then, The Hanged Man finished the stunt with ease, rolling forward, easily hopping up onto his feet.

"How's that!?" Pride inquired.

"A simple carnival trick," replied an unimpressed villager.

Magus stepped forward and menacingly predicted, "Then, look to the rock!"

Pride jumped down from The Square and took a sip from Magus' bottle. He walked over to a huge boulder nearby and wrapped his arms around the rock. The stunned crowd fell silent. As all of the villagers looked to The Hanged Man, Magus opened his eyes wide, his magic unnoticed by the crowd, and slowly raised his two hands up into the air. As he did so, Pride lifted the huge stone off of the ground, holding it high in the air, and then effortlessly threw it some twenty cubits away from him.

The crowd gasped in awe. . .

"We must get this to our men before they do battle with The Ace!" shouted one of the woman.

"Myra, with this elixir, they will surely be able to overpower The Ace's soldiers!" shouted another excited woman.

"You've judged wisely," said Pride, encouraging their line of reason.

The villagers mobbed Pride and Magus, who graciously accepted anything they humbly offered as payment for the powerful elixir. At first, Myra stood hesitant, but then relented and quickly joined her fellow villagers, buying one bottle.

#

The winds in The Forest again swirled near The Pond. Henry sat nearby on a fallen tree keeping watch on The Hermit, who continued his unyielding gaze upon The Pond.

"Quickly Henry, come here!" exclaimed The Hermit.

Henry rushed over to The Hermit who knowingly placed his hand on Henry's shoulder.

"I have seen Magus and The Hanged Man! I now know what Death's plan is!" The Hermit pronounced.

The Sun began its set on the horizon. The winds roared as The Forest sky blackened; thunderclaps boomed across the realm.

"Have you seen Phoebe? Is she alright!?" asked Henry.

"Henry, you must cross now!" implored The Hermit.

I saw a thunderbolt strike the tall tree overhead of The Hermit, slicing into its uppermost branch. I could hear the large limb slowly cracking; finally breaking free.

"Warn Chariot and the others not to drink. . !" said The Hermit, just as the falling tree limb hit him in the head. The Virtue fell to the ground, rendering him momentarily dazed. Henry frantically tried to revive him.

"Not to drink what Hermit!?" he shouted, still shaking him.

The dazed Hermit regained his focus, leaning on Henry as he rose. His eyes saw Death, riding on his horse, thundering into the clearing; heading right for The Pond!

"Into The Pond now!" commanded The Hermit.

The sight and sound of Death charging, momentarily mesmerized Henry; he stood there frozen. The Hermit quickly grabbed Henry and threw him into The Pond just as Death jumped off his horse, lunging after him. The light flashed!

I watched Death reach for Henry a second time; his hands swiping unsuccessfully into thin air. Henry had crossed back over. Furious, a defiant Death scowled at The Hermit, making ready to jump into The Pond.

"I will follow him and destroy him!" raged Death. "You cannot stop me, Hermit!"

I could not believe my eyes as I saw The Hermit block Death's way, knocking him to the ground. Quickly, The Hermit reached into his pocket and threw a handful of blue powder into The Pond. Enraged, Death got up and stood right up in The Hermit's face. The Hermit held his ground, not yielding an inch.

"The portal has closed!" declared The Hermit, triumphantly, as he brushed the mysterious colored powder from his hands.

The natural elements raged out of control as the two men stood unflinching, one to the other.

#

My eyes shuttered momentarily at the sight of The Jack of Diamonds, barely alive, being dragged by two of The Ace's soldiers into one of the open cells in the Tower prison. His body had been viciously tortured, bleeding badly from head to foot. The soldiers threw him face down onto the cell floor. The Jack did not move or make a sound.

Then, curiously, The Ace of Spades entered the prison alcove carrying a sumptuous tray of the finest foods; he smiled broadly at the sight of his brother lying there on the ground—near death. He purposely walked over to The Jack's cell, its door open, and motioned for the soldiers to leave; they did so quickly, saluting him as they passed by. The Ace walked into the cell and placed the tray on the floor next to The Jack's battered face. . .

"Do cheer up brother. . . I have decided to let you live. . . just a little longer," mused The Ace.

The Ace shoved the tray of sustenance with his foot: sliding it closer to The Jack's mouth. Again, The Jack did not react.

"But before you die, there is something I truly want you to see," offered The Ace.

The Jack remained motionless. The Ace playfully sighed, savoring his forthcoming words.

"If you do not eat, you will surely die within the hour. Sadly, you will not live long enough to see your precious. . . *Queen of Hearts!*" he declared.

The Jack's body twitched. Now he summoned all of his strength, barely managing to lift his head, attempting to look at his brother.

"Yes brother, it seems as though The Lady Justice has returned! And at this very moment, she is riding to join the rebel villagers," informed The Ace.

The Jack's face expressed his horror upon hearing this news. His head fell back to the floor.

"Oh, you are right brother. . . I will slaughter them all, all except your Lady Justice! As for her my dear bother, she will be brought back here to my castle. . . and I will kill her right before your very eyes!" savored The Ace.

I watched as The Jack tried to move but could not. His brother looked down at him lying there broken, his face filled with disdain. The contemptuous Ace turned and walked out of the cell, flippantly closing the cell door with just one finger. As he approached the staircase about to descend, he turned one last time to The Jack. . .

"Do enjoy your meal!" taunted The Ace, as he entered the staircase, closing the alcove door behind him.

The Jack struggled with all his might, trying to force his bloodied hand to reach out for the tray—it could not. I could sense his mind filling with thoughts of the woman he loved, and the horrible things that would happen to her at the hands of his brother; he would not let that happen! Incredibly, there before my eyes, I watched as he managed to grab hold of the tray with his teeth, pulling the tray close to his lips! The Jack stuck out his tongue, lapping at the nourishment he so desperately needed. The image faded.

Before I wrote in the scrolls, again I marveled at the power of love, human love. This miraculous emotion that makes one do willingly, anything and everything for the other; even the giving of one's own life if need be. I do not know if I have the capacity to really understand this fully, but each time I encounter it, I glorify my Creator.

23.

A LOVE DESTINED BEFORE TIME

Two more celestial rotations had passed. I could see The Jack sitting on the floor of his cell with his back against the stone wall. There were two empty trays, once filled with food, next to him. The Jack looked stronger, the nourishment fulfilling its purpose.

The Prison Alcove door burst open. Two 10's forcibly brought Justice, with her hands bound and her mouth gagged, into the Tower. Behind Justice, The Ace followed. As soon as Justice saw The Jack, she tried to break free from the soldiers, attempting to run to the man she loved.

The Ace quickly restrained her. Jack awkwardly rose in his cell.

"Take your hands off of her!" demanded The Jack.

The Ace ignored him, turning to the soldiers.

"Leave us," he ordered. The two 10's left.

"Well brother, this is good, very good indeed. <u>You</u> are the one who is locked in a cell, and yet. . . you give me orders!" scoffed The Ace.

The Ace put his hands on Justice's face and then looked back to his brother, enjoying The Jack's anguish. Then he turned once again, looking directly at Justice.

"If you promise not to scream or utter not one word till I am finished speaking. . . I will remove this gag from your mouth. If you disobey. . . I'll kill him now!" warned The Ace.

At first, Justice defiantly stared back at him. In response, The Ace put his hand on his sword's handle, warning her. Justice yielded.

"I'll take that as a yes," said the arrogant Ace.

I watched as The Ace of Spades softly pulled Justice's hair back from her face, removing the gag. Then he raised his finger, pointing, reminding her of his instruction. Justice stood keenly silent. The Ace turned to The Jack. . .

"My dear brother, listen well, for I have a kind and gracious proposition for you. It is most obvious that this woman loves you. And, it is even more evident that you love her! Truly, look at how you've gained some of your strength back in a feeble attempt at somehow protecting her. . . most admirable, I must say," said the condescending Ace. "Most admirable."

"What do you want with her? You have me!" snapped The Jack.

"No. . . I have you both!" corrected The Ace. "And rest assured, you two will die, for that is certain; but how. . . that is up to you!" he proffered.

I could feel anger and rage welling up inside of The Jack; I marveled at his outward composure. The Jack's eyes remained fixed on The Ace as if Justice were not in the room. Her eyes held steadfast on The Jack.

"Consider these two choices brother—carefully. . . I will kill your Queen of Hearts before your very eyes. I will torture her for days, right here in this very alcove; only inches away from your grasp. She will know pain far worse than that which you have endured!" offered The Ace.

The Jacks eyes momentarily closed, seeing the horrible sight in his mind. . .

"Or. . . YOU can kill your precious Justice yourself, as I standby and watch! But consider this choice carefully, for in this way, you are assured that the death of the woman you love will be *quick*. . . and as *painless* as possible!" said The Ace, in the alternative.

Justice hung her head to the floor.

"Choose now!" railed The Ace.

The Jack looked at Justice, who lifted her head back up to him.

"I love you Jack. I love you," she said, with a quiet passion.

The Jack did not take his eyes off the woman he loved as he answered his brother.

"I will kill her," said The Jack, showing no emotion. Then his eyes began to tear—something The Jack had never experienced before.

"Excellent brother, most excellent! And to show you that I am a compassionate man, and a lover of romance. . . I'm gong to let you two be together for one night. I trust you will have much to talk about. But I humbly beseech you both, do try not to think about unpleasant things," said The Ace, delighting in the grotesque irony.

"Guards!" shouted The Ace. The two 10's immediately re-entered the Tower Prison, swords in hand. The Ace led Justice over to The Jack's cell, opened it, and pointed to him.

"My lady, your executioner awaits you," said the sardonic Ace.

Justice ran to The Jack, throwing her arms tightly around him. The Jack momentarily grimaced from the bruises that stained his body.

"You will kill her at Sunrise tomorrow!" scowled The Ace. Then he paused and playfully mused in thought. ". . . right after I have had my breakfast, I should think. Enjoy your time together," declared The Ace.

The Ace of Spades turned and walked out of the Prison, his men following close behind. The Alcove door slammed shut.

The Jack put his hands on Justice's shoulders.

"Justice, why did you come back!?" he asked.

"To be with the man I love. . . the man who gave his life for me so I could live. And Jack, I would rather die at your hand then. . ." said a fervent Justice.

The Jack quickly put his arms around Justice, holding her tightly in a torrid embrace; his charging emotions rendering him oblivious to his physical pain.

"I love you Justice! I've loved you from the moment I first saw you!" said an impassioned Jack.

I too had been overcome with emotions I did not know I had. I watched The Jack of Diamonds open his shirt and remove the red diamond necklace from his neck, softly placing it around Justice. . .

"This was my mother's. . . I never knew her, but I know she would have loved you as I do," said The Jack.

An overwhelmed Justice took a few steps back from The Jack. She looked deeply into his eyes: the look only a woman can give.

"I give you my heart. . . and my soul," she said.

Justice loosened the top of her robe. Her shoulders were now exposed.

"I give you me," said Justice, with overwhelming earthly passion yet still filled with love.

She went to her Jack; they passionately kissed. Justice threw her head back as The Jack's lips burned into her neck. Both their eyes were aflame with desire. Justice took her lover's hands and placed them on the cinch of her robe. The Jack pulled on the cord, her garment fell to the ground. The two were about to became one. . . both in body and in spirit.

I quickly lifted my eyes, for this union was theirs alone. . . not mine. I cried intensely for the first time; but they were both tears of joy in their completed love, and tears of sorrow for what The Jack must do to Justice—only but a precious few hours from now.

I looked out into the firmament, and with all my being, I wished that I had the power to stop time. With all the beauty of creation before me, my heart weighed heavy with sadness as I considered Justice's fate at the hands of the man she loved. I did not realize it then, but somehow, I blamed my Creator.

As I looked out into the firmament again, the Sun's rays seemed brighter than before. Again, like days past, I followed their course down to the Earth—to the Tower Prison. I saw Justice and The Jack awake, lying quietly in each other's arms.

Small beams of morning Sunlight shone in through the tiny opening in their cell wall, the rays glowing beautifully on Justice's face. For a moment in time, all seemed as it should. Then, I heard the sound of iron, the sound of bondage...The Ace's soldiers unlocked The Prison alcove door.

The two lovers got up, Jack whispered to Justice...

"Remember, in his neck, as hard as you can," he reminded her.

The alcove door burst open. The Ace of Spades, dressed in the finest black silk, and two of his 10's entered the prison. . .

"I trust the night went well?" mused The Ace, looking at the disheveled straw on the cell floor. "But now it is time."

"Get them, the woman first," The Ace ordered his 10.

The 10 went into the cell and brought Justice into the center of the alcove. The other 10 escorted The Jack out, stopping near to Justice. The Jack stood calm. The Ace looked to his brother, as if peering into his psyche. . .

"You hide your nerves well brother," The Ace said, somewhat disappointed.

The Ace turned to his men, pointing his finger.

"Be at the ready!" he ordered.

The soldiers trained their guns on The Jack. I watched as The Ace removed a small blade from his waist and carefully handed it to The Jack, blade first.

"This should do rather nicely, and not leave too much of a mess, offered the sadistic Ace.

The Jack took the knife, unconsciously rolling the blade between his thumb and forefinger; he spoke not a word.

"Nothing profound to say. . .? Very well," said The Ace. **"You will kill her now!"** he ordered.

The Jack turned and faced Justice; their eyes locked but for a moment. Then she put her arms around The Jack, holding him tightly. Without hesitation, Justice willingly placed her head on his shoulder. I could sense that Justice wanted to make this horrifying act as easy as possible for the man she loved.

I watched The Jack slowly raise the knife to the side of Justice's neck. With his other hand, he gently lifted her hair off of the skin, exposing the flesh of her neck.

"Yes brother, go on. . . kill her, kill her now!" said The Ace, in a sadistic whisper.

Without wavering, The Jack made a quick cut. Justice's eyes snapped closed in response; she fainted in his arms. Her blood ran down from her neck, falling to her arms, and then onto the prison floor. The Jack knelt down, still with Justice in his arms, and gently laid his love onto the floor.

"You are good brother! That was swift and painless. . . She will quickly bleed to death while she is unconscious. . . *If* you've cut the main artery," said the overjoyed Ace.

The Jack remained over Justice, staring at her.

"Move him," The Ace ordered.

The soldiers grabbed The Jack, pulling him up and away from Justice. The Ace walked over to her and bent down, looking at her closed eyes. As he was about to examine her wound, shots rang out! Two 7's burst into the alcove.

"My Lord! The castle is under attack! Our forces have been defeated in the field! The Village army is now advancing on the castle!" said The 7.

"Go and secure the front wall, now!" commanded The Ace.

The soldiers ran out of the prison, hurrying down the stairs. The Ace drew his gun, pointing it at The Jack, as he bent down to examine Justice's wound.

That's when I saw it, secretly clenched in Justice's right hand—the red diamond. As The Ace pulled back her hair, Justice's eyes suddenly opened wide, staring right at The Ace, but a mere half a cubit from his face. The Ace of Spades startled. Justice quickly jammed the precious stone into his neck! His blood gushed out.

The Ace reeled back in pain, dropping his gun to the floor. Immediately, The Jack lunged for him. The two men fought hand to hand; The Ace's blood slinging wildly all over the room. I watched The Jack beat his brother mercilessly!

Justice picked up The Ace's gun, but could not bring herself to shoot. She stood by overwrought, watching the two brothers brawl about the alcove. The Jack hit him one last time, knocking him stupefied and dazed against the back wall, barely conscious.

The Jack ran back into his cell and peered through the tiny opening to the outside.

"It's a mess!" he yelled.

The sound of gunshots and soldiers yelling grew louder. In the corner, I saw the beaten Ace come to his senses, unnoticed; he grabbed one of the fire torches from the wall. The Ace charged a distracted Justice and, using the lit torch as a sword, lunged at her face. Justice managed to turn away from the front of impending horror, but the torch's flame still managed to singe her skin on the right side of the face.

"J-A-C-K!" Justice screamed out, in excoriating pain, raising both hands to her burned flesh.

The Ace bulleted out, fleeing down the spiral staircase. The Jack rushed to Justice, taking her in his arms. He pulled her hands away from her face and grimaced at the wound. Justice, seeing the look in his eyes, broke free of his hold and ran away from him!

She ran out the alcove, scurrying down the staircase into the main hall. There she passed a large mirror and stopped to look at her face.

"N-O!" Justice cried out, in revulsion at the sight of her burned flesh.

She ran wildly out the hall door to the outside. Justice looked around in panic, not knowing for what or who, just wanting to get away!

Moments later, The Jack came running out the door and saw Justice mounting a nearby horse. He looked to the front wall of the castle and saw the village army under attack. They were pinned down from The Ace's soldiers stationed on the high walls. Then The Jack turned and saw Justice ride off. Without hesitation, he took cover, choosing not to follow Justice, but instead, grabbed a gun from a nearby dead soldier and began picking off The Ace's men, one by one. Nearby, Phoebe saw Justice ride off and quickly mounted her horse, following after her.

As The Jack continued to decimate the castle sharp-shooters, Chariot seized the momentary advantage and led a heroic charge against the castle's front wall. The soldiers, now overpowered, dropped their weapons and surrendered.

Kellin and Henry ran triumphantly from the front line to The Jack, who raised his hand to Chariot, expressing his gratitude and respect for his bold and courageous move. The Jack uncharacteristically embraced Kellin.

"You've done well Kellin, and shown great courage!" The Jack said.

"Jack, thank God you're alive! But it was Henry who figured out that the elixir was a sleeping potion. . ." said an impassioned Kellin.

"Elixir? What elixir?" The Jack asked.

"From Magus and Pride, the Hanged Man," said Henry, to a still confused Jack.

"Jack, as I said, it was Henry who figured out that the elixir was really a sleeping potion, and then Henry figured out a way to trick the soldiers into taking it! Jack, that elixir was meant for us!" said Kellin.

The Jack shook his head in amazement.

"You should have seen it Jack, one by one, they all just fell asleep, right there on the front line! All because of Henry!" Kellin concluded. "It could have been us!"

Henry blushed a bit.

"That's true Jack, but it was Kellin who led us. He was determined to save you, and he would not give up no matter what. He gave all the villagers courage!" said Henry, correcting Kellin.

"No Henry, if it wasn't for Chariot. . ." Kellin contradicted.

Then Chariot appeared, seemingly from nowhere.

"Kellin is being too humble, Jack. He is a true leader," praised Chariot. He extended his hand to The Jack; the two men shook. "I am Chariot, from The Forest."

The Jack and Chariot embraced as compatriots.

"I never heard of you. . . But I like your style," said The Jack.

"And I yours, Diamonds," Chariot replied.

The Jack walked over to a nearby stray horse and mounted up.

"Kellin, you are now King!" declared The Jack, matter-of-factly.

"What?!" exclaimed Kellin.

"Yes Kellin, King. You've earned it. The villagers respect you, I respect you. . . and it's now mine to give," said The Jack.

Chariot and Henry nodded their approval.

"And If you're smart Kellin, maybe you can convince Henry and Phoebe to be your counselors," The Jack suggested.

The Jack turned to Chariot, still smiling at him, "Can you stay long enough to whip his men into better shape?"

"Yes, Jack, I will," Chariot replied.

I watched The Jack of Diamonds spur his horse and ride off.

I took in deep breath and quickly readied my quill; determined to record all of the day's events, missing not a one.

24.

VANITY

Justice sat alone inside the deserted Jack of Diamonds' hideout. I watched as she reluctantly looked at herself in a mirror. Over and over, she repeated her actions. She would look, then cower away in disgust, and then raise her hands, covering her face. Justice could not stop her tears.

With each glance at her scarred flesh, I could feel her utter disgust for what her face had become. Justice took one last long look around the room, instinctively picking up things that were once held by the man she loves. Her tears deepened; a silent decision had been made—She was prepared to die.

Justice pressed the red diamond into her chest and looked toward the corridor leading to the crossover point at the top. Once back in The Forest, and now mortal, she knew that she would die within hours.

As Justice took her first steps, the escape tunnel door opened; Phoebe came bursting into the room. Justice, startled, and realizing she had left her face uncovered, quickly raised her hands, covering her wound. Then upon recognizing Phoebe, she burst out uncontrollably, as she lowered her hands to her friend. . .

"Phoebe! My face! Look at my face!" Justice cried out.

A calm and inquisitive Phoebe came up to Justice and sat her down in The Jack's chair, seemingly not hearing a word she said. Justice was confused. Phoebe ripped off a piece of Justice's sleeve and dipped it in a nearby basin of water. Then she took the wet cloth and washed off the burnt ash that lay on her wound. Next, Phoebe opened a pouch around her waist and removed a bottle of cream, softly applying the balm with her hands onto the burn. Curiously, Phoebe, now only a cubit from Justice's face, moved her head from side to side, scrupulously examining the wound from every possible angle.

"Well. . . You'll have a scar, but in time it won't be near as bad as it looks now. . . But you will have a scar," said Phoebe.

"Phoebe, my face is burned! It's horrible!" argued Justice.

Phoebe paid her outburst no mind. Her brows furrowed.

"Justice, where were you going when I came in, and why did you leave us and The Jack back at the castle?" asked Phoebe.

"Phoebe! Are you blind?! I am ugly! I have no choice now but to go back to The Forest and die. I saw the look of horror in Jack's eyes when he looked at my face!" raved Justice.

"Oh Justice, do you really think The Jack of Diamonds will no longer love you just because you are scarred!?" scolded Phoebe.

"Yes, Phoebe! How could he? Look at me!" answered Justice.

"Now let me get this straight. Your Jack of Diamonds willingly gave up his life so you could live, enduring inhuman tortures! Then, upon hearing of your return, he suffered hideously yet again in order to protect you. . ! And now, just because you are scarred, this same man now wants nothing to do with you!? Do you really think he is that shallow, Justice!?" chastised Phoebe.

As Justice took a breath to answer, the escape tunnel door creaked open. The Jack entered the room.

"Well, Justice... answer her," said The Jack.

Justice quickly raised her hands to her face, turning away from him. The Jack nodded approvingly to Phoebe.

"Phoebe, Henry is waiting for you back at the castle, they need you; he needs you" said The Jack.

Phoebe smiled at The Jack and then looked hard to Justice.

"I told you Henry would be back," said Phoebe, as she entered the escape tunnel. "I told you Justice!"

I watched as The Jack came up to the woman he loved. His hands took her arms and forcibly pulled them away from her face. Justice looked away, turning her head in shame. Then The Jack took his hand and softly put it under Justice's chin, lightly turning her head back to him. Justice did not resist. Instead, she looked to the ground, crying.

"Jack, I am no longer beautiful. How can you bear to look at me?" she said, sobbing.

"If it had been me who was scarred rather than you, Justice... would you no longer love me?" asked The Jack, softly.

Justice remained silent, pondering what she had just heard. The Jack lifted her face upward and gently kissed her scar. Justice closed her eyes. The Jack stepped back and stared at her.

"Justice!" said The Jack.

She reluctantly opened her eyes, still tearing.

"Forgive me Jack, please forgive me!" she pleaded.

The Jack's fervent eyes burned into her. Justice took him in, her heart pounding.

"Justice, you are the air that I breathe, the blood in my veins! You're the fire in my heart, and the passion in my soul! You are my Queen of Hearts and I am your Jack of Diamonds! Now and forever!" said the impassioned Jack.

Then The Jack ripped his woman into his arms and passionately kissed her lips, pressing through to her very soul! The two lovers clawed at each other, practically squeezing the air from their lungs, as they feverishly kissed each other's lips, face, and neck.

"I love you Jack! I love you!" screamed an overwhelmed Justice, her body pressed tightly against his.

Suddenly, The Jack pushed Justice away from him, his hands tightly holding her upper arms. His gaze riveted upon Justice; her being totally captive. . .

"I love you Justice!" he again fervently declared, speaking to her soul as well as her body.

Then The Jack pulled the woman he loved back into his arms; the two lovers entwined as one. Justice was overcome with spiritual joy and earthly passion, her fears completely gone.

I looked down at my scroll and saw that my words were obscured. I realized that my tears of joy had made the ink run all over the Scroll's page. I quickly re-wrote all that I had written; my eyes still joyously tearing as I did so.

#

I could not believe my eyes—The King of Clubs was alive. I saw him there in the snow covered wasteland, heading toward The Keeper's mountain: unconscious and still tied to his horse that ambled through the ice and snow. The King's whiskers, eyebrows, and beard, were encased in a thick layer of ice.

As the horse reached the entrance to the mountain, the ground began to shake. I could feel the Earth rumble from my vantage point, or so it seemed. The King's mount reared up in fear, snapping The King's head backward. The powerful stead's front legs came smashing back down to the ground. As his hooves hit the Earth, the frozen ropes that bound The King to his horse snapped.

The King of Clubs' body toppled off the animal, falling into the snow. The Quake intensified, shaking loose rivers of heavy powder that slid down the side of the mountain onto his face. The freezing flakes quickly awakened him. As his eyes focused, he looked up, startled by what he saw!

"Where am I!? And who are you?!" demanded the terrified King of Clubs.

There, staring down at him, staff in hand, was Augustanian.

"YOU are where you need to be. . . and I am The Keeper of The Cards; my name is of no importance, said The Keeper. With emphasis, he planted his staff into the snowdrift. "Clubs, mark well what I say. . . The choice you make this day, will determine whether your grandson to be. . . will live to take the throne!" he warned.

"I do not understand!" replied The flabbergasted King.

The Keeper pointed to the open passageway that led into the underground cavern. Then he pointed off on the horizon.

"Choose your path!" said The Keeper.

#

Light flashed before my eyes, again, momentarily hindering my sight. When my vision returned, I saw The Pond and could see as The Hermit saw: the vision of The King and The Keeper. They were inside the mountain, walking down the underground cavern pathway past the blue waterfall, approaching the door to The Keeper's chamber room.

I watched the awestruck King read the parchment scroll nailed to the door. I could tell, even from here, the bewildered King was apprehensive; yet something kept him there, willingly. He seemed somehow different, of that I was sure; but of what cause—I did not know.

The Keeper opened the door and entered. The King of Clubs followed close behind. The door closed and like before, its sound echoed off the cavern walls, rippling across the blue waters of the falls.

As The Hermit continued to observe The Pond's images, he smiled; it was one of shrewdness. He nodded his head in agreement, but with what and why. . ? I did not know.

Then The Forest winds began to howl, swirling leaves all about. The Hermit knew that Death must be near. He quickly waved his hand over the water; the images disappeared. Now satisfied, he knowingly turned around. Death approached slowly, riding on his horse. He looked hard at The Hermit and then dismounted. . .

"It is not over Hermit. In time, The Ace will be back!" proclaimed Death.

"So will The Jack. . . **and The King!**" asserted a bold Hermit.

I could tell that Death had been caught off guard by The Hermit's cryptic response. As Death's frustration grew, the element's rage increased. Purposely, he tried to collect himself, not wanting to show The Hermit his weakening assuredness.

"What does it matter if The King is alive or if he should return?! He is one of us! The King is of evil!" countered Death.

"Are you sure?" said The Hermit, meaningfully.

The two virtues stood defiantly, face to face, neither man moving for what seemed like a moment locked in time. Then Death, unnerved, broke off in a rage and quickly mounted his horse, ranting, "It is not over Hermit!"

Death spurred his horse hard, his mount thundered off. The Hermit walked back to The Pond and once again waved his arms over the water. I saw as he saw, the entrance to The Keeper's mountain slowly being covered by heavy falling snow. In a matter of minutes, the blizzard completely engulfed The Keeper's mountain, hiding it from the world, as if it never existed. Time stood still. . .

I had faithfully made record of all that I saw and all that I felt in the <u>first</u> book scrolls; of which there were three. Then my eyes grew weary, I rested for but a brief moment. . . or so it seemed to me.

PART III

DANTE

25.

THE KINDNESS OF STRANGERS

W hen I heard the voice, I was sure I had been dreaming. It sounded frail, soft in volume, but yet, its spirit strong. . . very strong indeed.

"My time has been fulfilled. Soon, another will come in my place," the voice said.

I could not awaken. Before my unconscious eyes. . . blackness. Yet I still heard the more. . .

"Who and what will come to be. . . now passes into the hands of the next," the voice continued.

I sensed that I had heard this voice before, but now it sounded different. My eyes began to clear, the blackness slowly lifting, light filling me up. I awoke and looked out across the void. At first I was not sure of what my eyes beheld; then all became clear.

I saw The King of Clubs, older, seven decades plus in age. He had become thinner, now modestly dressed. The King sat at the bedside of Augustanian, The Keeper, whose bed curiously had been set up near the purple waterfalls in the underground cavern that lay deep inside The Keeper's mountain. The chamber room door, still nailed with the yellow parchment, had been left wide open. The King of Clubs reverently attended to Augustanian's needs—The Keeper was dying.

"I am proud," said Augustanian, as he looked up to The King.

Now I recognized fully. . . his was the voice that I had heard in my dream.

"What name will you now take?" asked Augustanian.

"I will give honor to you my teacher and take one born of yours. I will be called: August, The Lesser" said The King of Clubs.

Augustanian mustered his last ounce of strength and touched The King's arm. "My staff is now yours, August," said The Keeper, softly smiling. "You have learned well," he said, closing his eyes for the last time.

The King of Clubs sat silently, looking at his teacher; his eyes filled with tears. He leaned over and gently stroked Augustanian's white hair, brushing it back from his face. Then he picked up his frail body and carried him up the winding cavern passageway. Teardrops marked his path.

I realized that much time had passed in the blink of an eye; the length of which, I did not know; But why I slept so long remained a query I could not answer. As I picked up my quill, preparing to write the first scroll of the second book, I saw my Creator. I stood in awe. . .

"Do not be troubled Acellus, soon all will be clear. Continue to write what you see, and that which you feel," he said. "I am well pleased."

Upon hearing his words, my being filled with love. I held the quill, joyously; certain I had been exacting and faithful to my purpose. He looked at me and smiled. My heart overflowed.

I looked back out across the void and saw August, once called The King of Clubs, standing outside of The Keeper's' Mountain, near the entranceway. He stood, staff in hand, surveying the frozen wasteland, carefully watching. As I looked harder off in the distance, I saw a departing caravan of fourteen men, dressed in brown robes similar to Augustanian's, walking in pairs across the frozen wasteland. Their feet left footprints in the pristine powdered snow that covered the ice.

The last pair of men pulled a stretcher made of cloth that wrapped around two long wooden poles. Attached to the end of each pole was a long leather strap that hung over the shoulder of each man. The opposite end of the poles dragged across the terrain, leaving a chiseled trail in the snow and ice. Tied to the stretcher, I could see the body of The Keeper, Augustanian. As the caravan disappeared from August's sight, a small tear ran down his cheek, quickly freezing on his face. . .

"Who will teach me?" he mused, softly.

Then, seemingly from nowhere, a woman appeared. She was young, some two decades plus five. Her dress was that of a Keeper, wearing a long hooded brown robe. She was small in height, her skin fair. Her eyes were blue and her hair's color, that of onyx black. . .

"Who are you?" said August, startled by her sudden appearance.

"I am the new Keeper," she said. "Can you not feel Augustanian's spirit within you?" she asked.

August, The King of Clubs stood motionless, somewhat bewildered by the woman's remark.

"You doubt that you are prepared. . . Did he not say that you were?" she asked.

August smiled. Her wise words as well as her uplifting countenance reassured his lingering doubts.

"May I ask your name?" said August.

"I am called Aurora," she replied.

"You have come to interpret the cards?" he asked.

Yes. I must sign my name and take my place."

"But. . . you are so young," he said, smiling at her.

Aurora smiled back, speaking his unfinished thought, "And a woman, no doubt."

August, respectfully nodded. His gaze now looked out over the frozen wasteland. His countenance fell.

"As for you, August. . . You already know what destiny lies ahead," she said.

August nodded his head with slight apprehension.

"Keep Augustanian close to your heart," she proffered.

With that, Aurora turned and entered into the mountain tunnel opening. She did not look back to The King. August stood there watching her go into the passageway and then he turned and began walking out onto the frozen wasteland. He purposely followed the snow trail left by the poles from his teacher's stretcher. The tundra's winds swirled, severely buffeting him from every cardinal point. Steadfast, August continued on, steadying himself with his staff.

I watched August, The Lesser, until the swirling snow obscured my sight. I now fixed my gaze beneath Keeper's Mountain where I saw Aurora inside the underground chamber room, her hand on the closed book. As before, I read its title: THE KEEPERS OF THE TAROT. I watched her open the book and turn the pages, one by one, until reaching the last entry; that of The Keeper, Augustanian.

She mused for a moment, staring at his handwriting. Softly, she ran her fingers across his inked signature. Then she picked up the feathered quill from its well and wrote:

The Keeper Aurora—During the twentieth year's reign of KING KELLIN.

Aurora entered the chamber room and stood next to the table, surveying the geometric shape of the room. She marveled at how the huge stones had been precisely fit together. Curiously, the room appeared as if no one had ever lived there before; no trace of Augustanian nor The King of Clubs could be found.

Aurora sat down at the lone table and spied the box. Its jewel laden top glistened from the single shaft of light that radiated down from the ceiling's center. She slid the box close to her and opened it. As before, I saw the cloth that wrapped the cards. Aurora removed the cloth and spread the cards out onto the table. She placed her hands on top of the cards, feeling them as much as reading them. She seemed to be taking in their essence—their spirit. She picked them up, shuffled them, and unfalteringly dealt the first three onto the table.

I could not clearly see their names nor their number, as the image quickly faded before my eyes. As I wrote in the second book, I diligently noted that **twenty Earth years had passed...**

#

The Sun beat down hard, parching all that it touched; the terrain before my eyes, familiar, yet different. These were the Southern Hills in No Man's Land; deep in the Outlaw Territory. I could see the birds of prey circling high in the air. It had been their shrieks that caught my attention as they circled the quarry that lay motionless on the dirt road below. My eyes widened as I recognized August, lying in the road. He managed to turn on his back and then I saw his face, scorched by the Sun. His life force... fading.

I could hear the sound of hoof-beats, and watched August turn his head toward the sound, hoping that fate had saved him from certain impending death. The rays of the Sun filled his eyes, obscuring his vision; he barely could see the approaching rider. But from my vantage point, I could see him... The Ace of Spades!

The Ace, now four decades and five in age, rode up alongside August, stopping next to him. August looked up from the ground and recognized his son. His heart leapt, but he held his tongue. The Ace looked down at August with contempt in his eyes for the old man. It was obvious that he did not recognize his father. August raised his hand up to his son. . .

"Some water please!" asked August, The King.

The loathsome Ace leaned back in his saddle and laughed. "You are very lucky that I'm feeling generous today, OLD MAN. I won't even waste a bullet on you. After all. . ." said The Ace, as he sarcastically gestured to the birds circling above. "You wouldn't want to deny the vultures their due now, would you!?

The King's heart ached. He closed his eyes in helpless resignation. His death imminent, his purpose, unfulfilled. The Ace looked up to the vultures.

"Your meal awaits!" said The Ace, gleefully. He pointed to August. "Finish him, and enjoy it!"

The Ace sneered at The King, and then kicked his horse, riding off. The vultures continued their death spiral. With each revolution they flew closer to the ground, closer to their prey. August fell unconscious. He laid there for hours. . . Finally, the vultures made their move.

The birds descended on August, their talons open. The first pass a test of their prey. The claws of the vultures ripped into his chest. August awoke in pain, bewildered and confused. His arms naturally flailed at the birds. They quickly circled for another run, this time heading for his eyes!

A shot rang out! The vultures scattered at the sound, and I saw Justice approaching, riding hard, gun in hand. Her horse quickly reached August. Justice pulled up and holstered her gun. She jumped off her mount and quickly came to his aid.

August recognized her immediately, again choosing for the moment not to speak. However, like The Ace of Spades, she too did not recognize The King of Clubs, once her arch nemesis. August took her in, respectfully; her beauty deeper than before. She wore her hair long, still vividly reddish brown in color. Justice bore a small faint scar on her right cheek and her curvaceous figure was still that of a woman in her twenties. Her age, four decades plus five.

Justice removed a canteen from her horse and gently poured some water on August's face and parched lips. Momentarily, August's eyes closed in relief, taking in the much needed liquid of life. . .

"Dear God, I hope I am not too late!" she said.

Suddenly, a young handsome man, virile and strong, one decade plus nine in age, came riding up from behind, his horse thundering. He held a gun in his hand and brashly jumped from his mount before it had stopped. August's eyes had just opened again, seeing him arrive.

"Mother, I heard a shot. . . I thought you were in trouble! Who fired at you?" implored the young man. He gestured to August. "And what happened to him?" he asked.

"Dante, I just fired my gun to scare away the vultures. They had begun to descend upon this poor man," she replied.

Dante laughed uncontrollably. August could tell that he tried not to laugh, but could not contain himself.

"Mother, you mean the shot I heard was from **your** gun!?" he asked.

"Yes, Dante. . . and does this somehow amuse you?" she asked, matter-of-factly.

Dante took great care, measuring his forthcoming words, still smiling, "Well, you know what Father says. . ."

Dante took the canteen from his horse and dutifully aided his mother. He gently sprinkled water all over August's body, reviving his spirit.

"Yes, I know. . . Hades will turn to snow before Justice will ever fire her gun," she said, somewhat playfully, mimicking The Jack's phrasing.

"Well then mother, why even carry it?" he asked, as they both continued ministering to August.

"Because, it makes your father feel better knowing that I am armed whenever I am in these hills alone," she said.

August then fully realized that he was looking at his grandson; his inner spirit waxed, jubilantly. August raised his arm up to Justice and Dante.

"Not too fast my friend, you still are very weak," said Justice. "Dante help me get him up, but slowly."

"Yes Mother," replied Dante, respectfully.

The twosome finally got August up on his feet; his body still weak, but his composure, regained.

"Thank you! Thank you both for saving my life. How can I ever repay you?" said August, with humility.

"You wouldn't happen to have a beautiful daughter would you? Someone my age?" asked the roguish Dante, smiling.

"Dante please. . . I apologize for my son's indiscretion. He really is a wonderful son. No parents could ask for better," she said. Then Justice turned to Dante, her face somewhat stern, "But he is at the age where beautiful young girls are all that he thinks about."

August could not help himself, smiling the smile of a proud grandfather.

"My Lady, even an old man like me. . . was his age once," he said.

"Sir, if I may. . . What are you doing alone in these hills? It's not safe to travel here," asked Dante.

"Yes sir, Dante is right. There are many outlaws and rebel soldiers who will attack anyone who wanders in through here alone," Justice added.

"Are we still in danger from them?" August asked.

"Fortunately, my son is here. He has learned well from his father who. . ." said Justice, as Dante cut her off.

"Is the best! Nobody is better than my father. You must have heard of him? He is The Jack, The Jack of Diamonds!" finished Dante, proudly.

"Yes, I think I have," said August. Again he looked fondly to his grandson. "Please forgive me, my name is August. Actually, my full name is Augustanian, The Lesser; but August will do, he said.

"Augustanian is such a beautiful and most unusual name," said Justice.

"Thank you. I have taken the name of my teacher of many years," said August.

"My name is Justice. I am the wife of The Jack of Diamonds. . . and this is our son, Dante. We live in the northern hills," Justice said.

August gently took Justice's hand into his and bowed his head, respectfully. Then he put his hand on Dante's shoulder, proudly.

"Sir, do you need any help in where you are going?" asked Dante.

"No, Dante, but thank you. However, I best be on my way, there is much for me to do," August said.

"Are you sure you are strong enough?" asked a concerned Justice.

"I think so," August answered.

"August, please take this water and some provisions for your trip," Justice said, handing him her canteen and a pouch from her horse.

"And August. . ." said Dante.

Justice flashed him a scowl.

"Excuse me. . . *Sir*, please stay close to the road's edge. Use the rocks for as much cover as possible," said Dante.

"Thank you, Dante, that is good advice," said August. He turned to Justice. "My Lady Justice, thank you for your kindness, not to mention for saving my life."

"You are quite welcome. . . Have a safe journey and may God go with you," she said.

"Thank you both," August said, yet again.

He bent down and picked up his staff, turned, and began his walk. After only a few steps, he turned back to them. . .

"My Lady, I'm sure young Dante's heart will soon be captured by a fine young woman," said August. Then he looked to Dante. "And Dante, if you are as fortunate as you father is. . . She will have the spirit of your mother," he concluded.

"Sir, I truly hope so. . . Or at least let me die trying!" Dante replied, laughing in jest.

"D-a-n-t-e," warned Justice, trying not to show her subtle smile.

"Yes mother," Dante replied, straightening up just a bit.

August and Justice could not help but laugh at Dante's good humor and his brashness. Dante and Justice mounted their horses; August walked on. I saw a curious look cross Justice's face. . .

"How odd. . . "There's something about August's voice. I can't quite place it Dante, but is sounds quaintly familiar, yet something is different about it," Justice said.

"Well, I liked him mother. Maybe father will know who he is? But if we don't get moving soon, we'll lose the Sun," cautioned Dante.

Justice nodded to her son. They gently kicked their horses and rode off.

"You know mother. . . Father is never going to believe you actually <u>fired</u> your gun!" said Dante, teasing his mother.

I watched them disappear from my sight. The magnificent rays from the setting Sun gently basked the canyon hills with a beautiful reddish glow. I took up my quill and wrote, nearly filling the first scroll of the second book.

26.

THE RETURN OF THE KING

The Jack stood with his arms entwined around Justice, outside of the hideout hidden in the northern hills; his age, four decades plus six. The Jack dressed in black as before, his face still chiseled and rugged, his body tight and strong; he wore his jet black hair pulled back tightly.

As The Jack stood behind Justice, he teased her romantically; she was home in his arms. Nevertheless, Justice purposely fought off her mounting desire for him; attempting to keep her mind and gun focused on a distant target of rocks. As she held the gun outstretched in her arms, her hands kept trembling. The Jack held her tighter, now calming her.

"Justice, if you don't stop your hands from shaking. . . you'll shoot yourself instead of the rocks!" said The Jack, seductively as much as instructing.

"Please, Jack, help me learn to do this!" she implored.

"Now, after twenty years, you want to learn how to shoot?!" he said, shaking his head. "I've tried to teach you a thousand times in the past and you always refused to learn. . . Why now Justice?"

Justice fired one shot, completely missing the target. The bullet ricocheted back off the boulder, flying backwards, nearly hitting them. The Jack found it amusing, and held her even tighter, yet more romantically. . .

"Justice, I love you more than ever. . . But. . ."

Justice, gun in hand, turned around and fervently threw her arms around her husband, passionately kissing him as if she were not practice shooting. The Jack responded in kind, kissing her deeply, and then softly whispered into her ear.

"Justice, you're holding that gun at my head, you're going to kills us both," he said.

Justice quickly snapped to, composing herself. She turned back around, facing the rock targets.

"Jack, you must teach me to shoot! I don't know why, but I feel that it's something I must learn now!" she said.

"Alright Justice. For now, just place both of your hands on the handle of the gun, and relax. . . Now, look at the target and hold your arms outward, and please. . . stop shaking," he said.

Justice spurred her eyebrows. Determined, she collected herself and keenly focused on the target, firing one shot, hitting her mark! Proudly, she turned around, oblivious to the loaded gun's barrel that pointed straight at The Jack.

"Well?" she demanded, impressed with herself.

"The Jack smiled and then gently pushed her arm that held the gun away from him. He turned Justice back around, pointing her body and gun back at the targets. She stood steadfast, her arms still outstretched.

"You did well Justice. . . But remember this. . . always try to aim your gun at something you are trying to hit!" he said, playfully.

Dante entered the shooting area, approaching his parents from behind.

"Mother, that's twice in two days. . . you with a gun in your hand!? I can't believe it!" said Dante, playfully teasing her.

"Stand back Dante... She's gonna kill us both!" said The Jack, impishly laughing along with Dante.

"Very funny! I hope you two are enjoying this!" she said, steaming.

A defiant and determined Justice pulled away from The Jack and began firing rapidly at the stone targets, hitting them repeatedly. Father and son stood by astonished, yet smiling, as they watched a resolute Justice thrash the rocks, chips flying about.

#

The castle, once the fortress of The King of Clubs, now belonged to the people. While time had gone by, it looked very different than before; more open, inviting, not oppressive. Villagers were able to come and go into the open courtyards as they pleased. The front drawbridge had been kept open, day and night, for two decades.

Access to their king, King Kellin, could always be arranged by his chief counselor, Henry; or his wife, counselor Phoebe. Those soldiers that were loyal to Clubs had departed soon after the uprising, most following the ruthless Ace of Spades. Of the soldiers that remained, they were young and skilled, but most importantly, loyal to King Kellin and his just and kind ways. Justice, tempered with understanding and mercy, always guided King Kellin's royal decrees. It truly was a time of peace and happiness.

Henry and Phoebe had become King Kellin's trusted advisors as The Jack had suggested. The King's nephew Kent grew to be a skilled soldier, fiercely loyal to his uncle as well as Dante's most trusted friend. The King's sister, Myra, never remarried, instead choosing to oversee all the castle's domestic and culinary requirements. Sadly, she died during King Kellin's third year. Kellin had never taken a Queen in marriage, instead choosing to devote his life to his subjects.

I saw Henry, now near the end of his third decade in age, sitting behind a large desk inside one of the castle chamber rooms. Papers, quills, and partially opened scrolls were strewn about. Henry had gained some weight over the years, but still remained of good nature, and usually full of cheer. As before, he dressed in clothes that were considered odd by most. Henry had been in deep thought, pondering over the latest forthcoming proclamation. His thoughts were interrupted by an impassioned knock at his door. . .

"Come in," he said.

The door quickly opened and one of The King's 9's entered, approaching Henry's desk. His face expressed shock.

"What is it 9, you look like you have seen a ghost!?" said Henry.

"My Lord. . ." said The 9.

"Please 9! You must stop calling me that, Henry will do," said Henry, correcting him.

"Henry, there is an old man who seeks an immediate audience with King Kellin! He says it is a most urgent matter! And. . ." said the agitated 9.

"Well let me see, " said Henry, looking down at The King's schedule. "His register is complete for this day, but I'm sure if the gentleman will come back in the morning, I will arrange for The King to see him first thing."

The 9 struggled to continue. . .

"Henry, it's HIM!

"It is who 9?" Henry asked.

"The King. . . Henry, The King has returned!" he exclaimed.

"You're not making any sense 9. First you said there is an old man wanting an audience. . . And now you say King Kellin has returned?" said Henry, totally confused. "9, The King is in his chamber room now. . . Have you been drinking!?"

"Henry, It's **The King of Clubs**. . . **He is alive**, and waiting outside your door this very instant!" said The 9, in disbelief.

Henry looked at him dumfounded, shaking his head.

"Have you gone mad!? Now I know you've been drinking. . . 9, The King of Clubs is dead!" said Henry, authoritatively.

As Henry concluded his words, August, The King of Clubs, gently made his way into the room. With a sense of respect and humility, he stepped forward stopping behind The 9. . .

"Excuse me your grace. . ." said August.

The 9 immediately turned and drew his sword, protecting Henry.

"Put that away 9! Have you no respect for your elders?!" chastised Henry.

"But Henry!" implored The 9.

Henry scowled at him. The 9 reluctantly lowered his blade.

"We have never met, but The 9 speaks the truth. . . I am, or more aptly <u>was</u>. . . The King of Clubs," said August, softly.

The 9's eyes railed. I could tell he was afraid.

"Now shall I call the guards and throw him in the Tower Prison!?" snapped The 9.

Henry remained calm, trying to understand exactly what was actually happening.

"No, stand fast 9," said Henry.

"If I may. . ." said August.

"Do not trust him Henry. He is evil!" ranted The 9.

"We must let him explain, but be at the ready," answered Henry.

"I see you reason well, with clarity and calmness. King Kellin and his subjects are blessed to have counsel such as yours," said August.

"Sir, please explain what you mean by. . . 'You were The King of Clubs?'" questioned Henry.

"Your grace," said August.

Henry instinctively frowned.

"It is good to see a man who is not possessed of vanity. . . Let me explain," said August. Henry nodded for him to continue. "Many years ago, two decades to be exact, The Jack of Diamonds came to this very castle and rescued The Lady Justice from the Tower Prison and took The King of Clubs captive in his escape. . .

"Yes, everyone knows of this. . ." replied Henry.

"As I told you, you see before you, The King of Clubs. . . But," said August.

"You see! He freely admits it!" interjected The 9, still in fear. "I told you Henry! Shall I arrest him know!?"

"Calm down 9! No one is being arrested," said Henry, still puzzled. He calmly turned to August. "Please continue. . . kindly explain your words further."

"It's what happened to me afterward that no one, save my deceased teacher, knows. But, I have not come here to tell you that. I have come to warn you and King Kellin and. . ." said August.

Henry quickly bristled, "Warn us!? Warn us of what!?

". . . and most importantly, to protect the life of my grandson, Dante!" concluded August.

"The life of Dante!" said Henry, now extremely agitated. "Explain yourself fully sir, and quickly!"

At that very moment, King Kellin, now four decades plus one, dressed in simple royal garb, entered the room with his nephew Kent, two decades and two in age, wearing a sword.

I watched as King Kellin's eyes expressed shock and disbelief upon seeing August, The King of Clubs—Alive! August remained calm and humble.

"No my Lord, you have not seen a ghost, but I am now not the man I once was," said August.

Kellin remained calm, looking August up and down. "It may have been many years passed. . . But I see before me The King of Clubs, who was thought to have been dead!" said King Kellin.

"Is this true Uncle?" said Kent, his hand upon his sword.

"Yes, Kent, it is him," Kellin replied.

"I told you Henry!" exclaimed The 9.

"Kellin, he says he comes here to warn you. . . and to protect Dante's life!" offered Henry.

"From WHAT?" asked King Kellin, cautiously.

"From The Ace of Spades and the evil which still possesses his heart. This evil is about to strike its wrathful revenge. . . On all of you, especially Dante!" revealed August, insightfully.

Both Kent and The 9 drew out their swords, ready to strike. King Kellin waved his hand at them; they relented, lowering their swords. King Kellin and Henry both looked bewildered, trying to fathom what they had just heard. . .

"We do not have much time, please your grace, summon my eldest son to the castle. It is imperative that I speak with him now!" implored August.

"You and The Jack of Diamonds, face to face. . . Again!?" exclaimed Henry.

"Yes, Henry. If he loves Dante as much as I already love him. . . He will overcome his well-founded hatred of me, and come to the castle," August said.

"Dante and I are like brothers. . . I would protect him with my life!" declared Kent.

August smiled admiringly at Kent as King Kellin ordered The 9. . .

"Take this news to The Jack and Justice! Ask for their presence, immediately!" said King Kellin.

"Yes my Lord," answered The 9. He turned and hurried for the door. Henry quickly stopped him.

"9, you had better inform counselor Phoebe of this news and take her with you. She knows all the shortcuts in the hills of No Man's Land," instructed Henry.

"I will go with them uncle," said Kent, to King Kellin.

"Very well, Kent" said The King. The 9 and Kent quickly took their leave.

King Kellin and Henry were now alone with August; they were not afraid. Kellin inquired further. . .

"Tell me all that has happened, and as you say. . . will happen. . . and how you have come to know this. . . Explain all fully," said King Kellin.

"I have taken the name of my teacher, my name is August. He was The Keeper who saved my life, and more importantly, restored my soul, rescuing it from darkness!" revealed August.

"A Keeper you say? Then they are indeed real and not folklore?!" questioned King Kellin.

"Indeed they are your grace," answered August.

"I told you Kellin. . . They do exist!" said Henry, assuredly.

Their voices faded until I could no longer hear. However, I observed them in conversation for quite some time, their words cut off from my ears. Then the image disappeared as well. There was much for me to write; I wasted not a moment.

27.

DANTE AND ALYSANDRA

The wheels of the carriage turned, furiously, as it raced along a pathway in The Forest, my eyes heretofore had not yet seen. I could clearly see them both, The Hermit and Chariot. The military Virtue skillfully drove his carriage along the bluff, the roadway barely wide enough for the chariot's wheels. The Hermit stood next to him, fixated on the upcoming destination, paying no mind to the danger. He held out his arm, pointing.

"There it is! Turn there!" he shouted.

Chariot quickly yanked on the right side of the reigns, guiding his thundering horses into a hidden pathway. The carriage swerved hard right, its wheels digging into the dirt. The two men were now racing down a steep road leading to a small rise where THE TOWER stood.

As soon as the carriage entered the rise, the elements in The Forest began to rage. Lightning bolts repeatedly struck the top of The Tower, impaling into its number, XVI, that had been carved into the top. . .

"In all my time in The Forest, I have never seen The Tower like this," said Chariot.

"Quickly, Chariot, now I must see The Wheel," said The Hermit, with grave concern, pointing to another road.

Chariot snapped the reigns and again the horses raced. The two Virtues continually ducked as tree limbs flew at their heads being tossed through the air by the storm's intensifying rage. I sensed that this fury of nature had not been of its own doing, but rather from that of machinations more sinister.

The carriage came to the next clearing; Chariot pulled up. I saw Fortune's Wheel just as it turned upside down, as it had done two decades past. . .

"Chariot, your courage and skill may once again be needed both here in The Forest, and in King Kellin's realm," said The Hermit, somewhat cryptically.

"Of course Hermit, I will do whatever is needed, this is my purpose," replied Chariot.

"You must bring Jupiter and Juno back to The Pond as you once did many years past. Then, you must find Temperance and Strength and do likewise," said The Hermit.

"Hermit, how do you interpret this turning of The Wheel?" asked Chariot.

"The forces of Darkness are once again realigning, this time more certain than before," he answered. The Hermit looked hard at Chariot, and said, "Snap your whip!"

Chariot pulled back hard on the reigns, his powerful arm muscles flexed. Then he leaned forward and ripped his whip into the air, cracking it near the horse's ears. The carriage raced off.

I could feel the impending confrontation of Good and Evil. Once again, Darkness would challenge The Light.

This time I wrote more of what I felt as well as that which I saw.

#

The snow flew in every direction, swirling across the Tundra at will. The Earthly elements railed against The Keeper's mountain. I had begun to wonder if these two realms were somehow connected. I considered the possibility, and still not sure of the answer, put away the conundrum, and looked further inside, down into the underground chamber room.

I saw The Keeper, Aurora, sitting at the table, the deck of cards in her hand. She dealt the top card to the table. I read its name—THE PAGE OF DISKS.

"Ah. . . Young Dante, no doubt," she surmised.

With a sense of purpose, Aurora dealt the next four cards, forming a square around THE PAGE OF DISKS.

First, on the top left: The ACE OF SWORDS. Opposite The Page, on his right: MAGUS, THE MAGICIAN. To the bottom left of The Page: PRIDE, THE HANGED MAN. The square closed on the bottom right with the card of: DEATH.

Aurora carefully studied the four cards of the square that surrounded Dante, THE PAGE OF DISKS. Then she quickly dealt four more cards to the right of Dante's square. She placed these cards onto the table forming its own square, to the right of the first.

THE KING OF WANDS was the first card of the second square placed on the table. When she saw it, her eyes opened wide.

"August, I knew it. There could be no other meaning," she said, staring at the card.

Next she dealt THE KNIGHT OF DISKS, placing it on the top right, followed by: LADY JUSTICE, placing this card bottom left. She paused for a moment and then considered. . .

"Justice and The Jack of Diamonds. . . together with August!? It must be, for there is no other way," she said.

The next card dealt was that of: THE FOOL, completing the second square by placing it bottom left.

"A Fool no more, for Henry has learned wisdom!" she proffered.

Then, curiously, Aurora took Dante's card (THE PAGE OF DISKS) out of the center of the first square and placed it into the center of the second. She stared at it as she measured further, her eyebrows furrowed.

"Strange that I do not see King Kellin represented . . . how very strange," she said, uncomfortably.

I watched as Aurora dealt one last card, which she placed right over and on top of Dante's PAGE OF DISKS. I saw the card of: THE LOVERS—its number, VI. Aurora shook her head.

"NOW, of all times, *Love* is to enter Dante's life. . . when his own life hangs by a thread!? The forces of good and evil are again out of balance, and are ALL centered on young Dante!" Aurora shook her head more forcefully. "And why do I not see King Kellin represented!? W-h-y?!

As I considered the events, I found it most odd how different the two Keeper's were. I carefully recorded all, starting a new page of the scroll.

#

Alysandra was young, beautiful, and most alluring. Her age, one decade plus nine. The blonde chestnut color of her hair flowed long, down her back. Her feminine form curved, beautifully.

Dante held her in his arms, about to kiss her. Alysandra had all to do to resist his sensual stare as well the touch of his lips. She pulled away from his embrace with great difficulty. . .

"Dante, please do not toy with me," she said, breathing hard.

"Why do you say that Alysandra? You know how I feel about you," he said.

"No I don't, Dante! And what about the other girls? You openly flirt with all of them! Do you tell them the same as me?" she asked, with conviction.

I could tell the young man had become uncomfortable at the challenge. I became quite amused as he poured out his masculine charm, a trait he most certainly had acquired from his father; of that I was sure.

"Alysandra. . . It is true that I do. . . well. . . have a bit of fun with the others, but it is innocent. You know that I. . I. . ."

With that Dante pulled her nearer to him, staring fiercely into her eyes. Alysandra's passions rose again, slowly subduing her stated concerns. Now she too looked with wanting into his eyes. . .

"That you what Dante?" she said, breathing heavier.

A resolute Dante looked at her, taking her in.

"That I truly love you Alysandra. . . Only YOU!" he said, passionately.

Dante took hold of her forcefully and fervently kissed her lips. Alysandra threw her head back and Dante kissed her neck. She became overwhelmed with her passion for him. The two lovers repeatedly kissed each other at will. . .

"I would give up my life for you Dante!" she ardently exclaimed.

Dante's passion turned to a deeper love. He softly spoke while still staring into her eyes. . .

"And I would die for you Alysandra. . . I swear it!" he said, as he pulled her body back against him, now just holding her.

Alysandra held him tightly, resting her head on his shoulder. She cried tears of joy that were born from finally hearing the words she secretly longed for.

"I love you Dante. I always have! I am yours, only yours!" she fervently declared.

The young lovers' attentions had been caught by Kent who had just come up over the hill, galloping on horseback. They hastily straightened up as Kent rode up to them, quickly dismounting.

"Dante, thank God I found you! I thought you would be here!" said Kent. Her turned to Alysandra. "I'm sorry Alysandra, but this is urgent!"

"What is it Kent. . ? What's happened?" asked Dante.

"It's your grandfather Dante. . . He is alive and has returned to the castle!" answered Kent.

"My Grandfather!? Kent, he is dead! What are you talking about!?" demanded Dante.

"My word Kent, how can you joke about such a thing?" scolded Alysandra.

"This is no joke, Alysandra! And your grandfather Dante, has just had an audience with my uncle; I tell you now, he is very much alive!" said an unwavering Kent. "Your mother and father are on their way back to the castle as we speak. They sent me out looking for you. We must hurry!" exclaimed Kent, to the stunned lovers.

Alysandra's attention had been caught by a rising cloud of smoke off on the horizon.

"Look. . . out there!" she said, pointing to the smoke.

"I hope it's not what I think it is!" said Dante, with increasing concern.

The two men looked knowingly at each other; Alysandra stood confused.

"You hope it's not what, Dante?" she asked.

"Renegade soldiers!" replied Dante.

"On their way to attack the castle!" concluded Kent.

Quickly, Kent and Dante mounted their horses. Dante extended his arm down to Alysandra, pulling her up on his mount, sitting behind him.

"Hold on well, Alysandra!" said Dante.

Alysandra put her arms around Dante, holding him tightly. Dante nodded to Kent. The two young men kicked their horses and bolted off.

28.

UNFINISHED BUSINESS

I saw Phoebe pacing back and forth by the castle drawbridge; still dressed in clothes that were most odd.
Anxiously, she gazed up to the lookout posted on the tower.

"Can you see them yet!?" she asked.

The lookout peered into his spyglass, carefully surveying
the landscape.

"Yes! I can see them now. They will be here shortly!"
replied the lookout.

Phoebe turned and called to a nearby 7, instructing,
"Go and tell Henry that Justice and The Jack have arrived,
quickly!"

The 7 darted off. Justice and The Jack galloped up to
the drawbridge. Phoebe ran up to them as they dismounted.
Justice hugged her.

"Phoebe, is it really true?! The King of Clubs is alive?!"
asked Justice.

Phoebe looked to The Jack with trepidation, measuring
her forthcoming words.

"I'm afraid it's worse than that. . ." Phoebe answered.

Phoebe broke out in tears. Justice put her arms around
her, consoling. The Jack grew impatient. . .

"What is it Phoebe!?" implored The Jack

"Your brother sent four of his men here to the castle, they were disguised as Kellin's soldiers. They managed to fool our guards, and. . ." she said, pausing.

The Jack's patience waxed. He looked hard at Phoebe.

"And what Phoebe!? WHAT!?" demanded The Jack.

"Jack, Justice. . . Kellin has been shot and stabbed! The physicians are with him now. They say it is hopeless and that he will die within the hour," said Phoebe, sobbing.

Justice gasped in disbelief. The Jack's fury grew.

"So my father's return was just a diversion so he and my brother could murder Kellin and re-take the throne!" proffered The Jack.

The Jack spoke as if he knew all along that the story of his father's conversion had been an elaborate ruse.

"No, Jack, your father tried to save Kellin's life, he too has been wounded! Your father had nothing to do with this!" said Phoebe, clarifying. "August came and. . ."

"August?!" exclaimed Justice.

"Yes, Justice," replied Phoebe, as she pointed to The Jack. "His father has taken this name, it was his teacher's."

"The only teacher he ever had was the devil himself! He is evil and always has been!" said The Jack, challenging Phoebe's defense of August.

Phoebe stood resolute, continuing. . .

"Jack, your father came here to warn King Kellin about The Ace's plan to attack, as well as to warn you and Justice about Dante!" insisted Phoebe, assured of her words.

Justice panicked upon hearing Dante's name.

"Dante!? What about Dante!? What did he say!? Tell me Phoebe!" implored Justice.

"I do not know the details. We must go inside. . . King Kellin is waiting, he must see you both. Henry and August will fill you in on everything that has transpired," concluded Phoebe.

The Jack put his arm around Justice, reassuring her. Without a word, the threesome hurried into the castle.

My soul ached when I saw him, lying on his bed, weak, and covered with bandages. King Kellin's physicians all hovered about him, doing what they could. Kellin's eyes were more closed than open. Henry sat on the edge of The King's bed, his eyes tearful.

As Justice and The Jack entered the room, King Kellin's eyes opened wider upon seeing them. Phoebe entered after them and stood behind Henry. As soon as Justice laid her eyes on Kellin, she broke down crying into Phoebe's arms.

The Jack remained unemotional as he walked over to Kellin's bedside. Justice and Phoebe now stood behind The Jack. The frail King motioned for his doting physicians to leave; they bowed and departed. The weak King took The Jack's arm. . .

"Jack, it was an ambush. . . and I will not live much longer," Kellin said, with acceptance. The King began to cough. Justice and Phoebe's tears deepened. The Jack remained stoic. "No man could have had more loyal and true friends than you four. . ." Then Kellin looked directly at The Jack. "But Jack, you must listen to what your father has to say." The Jack remained silent, staring intently at Kellin. "Jack, your brother is coming back, intent on retaking the throne. Dante is in danger, grave danger. . . His death is the revenge The Ace seeks upon YOU for his mother's death!" said Kellin, fighting for strength to speak.

"She died at his hand, Kellin, not mine! Everyone knows that!" said The Jack.

"Nevertheless, he still blames you," answered Kellin. "Jack, Justice. . . It is time for Dante to take his rightful place on the throne. He must lead and guide our people now."

"Kellin, we knew this day would come, but I never dreamed it would be like this," exclaimed Justice, as she burst out crying, leaning over Kellin, warmly embracing him.

Henry wiped the tears from his eyes and turned to The Jack. . .

"Jack, your father has warned us of The Ace's evil obsession with you and Dante. August has told us that your brother will stop at nothing until Dante is dead!" warned Henry.

"How can any of you trust my father. . .? He ordered the death of my mother, his own wife. . . so he could marry his mistress! And you actually trust the words of this man!?" exclaimed The Jack. "I should kill him right now! Where is he!?"

"Jack please!" pleaded Justice.

Before The Jack could answer, Dante and Kent hurried into the room. Alysandra stood bashfully behind them. Kent immediately went over to his uncle, Dante followed behind him. Alysandra remained near the doorway. All in the room looked quizzically at her, then to each other.

"Uncle!" cried Kent.

King Kellin held his nephew's forearm, looking directly into his eyes.

"Kent, you have been like a son to me and I hope I have earned your love and respect. If only your mother could have lived to see you as a fine young man. I have missed Myra almost as much as you have," said Kellin, profoundly.

"Uncle, you must rest, you will recover," Kent said, trying to muster conviction.

"Kent hold out your right arm to Dante," said Kellin, with as much royal demeanor as he could muster.

Everyone watched, confused, as Kent held out his arm to Dante.

"Since you were infants, you two have grown up closer than brothers. . . Kent, swear before me your complete allegiance to Dante, who will now take his rightful place on the throne, as King. . . Swear before God and all that are present" declared King Kellin.

"Uncle Kellin. . . Your grace. . . There is no need. Kent is right, you will recover!" said Dante, hoping his words would come to pass.

King Kellin smiled at Dante, pleased with his compassion.

"Dante, rule with the heart and soul of your mother, and with the strength, passion, and honor of your father. . . who has taught me well," said Kellin.

The Jack's eyes filled with tears.

"Be fair, be kind. . . have compassion and rule with gentleness. . . But know that there will be times when force must be used, but only as a last resort! And even then, Dante. . . No more than is absolutely necessary!" instructed King Kellin.

The weakening King coughed, looking to Kent. . .

"Kent, swear your allegiance before I die," said Kellin.

"Uncle, I swear before you and God above, my complete allegiance to Dante," said Kent, with fervent reverence.

Kent firmly took Dante's forearm into his. Dante followed by placing his other hand on top of Kent's, signifying the oath. King Kellin smiled, proudly. Justice put her arm around The Jack as Phoebe held Henry's hand.

Then Kellin noticed Alysandra standing quietly in the doorway. He quizzically gestured to Dante. . .

"Your grace, Mother, Father. . . counselors Henry and Phoebe. . . may I present: Alysandra DellaSalle, the woman I love and will soon marry," said Dante, beaming with pride.

The entire room gasped. Dante looked to his parents, then to Alysandra. King Kellin smiled fondly at Dante and beckoned for Alysandra to come forward. Dutifully, she went up to his bed, standing alongside of Dante.

"Do you love him child?" asked The King.

"With all my heart and soul your grace," she ardently answered.

"Aha... Isn't love wonderful," Kellin mused to the room.

The King looked at Dante and Alysandra's hands which were now clasped. Then he smiled lovingly to Justice and The Jack, finally turning to Henry and Phoebe.

"Henry, you and Phoebe have been my counselors for all my years as King. But most of all, you are my treasured friends. And now you must advise Dante with the same skill and wisdom with which you have counseled me," instructed Kellin.

Henry could not stop his tears from falling.

"Yes Kellin. . ." said Henry, not being able to continue.

"We will your grace," concluded Phoebe.

The King's cough deepened, now barely able to breathe. He summoned his last ounce of strength, looking to The Jack.

"Jack, it is once again your time. . . Only you can do this. . . They will all need you!" declared Kellin.

"I know Kellin. . . I know," said The Jack, as if he knew all along this day would eventually come.

With The Jack's assurance, King Kellin closed his eyes and took his last breath. His head slumped slightly to the side. King Kellin had died. The room fell silent. Then The Jack's face burned with anger. He stormed toward the door.

"Jack! Where are you going!?" asked Justice, confused.

"To speak to the man that killed my mother, and who probably arranged Kellin's assassination as well!" said The Jack.

"Jack, August nearly died trying to help Kellin, his wounds are many!" countered Henry.

"What a pity!" said The Jack, his sarcasm filling the air.

As The Jack turned to leave, one of The King's physicians came hurrying into the room. . .

"Counselor Henry. . . He is gone!" exclaimed the doctor.

"Who sir... Who is gone?" asked Henry.

Before the physician could answer, The Jack answered, knowingly, "Your precious, August. . . That's who!"

"He is seriously wounded! It's a miracle that he is even alive!" offered the befuddled doctor.

"Father, why would August leave us?" questioned Dante.

"And where could he be going?" questioned Phoebe.

The Jack shook his head, again, sure of the reason.

"To report back to The Ace and help plan his return to power!" said The Jack.

"Jack, your father is not the same man he once was. . . August has changed, I truly believe this in my heart!" said an impassioned Justice.

"Father, I agree with mother. The man I know as August, could not be evil. . . he was so humble," reasoned Dante.

"Jack, would Dante's own grandfather plot against him. . . his own flesh and blood!?" offered Henry.

The Jack stared hard at Henry, choosing not to answer. He turned to his son.

"Dante, now you are King, and The Ace of Spades wants you dead. Make no mistake, he and his men will attack, and soon! Your marriage to Alysandra will have to wait." said The Jack, matter-of-factly. "You and Kent must make the necessary preparations for the defense of this castle. I will be back as quickly as possible. If I do not return in two days, be prepared for all out war without my help!"

"Jack, what do you mean, not return. . . what are you going to do!?" asked a concerned Justice.

"What I should have done years ago... Kill my brother and end this right now!" said The Jack, his voice filled with venom.

"Jack, NO!" pleaded Justice.

"Justice, his single death will save the lives of many," insisted The Jack.

"I will go with you!" Justice said.

The Jack smiled lovingly at his wife. . .

"No you will not, Justice! You are needed here," replied The Jack.

With that, he abruptly turned and stormed out. All in the room were overwhelmed. Dante took charge.

"Henry, prepare the hall! Kent, round up The Captains of each rank and bring them there; we will meet to discuss our strategy. Phoebe, you ride to the nearby villages and put them on alert," said Dante, as King.

Kent, Phoebe, and Henry quickly departed.

"And what would you have me to do?" Justice softly asked her son.

"And me as well, Dante?" interjected Alysandra.

"Mother, take Alysandra to the secret tunnel in our home. You will both be safe there till this is over," replied Dante.

"I will not be hidden away like some child," snapped Alysandra. I will stay here with you! No matter what, Dante, I stand with you!"

Justice smiled with admiration and respect for what she had just heard.

"And I Dante, go to be with your father, whether he likes it or not! You may be King. . . but I am still your mother!" Justice said.

Dante had been taken back by both Alysandra and his mother. Justice went over to Alysandra and hugged her, warmly.

Alysandra whispered into Justice's ear, "My Lady, I do love Dante with my whole heart and soul. . . I truly do, I swear on my life"

Justice kissed her cheeks.

"I know child. It is plain to see. And I already love you!" said Justice.

Dante came over to his mother. Justice took both of their hands into hers.

"Now stand together as one. . . and grow in each other's love," she proclaimed, as only a mother could do.

"Since I cannot stop you mother. . . please be careful, and whatever you do. . . don't use that gun!" said Dante, somewhat playfully.

"Your father and I will be back soon, and when this is over. . . we will celebrate your wedding!" said Justice, as she departed the room.

Alysandra turned to Dante, "Dante, I will help Phoebe and ride to the other villages."

"Are you sure?" asked Dante.

"Yes, Dante. If am to be your wife, I must lead by example," replied Alysandra.

"Very well, Alysandra, but please be careful!" said Dante.

Dante took her into his arms and they passionately kissed. Alysandra then turned and took her leave. Dante, now alone, went over to King Kellin's body. A solemn silence came over the room. Dante eyes teared as he looked upon King Kellin. He lightly touched his hand. . .

"I will burn your words of wisdom in my heart. . . I hope I am worthy," said a reverent Dante. Then he turned to the hallway. "Physicians, come and prepare the body for a royal burial!"

Dante left the room as two physicians came in, attending to The King's body.

As I took up my quill to enter the record, I paused to consider my inner thoughts.

Something was happening to me that I did not understand. More and more I found myself feeling emotions. . . like those of the Earth; getting stronger with passing full moon. I had been troubled by this awareness, puzzled as to its meaning.

I knew my purpose well. The Creator's instructions, perfectly clear. "Write all that you see," he said. But I found myself only wanting to write all that I felt. My emotions seemed to be taking my being captive; an imprisonment that

I welcomed. Nevertheless, I wrote all that I had observed as well as that which I felt.

I struggled with the dilemma. Then I realized its true meaning. . .

29.

A FALLEN STAR

eath sat on his magnificent white steed, high upon a
hill in The Forest of Cards; his black armor reflected
the Sun's morning rays. Death still held the banner in
his hand that bore the emblem of the mystic rose, and its
number—XVIII.

Kneeling on the ground, almost escaping my vision, I
spied Magus, The Magician; and Pride, The Hanged Man;
who were keenly observing a Forest trail off in the distance. . .

"It is once more our time," said Death "And this time,
we will not fail. Good will be vanquished, and love shall be
destroyed. . . Darkness will again reign supreme!"

Pride jumped up, pointing his finger outward on the
horizon.

"Look there! It's Chariot!" he said.

Death and Magus turned their eyes to a rising dust cloud
below. Death pointed his banner to the plume.

"His skills are wasted. Foolishly, he brings Jupiter and
Juno with him," said Death.

"Do you think they know?" asked Pride.

"It is of no matter if they do," answered Death.

"Look at the speed at which he races, no doubt headed for The Hermit's Pond," said Magus, looking up to Death.

"And so are we," Death answered.

#

The Moon ruled, its light bathed all of No Man's Land. There, nestled in a remote clearing, high in the Northern Hills, I saw The Ace's compound. The space had been designed perfectly by nature, surrounded on three sides by huge fir trees, fifty cubits in height. The trees camouflaged the stronghold, completely. The rear of the compound backed up to a cliff that jutted out over a raging river, whose white-capped rapids ran violently, some two hundred cubits below!

Arrayed throughout the compound were small make-shift wooden structures and cloth tents. Renegade soldiers and thieves milled about. The Ace of Spades stood at the edge of the precipice, looking straight down the sheer rock face at the fierce river below. Next to him stood one of his lieutenants. . .

"This will be like taking sugar from a child, he is but a boy!" said The Ace, salivating.

"That <u>boy</u> your grace, is the son of The Jack of Diamonds, and rumored to be almost as good as your half brother!" said The Lieutenant, fearlessly correcting him.

"It is true, young Dante is most skilled. . . but he is most certainly not his father," countered The Ace of Spades.

"My Lord, you once underestimated The Jack, and it cost you the throne. . . Are you certain you are not making the same mistake again?" cautioned the bold Lieutenant.

Instantly, The Ace snapped, grabbing the throat of The Lieutenant. He squeezed his neck hard, holding him on the edge of the precipice, the perilous fall to his back. A crowd of soldiers quickly gathered.

"Shall I drop you, Lieutenant!?" mused The Ace.

"If you must your grace. . . but my question still stands!" answered The Lieutenant, incredibly, more defiant than before.

The Ace pulled him forward, staring straight into his eyes. . .

"This is a man of true courage!" shouted out The Ace, to his soldiers while still looking at his Lieutenant. The Lieutenant smiled triumphantly. With his free hand, The Ace quickly drew his sword and ran him through! He raised his foot and pushed The Lieutenant back and off of his blade. His bleeding body fell helplessly through the air, hitting the sheer rock façade three times before landing into the river below. The furious rapids quickly sucked his lifeless body under. The Ace of Spades then turned back to the soldiers, still standing only a cubit from the cliff's edge.

"But he was also a man of great stupidity for daring to question me!" The Ace declared, subtly warning his men. He sheathed his sword. "Captains, prepare your men! In two days. . . we take back the castle!" he said, holding his clenched fist before them.

The renegade soldiers cheered their leader, hurrying off, organizing. The Ace stood defiantly close to the very edge of the precipice, almost inviting certain death.

"Finally. . . I will have my revenge," he said, his voice barely above a whisper.

The image faded. . .

#

I watched as Chariot raced his carriage up to The Pond. Skillfully, he pulled up; the carriage's wheels dug into the dirt as before. Jupiter and Juno got out, hurrying over to The Hermit, Temperance, and Strength who were all earnestly awaiting their arrival.

"Hermit, please tell us what has happened?!" asked an anxious Jupiter. "Chariot reports of strange signs you have observed."

"Is Justice safe? And what of The Jack? And. . ." interjected Juno.

The Hermit interrupted, remaining composed.

"King Kellin is dead. He has been killed by assassins sent by The Ace of Spades," informed The Hermit.

Strength and Juno hung their heads. Temperance put his arms around them, comforting. Jupiter's anger rose.

"The King of Clubs is alive," continued The Hermit.

The group all expressed shock, all except Chariot.

"It seems as though Clubs has had a rebirth of Spirit. He has taken the name of his teacher for all these years, Augustanian, The Lesser; and is now known simply as August. He has come back to warn King Kellin about The Ace's impending attack on the castle as well as his son's blood lust for Dante," revealed The Hermit.

"Dante?! What about Dante?!" exclaimed Juno.

"Hermit! Where is The Jack? He will not fall for this trick of Clubs!" declared Jupiter.

The Hermit paused for the group to take in all that had been said, then methodically proceeded, "There is more. . . Dante is now King. Before Kellin's death, The King's nephew Kent swore his allegiance to Dante. . . and The Jack promised Kellin to once again defend all against the evil that rules the heart of his brother!"

"I knew this day would come, two brothers face to face, yet again," mused Chariot.

"Hermit, is this August truly The King of Clubs?" asked Temperance.

"He is."

"But surely he cannot be trusted? How can a man that evil change? It just can't be," questioned Jupiter.

"What is of greater concern, Jupiter, is the manner in which The Jack will react to his father! This is the key!" offered Strength.

"Strength has reasoned correctly. . . for The Jack does not believe that he is a changed man as Justice and Dante do believe. Instead, he is convinced of his trickery, and is at this very moment on his way to find his brother to kill him. . . and possibly his father as well!" declared The Hermit.

"Hermit, you have not mentioned Justice. Where is she? Is she safe?" asked Juno.

The Hermit ignored Juno's question. He drew in another breath and matter-of-factly declared, "There is yet another complication."

The group waxed more quizzical, especially Juno.

"As Justice and The Jack found true love. . . It seems Dante has found his. Her name is Alysandra DellaSalle, and they are to be married!" he said.

"Married?! Now is not the time for Dante's mind to be preoccupied with love. He has a castle to defend and will need all his attention on that, and that alone!" said Chariot, uncharacteristically emotional.

"Hermit, please. . . What about Justice!?" implored Juno.

"Juno, she has left to join The Jack and stand with him. She truly believes that August's spirit has changed. However, she is now apart from him, and The Jack does not know that she seeks after him. She is alone and unprotected, and has chosen not to follow his instructions," answered The Hermit.

"Justice will surely find him and he will protect her. . . I know it," said Juno.

"Justice truly admires Alysandra, who chose to stand with Dante, helping him, rather than go into hiding," concluded The Hermit.

"It would appear that the apple does not fall far from the tree," said Temperance.

Everyone except Juno expressed bemusement. . .

"As The Jack fell in love with Justice's spirit. . . It seems young Dante has found a love with similar qualities," clarified Temperance.

"The boy is too young to get married! This must be stopped!" declared Jupiter.

"If Alysandra is anything like Justice. . ." said Strength.

". . . as Dante is like his father. . ." said Juno.

"Their love Jupiter, will not and cannot be denied!" concluded Temperance.

Jupiter softened, yet still showed much concern.

"Yes, that very well may be. . . If they live long enough to share it," said Jupiter.

"Chariot, Dante is quite skilled and so is Kent. . . However, they are young and will need your help," proffered The Hermit.

"I agree, Hermit. I must again cross and go to the castle!" said Chariot.

"What about The Jack, Chariot? He is but one against many?" asked Temperance.

"Don't worry about The Jack of Diamonds. . . He is the best I've ever seen! And even though it is one against many. . . I'd still say the odds are about even," stated Chariot, with great admiration.

"I fear for my daughter," said Juno

"Juno, do not let fear take hold of you. . . The Jack will not let any harm come to her, you know this to be true," reassured Strength.

"Yes. . . but they are separated. Strength, The Jack does not even know that she has left to follow him," countered Juno.

The Hermit suddenly looked out to The Forest, as if provoked. His brows furrowed. Quickly, he raised his hand into the air. . .

"That is enough. . . It is apparent that all is not happening of its own accord," he declared. The Hermit looked around The Pond, his senses sharpened. "The forces of evil, and those in league with them, are once again secretly at work."

"Death and his disciples. . .?" offered Temperance.

The Hermit nodded, still looking out into The Forest.

"We must as once before, foil their plans, and ward off this new attack of evil," said The Hermit.

"Where will you begin, Hermit?" asked Chariot.

"I already have," answered The Hermit, cryptically smiling to the confused group.

As I wrote in the scrolls, time passed by. The quartered Moon now ruled The Forest night; its cold rays of light obscured by heavy clouds. I heard the voices of Darkness covertly filling the air a little ways off from The Pond. As the breaks in the clouds rolled by, I could see their faces, barely.

I saw Magus wave his hands outward in mid air. Out of the dark, his magic created a thin blanket of light that revealed their faces and nothing else.

"First we must distract Dante. In that way we make him vulnerable!" said Death. "Then, we'll attack him where it hurts the most. . ." Death's eyes widened. "The love in his heart!" he said, sarcastically.

Magus and Pride smiled, contemptuously.

"What would you have us do?" asked Pride.

"When do we cross?" asked Magus.

"You both cross tonight!" answered Death. "Pride, you will go to the nearby villages and search out Dante's precious Alysandra DellaSalle!"

Pride's eyes lit up, savoring the impending deception.

"She is young and fair. . . and most impressionable," continued Death. "You will appeal to her vanity as Queen to be! In that way, she can be tricked. I'm sure you will have no problem accomplishing this!" affirmed Death.

"If she has any pride in her. . . I will find it!" declared Pride. "What will you have me do, once I have it?"

"You will feed her vanity and deceive, leading her to The Ace of Spades; he will be waiting for her at the portal. The Ace will use her as the bait to capture and eventually kill Dante; the prize he has been wanting for throughout the years! The Ace has been loyal to our cause and he most decidedly has earned that reward!" declared Death.

Magus shook his head, challenging Death, "I do not think Dante will let Alysandra out of his sight long enough for all that to be accomplished!"

"As always Magus. . . you are extremely perceptive. . . and yes, you are indeed correct," said Death. "However, I have a surprise for you both. . . but first Magus, give us more light."

Magus waved his arms yet again. Now I could see all of their form standing in a tiny pool of light. Then Death turned his head to the blackness behind him.

"Come child. . . show yourself," he said.

From out of the blackness and into the light came Star. She had been dressed in beautiful flowing silks, her years one decade plus eight. She held a pitcher of water in her left hand. Around her neck she wore a gold locket bearing her number—XVII. I could sense that Magus and Pride both knew of her, but yet they seemed totally confused by her presence. . .

"It seems as though we have a fallen star who now has abandoned the Light for the powers and the pleasures of Darkness!" proclaimed Death, savoring his every word.

Star took her pitcher and smashed it to the ground.

"I am tired of being a beacon of light and getting nothing in return! I want power and pleasures for myself. . . I want what you have!" she declared.

Magus and Pride smiled one to the other; knowing full well of what she spoke.

"Now, Magus, listen carefully. You will use your powers of illusion to make Star *look* like Alysandra. Then, appearing to all with her form as Alysandra, Star will confuse and distract Dante making him weak in spirit. . . She will beguile him just long enough for *The Ace to kill him!*" said Death.

Magus, still had his concerns, countering, "Her appearance I can change. . . but as soon as she speaks. . . Dante and all will surely know her to be an imposter."

Death smiled at Star, urging her to speak. Magus and Pride were stunned as Star's voice now sounded exactly as Alysandra's. . .

"Oh Dante," she said, acting capriciously. "I don't think you really love me as you say. . . and there are many other suitors who find me most attractive and ask for my hand."

Star raised her skirt and showed a little bit of her legs, mocking Alysandra's movements exactly, as well as her voice. Magus smiled broadly, nodding his approval to Death.

"Yes, but what of The Jack of Diamonds?" asked Pride.

"Do not worry about him," replied Death. "He will meet his fate soon enough. . . Isn't that right Star? Or should I say, Justice?"

Star changed her demeanor and voice yet again, now sounding and acting just like Justice. She spoke, sarcastically, "Oh Jack. . . I love you more than life itself!"

The conspiring foursome laughed, anticipating their ultimate conquest. Then Magus considered further. . .

"Death, that Star can fool young Dante, of that I am sure. But do you really think she can beguile The Jack?"

Star stood right alongside of Magus and teased him with her body movement.

"Oh Yes!" she said.

"And the fate of Justice. . ?" asked Pride.

"SHE is the prize that I want! Her death here in The Forest!" said Death. "Once that is done, The Hermit and all the virtues of his ilk will be crushed! Goodness will perish forever! We will rule The Forest. . . And Darkness and the spirit of Evil will once again engulf The Earth!"

I watched as Magus waved his hands in the air as before; their faces disappeared into the blackness of the night.

30.

SOWING THE SEEDS

K ent stood boldly outside the main gate of the castle. He held his sword high in the air as he stared at a cloud of dust rising off in the distance. A garrison of his soldiers were arrayed behind him in two columns, one kneeling the other standing; their long rifles aimed outward at the rising dust. They were all very young. . .

"Prepare to fire! Wait for my command!" exclaimed Kent.

The soldiers readied their weapons, pulling back the iron hammers. Kent sensed their uneasiness as the dust column drew nearer, still obscuring what was contained within. . .

"Wait. . . Wait. . ." ordered Kent.

As the cloud drew even nearer, it began to break up. There in the front of the plume, I saw Chariot whipping his team of horses as they pulled his makeshift carriage made from a farmer's wagon. Chariot now saw the soldier's weapons pointed at him and immediately knew they thought he was the enemy.

"Must I go through this!" he mused to himself.

Then Kent lowered his sword, commanding, "Fire!"

The soldiers fired their weapons. Chariot skillfully swerved his carriage left and right. The young soldiers continually missed their mark. Some bullets hit the side of the carriage, others harmlessly flew by Chariot.

Kent, frustrated by what he was seeing, advanced on foot toward the intruder, not paying any mind to the flurry of bullets still being fired behind him. As he walked, one of the stray bullets grazed his arm.

Then I saw Henry run out from the castle. Immediately, he recognized Chariot and yelled to the soldiers as Kent continued his charge on foot.

"Cease fire!" Henry commanded.

The soldiers obeyed. Henry saw Kent take hold of his pistol only 25 cubits from Chariot who pulled up on his reigns, ignoring Kent's weapon pointing at him.

"No, Kent! Stop! He is our ally! Stop!" shouted Henry, as he ran out to them.

Chariot's carriage came to a sliding stop right in front of Kent. The side of the wagon hit Kent who stood his ground but dropped his gun from the impact. Without hesitation, Kent drew his sword on Chariot. . .

"Defend yourself, renegade!" commanded Kent.

"Must I?" answered Chariot, somewhat whimsically.

Henry reached them, doubling over trying to catch his breath.

"Kent, please put away your sword. . . you will most certainly get killed," he said, gasping, as he drew in great gulps of air.

"Killed!? What do you mean, Henry?" replied an insulted Kent. "This man is a coward. Do you not see that he draws not on me!?"

Chariot stood by patiently, admiring young Kent's misplaced courage.

"No, Kent, he is our ally. . . He has come to lead our forces," explained Henry.

Henry and Chariot warmly embraced as a confused Kent looked on.

"Please excuse him, Chariot, he is young," said Henry. "However, no one could be more loyal to Dante than Kent, nephew of King Kellin."

Chariot extended his hand out to a surprised Kent; they shook.

"Your bravery and courage are admirable. . . as was Kellin's," said Chariot. "But now I must get you to think before you act. . . And as for them," Chariot pointed to the young soldiers. "I must teach them to shoot the enemy. . . not their commander. Is your arm alright?"

"Yes," said Kent, smiling, somewhat embarrassed.

"My name is Chariot, I have come to help you and Dante protect this castle from evil. . . from The Ace of Spades and his men."

"I am Kent, your help will be most welcomed. My uncle has often spoke of your exploits."

Chariot turned to Henry, and said, "Any news from The Jack?"

"There is none. Only that he has gone in search of his brother," answered Henry.

"Let's hope that he finds him in time. . . Otherwise, we will have to do this the hard way," Chariot said.

"Chariot, Henry and I will take you to Dante," said Kent.

"Excellent, together we will plan our defense," replied Chariot.

The threesome walked to the castle gates. As they passed the soldiers, Chariot saluted them. Instinctively, they returned a respectful signal back.

"Men, break from your ranks and spread out along the perimeter of the castle. Each one of you must keep contact with his eyes," said Chariot, as he pointed up to the top tier of the castle where the lookout stood.

The soldiers dispersed immediately as instructed.

#

She stood in the middle of The Square, young, impassioned, beautiful, and most determined. A throng of curious villagers had gathered to hear this stranger speak. I could see Pride, The Hanged Man; inconspicuously dressed as a villager, standing near the front of the crowd, listening quietly.

"And so my friends. . . we must be on our guard and prepare as best as possible for The Ace's impending attack. No one knows by what route he and his men will take," said Alysandra. "After I speak here, I am going to the nearby villages to warn our neighbors as well."

I could sense the villager's apprehension as they looked with uncertainty to one another. . .

"Why has Dante sent you and not Henry or Phoebe?" asked a not so sure villager.

"Counselor Henry remains at the castle to advise Dante and Kent, while Counselor Phoebe rides to the outer villages to warn them as well," answered Alysandra.

"How do we know we can trust you? We have never seen you before!" shouted one of the elders. "You could be an imposter; maybe one of The Ace's women!"

The crowd quickly became unruly, shaken by what the elder had said. They began to shout at her, raising their hands into the air. Pride quickly sized the opportunity, stepping forward to the front of the crowd. . .

"Wait my friends, I have seen her before!" he shouted. "She is Dante's betrothed! She speaks the truth!"

The crowd gasped upon hearing Pride's words. Alysandra herself was taken aback as well.

"Why should we trust you!? You dress like one of us, but you too are but a stranger here!" said another villager. Maybe you and she are in league together?!"

The crowd became even more unruly and closed in on Pride, forcing him to step back against The Square. They were about to climb in and bring Alysandra down from The Square when I heard Phoebe's voice. . .

"Wait! Wait!" she shouted.

The unruly crowd hesitated, looking to see who spoke. Phoebe fought her way through the mob.

"It's Counselor Phoebe! Let her pass!" shouted one of the village women.

As soon as they recognized her, the assembly made a clear path for her to The Square. Phoebe quickly climbed up and onto The Square, standing next to Alysandra. She raised her hands into the air asking for silence. The crowd hushed.

"My fellow villagers. . . you all know me," said Phoebe.

The crowd murmured, approvingly. . .

"Tell us Counselor Phoebe, does she speak the truth?!" shouted another villager.

Again, the crowd blustered, Phoebe calmed them with her hands. The assembly hushed. She waited for complete silence. Now one could hear the sounds of nature clearly.

"It is true my friends. . . May I present to you, Alysandra DellaSalle, King Dante's betrothed."

Alysandra respectfully curtsied to the crowd.

"And may I remind you all. . . soon to be the next Queen!" said Phoebe, gently chiding them.

The assembly, now embarrassed by their mob behavior, dutifully bowed to Alysandra. I could tell that Alysandra had been taken back by their gesture, feeling uncomfortable at the sudden attention paid to her.

"Oh no. . . Please do not bow," she said.

The demeanor of the villagers had completely changed. Their Queen to be was in their presence.

"We will prepare as you ask Alysandra," spoke one of the villagers, with a sense of homage.

"Thank you all. . . Phoebe and I must go and warn the other villages," concluded Alysandra, now more comfortable.

The crowd dispersed, all bowing to her as they passed The Square.

"Thank you Phoebe for speaking up for me," said Alysandra. "Now I must go to the village on the North."

"And I to the village in the South. . . Will you be alright on your own?" asked Phoebe.

"Yes, Counselor Phoebe," replied Alysandra.

Phoebe smiled at her.

"A woman of courage. . . Dante has chosen wisely. You will indeed make a good Queen. . . as well as a loving wife," declared Phoebe.

Alysandra blushed as Phoebe jumped off The Square. Pride then approached, unnoticed. He nodded his head to Phoebe as she quickly departed. He looked up at Alysandra in The Square; she recognized him. . .

"And thank you my friend for speaking on my behalf," said Alysandra.

Pride bowed deeply, then rose, "Anything for my Q-u-e-e-n."

It was at that instant, I could sense the seeds of Vanity had taken root. Alysandra smiled in response to Pride, but now it contained fragments of the deadly attribute.

"Why Sir, you must not address me as such. . . King Dante and I are only betrothed. . . I am not yet his Queen," she said, with an air of royalty in her voice.

"Nevertheless, you are most courageous, and your beauty unequalled in all the land. YOU are my Queen, and I pledge my undying loyalty to you," said Pride, gushing over her.

Alysandra, again had been taken back; Vanity's roots growing yet deeper within her. . .

"May I accompany you to the next village?" asked Pride. "I will serve and protect you with my life, Q-u-e-e-n Alysandra," sowed Pride, yet deeper.

Before she responded, Alysandra's attention had been caught by a few villagers who respectfully bowed to her as they passed by. With only her eyes, she acknowledged their gesture. Then she looked back down to Pride. . .

"What is your name?" she asked, now with a hint of superiority in her voice.

"My name is William, I am a loyal friend of Dante's," he said, humbly.

"Very well, William, you may accompany me. . . Please get my horse, and be quick about it," said Alysandra, now under Vanity's growing rule.

"Pride, The Hanged Man, bowed, deceitfully. His cynical smile deftly hidden from his prey. When he rose, Alysandra extended her hand to him, beckoning Pride to help her down from The Square; her eyes now full of new-found pretentiousness.

I closed my eyes to take in what I had just observed; being careful to scrupulously find the correct words, that would describe the change that had begun to take hold of Dante's Alysandra. I took up my quill. . .

#

The blood ran red over the way. It marked a thin line, lasting for one league in length. Justice rode her mount carefully, following the blood trail that now turned in direction, heading off the trail, leading to a nearby riverbank.

As Justice neared the water's edge, she saw August leaning against a tree holding his shoulder; his hand covered in blood. Justice quickly rode up to him and dismounted.

"My God August. . . Look at you!" she exclaimed.

Justice took his arm and sat August down on a nearby fallen tree. She ripped open his shirt and surveyed his wound. There were two: one grazed his arm, the other pierced his side.

August pleaded with her, saying, "Justice, I must get to The Ace while there is still time!"

"But, you are in no condition to travel. August, if you keep moving, you will bleed to death!" she answered.

Immediately, Justice tore a piece of her waist cinch and tied it around his upper arm. Then she tore the hem of her garment and tied that around his chest and side.

"Justice, this is the second time you have come to my aid... And now I require your help yet again! Please, you must help me continue on!" he implored.

"But your wounds... they are too grave," countered Justice. "August, you will most certainly bleed to death."

August would not be deterred by the rational reasoning of Justice.

"I would rather die Justice, than not try and stop him!" exclaimed August. "His evil must come to an end. If I can just talk to my son, I know I will be able to get through to him."

"No August, you are too weak!" answered Justice.

"The revenge he seeks on his brother and you Justice. . . is the life of DANTE! He wants you both to live long enough, *only to see Dante's death before your eyes!*" revealed August. Justice grimaced in horror at the thought. "Now do you see why I must continue on!?"

"YES!" said an inflamed Justice.

She pulled his bandages tighter. August winced in pain, then nodded his approval.

"Jack and I would both die first than let anything happen to Dante!" said Justice, as she tied off the knot in his bandage. August again nodded his agreement.

"Take my arm and lean on me," she said.

August got up carefully, leaning on Justice for support. Then he hesitated. . .

"Justice. . . Once we are near to The Ace, I must go on alone," he said.

"Don't be foolish, August. . . I will not leave you," she answered.

"No, Justice, If I should fail to get through to him. . . The Ace will surely use you as bait to lure The Jack as he did once before," explained August. "We cannot let that happen." Justice silently took in his words. She looked up at the setting Sun. . .

"Let's continue on while there is still light. We must find Jack. . ." said Justice.

"Do you know where he is, Justice?" asked August.

"Yes, somewhere in these hills. . . on his way to kill his brother," she said, ominously. "August, he does not believe that you have changed."

"I know," he replied.

Justice bent down and picked up his staff, handing it to him.

"Which way?" she asked.

"I do not know."

Justice put her arm around his waist. . .

"Very well, we go North!" she said, as they began to walk.

#

Alysandra and Pride stood in The Square of Vexilla village. There too, a crowd had gathered, listening to her speak. Now I could see Magus, also dressed as an ordinary villager, standing near The Square, gesturing to many of the villagers. Pride stood next to Alysandra as her aide and bodyguard. . .

"Remember my friends. . . prepare yourselves and be at the ready. I must take leave of you now and return to King Dante," Alysandra concluded.

Then, from the center of the crowd, a voice shouted up. . .

"My Queen. . . You must stay here for the night. It is too dangerous for you to travel without the light. Let us prepare a royal banquet in your honor," said Magus, effectively convincing the villagers who murmured their approval.

Alysandra's face beamed at the continued accolades.

"Thank you my good friends. . . But my place is with King Dante," she answered.

Pride came up to her and nimbly whispered into her ear. . .

"My Queen, the villagers are correct. You are to be their new Queen. . . They only want to honor you and keep you safe from harm. My Lady, it would most certainly be an unintentioned insult to refuse them," said Pride, with great skill and cunning. "Listen to them."

"You must stay and be with us Queen Alysandra!" shouted many villagers, one over the other.

"We will prepare a great feast for you!" shouted another.

I could see as well as feel Alysandra being torn by the stealth and deception of vanity; the deadly vice that continued to grow stronger within her. She looked to Pride, her counselor, for guidance. . .

"My Queen. . . Dante would never forgive me if I let *the most important woman in the realm,* travel at night with The Ace of Spades and his men lurking about. My Lady. . . *Your people need you,*" spoke Pride, with the venom of an asp.

The last of Pride's poisonous seeds took firm root. At the same time, Magus led a group of villagers up to her who curtseyed before her. Alysandra's head swelled from within. . .

"Very well my people. . . I will grace this village and stay the night," she declared.

Then Alysandra looked down to Magus and pointed to Pride.

"This is my trusted aide, William. You will do whatever he commands. . ." she ordered.

Magus bowed deeply.

"Yes, my Queen" he replied.

Pride then shouted orders to Magus, "You! Go and prepare a royal tent for Queen Alysandra. . . and be quick about
it!"

"It has already been done my lord," said a dutiful Magus.
"If you would, please follow me."

Pride helped Alysandra down from The Square.

"My Queen, now you must rest while these peasants prepare your royal meal. . . I will see to everything My Lady,"
said Pride, doting on her.

"Excellent, William. I am a bit tired and in need of rest
and refreshment," she answered.

"Lead the way!" said Pride, to Magus, taking Alysandra
by the hand.

Pride led Alysandra through the bustling village crowd
that scurried about making preparations for her stay.

As I looked upon Alysandra, there could be no doubt,
Pride's seeds of vanity had taken their full root—and they
were growing.

31.

DARKNESS PRESSES

Isaw The Jack of Diamonds, alone in the Northern Hills, crouching down behind a large boulder methodically cleaning his gun. I could sense his mind considering many conflicting thoughts; his countenance changed. With a clear sense of focus, The Jack removed the bullets from his weapon and began pulling the gun's trigger over and over, making sure its hammer fired exactly as expected. Now satisfied, he reloaded and holstered his weapon.

The Jack stood and looked out over the huge rock. No one was around, yet he still seemed uneasy; but I sensed this concern was from a different cause. He turned and sat back down on the ground, his back against the rock.

From out of nowhere, a ferocious mountain lion pounced on him, savagely attacking, growling madly! The weight of the animal forced his body to the ground. The cat's sharp claws swiped at his face. The Jack raised his arms fending off the lion's strikes. With the heel of his boot, he repeatedly kicked the animal in its face. The lion's fangs caught hold of the boot, chewing deeply into the leather.

The Jack kicked him as hard as he could with his other boot. The shrieking cat momentarily fell backwards from a solid strike, and then lunged again; this time pinning The

Jack on the ground flat on his back, attempting to maul him further. The Jack's two hands were around the cat's neck; barely holding off the lion's open mouth only inches from his face, its teeth gnashing. The Jack squeezed his throat with all his might. The cat's paws, with it's razor sharp claws fully extended, were wrapped around his chest. And then I heard it! A lone gunshot rang out! I saw dirt rise from the ground, inches from the beast.

The mountain lion cowered in fear and jumped away from The Jack; the big cat ran off leaving his human prey wounded. The Jack grabbed his hip and chest; he was bleeding badly. A terrified Justice came running up to him, holding her gun in hand.

"JACK!" she screamed.

Justice threw herself on him, not knowing where to touch.

"I'm OK Justice," he said. "Help me up."

Justice put her arms around him, helping him stand. The Jack looked down at his bleeding hip. He began to laugh and wince at the same time.

"Jack!? What's so funny? You were almost killed!" implored Justice.

"Yes my love. . . And by YOU!" he replied.

The Jack pointed to his bleeding hip and then to the gun in Justice's hand.

"Oh my God! I shot you?!" she exclaimed.

"Not quite. . . It's only a flesh wound," he said. "The bullet grazed the skin."

Then he took her in his arms, his chest and hands bleeding. . .

"But you did save my life," he said, fervently kissing her.

Justice melted in his arms. Then The Jack pulled back. . .

"Justice, I told you. . . You have to stop shaking your hands when you shoot," he said, chuckling.

"Well laugh if you want! But I did save your life you know," said Justice, with an air of righteous ingratitude.

The Jack softly smiled, "That you did."

Justice suddenly gasped, as she spied a band of The Ace's men coming out of the woods, riding toward them.

"Jack! Look!" she exclaimed, standing dumfounded.

The Jack turned and saw the soldiers.

"Get down, Justice!" he shouted.

The Jack grabbed Justice by the arm and pulled her down next to him behind the boulder. The soldiers were riding in their direction. Justice curiously peeked around the rock. . .

"They have August!" she cried.

"They have who?" asked The Jack.

"Your father!" answered Justice.

Instantly, The Jack defiantly stood in plain view, his hands still bleeding as the soldiers thundered by. Quickly, they stopped and dismounted, all taking cover. Bullets started flying in The Jack's direction, ricocheting off the large rock; huge chips soared into the air.

The Jack stood his ground, holding a gun in each hand. Justice rose to help her husband, and immediately The Jack pushed on her head, forcing her back down behind the boulder.

"Stay down!" he shouted.

"Jack! Let me help you!" she pleaded.

The Jack bent down, momentarily taking cover behind the rock.

"Alright Justice. I need you to guard our rear. Go back behind us, where you came in from. Shoot anyone who approaches from my rear! Anyone Justice! Now, you will have to shoot that gun! Can you do that, Justice!?" he exclaimed.

Justice nodded, this time without hesitation.

"Good. I'll cover you. . . as soon as I stand and fire, you go!" he instructed.

The Jack stood and thrashed the soldiers, firing relentlessly as Justice ran off to the rear into the wood's edge, disappearing from his sight. The Jack held his position, yet he was pinned down. He turned to look back at Justice, but she was not there, already in the woods.

The shooting stopped. Both the soldiers and The Jack of Diamonds used the lull to reload. As The Jack did so, his attention was now caught by the voice of August. He peered around the rock and saw him, his hands tied, being guarded by one of the soldiers.

"Let me talk to him! There is no need to kill him!" implored August.

"Shut up old man, or I'll kill you now!" shouted the soldier, as he backhand slapped August across his face. . .

Quickly, I looked for Justice, and found her standing just inside the woods' edge, holding her gun in outstretched arms with hands that trembled. She pointed the weapon at a soldier who slowly approached her. . .

"Not another step! I'll shoot! Really," she said, trying to summon up conviction.

The soldier stared at her shaking hands and continued to slowly advance on her; more confident with every step.

"I swear it! Not another step! I'll shoot!" she exclaimed.

Ignoring her protestations, the soldier continued forward. Now only a few cubits away from her, Justice drew in her breath and squeezed the iron trigger of her gun. I watched the hammer slowly come back, the gun about to fire. At the very last second, Justice pointed the barrel of the gun into the air; the weapon shooting off its bullet into the sky; She could not kill the soldier. Quickly, he lunged and grabbed her. He positioned himself directly behind her, wrapping his arms around her, rendering her helpless.

"I knew you couldn't do it!" he mocked.

The soldier made ready to violate her, about to tear off her garment as The Captain came riding up. Instantly, The Captain's eyes widened, recognizing Justice.

"Stop! That is The Lady Justice!" declared The Captain. The stunned soldier promptly dropped his hold of Justice.

"Take her to the camp and do not touch her!" commanded The Captain. "The Ace will reward you well!"

As he spoke, four more shots rang out!

"Take her now!" commanded The Captain.

The soldier led Justice deeper into the woods as The Captain rode back to his men. Now in the clearing, he saw The Jack of Diamonds standing beside the rock looking down at the bodies of four dead soldiers. Off in the distance, I could see three soldiers riding off with August, whose hands were still bound together.

The Captain charged The Jack and fired at him, missing. The Jack took careful aim and fired his last bullet at The Captain, hitting him. He fell off his horse onto the ground. As The Jack walked over to him, he turned back to his rear. . .

"Justice! You can come out now. . . It's over!" shouted The Jack, as he came upon the smirking Captain lying on the ground, bleeding.

"Justice! Can you hear me?! It's over!" again shouted The Jack.

"I'm afraid all she will be able to hear is the voice of your brother!" The Captain sarcastically said, holding his wound.

As soon as The Jack heard the words 'of your brother,' The Jack knelt down and ruthlessly shook him by the collar.

"What do you mean?!" The Jack implored.

"She is his now!" said The Captain, with his dying breath.

The Jack grimaced at the thought of his brother having Justice his captive—again. He knew this time, his brother would not make the same mistakes as before. In anger, he threw the dead body of The Captain back down to the ground.

The Jack stood and looked around, methodically reloading both his guns...

#

The Sun's rays bathed the main road leading to King Dante's castle. Just off the path, in the deep brush, I saw two horses aimlessly grazing. As I looked deeper into the foliage, I could see Magus and Star in deep conversation...

"Star, you must get Dante to follow after you to The Jack's hideout!" insisted Magus.

"Don't worry Magus, I will," she answered.

"Good, now stand firm, hands at your side," he instructed.

I watched as Magus removed a pinch of red powder from his pouch, throwing it into the air in Star's direction. Then he waved his hands back in forth, faster and faster in a constant circular motion. The loose leaves that lay on the ground rose up into the air and began circling around Star, engulfing her; swirling around Star until I could no longer see her. Once engulfed, Magus abruptly stopped. The leaves floated back down to the ground revealing a transformed Star: now into the exact likeness of Alysandra!

"Remember, The Ace will be there, waiting, according to Death's plan," continued Magus.

"Yes, Magus!" she reassured, yet again.

I watched Star quickly mount her horse. She threw her head back and ran her hands through her long beautiful hair. Then she looked back down at Magus, as she purposely ran her fingers across her throat...

"The King will follow his Queen!" she said; her voice now sounding exactly like Alysandra's.

Star laughed sarcastically, enjoying her newfound sense of power. She nodded to Magus, spurred her horse and rode off, heading to the castle. I watched her until she disappeared from my sight.

I turned my eyes up to the Sun and followed its rays down to the dirt and sandstone of the Western plains of No Man's Land; and that's where I saw them: Pride, The Hanged Man, leading his Queen to be, Alysandra. They were riding on horses through the plains, traveling across the hard and arid salt lake. . .

"How much further William?" asked Alysandra, her being now somewhat disoriented.

"I see it now, my Queen," said Pride, stopping his horse. "Wait here my Queen, I'll be but a moment."

Pride dismounted and walked over to a lone stone well; a rusted iron handle stuck out the top, beckoning. It seemed to exist in its own world, isolated from civilization in the middle of the dry lakebed, almost a mirage. As Pride came upon it, he saw the old frayed rope that tied to the handle as well as a wooden bucket sitting on the dirt.

Pride leaned over the well's small circular opening and peered down inside the shaft. There below, some ten cubits down, was a shallow pool of standing water. Pride's eyes lit up upon seeing the water.

"My Queen, there is still a measure of water, come. . . refresh yourself," he said.

Alysandra gently kicked her horse and rode up to the well. She dismounted and raised her hands to her forehead. I could tell that her demeanor was slowly returning to her former self—so could Pride.

"William, I have been away too long. I must get back to Dante. . . I should have never left him this long," she said, more like herself.

"But your highness, I think that. . ."

Alysandra immediately cut him off and said, "Please, William, do not call me that. I truly do not know what came over me. . . I am not The Queen! All I know is that I love Dante with all my heart and soul, and my place is with him, by his side!"

Pride knew his influence would soon depart fully; it seemed as though the seeds he had sown were now dying. He had misjudged her true character; she was truly a woman of virtue. Nevertheless, he continued to disorient her. "My Queen, Dante would never forgive me If I did not address you properly and introduce you as Queen to the villagers. . . Come, My Lady, refresh yourself!" he said, with cunning.

"That is most strange, William, I never knew Dante to be possessed by such formality and ego?" she replied. Then Alysandra grew more faint, she held her head. . . "How strange, William. . . I feel as though a cloud is slowly lifting from me," she said, sighing.

Immediately, Pride seized the one moment he had left and lunged at Alysandra, picking her up off her feet and throwing her into the well; she fell down into the water below. The icy liquid revived her, bringing her back to her full senses. Alysandra stood, soaking wet and muddied, in two cubits of water, speechless. She looked up the shaft at Pride, in a complete state of shock!

"Dante may not be possessed by pride. . . But as for you Alysandra. . . you have been! And it is your short dance with vanity that will lead to the death of your precious Dante!" proclaimed Pride!

"Oh my God! Who are you?! And what do you mean by Dante's death!" demanded an overwhelmed Alysandra.

"You are but a pawn in a grand plan, woman! At this very moment, your betrothed is being led by Star to The Ace of Spades, who will kill him!" he explained.

"My God, William, I do not understand! Why are you doing this!? And who is Star!?" she exclaimed.

"Star is a powerful woman, as beautiful as you are my dear. In fact, she is you, and probably kissing your beloved Dante right now, as we speak!" he declared.

Alysandra became enraged; her confusion gave way to anger and fury! She extended her hands outward, pushing as hard as she could, trying to climb the smooth circular wall of the well. She rose but a few cubits and then fell back down into the water. . .

"Tell me what is happening! Why are you doing this!?" she demanded in a frenzy.

"There are forces at work my dear that you do not understand. . . The Dark will once again rule the Light! Goodbye Q-U-E-E-N Alysandra. . . your usefulness is over!" said Pride, as he pulled his face away from the well's opening. He walked away and mounted his horse, briskly riding off.

"William! William!" shouted Alysandra. "You bastard!"

Alysandra's spirit raged, furiously. She extended her hands yet again, this time digging her nails into the old mortared walls of the well. She managed to climb higher than before, but yet again still fell back down into the water; her fingertips bleeding under her painted nails. She pleaded to herself. . .

"Dante, please forgive me. . . Please, Dante. . . forgive me."

Undaunted, she swirled her bloodied hands in the water, cleansing the blood. Then she positioned her back against the wall and extended both her legs to the opposite side, pushing as hard as she could, holding herself in mid air by the force of her legs. Next, she placed both her palms against the mortared bricks and pushed her back up the wall but a half cubit. Then she moved up the same distance with her feet, slowly rising her body higher. The blood from her fingernails ran down the bricks mixing with the water below.

I could feel her being running through a gamut of emotions. Her fears for Dante's life surprisingly gave way to the passions of her youth, taking over her thoughts completely; she shouted defiantly, "Who is this Star!? I'll rip that harlot's eyes out if she thinks she will have my Dante!"

Undaunted, Alysandra was determined to escape from her circular prison and pressed even harder with her legs, using her hands to push herself up one brick at a time with each thrust of her legs.

I wrote like the wind as the visions were coming faster. . .

#

Dante had chosen a little used room in the castle to gather his counsel. He could remember as a child playing soldier there with his cousin Kent. The soldiers would give them sawed off broomsticks as makeshift swords and the two children would go around the castle slaying their imagined enemies. King Kellin would often sit and watch them for hours, loving their friendship.

Now King Dante, Chariot, Kent, Henry, and Phoebe all sat at the long table listening to an impassioned Star, who Dante and everybody else thought to be Alysandra. Her appearance and speech were perfect. . .

"Oh Dante, you must hurry!" Star swooned. "They have captured your parents and are taking them to your compound!" She turned to Dante, holding her face in her hands. . . "The Ace is going to kill them there! Oh, Dante!"

Star threw herself into Dante's arms; he held her tightly. She wrapped her arms around him, drawing him closer to her body.

"You must hurry Dante!" she said, still holding on to him.

Dante purposefully pulled back from the embrace.

"Chariot, you will command the soldiers here at the castle! I will go to the compound!" said Dante, with authority.

"I don't like it, Dante. . . It smells like a trap!" warned a reasoned Chariot.

Henry's eyebrows bristled.

"Chariot is right," said Henry. "We must marshal our forces and overpower them there at the compound."

Star sighed at Dante, forcing his thoughts to be at cross purposes.

"No, Henry. . . I will go alone. I am the only one who knows the many secret passageways my father had built. I could get in unseen," said Dante. "Henry, we cannot leave the castle unprotected."

"And if you should get in unseen, then what Dante?" asked Phoebe.

"Somehow, I will free them," replied Dante.

"Dante, do not let your love for your parents blind your good judgment," reasoned Henry. You are now King! Your place is here at the castle. This is too dangerous!"

"Yes, Counselor Henry, that it may be; but my skills are many. Would not my father expect nothing less of me?" said Dante.

"Dante is right, Henry. The castle must not be left unprotected. Kent, array the men around all four walls," said Chariot.

"Immediately!" replied Kent, who started for the door.

"No, Kent! Do not!" interrupted Henry. You will accompany Dante to the compound. Chariot will command our soldiers here. If you agree Dante. . ."

Dante looked to Chariot and Kent, who both nodded their approval.

"Very well, Henry," said Dante as he looked to Star, who flashed her eyes at him.

"Counselor Phoebe, will you watch over Alysandra?" asked Dante.

"Of course," she replied.

"Star bristled ever so slightly, momentarily loosing Alysandra's demeanor.

"No, Dante. . . I will go with you and show you the road they took. You will need to know this," she countered, quickly regaining Alysandra's countenance.

Dante paused, considering Alysandra's words. As he did so, Henry quizzically stared hard at Star, somewhat bewildered. He turned to Chariot.

"What do you think of that strategically, Chariot?" asked Dante.

Chariot too seemed uneasy as he answered, "Well, knowing the exact route would be a help."

Dante turned to a beaming Alysandra. . .

"Very well my love. . ." said Dante. "But once we are there, you will return to the castle, I will go in alone."

"Yes, Dante," she said, smiling at him with her eyes.

"Then it's settled," said Chariot.

"Not quite," said Henry, as he turned to Dante. "Maybe it would be best if Phoebe rode with you as well. It may be too difficult for Alysandra to find her way back alone at night."

Dante smiled.

"As always, Henry, your counsel is wise," said Dante.

Henry bowed humbly.

"We had better hurry!" interjected Star.

Dante and an overeager Star went to the door. Henry came over to Phoebe and purposefully hugged her, drawing her uncharacteristically close in public for him; he whispered into her ear. . .

"There is something strange about Alysandra. . . Watch her closely, Phoebe," warned Henry.

Chariot took notice of Henry's demeanor as Phoebe pulled back from Henry's embrace, subtly nodding to him. Dante, Alysandra, Kent, and Phoebe quickly exited the room. Chariot, now alone with Henry, came over to him. His face expressed concern.

"You noticed it too?" asked Henry.

"Yes!" Chariot answered.

The visions before my eyes, darkened, then disappeared. I made record of all the events that had transpired.

32.

TWO SIDES OF THE GLASS

August stood lashed to a post with his hands tied tightly behind him. His face had been severely bruised, his body weak and bleeding. Standing before him with contempt in his eyes, his son, The Ace of Spades. The Ace paced to and fro, furious, ranting. . .

"What has happened to you?! You were once powerful and strong. . . There was none mightier than you. Now, you speak like a priest!" railed The Ace.

August forced himself strong, undaunted by his son's rebukes.

"I now only speak the truth! A truth which I am trying to make you hear!" exclaimed August.

The Ace shook his head in utter disgust.

"Well hear this old man. . . I will have my throne, and my r-e-v-e-n-g-e! And if you once again get in my way. . ." warned The Ace, as he pressed into his father's face. "You too will die!"

August still stood unnerved, determined.

"No son, I cannot let you do this! You must listen to what I have to say!" said August, with passion. "You must find a way to let go of the venom in your heart! A poison that I put there!"

The Ace drew his hand back and slapped his father across the face. August remained steadfast.

"I like my heart just the way it is father!" replied the sarcastic Ace.

"No you do not, Son! You think you are mighty because you live by force! But you never know if today is your day to die at the hand of someone just like you!" exclaimed August.

The Ace shook his head in contemptuous disbelief.

"You are indeed a pathetic old man," scowled The Ace.

"That very well may be, but tell me this. . . Your men, do they follow you out of fear. . . or out of respect?! Tell me!" August railed back.

I could tell that the weight of August's words rang true somewhere deep inside The Ace's poisoned being. Now, losing more of his control, he grabbed his father by the throat. . .

"What does it matter HOW. . .?! That they do obey my every command is all that matters! And you old man, would have been better off staying dead!"

The Ace turned in anger to the guard.

"Whip some sense into him!" he shouted.

The guard took hold of his lash and approached August. He drew the leather back, about to slash him. . .

"Wait! You want to hurt me?! Do it yourself—coward!" shouted August, to his son.

The enraged Ace grabbed the whip from the guard and mercilessly thrashed his father across the front of his body. With each lash, August stood firm, unflinching, staring into the eyes of his possessed son. As the whip lashed across his face. . .

"Forgive me my son," August said.

The Ace ripped him again. August passed out.

The words from his father sunk deep into The Ace's soul yet he continued to thrash the unconscious body of his father. But now, for the second time in his life, his eyes welled up with tears as they did years past when he accidentally ran his mother through—killing her.

A soldier came bursting into camp on horseback. Justice sat in front of him, her hands tied and her mouth gagged. The surprised Ace momentarily forgot about his father. His eyes raved in euphoric disbelief upon seeing Justice...

"Get her down and bring her to me!" he commanded.

The soldier quickly dismounted, and took Justice down from his horse. He grabbed her arm and forced her over to The Ace...

"A present for you my lord," said The Soldier.

Justice looked behind The Ace; her eyes expressed horror at the sight of August's mangled body. The Ace of Spades placed his hands on the soldier's shoulders.

"You have not touched her. .?" asked The Ace, his eyes demanding the truth.

"No my lord!" I swear!" said the soldier, beating his breast with his clenched fist for affirmation.

"Good! A hundred gold coins for you! Now, tie her next to him," said The Ace, pointing to August.

The soldier took Justice by the arm and dragged her over to the post next to August. He quickly tied her to the wood, bowed to The Ace and walked to the men. The Ace strutted around her, looking Justice up and down, savoring the vision before his eyes. He tried to contain himself but could not...

"Gentleman! Look! The Queen of Hearts... Back where she belongs!" shouted the sarcastic Ace, smiling, almost gleefully.

Then his face turned cold. The Ace hauled back and slapped Justice brutally across her face! The soldiers looked on, roaring with glee. Next, The Ace came up from behind Justice. He let his hands wander over the front of her body, pressing them against her waist. Justice tried to move, to scream, but could not.

Her eyes closed in horror as The Ace slowly slid his hands up and across her breasts, finally raising them up onto her face. He squeezed her checks together and ripped his nails across her skin. Then he took his hands off of her and menacingly whispered into her ear. . .

"Welcome home my Q-u-e-e-n."

Justice, dazed and bleeding, passed out.

The vision faded. I quickly wrote the account; being ever mindful to not let the emotions I felt, obscure the record. When I looked back out, The Sun's arc had neared its set. The celestial body's golden rays illuminated the sheer walls of the precipice that jutted out from The Ace's camp. That's when I saw him, The Jack of Diamonds, there on the other side, some one hundred cubits across the ravine.

The Jack looked down to the gorge's bottom, the drop all of two hundred cubits. He could see the river running swiftly, its rapids continually white capped. As he looked across, he thought he saw movement. The Jack took a small spyglass from his belt and peered through.

My eyes followed the path of his, and I saw through the glass as he did. There across the gorge he saw Justice, bound and gagged, sitting on a horse being led by his brother; behind her followed a small band of soldiers. The Jack expressed no outward emotion upon seeing his wife captive. Still looking, The Jack watched The Ace ride by his unconscious father tied to the post. The Jack holstered his spyglass and searched for a way across the divide—there was none.

As The Ace passed his father by, he saw him coming to. Quickly, The Ace held out his hand, stopping his men behind him. He looked down at August, who was barely conscious; contempt filled his eyes. . .

"It was **you** father who taught me to despise weakness. . . AND I DO!" he shouted, as if justifying his sadistic behavior.

The Ace spit on his father. Justice tried to speak but could not. August now recognized that she too had been taken captive by his son, exactly what he had feared.

"Oh Justice, forgive me!" he implored, up to her.

The Ace, infuriated by his father's outburst, took his gun, about to shoot him. At the same time, the camp lookout spotted The Jack of Diamonds through his spyglass. He ran to The Ace...

"Your grace! I believe your brother has found us! Look, across the ravine!" he said, handing the spyglass to The Ace as he pointed to the spot.

Again, I saw through the glass... The Jack of Diamonds, determined, on the other side of the gorge, methodically looking for a way across. Curiously, The Ace took his pistol and fired three quick shots into the air...

"Come on brother... Look this way!" mused The Ace.

The gunfire immediately caught The Jack's attention. Now he looked back through his glass and saw The Ace taunting him.

Spades tossed the glass back to the lookout, and said, "Let me know what he does."

The Soldier nodded, went back to the edge of the precipice and looked back across at The Jack. The Ace rode next to Justice and placed his hands onto her cheek.

"Is he still watching?" asked The Ace.

"Yes my lord," replied The Lookout.

"Excellent!" said The Ace of Spades.

The Ace leaned over and took Justice by the hair. He pulled her head back and forcibly kissed her. The Ace turned again in The Jack's direction and waved goodbye to his brother, taunting him across the divide.

"And now?" asked The Ace.

The Lookout stood still watching, as The Jack now enraged, took four steps back and then ran at full speed, launching himself out and over the cliff. The Lookout leaned over the precipice and followed The Jack's fall all the way down into the icy cold water. He watched his body splash into the raging river. The rapids quickly grabbed hold of The Jack propelling him into the side of a standing rock. His body disappeared into the water, sinking below the raging rapids. . .

"W-E-L-L?!" shouted The Ace.

"My Lord! Your brother jumped off the cliff!" exclaimed The Lookout.

"And?" demanded The Ace.

The Lookout again looked hard through the glass down to the river.

"I don't see him my lord," he said.

The Ace turned to a struggling Justice, who expressed horror at what she had just heard.

"What is it about you my dear that compels my brother to constantly risk his life?" asked The Ace.

Justice continued in vain to try and break her bonds. The Ace paid her attempts no mind.

"No matter My Lady. . . I shall soon know all, first hand!" he mused, taunting her.

The Lookout pulled the glass off his eye, turning to The Ace.

"He's surfaced my lord!" exclaimed The Lookout, in disbelief.

The Ace matter-of-factly turned to Justice. . .

"Well my dear, yet again he survives. . . But not to worry. . . I will kill him soon enough!" he declared.

The Ace dismounted and walked over to the precipice. He took the glass from The Lookout who pointed down to where he saw The Jack last. The Ace looked down and saw his brother banged up, limping out of the raging river onto its bank.

Unbelievably, The Jack looked straight up the sheer rock face, desperately looking for a way up the vertical climb.

The Ace watched as his brother put his hands on a jutting rock near the bottom of the face. Incredibly, he began to pull himself up with tremendous upper body strength. As he climbed the first six cubits, undaunted, The Jack screamed in pain from the wound on his side. The Ace marveled at this sight, turned and proclaimed to all. . .

"I can't believe it! He's actually trying to climb the façade!" declared the stupefied Ace.

Justice again expressed shock as she took in his words. The Ace turned to his Captain, pointing to August.

"Wake him!" he commanded.

The Captain threw a large bucket of water onto August who immediately came to. August saw Justice captive on her horse and knew his son would be taking her away to violate her and eventually kill her, as he had warned Justice.

"Let her go!" he demanded of The Ace, barely alive.

"Soon, Old Man. . . Very soon. But first thing's first," replied The Ace, pointing to the cliff's edge. "Father, it seems as though you too may soon have a visitor. . . Your eldest son is actually trying to climb the façade!"

August's eyes expressed shock.

"If he should make it, maybe you can convince him how you have changed, and reassure him that you are not the man you once were. . . And then, try to explain why you had his mother killed!" continued the sarcastic Ace. "I'm sure he will be as amenable as I was!"

The Ace motioned for his men to move out.

"And one last thing dear father," continued The Ace. "Be sure to tell my brother that I will have my way with his wife! After all, shouldn't brothers share!?" The Ace of Spades laughed, pleased by his own words.

"No, Son! This madness must stop!" implored August.

"Madness father? You misspeak! This is not madness. . . This is revenge!" answered The Ace. "Tell The Jack, after I kill Dante, I will kill him as well! And then Justice will be sent back to The Forest from which she came to be delivered into the hands of Death. There he will make all in The Forest watch her die before their very eyes; everyone helpless to stop it. All of this will happen Father. . . starting with Dante!"

Justice finally broke the cloth gag, screaming. . .

"N-O!"

The Ace rode over to Justice and shoved the cloth back into her mouth.

"My dear. . . there will be plenty of time for screams soon enough!" he said, laughing. "Screams of delight no doubt."

The Ace grabbed the reigns of her horse and led Justice and his men out of the camp.

33.

REPENTANCE

C hariot and Henry were in the great hall of the castle. Before them, stretched out on the round table, laid an intricate map pinpointing all the known roads that led to the castle. Many soldiers hurried about, all making ready the defense preparations. Henry anxiously paced to and fro as Chariot drew bisecting lines on the parchment. The hall's doors opened; Kent entered quickly. . .

"Kent, what has happened? Why are you here? And where are the others?" asked a confused Henry.

"Counselor, on our way to The Jack's hideout, Dante and I spotted renegade soldiers heading toward the castle," replied Kent. "The band was small, but Dante ordered me back here to the castle, to aid Chariot in its defense while they continued on."

"How close are they?" asked Chariot.

"About two hours ride," answered Kent.

"And their numbers. . . small I hope?" interjected Henry.

"Yes Counselor Henry, no more than five."

"Good!" said Chariot. That is only the advance scouting party. . . We still have some time." Chariot looked closer at the map. "Henry, I think we should seize the moment and take the offensive now."

Kent came over to the map and looked where Chariot pointed. He studied the area carefully. . .

"Judging from what I saw, I'm certain the full force of The Ace's men will come from here and here," said Kent, pointing on the map. "I believe they will soon make a charge along our Southern wall. If we advance and attack now, surely we will cut their ranks in half; long before they've had a chance to fortify and dig in securely."

Chariot came up to Kent and put his hand on his shoulder. "Kent is correct," said Chariot, with much admiration. "I can lead a garrison around their flank and force them to the castle wall. There, Kent and the rest of our soldiers can pin them down. They will have no means of escape! They will surrender, or all be killed."

Henry listened attentively to the two military men, fighting hard to keep his focus.

"Why have we not heard from Dante. . . or Alysandra, or Phoebe? Why?" said Henry, with much concern. "Surely by now, Dante would have sent back a report with one of the two women."

"Henry, if this plan is to work. . . we must act now," interjected Chariot. I must get my men out and behind the advancing front force, unseen, using The Forest as cover, before The Ace's men reach the open ground.

"Very well Chariot," answered Henry. He briskly turned to Kent. "Kent, you will take your *military* orders from Chariot!"

"Yes Counselor Henry!" answered Kent, smartly.

"However. . . Until King Dante or I return to the castle, the palace and all who reside therein, are under your command," instructed Henry. "Do you understand?"

Kent took in a deep breath and replied, "Completely, Counselor Henry."

"I am going to look for The Jack and Justice. . . I'm most uneasy," explained Henry.

"Going out alone. . . Is that a good idea, Henry?" asked Chariot, with delicacy.

"No, Chariot it is not!" Henry replied. "Nevertheless. . . You two make us proud!" said Henry, who turned and exited the hall. . .

"Are you ready Kent?" asked Chariot.

"Yes, commander. . . Where do you want my men?"

Chariot carefully pointed to positions on the map. "Put a platoon here, and another there," instructed Chariot. "I will take a garrison and depart from the rear of the castle. If there are indeed spies in front, we will be able to get out unseen."

Kent nodded.

"Chariot, just to be sure," Kent said. "I will have my men shoot off their guns into the air on the tower front wall. I'm sure The Ace's men will look there, trying to figure out what we are doing. That should give you and your men a sufficient window to ride out unseen."

"Excellent Kent!" said Chariot. "We will ride through The Forest along this road and then wait for The Ace's men in the deep woods at night. Once they pass us, we'll follow them from behind, just far enough back not to be seen."

"They will probably attack at first light!" said Kent.

"Yes, but this is the key, continued Chariot. "When they attack, do not be unnerved. You must let them advance right up to the castle's walls. . . close enough to scale them. Then, I will charge with my men from behind, leaving them no room to escape! Your soldiers will then rise from behind the tower walls, shooting down, while me and my men attack from their rear!"

Kent nodded. Chariot saluted young Kent, who snapped back the respect to his commander.

"Lets get this done!" said Chariot, as the two men went off in opposite directions.

#

My eyes followed a flock of vultures that flew high in the sky over the Western plains of No Man's Land. The birds circled tighter and tighter; their eyes fixed on some kind of prey below. As I looked out further, I spotted Dante, Alysandra, and Phoebe riding South, some distance away from the birds. . .

"Dante! Look there!" exclaimed Phoebe, pointing at the circling vultures off to the West.

"Someone is hurt, probably near death!" said Dante. "If we hurry, we might be able to save him.

"No Dante, there is no time! We must get to the hideout!" exclaimed an anxious Alysandra. "Besides, it's more likely only a dead animal."

Dante looked to Phoebe: "What do you think Phoebe?" he asked.

Phoebe thought for a moment. . .

"Alysandra may well be right," she said. "But still. . ."

"No, we can't take a chance," said Dante. "We must make sure."

Alysandra quickly interjected, "Dante, why don't we go on alone while Phoebe rides over to check. This way we will not waste any more time! We can meet up later."

"What do you think Counselor Phoebe?" asked Dante.

Phoebe knew Alysandra's suggestion made good sense, yet I could feel her pangs of uncertainty growing. . .

"Very well, I'll go alone and meet you at the hideout as soon as I can," said Phoebe. "You two be careful!"

"Don't worry Phoebe. . . we will," replied Alysandra, smiling a grin of smug satisfaction that did not go unnoticed by Phoebe.

"We'll wait for you at the hideout," said Dante.

Phoebe nodded to Dante as she turned her horse and darted West toward the birds. Dante and Alysandra headed South.

#

The Jack of Diamonds hung perilously on a limb two hundred cubits in the air. The outlaw's hands clung to a lone branch that jutted out only a few cubits before the top of the precipice that darted out from The Ace's compound.

At first, The Jack's body swung aimlessly in the raw cold air. Then The Jack began to rock his body back and forth, out over the gorge. With each inward swing, The Jack winced in pain as he hit the rock face. Yet, with each successive thrust, his boots came closer to the top. Finally, he managed to hook his left boot on the top of the precipice.

Now with but a tiny toehold on the top, The Jack pulled his body upward with his arms, his eyes now level with the top edge of the cliff. With one hand he let go of the branch and jumped into the air, reaching for a small handhold at the top. Then The Jack let go of the limb completely, digging his nails into the dirt with both hands. I watched in amazement as he managed to pull himself up and over the precipice. Now on the top, The Jack laid on the ground right at the cliff's edge, motionless, exhausted; His body dangerously close to falling back over the precipice to certain death below.

Finally, with his breath caught and his side bleeding, The Jack rolled over away from the edge and stood. His eyes now stared straight at his unconscious father, sitting on the ground, still tied to the post. August's face had been sorely beaten.

He looked around and spotted the bucket of water and quickly went over, cupping a handful of the cold liquid in his hand, splashing it on his father's face. August slowly came to. His eyes widened upon seeing his son. . .

"Son!" exclaimed August.

The Jack methodically untied him.

"Where did he take her?!" demanded The Jack.

"I'm not sure. I think he is headed to your hideout. . . Jack, he wants to kill Dante, and then you!" said August. "It is the revenge he seeks for his mother!"

"Her life is on him! Not me!" The Jack bristled back.

August hung his head. . .

"No son, it is on me," said August, somewhat shamefully. "Now we must hurry; there is still time: For your brother will not harm Dante or Justice until he has you!"

"I'm gong to kill him, like I should have done a long time ago!" snapped The Jack.

"No son, do not! Let me reason with him. All of this is my fault," said August, with remorse.

The Jack did not know what to make of his father; he stared him down hard. . .

"Before I die," said August. I must right all the wrong I have done to you and your brother."

"Really? And what of my mother. . . no remorse there?" said the sarcastic Jack.

August's eyes teared.

"And most of all for her. You son, have the very best of her," said August, sincerely.

The Jack pensively caressed the red diamond around his neck.

"I have to go!" said The Jack.

August struggled to stand and then picked up a nearby sword from the ground. The Jack stood still, just watching him, saying not a word. August handed the blade to The Jack, handle first.

"I don't need this," said The Jack.

August paid him no mind and knelt directly in front of him. He lifted his head up to his son. . .

"I beg of you son. . . Do not kill your brother! If you must kill. . . then let it be me, for I deserve it! Spare his life. Do not blame the evil in your brother's heart for the sins of the father! I made him that way; I put it there. . . And you,

I deserted. But worst of all, I am guilty of your mother's murder. . .All for my ego and my lust!" said August, who now looked directly in his son's eyes. "I deserve to die—and by your hand."

August, the once King of Clubs, now hung his head in submission, waiting for The Jack to strike. The Jack just stared at his father who remained motionless with his head hung low, waiting to die—willing to die for his sins.

The Jack became overwhelmed by his father's humility and contrition. He jammed the sword in the ground with all his might; it was as if the fierce rage and tremendous hurt he carried deep in his soul all his life had been purged with the one strike. August knelt there silently, accepting whatever his son would do. The Jack reached down and took his father by the arm, helping him up.

"Justice was right. . You truly are not the man you once were," said The Jack.

He stared long into the eyes of his father. . .

"I will not let any harm come to Dante or Justice! But father, hear this. . .I will kill my brother!" declared The Jack.

"Please son. . . Only if you have to! Promise me son, a promise I have no right to ask, but I do. . . Only if you have to!" pleaded an impassioned August.

The Jack silently considered his father's words. . .

"Will you not take me with you?" asked August.

"No, you are too weak, you'll only slow me down. And besides, my brother already has a huge head start. If I am to catch him in time, I must go back the way I came," said The Jack, pointing to the cliff.

"No, Son, you too are weak. You will never survive the fall," warned August.

"Father, I am The Jack. . .The Jack of Diamonds! I trust you have heard of me!"

"Yes, I have! And only he could do such a thing!" said August, beaming with pride. "Jack, I have met Dante, he will make a good King! One who is loved and respected," declared a proud August.

"That he will. . . farewell. . . FATHER," said The Jack. August's eyes welled up with tears. He extended his open arms out to his son, pleading for The Jack's affection. I could feel all the years of pent up emotion swelling inside The Jack. Finally, the surging emotions overflowed—The Jack came to his father, embracing him deeply.

"I love you son!" said an impassioned August, as he kissed his son's cheeks.

This was a new feeling for The Jack, one he so desperately needed.

"Be careful Father, you're still very weak," said The Jack.

"Yes son. I will follow as fast as I can; there is a wagon," said August.

Then The Jack turned from his father and ran at full speed toward the cliff's edge, launching himself out over the precipice into mid air as far as he could from the rock face.

I watched him fall through the air with his legs and arms pumping for balance, nearly hitting the rocks that jutted out from the sheer cliff face. The Jack splashed into the icy water, two hundred cubits below, submerging upon impact and then surfacing. The furious rapids took his weakened body far down stream. Finally, his arms began to move— The Jack of Diamonds had survived the fall!

#

Phoebe drove her horse hard across the Western plains of No Man's Land. The vultures were close now, still circling high above. Then, incredulously, she saw Henry, riding his horse quite precariously from the opposite direction, heading directly toward her. They were no more than a half stadia apart; both riding toward the lone well that stood in the center of plain. The two Counselors finally met near the well, surrounded by nothingness, save the vultures that flew above the humble oasis. Henry pointed to the sky. . .

"You saw them too!?" he exclaimed.

"Yes Henry!" she replied. "Dante thought it best for me to check on it. He and Alysandra went on alone."

Phoebe dismounted first, and then helped Henry down off his horse. He looked around, confused; his brows furrowed. "I don't understand why they are circling," he said. "There's nothing here."

Phoebe looked skyward and spied a lone bird breaking from the circle. It dove down from the sky, flying toward the well.

"Henry look!" she shouted.

They watched the renegade bird dart down and into the well. They ran over about to look in, when two bloodied hands reached out from within the well, grabbing onto the top row of stone. The startled twosome looked in and saw Alysandra, bruised and bloodied, clawing her way out.

"Oh my God! Alysandra!" exclaimed Henry, as he and Phoebe took her arms and pulled her out. She fainted in Henry's arms. Phoebe's face expressed disbelief.

"Henry! I just left her!" exclaimed Phoebe.

"What do you mean, 'Just left her!?'" he asked.

"There Henry!" answered Phoebe, pointing back from where she had just come. "A few stadia back there!"

Both of them shook their heads in confusion.

"Unless she has an identical twin. . ?" continued Phoebe.

"One of these women is an imposter!" reasoned Henry.

Phoebe lowered the bucket down into the well and drew out some water. Next, she tore off a piece of her garment and dipped it in the bucket, lightly washing Alysandra's face. The cold water momentarily brought Alysandra around.

"Hurry. . . Dante is in danger," she said, deliriously. "Please William, tell me, who is Star?!"

Alysandra, looked up at Henry and then passed out.

"She's talking gibberish," said Phoebe, taking Alysandra from Henry's arms and resting her on the ground. Henry gently placed Alysandra's back against the well; he thought hard. . .

"Is it possible?" he mused out loud.

"Is what possible, Henry?" she asked.

"Star?! Here?! Now aligned with Darkness?! Could it be?!" proffered Henry,

"Henry, have you gone daft too?" exclaimed Phoebe, as she continued to sprinkle Alysandra's face with water. Henry became resolute.

"Phoebe, I can't explain everything now. . . You must take care of her. She is the real Alysandra! I have to get to Dante!" he cryptically exclaimed.

Henry, what is it? Tell me! And who is this Star?!" she implored.

Henry paid her no mind and awkwardly mounted his horse.

"Take care of her Phoebe!" he shouted, as he rode off. "She is the real Alysandra!"

Phoebe looked at Alysandra, still incoherent. . .

"What happened to you child?" she said, as she sprinkled water on her arms and legs.

34.

PICTURES AND SYMBOLS

Twelve cards lay on her table face up, forming the letter Y; Aurora stared in shock at the surprising formation. Each of the three spokes of the Y had four cards touching the other. Spread above the Y, laying left to right, were three new cards I had never seen before: THE DEVIL, its number—XV; JUDGMENT, bearing the number XX; and the last card, THE WORLD; it bore the final number—XXI.

The position of these new cards seemed to exert influence on the three spokes of the Y below them. The first spoke of the Y on the upper left consisted of: DEATH'S card at the top, followed by MAGUS, The Magician; Then PRIDE, The Hanged Man; and finally STAR. Aurora carefully ran the index finger of her left hand down these four cards and then recoiled. . .

"The Spoke of Evil!" she declared.

Aurora's gaze now went to the upper spoke on the right of the Y, surveying these cards: THE HERMIT at the top, followed by the cards of TEMPERANCE and CHARIOT, finishing with the card of THE FOOL: a simple-hearted bumpkin no more. She smiled to herself and then mused. . .

"The Spoke of Light and Righteousness—eternal enemies of Evil."

The two top spokes of the Y both pointed to and joined the bottom spoke of the Y, forming the spine of the formation. Its cards: THE LADY JUSTICE, THE JACK OF DIAMONDS, and the cards of ALYSANDRA, and DANTE. "Everything centers here!" she said.

As I looked around further, strewn about the floor, I saw many opened books with pages carefully marked. Curiously, I saw scrolls that were similar to mine as well as loose papers that had drawings of various card formations.

Aurora got up from the table and walked back and forth in great distress! She began rummaging through many of the books, seemingly looking for something specific. Finally, Aurora grabbed an unopened scroll hidden in the corner.

"It must be in here! I know I've seen this formation before; I'm sure of it!" she cried out.

Quickly, Aurora untied the leather strap that held the scroll closed, letting it fall to the ground. Then she sat down in the corner on the stone floor and began reading. I watched her eyes devour each and every picture and symbol. Finally, she stopped and gasped, loudly. . .

"Oh My God. . . Can this really be?!"

At that very moment, the room started shaking violently as if Aurora had uncovered something she should not have. Blocks of stone loosened from the ceiling, falling down and breaking into pieces right next to her as she moved about. It seemed as if some unknown force was trying to stop her.

Quickly, Aurora scrambled about the room, gathering up all the cards on the table as well as those on the floor. She grabbed the silken cloth purse from the table and put the full deck into it. Then, without pause, she put the shiny bag back into the jeweled box and then shoved that into the pouch she wore around her neck. The ground continued to shake violently. . .

Aurora ran out of the room into the alcove, purposely darting to the iron stand; but the secret book of The Keeper's was not there. Undaunted by the falling stone, she searched for the tome, finally finding it on the floor. Aurora grabbed the book and placed it into her pouch. Now satisfied, she quickly ran out the alcove door and began her climb up the dirt pathway to the top. The pools of water from the waterfalls were overflowing down onto the lower pathway making her climb extremely difficult. The entire underground cavern was shaking, caught in a violent earthquake. Strangely, I watched in amazement as Aurora suddenly stopped, looking into her pouch. . .

"The Scroll!" she shouted.

Without hesitation, The Keeper ran back down the pathway into the crumbling chamber room that was filling rapidly. She lunged for the precious scroll that held the covert interpretation and quickly removed the parchment from the wood roll; stuffing the ancient paper into her bulging pouch. As Aurora ran back out of the room and cleared the door, the final portion of the ceiling gave way, smashing down into the room. The enigmatic space, known to no one save The Keepers, had been buried completely under dirt and piles of massive rock.

She ran as fast as she could up the muddied pathway, heading to the top, but the force of the quake had separated the narrow footpath into sections, leaving four rifts of three feet each between fissures. The young Keeper ran as fast as she could, jumping each of the four breaks in succession. As Aurora neared the top, she took one look backward; the entire lower cavern had disappeared, completely, its ceiling finally collapsed.

The cavern ice tunnel entrance lay just ahead; across the divide. She could see small rays of sunlight peering in from the outside. Aurora knew she had but only a precious few moments left to escape. Fearlessly, she jumped across the divide, desperate to get to the Ice Tunnel's outside opening before the entire mountain collapsed. Her body crashed down onto the freezing ice on the other side, sliding on her stomach, outward and away from the cavern. However, the force of her fall broke the strap of her bag; she watched in horror as the cloth pouch, with all its precious contents, slid perilously backwards toward the imploding cavern.

Aurora dug her nails into the ice, slowing herself down to a stop. Quickly, she rose up onto her hands and knees and crawled back on the ice as fast as she could; trying to reach the sliding bag before it fell back down into the cavern. The Keeper watched in horror as the pouch slid off the ledge. Aurora made one final lunge and caught the end of the bag's broken strap as it was about to disappear into the secret grotto. She yanked hard, and snapped the pouch back up over the ledge, and then quickly rolled backwards into the safety of the ice tunnel. In an instant, the entire underground cavern filled in—as if it were never there.

Aurora crawled her way to the tunnel's entrance, stood, and went through the mountain opening into the tundra's daylight as the frozen ice tube collapsed behind her. The Keeper's mountain was gone! All that remained was a small hill; the ice tunnel and underground cavern had been completely sealed by the earth! Heavy snow began to fall. In no time the entire area was covered in pristine white powder as if it had never existed.

Aurora carefully retied the loose strap to her pouch. Satisfied of its security, she put it back around her neck. Then she looked out in every direction and saw nothing but the snow covered emptiness. The white flakes quickly gathered in her hair. Unconsciously, she placed her hand on the pouch, as if to protect it, and began to walk. . .

But to where, I did not know—neither did she.

35.

DARKNESS STRIKES

The soldiers were arrayed across the front castle wall; the morning Sun but a few minutes away. Kent walked the Tower's ledge, being careful not to knock over the many standing quivers of arrows made ready by the second row of archers.

"Archers, form a second line behind the rifles," said Kent, to his commanding 9.

"My Lord, should not the archers fire first, then the rifles?" asked The 9.

"Captain, array the men as instructed, and be at the ready," answered Kent, firmly.

The bewildered 9 turned to his men. "Archers to the rear!" he shouted. "Rifles on the wall!"

The soldiers murmured their confusion among themselves but quickly re-deployed as instructed. I could tell that many of the men secretly questioned the wisdom of such an order, now wondering if young Kent was up to the task of leading.

I looked further out from the castle searching out Chariot; fining his garrison of soldiers walking on foot through the thick woods that bordered the road leading to the castle. Each man guided his horse, holding the reigns to their mounts, following Chariot's lead. Then, instinctively, Chariot held up his hand. . .

"We will break up into three companies," said Chariot, to his two Captains, Braxus and Pen, both 10's. "I want three companies of twenty men. . . one hidden just off the path's edge on the left side of the road, the other concealed on the right.

"I will continue on with the third company a little further. Once The Ace's men pass me by, I will attack from their rear, pushing them down the road toward your companies. As soon as my men get there, your two companies will come out and attack them from their left and right flanks. They will be trapped on three sides and have no other choice but to make their escape to the castle—exactly where we want them." With that, the two 10's broke up the ranks and deployed as Chariot had instructed. Chariot nodded and led his company further down, still camouflaged by the woods.

The Sun's light had just peeked over the horizon. Its warmth heated the dew-laden grass and bushes. A thin water vapor now rose into the air. I could hear the tiniest of twigs breaking. Then I heard them. . . the voices of The Ace's men riding on horseback, approaching.

"Not a sound!" said Chariot, whispering. "As soon as they pass us, mount up and wait for my command."

I watched The Ace's men ride by Chariot's company, completely oblivious to their presence. Then Chariot gestured with his hand. The soldiers of The King Dante, quickly mounted their horses. . .

"Charge!" commanded Chariot, as his horse broke from the woods onto the path.

Chariot's men quickly followed at full gallop, advancing on The Ace's men from their rear.

"Fire!" ordered Chariot.

Chariot's soldiers began firing at will toward the rear of The Ace's company. Immediately, the element of surprise worked to their advantage; killing four of The Ace's men with the first volley.

The Ace's men were caught unawares. Most of their rifles were still in their sheaths on their horses. Trying to buy time to arm, they galloped further down the road toward the castle. Chariot wisely slowed his men down, allowing The Ace's men to get into position right alongside Chariot's other two companies that were veiled and waiting just off the roadway. . .

The Ace's Captain shouted, "Quickly into the woods for cover!"

Chariot's company now approached as The Ace's men were about to disband into the woods. Instantly, Braxus led his company out of the woods, charging and firing at will. Moments later from the other side, Pen led his company as well. At first, the outlaws tried to stand their ground, but were overpowered by Chariot's forces on three sides. The Ace's Lieutenant, still wearing his torn 7's uniform from under The King of Clubs, rode up to The Captain as bullets flied in all directions. . .

"Captain, the castle is surely left unguarded, lets make a ride for it now!" said The Ace's Lieutenant. "We'll storm the ramparts and then shoot from behind the walls! Surely, the tide will turn; we'll kill them all!"

With that The Captain reared back his horse on its hind legs, shouting, "Forward, to the castle! Ride to the castle!"

The Ace's company turned away from Chariot and his men, and rode at a full gallop to the castle, with Chariot and his soldiers in full pursuit not far behind—exactly as planned.

The sounds of all the mighty horses' hooves pounding the earth filled the morning air, spreading across the realm as far as the eye could see.

#

The winds of The Forest of Cards roared defiantly. The skies burst forth with torrential hail, the size and shape of which resembled that of small stones. Tree limbs were ripped apart by the gale force winds. The entire Forest was again in chaos as if being pulled in two divergent directions—and it was!

Once again, Death rode into The Hermit's realm, confident, arrogant—Evil. He saw The Hermit alone, staring steadfast into his pond, oblivious to the raging elements; he seemed disappointed. . .

"Stare into the water all you want, Hermit. . . Nothing will change, it is hopeless," said Death.

The Hermit did not turn around. . .

"Move on, Death! Your words mean nothing to me," replied The Hermit.

Death quickly trotted his horse to the other side of The Pond, now staring at The Hermit's face.

"Nothing!? Hermit!" shouted Death, in anger. "Do you not see how the elements rage at my doing!?"

"And do you not remember many years past how you boasted yet these same words to me. . . 'It is over Hermit, the forces of Darkness have won?'" said The Hermit.

"What of it, Virtue!?" replied Death.

"You were wrong then, and once again, you make the same mistake," said The Hermit.

"R-E-A-L-LY?" said Death, salivating. "Watch!"

He raised his hands up to the sky and clenched his fists. . .

"More!" he railed.

Nature seemed to obey his words, as lightning bolts struck the ground circling The Hermit; scorching the earth in spite of the torrential rains. The Hermit stood fast, unaffected by the Death's display of power.

"You are the son of perdition. You are strong. . . you are powerful. . . But you and your ilk will NEVER overcome The Light!—Never!" decreed The Hermit.

With that, The Hermit simply waved his staff in small circles above the ground. Before my eyes, I saw the earth just below Death's horse form a circle encompassing him, as if the dirt outline had been actually dug by The Hermit's staff. As soon as the ring's outline around Death completed, the ground just within the circle began to quake. Death's horse trembled at the cracking ground beneath its encircled hooves. Death could not control his mount as the magnificent animal reared back in fear.

"Be gone Death! Or sink back into the Abyss from which you were born!" ordered The Hermit.

Death yanked on the reigns of his horse and kicked his heels. His pale white mount jumped into the air, leaping out of the quake circle. He steadied his horse and turned back defiantly. . .

"Virtue. . . Go back to your pond, and watch helplessly at what I am about to do!" scoffed Death.

Again, The Hermit drew circles in the air with his staff, and as before, the new ground beneath Death's horse also began to quake. Thwarted, Death spurred his horse, quickly galloping out of The Hermit's sphere, back into the deep Forest. . .

#

Dante and Star, riding on horseback, approached the escape tunnel exit of his father's compound. Though many years ago, my eyes still could recall the vision of Lena's tragic death and her fervent declaration of The Jack's love for Justice. Yet again, this ground held destiny in its embrace.

Dante halted his mount and dismounted. He went over to Star and extended his arms upward. Star smiled at the handsome King and leapt into his arms. Dante kissed her passionately. Star's carnal passion exploded. . .

"Dante, I love you!" she sighed. "Take me now!"

The Young King was taken back by the boldness of his betrothed's pleading. Unthinkably, for a brief moment, he forgot about the fate of his parents. His youthful passions took over, overriding his utmost respect for her; as he allowed himself to contemplate their consummation before marriage. . .

"I am yours, forever!" breathed Star.

Dante quickly regained his composure, breaking off their torrid embrace. He took her hands into his. . .

"Alysandra, my love, I want you more than life itself," said Dante, deeply.

With that, he smiled his roughish smile and kissed her more playfully. . .

"Although, I do not know how long I will be able to protect your honor, if you kiss me like that again."

As Star was about to answer, Pride rode up to them, seemingly from nowhere. Instantly, Dante took out his gun, about to fire. Star grabbed his arm, pulling it down. . .

"No Dante! This is my friend," she said. "This is William, the man I told you about who helped calm down the villagers and vouched for me at The Square!"

Dante holstered his gun. Pride dismounted and respectfully approached Dante and began to bow. . .

"No William, no need of that," said Dante, as he extended his hand, warmly shaking Pride's hand. "I want to thank you for the kindness you have shown my fiancé," continued Dante. "How do you know her?"

"My King, our fathers are best of friends, our families have known each other for many years," replied Pride.

"May I ask. . . what are you doing out here alone, William?" asked Dante.

"Alysandra?" said Pride. "Did you not tell, Dante. . . excuse me your grace, King Dante. . . that I was to meet you here?"

"No, William, forgive me. With all that is happening, I simply forgot," replied Starr. She turned to Dante, explaining further, "Dante, after I left William and came back to the castle, I asked him to ride out here and wait for me. I was not sure whether you would decide to leave the castle. In the event you stayed behind, I welcomed his protection yet again. He is a trusted friend."

"Your grace, I am at your service," said Pride, bowing deeply.

"Very well, William, I am in need of your service," said Dante. "Once I go into the tunnel, I want you to accompany Alysandra back to the castle until I return."

"No, Dante! I must stay with you," protested Star.

"Not another word, Alysandra. . . you are going back!" said Dante, forcefully. "I will meet up with you as soon as I free my parents."

"My King, do you not need me to help you once you are inside?" asked Pride.

"No, William, I need to be alone. No one knows the secret tunnels inside the compound but me and my father," said Dante. "However, you can help me open the passageway door. It has not been used in years."

The two men, with Star looking on, used their hands and small stones to remove the overgrown brush and dirt that had overtaken the secret door. Then, Dante kicked the door at the bottom and its earthly seal broke.

"Very well, now ride quickly and be careful!" said Dante.

Pride nodded to Dante. The King took Alysandra into his arms and kissed her. Without saying another word, he turned and went into the passageway, closing the door behind him. . .

"What do we do, Pride?" asked Star.

"We wait, momentarily, and then go in behind him, unawares," scoffed Pride.

#

The battle at the castle wall raged furiously. The Ace's men were trapped between the fortress wall to their front, and Chariot's three companies to their rear. The fighting had been costly. The grounds in front of the castle were strewn with many wounded or dead soldiers from both sides.

Chariot's forces continued advancing forward, pressing the outlaws into an ever tightening vice. Kent skillfully commanded his soldiers on the tower wall. Curiously, he still would not let his rank of Archers shoot. His riflemen were perplexed at this decision—so was Chariot.

Then, it happened. Another full garrison of The Ace's men approached from Chariot's rear! They fired mercilessly, hitting many of Chariot's soldiers with their opening barrage. I watched as the tide of the battle quickly turned. King Dante's men were now trapped as well, and now, there was no escape route for Chariot.

"Braxus!" commanded Chariot. "Hold the castle wall! Get Pen, and send him to join me at the rear. Our two companies will cover you!"

Braxus quickly rode to Pen, charging forward as ordered. Pen rounded up his company and joined Chariot. Kent looked through his spy glass and saw Chariot's men trapped from his rear. Immediately, he defiantly stood on top of the Tower wall. . .

"Archers! To the front!" Kent commanded. The Archers, without delay, positioned themselves in front of the exhausted riflemen. "Aim high and long! Over Chariot's head! Pull back with all your might men! I want you to shoot as fast as you can; empty your quivers! Fill the sky with your quills! Make sure you fire long or you will hit our own men!"

With that Kent flagged his hand and jumped off the Tower wall. The Archers, to a one, pulled back hard on the strings, practically breaking the bended wood of their bows in two! The first volley of arrows flew high into the sky, disappearing into the Sun; followed by a second volley of darts launched before the first shots even landed.

I watched in amazement as a hailstorm of arrows fell back to the earth, just behind Chariot and Pen's companies. The darts hit their mark, felling the outlaws in large groups. Over and over, the archer's deadly arrows fell back to Earth, hitting The Ace's men. As fast as the tide had turned against Dante's forces, it had changed yet again to the advantage of Chariot and Kent.

Chariot could not believe his eyes as the multitude of arrows continued, relentlessly. He turned and saw young Kent high atop the Castle tower who waved his hand in his direction. . .

"Well done Kent!" Chariot said to himself. "Very well done indeed!"

For now, the first attack of the castle had been repelled. There would be nothing left to do but bury the dead, wait for the news from anyone, and be at the ready—It was an uneasy calm.

As I finished writing the second scroll of the second book, I wondered what fate would befall all those that were still in peril: For The Ace had only been wounded, certainly not defeated—of that I was sure.

36.

PERSEVERANCE

As the Sun began its set over the Hills of No Man's Land, I saw it anew. It had been many Earth years since my eyes beheld the compound of The Jack of Diamonds—the hideout had changed. No longer just an underground fortress secretly dug into and under the mountain for The Jack and his men; but now a serene site laden with various colored plants growing all around.

Above ground, standing in the center of this beauty in the open courtyard near to the entrance of the underground stronghold, The Jack built a home for Justice and their new-born son, crafted of redwood and stone; their love grew here—more and more with each passing year.

Then my eyes sharpened and beheld the stains that now infected this beautiful place. All over the courtyard, outlaws of The Ace milled about; their horses tied nearby. Not too far from the house, Krispen, The Ace's second in command and Selwyn, an outlaw 7, sat by a fire drinking. . .

"She'll get hers tonight," proffered Krispen.

"Yes, and in her own bed! How fitting for a trollop like her!" spewed a drunk Selwyn.

The two men laughed as the night deepened; the strong drink finally closed their eyes. From across the courtyard,

I saw him, The Ace of Spades. He had just come out of the door leading down to the hideout. Quietly, he walked up to Arcus, a mercenary with no past that any one knew of, who stood guard not too far from Justice's house where she had been imprisoned.

"Keep a sharp eye, Arcus," said The Ace.

"Always," he replied.

"Good. Now, I'm going inside, and no matter what you hear. . . stand your guard," said The Ace, forcefully. Arcus nodded, as The Ace's expression turned malevolent, continuing, "You see, a certain lady has need of me. . . and I do not want to disappoint!"

"Of course your grace," replied Arcus, smiling coldheartedly.

With that, The Ace turned and walked to the front door. With the stealth of a cat, he carefully opened it and went in; quietly closing the door behind him. I watched him walk softly through the dark house to the rear bedroom—her bedroom, where earlier he had put Justice. The only light that shone came from a lone candle that flickered through the doorway. Not a sound could be heard in the house.

From out of the silence, The Ace kicked the door open and stood in the doorway, staring rabidly at Justice, who was gagged and tied in a chair near her bed. At first, she shuddered at his presence; then got hold of herself, her eyes riveted on his every move.

The Ace slowly closed the door, seemingly pleased with himself at being able to unnerve her, if even for a moment. He walked up to her and removed his gloves, tossing them onto a nearby dressing table. . .

"My Queen, why how beautiful you look tonight," he said, sarcastically. Then he walked behind her, just standing, not saying or doing anything. Justice sat there inwardly terrified at what he would do.

Still standing behind her, The Ace took his hands and softly ran them through Justice's hair. His fingers slowly caressed her face. Then he leaned over and put his cheek next to hers as he let his hands wrap around her waist. Immediately, Justice squirmed and tried to break free from her bonds, but could not. The more she struggled, the more The Ace seemed to enjoy it.

Next, he let his hands rise up and cover her breasts. Justice shook with all her might, moving the chair away from him. The Ace forcibly held her still, pushing down hard on her shoulders. Momentarily, Justice kept still.

"That's better my dear," he said. The Ace walked in front of her and ripped the gag out of her mouth. Before Justice could say anything, he pressed his lips hard onto hers, kissing her brutally! Justice desperately turned her head back and forth, finally managing to break his lips off of hers. . .

"What my dear, better than my brother no doubt!?" he said, laughing in her face. "Say it, trollop. . . Tell me you want me to take you!"

Justice spit on the floor, expelling his arrogance.

"I'm going to have you—rape you. . . over and over! You can scream all you want, Justice. . . but there is no one who can help you!" he declared.

"You call yourself a man!?" she exclaimed. "You are anything but. Your brother, my husband, is the essence of my life! He is inside of me, outside of me, all over me; and I likewise in him. There is nothing you can do to me; nothing at all that can hurt me. I am bound in his love forever! I am his Lady Justice now and till the end of my days.

"Oh really bitch!" screamed The Ace. "Lets put that ardent declaration to the test!" The Ace reached over and slowly opened the top of her tunic, waiting to see her reaction. Justice did not move. Then The Ace took out his knife and slowly outlined her breast and then ran the blade alongside her faint scar. . .

"Remember this my queen?" said The Ace, salivating. Suddenly, he took the knife and cut the ropes. He grabbed Justice by the hair, lifted her up and threw her onto the bed. Justice fought him and managed to get away, now standing along side of the bed. . .

"So you want me to chase you, to ease your guilt!? How noble," he said, laughing.

Then Justice calmly walked right up to him. . .

"You arrogant bastard!" she said, with disgust not fear. She defiantly took her hands and ripped open the top of her tunic exposing her breasts fully. The Ace was taken back, dumfounded! Then Justice ripped off the lower portion of her tunic and got on the bed, lying on her back. The Ace could not believe his eyes. . .

"Do what you want! Take what you want! I will feel nothing!" she exclaimed. "I am my husband, and there is nothing you can do to me to change that. Go on! Rape me if you must, you pathetic weak little man! I do not fear you!"

"I will kill you!" screamed the enraged Ace, not knowing what to do.

"So be it!" she replied, with complete serenity and confidence.

Immediately, The Ace picked up the chair and came right alongside of her, staring down into her eyes. He raised the chair high into the air, threatening her with the forthcoming blow. Justice stared back, defiant, calm, assured.

Infuriated by his loss of control, The Ace smashed the chair on the wood posts of the bed right next to Justice; she did not even flinch. Still furious, he walked away from her back to the door and turned. . .

"You may not fear me now, but when I have Dante, and am about to kill him. . . You will beg to me, asserting you will do anything to save his miserable life," he said. "But I will not! I will kill him before you and my brother, your precious Jack of Diamonds' eyes! Of that you can be certain woman! And then, I will send you back to The Forest where you came from, where Death will watch you die while he tells you in perfect detail, all of the unrelenting tortures I am inflicting on my brother, before killing him! Then my revenge will be complete!"

The Ace stormed out. Justice broke down and got on her knees. She prayed in silence as her hands fervently clutched the red diamond she wore around her neck.

I turned my gaze from her words with my Creator; For they were not mine to hear. Now I saw Star and Pride, sitting at a campfire just outside the escape tunnel door. Time had surely past. . .

"It's time," said Pride.

"What will we tell Dante?" asked Star.

"If he suspects, we will tell him that we encountered one of the renegade patrols of The Ace, he replied. "And that all we could do was turn back and hide inside the tunnel."

"Excellent!" she said. "Do you think they are all there?"

"Except for Justice, of the rest I do not know. . ." offered Pride. "But I'm sure The Ace's men have Dante captive by now."

Pride picked up a long piece of wood and lit one end.

"We'll need some light inside," he said.

The twosome kicked dirt into the fire and walked to the tunnel door. Making sure they were not seen, they opened the door and entered. Inside, the tunnel was dark, even with the torch; I barely could see. Pride led Star deeper inside the tunnel. After only fifty cubits, their path was blocked by a cave-in from the tunnel's roof. A wall of dirt filled the burrow. . .

"Listen! Do you hear something!?" asked Star.

Pride turned his head slightly. . .

"No, nothing," he replied.

"It's coming from inside that dirt!" she insisted.

Pride put his ear to the earth. . .

"Yes! You're right. There's someone in there," he said.

"It must be Dante!" she exclaimed.

Pride began digging into the mound with his hands, throwing the dirt behind him.

"Help me, Star! We must dig him out before he suffocates to death! We wouldn't want him to die before his appointed time now, would we!" Pride said, laughing.

"Oh D-A-N-T-E, thank god you're alive!" she said, mimicking Alysandra.

As they dug, my vision turned to Henry; his horse galloping across No Man's Land in the dead of night. He desperately held onto the reigns as tightly as he could; his body bouncing up and down in the saddle. The dense clouds in the sky covered the moonlight, making it difficult to see the ground. Henry's mount strayed off the trail onto the rough ground on the side of the road; its front hooves pounded into a hole and the animal broke its stride. The Counselor went flying off his horse, thrown into the air. He hit the ground hard, banging his head. He lied there on the ground dazed and disoriented, and then passed out.

The sight of Henry on the ground brought forth to my mind, visions of The Jack of Diamonds I had seen earlier. When I looked back, The Jack still laid flat on his face by the river's edge. A trail of clotted blood had hardened on his cheek. The river flowed full and the cool water crept onto The Jack's face, waking him. The morning Sun felt good on his body. The Jack of Diamonds rolled onto his back, looking straight up into the sky, but not seeing it.

He laid there motionless, recalling his leap down from The Ace's camp into the raging river below; and how the tumultuous rapids waiting for him there, carried him helplessly downstream, eventually hurling him uncontrollably over the great falls. Unconsciously, he shook his head in his own disbelief, recalling how he had been sucked down under the churning water, smashing his head into a boulder that laid just below the surface.

I too recalled in amazement, how The Jack somehow managed to stay conscious long enough to swim to the river's edge once the rapids had calmed. My mind's eye still saw the visions of him crawling out of the water on his hands and knees, falling unconscious on the shoreline. He had laid there past out for more than one full day, bleeding from his head, on his stomach in the muddied dirt: only a few cubits from the river's edge.

Now fully conscious, The Jack saw a flock of buzzards circling high above him—waiting. . .

"Today, will not be your day!" he said, defiantly.

Still lying on his back, The Jack reached for his gun, shaded his eyes, and fired skyward. The scavengers flew off in fear of the noise.

I marveled at The Jack of Diamonds' inner will, the likes of which I had not seen in any of those of the Earth that I had observed thus far. As I wrote in the third scroll, an overwhelming sense of pride came over me; a feeling birthed from my continuing witness of The Jack of Diamonds.

#

A now conscious Henry roamed around No Man's Land, seemingly looking for something. He repeatedly bent down, peering under only those small rocks that glistened in the morning Sun, as if the glimmering stones beckoned to him. Yet, he threw each away in frustration. The Counselor's eyes lit up as he spied his horse grazing nearby.

"That's where it is!" he said, to himself.

Carefully, he snuck up on the animal and grabbed its front leg. Henry raised the hoof, shouting to the docile animal, "My wallet, where did you put my wallet!? I know you took it from me when I was sleeping!"

The horse paid his master no mind, continuing to fodder for plants.

"You're no help!" he said, turning around looking out to the hills. Then he started running toward a cloud of smoke off in the distance. Henry ran as fast as he could, wobbling a bit back and forth, holding on to his three cornered hat.

Phoebe and Alysandra were on horseback approaching. . .

"Look Alysandra! It's Henry!" shouted Phoebe.

"Why has he stopped!?" asked Alysandra.

"Come on!" said Phoebe, as she kicked her horse, bolting off ahead of Alysandra.

As Phoebe reached Henry, she jumped from her mount. Henry ran up to her and grabbed her by her arms, shaking her. . .

"Now listen here woman! I know you know where my wallet is! Give it back this instant!" he raved.

Phoebe was taken aback.

"Henry, what's wrong!? Are you alright? What happened to you!?" exclaimed Phoebe, as Alysandra rode up, quickly dismounting.

Henry paid Phoebe no mind and immediately went over to Alysandra, pointing his finger in her face, demanding, "You there woman! Give it to me now! I do not want to have to use force!"

Alysandra looked at a stunned Phoebe, totally befuddled. . .

"Phoebe, what is he talking about!?" questioned Alysandra.

"I don't know! Something has happened to him!" replied Phoebe.

"Look, Phoebe, his head! Look at the bump on his head!" shouted Alysandra.

Phoebe went up to her husband and began closely examining his head, running her hands through his hair.

"Unhand me woman! This very instant!" protested Henry.

Phoebe paid him no mind.

"What is your name?" demanded Phoebe.

Alysandra looked on, now more confused at Phoebe's strange question.

"Unhand me and I shall tell you, but only if you give back to me my wallet!" answered Henry.

Sir, calm down and tell us your name. We do not have your wallet, but we will most certainly help you find it," said Phoebe.

"Very well, Madame. . . I am called The Fool! But you two may call me Fool, without the 'The,' for I am one who stands not on formality," said Henry.

"Phoebe, what has happened to him!?" shouted an astonished Alysandra.

"He must have fallen from his horse and hit his head. The bruise is quite large," she said.

"Who is this Fool!?' asked Alysandra.

Phoebe's eyes began to tear.

"It is very complicated Alysandra. . . For now, my husband has returned to the man he once was; before we met many years past," explained Phoebe.

"Counselor Phoebe, I do not understand! What do mean, 'who he was,' many years ago. . ?"

Phoebe did not answer; instead, she put her arms around Henry and led him to a nearby rock.

"Come Henry, you need to get off your feet. I must attend to your bruise," said Phoebe.

"Madame, I told you, my name is Fool! I do not know this Henry. However, might he be the one who has stolen my wallet?" mused Henry.

"Yes, Fool, he is," answered Phoebe.

"Will you take me to him?" asked Henry.

"Yes. But you must rest first," answered Phoebe.

Henry pointed to Alysandra. . .

"Does she know this Henry too!?" he asked.

Alysandra looked into the eyes of her Counselor, somehow understanding without truly knowing, and softly answered, "Yes Fool, I do. As soon as you have rested, we will take you to him."

"May I ask your names?" inquired Henry.

"I am Phoebe, " said Phoebe.

"And I am Alysandra" continued Alysandra.

Henry's eyebrows tightened. . .

"Are you in league with Death, Magus, and Pride?" he asked, sternly.

The women looked at each other confused.

"No, Fool we are not," answered Phoebe.

"Be careful and mark my words well, for I will ask The Hermit and he will surely know," countered Henry. He paused and looked at them hard. "Now, knowing that, do you still give the same answer!?" he offered.

"Yes, Fool, we do," replied Alysandra.

"Come Fool, you need rest," said Phoebe.

"Very well," answered Henry.

The two women gently guided Henry to the rock and sat him down, attending to his wound.

"I must find my wallet. I know I put it somewhere," Henry mused, softly to himself, barely above a whisper.

Then he raised his hand to his head, and said, "I am feeling a bit dizzy."

With that, he passed out into Phoebe's arms. Her tears ran down her face onto Henry's head. Alysandra gently wiped the salted water from Phoebe's eyes; for her arms were holding her husband tightly, and she would not let him go.

I faithfully recorded all that I had observed, being careful not to let the tears that had formed in my eyes drop onto the scroll.

37.

THE CONVERGENCE

Star and Pride had cleared as much dirt as they could, one tiny handful at a time. They had not heard any sounds from Dante in over an hour, and there was still plenty of earth left to dig. Pride reached up and tried to move a large rock that had fallen down, blocking their progress further. . .

"Star, help me with this rock," he said.

Star squeezed alongside of Pride and they both pulled with all their might. The stone gave way, falling sideways. At the same time, the ground opened up a hole ten cubits deep. The huge rock fell through the opening and miraculously, the remaining dirt that entombed Dante fell into the hole as well.

Quickly, Star and Pride turned Dante over on his back. Pride put his face to his nose. . .

"He's still breathing," he said.

"Pull him back!" exclaimed Star.

The dark Virtues grabbed Dante by his feet and pulled him backwards, all the way to the door.

"Let's get him outside," said Pride.

Star quickly opened the door and they dragged Dante outside.

I could feel Dante's spirit refresh as the brisk morning air filled his lungs. His eyes opened, looking at Star. . .

"Alysandra!? What happened?" he said, still a little groggy.

Star hugged Dante, fawning over him as Alysandra.

"Oh my love! You could have been killed!" she exclaimed.

"There was a cave-in inside the tunnel," said Pride. "The two of us dug you out and pulled you to safety."

"But, I don't understand. Why were you two inside? William, you were supposed to escort Alysandra back to the castle," queried Dante, trying to stand.

Alysandra kept her arms around him, helping him up.

"My love. . . We rode back as you instructed, but soon after we left, we were spotted by The Ace's soldiers, a small patrol," explained Star.

"It was my idea to turn back and hide inside the escape tunnel, fairly sure that they would not find us and move on," finished Pride.

"Dante, now stable, put his hand on Pride's shoulder.

"Excellent William," he said. "You did as I instructed, you kept Alysandra safe. I will not forget this."

Pride bowed.

"Now, I must go back in and help my parents. I hope I am not too late!" exclaimed Dante. "William, take Alysandra back. If you run into more soldiers from The Ace, return as before to the tunnel and hide just inside the door. "Don't come after me. Stay by the door. Is that clear?"

"Yes my King," replied Pride.

"Dante," said Star. "I almost lost you once! I will not let that happen again. I must go with you!"

"My King," Pride interjected. "You will most certainly need our help to clear the remaining dirt that still blocks the tunnel. Maybe it would be safer for Alysandra to be with you than out in No Man's Land alone; with patrols from The Ace roaming about?"

Dante paused to think. . .

"Your point is well taken," replied Dante. "Once we get to the other side, you two will wait just before the door to the underground hideout. No one will know you are there. And when I return with my parents. . . we will all leave together."

"Thank you My King," said Star, looking at him with wanting eyes as she threw her arms around him.

Dante blushed a bit and turned for the door, opening it. The threesome went in.

"How far in was the breach?" asked Dante, as Pride closed the door behind them.

"Just a little further your grace," replied Pride. "Just a little further. . ."

#

The soldiers of The Ace gathered about the courtyard of The Jack's compound in small groups; they were restless. Krispen noticed a commotion brewing nearby; a crowd of outlaws had gathered. Quickly, he walked over to Selwyn who was scolding Lucian, a young outlaw of no more than one decade plus eight in years.

"Did you not hear what I said, boy!?" raged Selwyn.

"Do it yourself! Fool!" answered Lucian, with cold steel in his eyes.

Selwyn took out his sword and charged the young brigand. Lucian stepped back and drew his sword, welcoming Selwyn's advance. Krispen, seeing the impending fight, immediately stepped in to stop it. . .

"Enough! Both of you! Get back to work!" ordered Krispen.

"Krispen, I have had enough of his arrogance, the boy needs to be taught a lesson, now!" railed Selwyn.

"Yes, Captain, I truly need this lesson from this maggot who thinks he can insult me!" interjected Lucian. "And who foolishly thinks his sword is king!"

The fellow soldiers in the crowd laughed at Lucian's insults. Selwyn's face turned beet red. . .

"Did you not hear what I said, enough!" countered Krispen.

The crowd silenced, but not from Krispen's words. The Ace had entered the fray, unnoticed. . .

"Let them fight!" he said, calmly.

"The crowd cheered. Krispen acknowledged his order and stood back.

Selwyn charged the young lad, smashing his sword into Lucian's. The outlaws roared at the first blow; they were hungry for blood. Lucian just stepped back and let Selwyn advance on him again; another blow flew from Selwyn's blade onto the very handle of Lucian' sword.

Lucian smirked in Selwyn's face and then pushed him off. Now, Lucian charged relentlessly, striking blow after blow like a raging wind, all of which went unanswered by a surprised Selwyn. Lucian had Selwyn on his heels. The thrusts from Lucian's sword were unending. Quickly, he moved Selwyn all the way back against the Prisoner's Post at the far end of the courtyard.

The crowd followed them across the open yard. Lucian skillfully struck his next blow right at Selwyn's hands cutting his wrist. The older outlaw immediately dropped his sword. With that, Krispen stepped in. . .

"Enough!" he said, as he looked to The Ace.

"Not yet!" replied Lucian, defiantly to Krispen as he placed the tip of his sword right on Selwyn's throat. The young outlaw turned to Selwyn, railing, "Now, you pick up the dung!"

The beaten and humiliated soldier stepped back and picked up a nearby bucket and shovel, scooping up a pile of dung from the horses that were tied up nearby. The Ace turned and left not showing any emotion. After a few steps, the soldiers gasped. The Ace tuned back to see. Lucian had just run Selwyn through; his body laying on the ground. . . "Anybody else care to insult me!?" exclaimed Lucian, coldly.

The stunned outlaws stood silent, turning to their leader. The Ace said nothing, turned and walked toward the door leading to the underground hide out.

"Be on the lookout!" he shouted, as he went in The Ace closed the door. Krispen stared hard at the young outlaw, who boldly returned his glare. . .

"It's your kill, Lucian. . . now you bury him!" ordered Krispen.

Lucian took in Krispen's unflinching eyes, sheathed his sword, and dragged Selwyn's dead body by his hands, pulling him away from the compound.

#

August labored in the noon day Sun; his wagon had thrown a wheel. With only a stone for a tool, he continued to hammer the last of the broken wood spokes into place. Thoughts of The Jack ran continually through his mind: for it had been one full day since he left his son, not really knowing if The Jack even survived the treacherous leap.

August knelt down on both knees, closed his eyes, and began to pray. . . Refreshed from his spiritual infusion, he purposefully climbed into the wagon, snapped the reigns and continued on across the Western plains, heading to The Jack of Diamonds' compound.

The vision faded from my eyes as the wagon disappeared from my sight. My gaze now had been captured by a giant falcon flying high above the earth. I followed the magnificent bird to the farthest end of The King's Land and then I saw her, Aurora, standing atop of Falcon's Crest. No matter where one stood in all of The King's realm, this towering edifice could be seen. It had been said that all who dared to climb it—never came back. There was also a little known legend that told of a strange breed of people who lived there in the Valley of the Crest. . . They were called Keepers—Aurora had come home.

Boldly, she stood on the towering peak that loomed so high that it was above the cloud line. On the other side of the mountain, below her, there was a break in the clouds revealing a small, hidden shrine. From her lofty vantage point, she could see her teachers down below, gathered as they always did in circles, quietly studying the cards.

As Aurora began her steep decent to the shrine below, the lone golden falcon flew by her, circling, seemingly welcoming her back. She smiled at the huge bird as if she knew him, yet a strange feeling came over her. . .

"Dyami, hello my old friend. . . Aren't you glad to see me?" she said.

The Falcon began swooping at her from below, pushing her back. With each pass, the huge bird shrieked at her, backing her up towards the peak. Aurora did not understand. Then it happened. . .

The mountain shook violently, knocking Aurora to the ground. Dyami flew back and forth as if standing guard, making sure she would not descend. Giant boulders began falling from below her, rolling down the mountain onto the shrine. It was a terrible avalanche of rock and dirt.

A horrified Aurora stood helpless, as a sea of mountain innards completely buried the hidden shrine. This was the second earthquake that she had endured and survived. . . 'But why?' she mused, silently in her mind.

Aurora sat on the ground stunned, not knowing what she should do or where to go. She was the only Keeper left, and in her pouch contained the sacred deck of Virtues, The Book of The Keepers, as well as the ancient scroll which contained the meaning of the last card formation she had seen. The underground chamber room had been destroyed forever; The Keeper's shrine now buried as well. All that she had ever known or loved—was gone. Her eyes welled up with tears.

The great Falcon, Dyami, swooped down and landed next to her—protecting her, comforting her. The only thing she knew for sure was that somehow—Dyami knew. 'How could that be?' she wondered to herself. 'Who was in control of these events?'

I too had wondered the very same. I thought to myself, 'Why would The Creator do such a thing?' I considered one of the cards of the last formation: THE DEVIL. Could it be that he is that strong and capable of such devastation?

It had to be. . .

I wrote with a heart as heavy as the stones that buried The Keepers. . . I began to question everything.

38.

THE RING TIGHTENS

I looked to The Forest of Cards, and curiously, there too, the natural elements of its creation were raging, uncontrollably. I could feel a shift in the spiritual forces of Good and Evil; It seemed to affect everything in The Forest. I wondered to myself, 'Would this too be destroyed by a quake?' Unnerved, I looked for The Pond. . . And as before, they were all there. . .

"My God Hermit! What is happening!?" exclaimed Jupiter.

"It is the strongest attack yet!" said The Hermit, more to himself than Jupiter.

"This is Death's work, no doubt!" shouted Temperance, trying to be heard over the roaring of the wind.

"No, Temperance, it is not!" declared The Hermit, standing his ground, defiantly, as giant hail stones pounded The Forest. "As powerful as Death is, this assault is from one greater than he!"

"Can you see anything in The Pond!?" asked Juno.

"Yes, Juno. The convergence has begun!" replied The Hermit.

"The grand convergence!?" shouted Temperance.

"It would seem so," answered The Hermit. "And what we are experiencing here in The Forest, reflects that convergence."

"Can you affect it?" asked Strength.

"No, of this. . . we can only observe," answered The Hermit.

The ground shook violently. Many trees fell from the gale force of the crossing winds. Thunderbolts flashed across the skies, followed by a boom so loud that the shock of it knocked Juno to the ground. As Jupiter helped her up, she saw Death galloping out of the woods, heading straight for The Pond.

"Hermit! Look!" she shouted.

At that moment, Death's horse leaped over a large fallen tree and jumped right over Juno, landing directly into The Pond. The waters of The Pond splashed. Death gave a quick look of superiority to The Hermit and then disappeared.

Without hesitation, The Hermit shouted, "Quickly, hands into The Pond, bail the water!

The stunned group circled The Pond and cupped their hands, splashing the water out of The Pond as fast as they could. However, the pouring rain continued to fill The Pond almost as fast as they bailed. . .

"This won't work!" shouted The Hermit. "He's almost across! To the rock!"

The Hermit ran behind a huge round boulder that stood shoulder high, nearby.

"We must roll this into The Pond NOW!" he shouted.

The Five Virtues pushed the stone with all their might. It began rolling on a shallow dirt trench that had been previously dug into the ground. Once rolling, the weight of the huge bolder took over as it followed the pathway directly into The Pond: its weight and size splashed all of the water out of The Pond.

311

"What is the meaning of this Hermit!?" demanded Jupiter.

"The Convergence I can not affect. . . however, we have just trapped Death in-between both dimensions, in the void!" said The Hermit, allowing himself a tiny smile of satisfaction. "As long as we keep The Pond empty, he cannot move to nor fro."

Suddenly, the elements calmed. The group smiled at The Hermit's wisdom.

Temperance queried, "But now, without water. . can you see what is happening?"

"You are correct, Temperance. . . without the water, I cannot. However, not knowing the full of Death's plan, I thought it best to trap him in the void while we ponder further," offered The Hermit. "It is fate that all of you were here when he tried to cross. Alone, I surely could not have moved the stone in time."

"Hermit, don't you mean Divine intervention, not fate?" asked Strength.

"Are they not often, truly one and the same?" answered The Hermit.

"Indeed," replied Strength, smiling.

"Hermit, what will happen if we remove the rock and once again fill The Pond?" Temperance asked.

"Death will have no choice but to return here to The Forest: for one cannot cross dimensions without The Pond being full. When we are ready, we will refill The Pond, but only halfway," answered The Hermit.

"Will you still be able to see Justice?" asked Juno, her heart aching.

"Of that which I will be able to see, I do knot know. . . indeed some, but not all," answered The Hermit.

"Surely you can fill The Pond and see all; and then close the portal, stopping Death from attempting to cross yet again," reasoned Jupiter.

"Only with tricks, Jupiter, as before. The gateway of the portal is controlled by a force I have no direct influence on," answered The Hermit.

"Hermit, what can you tell me of Justice now?" asked Juno.

"Only that she is still captive of The Ace of Spades, and has survived his physical assault by being absent of fear. It was this absence that was the key in rendering his forthcoming carnal violation of her impotent," answered The Hermit.

"And what of Dante, The Jack, and the others?" asked Jupiter.

"There was not time enough to see further; I know nothing more—only that all the forces of Good and Evil are still converging," answered The Hermit.

The image before me began to fade. I could not hear or see any more in The Forest. Instead, my eyes beheld Death trapped in the void, raging in anger, trying to move, but unable to. The void filled with vicious words that spewed forth from his soul; but they carried no weight, instead, drifting uselessly in this realm.

For now, The Hermit, once again, successfully parried Death's evil strike. . .

#

Magus waited patiently inside The Jack of Diamonds' inner room, deep inside the underground stronghold. With him were Lucian, and three of The Ace's men; all sitting around the meeting table. The renegade soldiers sat admiring The Jack's guns that once lined the walls of this room. Spent shells lay strewn about the floor, exactly as they had been left more than 20 years past. The Ace of Spades entered. . .

"Are you sure Magus?" asked The Ace.

"Yes!

"A-n-d?" pressed The Ace.

"I have seen the vision. Soon, they will be coming through that door," Magus replied.

"Excellent! Bring Dante to me as soon as you have him! And remember. . . arrest the others in his presence to continue the charade," instructed The Ace.

"Of course," answered Magus. "I, for one, surely do not want to spoil the fun for all."

The soldiers laughed at the thought. The Ace of Spades turned and left the room.

"You three over there," said Magus, as he pointed to the rear escape tunnel door. "Lucian, in case he makes it past us, you wait outside in the passageway" said Magus. "And Lucian, if somehow Dante should best us and makes it to you, do not kill him! Is that understood?" pressed Magus.

Somewhat reluctantly, Lucian replied, "Yes."

Everyone moved into position. Magus waved his hands, and the candles that lit the room mysteriously blew out. The eyes of the renegade soldier's slowly adjusted to the dark. Within minutes, the escape tunnel's door handle slowly turned. In walked Dante, alone, carefully, holding a small candle.

He took not more than a few steps when the soldiers pounced on him from behind. The candle fell to the floor. Dante turned and kicked the first soldier in the stomach, knocking him back. The other two jumped him from each side. Dante gabbed one arm from each outlaw and dropped to the floor, causing the two men to butt heads, dazing them both. Magus could not believe his eyes. In seconds, Dante was able to break free from three soldiers. He ran through the doorway into the passageway leading to the top. It was pitch-black. A shot rang out. Dante froze. He could feel cold steel pressing into his back. Magus entered the hallway and waved his arms. All the candles lit. . .

"So this is the great King Dante!?" scoffed Lucian. "Second in skill only to his father!? How pathetic! Look Magus, he stands there not challenging—a coward!" Dante's pride got the best of him. Foolishly, and uncharacteristically, paying no mind to the gun pointed in his back, Dante quickly turned, catching Lucian off his guard. His left arm pushed the gun away, followed by his right hand that punched Lucian squarely in his jaw. Lucian fell to the floor. The guards from the inner room came rushing into the hallway, pointing their swords at Dante, surrounding him.

"What, nothing to say now. . . boy without a jaw!" said Dante, with a venom I had never heard before.

The outlaw soldiers could not help but laugh at Lucian.

"Take him back inside!" commanded Magus, to the soldiers. "There's something I want him to see!"

Lucian rose from the ground staring hatefully into Dante's eyes and said, "Magus, I'll search the escape tunnel for the others, we'll soon have them as well!"

Dante railed back, "There is no one but me! I came alone!"

"You must think us to be fools beyond belief," said Magus.

"Lucian, do not hesitate to kill Alysandra or her precious William if they resist!"

"With pleasure Magus!" replied Lucian, as he stormed back into the room.

"If you touch her I will kill you! I swear Lucian, I will kill you!" raged Dante. The soldiers dragged Dante back into the room. They sat him down at a chair with their swords at his neck.

In a matter of minutes, Star and Pride came out of the tunnel with their hands held high into the air. The blade of Lucian's sword was pressed tightly against Star's back. As soon as Star saw Dante, she called to him, "Oh Dante! Help me!"

Dante tried to rise but the surrounding blades kept him prisoner. "Let her go Magus! She is of no use to you!" implored Dante.

"Of that I am not so sure. . . your g-r-a-c-e," scoffed Magus.

Lucian laughed at Magus' sarcasm, and seemingly pushed his blade harder into Star's back.

"Get your sword off of her!" exclaimed Dante.

"Or what King? You're gong to kill me!" said Lucian. You may have got the best of me before, but in an open fight, I will cut you to pieces. . . M-Y K-I-N-G," spewed Lucian.

Before Dante could reply, Magus interrupted, "Lucian, take those two to their rooms; lock them in. You three, take Dante to The Ace; he has been waiting most patiently!"

Lucian pushed Pride and Star forward. . .

"Do not worry Alysandra! Be strong!" exclaimed Dante, as Lucian led them out. The remaining soldiers pulled Dante out of his chair, dragging him out of the room. Magus sat down and waited. Moments later, Star came running back into the room followed by Pride. She ran up to Magus, overwhelmed, thrilled. . .

"Oh Magus! Did you see me," she said. "He has no idea I am an imposter! Dante couldn't take his hands off his precious Alysandra. This is so much fun!"

Pride sat down.

"Good to see you W-I-L-L-I-A-M," said Magus.

"Never mind that. Where is the wine?" asked Pride.

"Yes, Magus, let us drink to our success!" said Star.

Magus waved his hands over an empty bottle on the table and then slowly raised his palms face up into the air. Wine began to fill from the inside of the bottle, rising higher and higher, as Magus' hands lifted into the air.

Pride's eyes widened, grabbing the bottle. He nodded to them both and drank deeply. Star, not to be outdone, took the bottle from Pride's hands and did likewise.

"It's very good, Magus," said Pride. "Now, when do we meet The Ace?"

"Soon enough!" replied Magus.

"Has Death crossed over?" asked Star.

"No, he is overdue," answered Magus, as Star took another big belt from the bottle.

"Too bad. . . he's missing all the fun," said Star, already feeling tipsy from the nectar. She got up and moved about the room, bottle in hand mimicking Alysandra, putting on quite a show for Pride and Magus. . .

I closed my eyes for but a brief moment; my thoughts turned to Dante. I too wondered if the young King would soon discover Star's ruse. When I opened my eyes again, I saw The Ace of Spades walking briskly across the court-yard. Following behind him were Dante, surrounded by Krispen, with his sword drawn; and Arcus, who brandished his gun. Dante's hands were tied behind his back. They entered the house and headed directly to the rear bedroom where Justice was being held. Posted outside her door were three soldiers. . .

"Open it!" snapped The Ace, to the soldiers.

One of the soldiers took out a key and unlocked the door; The Ace and his prized quarry went in. Justice ran to her son and was immediately restrained by The Ace. . .

"DANTE!" exclaimed Justice.

Dante tried to break free, but could not.

"Take your hands off of her, you filthy swine!" raged Dante.

"Not another word by anyone, or you both die this instant!" ordered The Ace.

"If you touch her I will kill you!" insisted Dante.

"Arcus, gag him now!" ordered The Ace.

Arcus took out a cloth from his side and wrapped it around Dante's mouth, pulling the gag as tight as he could before tying it. A small trail of blood flowed from Dante's lips. Then Arcus held his gun to Dante's head, warning Justice.

"Now, Justice, sit there and listen to me!" ordered The Ace.

Justice sat there helpless with Krispen's sword but inches from her. . .

"My Lady," said The Ace. "I want you to see with your own eyes that I have your son. But be of good cheer, for I will not kill him yet. As soon as I have my brother, and after I torture our young King a bit. . ." he said sarcastically. . . "Then I will kill him! In front of you both!"

Justice instinctively stood, Krispen quickly restrained her. . .

"Leave her be!" shouted The Ace.

Justice ran up to The Ace, pleading, "Spare his life! Take me! I will do anything you ask! "Kill me! Do what you want, but spare his life!"

"Well, well my dear, not so fearless now, are we?" said the sadistic Ace.

"Please, spare him!" said Justice, passionately.

"Sit my Queen. . . And hear me well," ordered The Ace of Spades.

The Ace motioned for Krispen to sit her back down in the chair. Justice complied.

"N-O Justice! I will not spare him! For I AM KING! Not Dante!" said the arrogant Ace. "He will die first as I said, and then, I will have you while my brother is forced to watch your rape! And finally, after I've taken my pleasure. . . I will send you back to The Forest to die at the hands of Death! For now you are mortal!" The Ace paused. "But I'm sure you will live long enough to reflect on the last of my vengeance—The murder of my brother, your precious Jack of Diamonds! Then my revenge will be complete!"

Justice launched out of her chair, completely out of control, and mercilessly began ripping at his chest. Krispen was at a loss to stop her. Dante again tried to break free, but could not. The Ace of Spades just laughed in her face, letting her beat him.

Finally, he grabbed both her arms and violently threw her to the ground! With that, he turned and walked out, taking a struggling Dante with him. Justice, now totally overwrought, passed out on the floor.

Outside the room, the guards re-locked her door. The Ace commanded Arcus, "Put our young King in one of the rooms down below."

"Yes, my Lord," replied Arcus, grabbing Dante from behind by his hair.

Arcus led him out of the house with his gun firmly in his back. Krispen and The Ace of Spades followed not far behind into the open courtyard. The Ace took in a deep breath, pleased with himself. Then he touched his stomach and turned to Krispen...

"It seems all this merrymaking has made me quite hungry," said The Ace. "Have the cook bring me some meat."

"Right away My Lord," replied Krispen...

#

Phoebe had made a makeshift camp in No Man's Land; she sat by the fire cooking some soup, her eyes never leaving her husband. Henry, still The Fool, had calmed down, but continued to walk about aimlessly murmuring to himself. I did not see Alysandra. Just off on the horizon, I could see August's wagon approaching.

As August neared, Phoebe spotted the trail of dust rising into the air from the wagon's wheels. Immediately, she called out to Henry, "Fool! Come here quickly!" Henry ran over, thinking she had found his wallet...

"You found it!? Where is it woman!?" he exclaimed.

"Quiet Fool! Stay close to me and do as I say!" exclaimed Phoebe. She hurried to her saddlebag and removed a gun.

"Is that it!?" shouted Henry.

"No! It is not! And do not speak unless I tell you, or I will not take you to your wallet. Do you understand?" she said.

"Very well," replied a confused Henry.

Phoebe slipped the gun into the pocket of her tunic. August's wagon approached. Now, recognizing August, she quickly went up to him. . .

"August!?" she said. "What are you doing here?"

"What is the news? Have you seen my son!?" asked August, as he got down from the wagon.

"Which one?" asked Phoebe.

"The Jack of Diamonds" August replied, looking quizzically to Henry.

"What happened to him?" he asked, fully realizing something was not right with The Counselor.

"My husband has retuned to his former self, as he once was in The Forest—He is again: The Fool," she explained, tears filling her eyes.

August went over to Henry who said not a word and then put his hand on Phoebe's shoulder. . .

"The man I met as Counselor Henry was a prudent, wise, and gentle man. . . He will again return to you Counselor Phoebe; I am sure of it," proffered August.

There was something in his voice that comforted Phoebe. Her countenance lifted a bit.

"And what can you tell me of my other son?" asked August.

"All I know for sure is that everyone is headed for, or already is at The Jack's compound. I also know that there has been much deception and trickery going on. It seems as though Dante's betrothed, Alysandra DellaSalle, has an exact double who is aligned with Darkness; she goes by the name of Star," answered Phoebe.

"August, this woman looks and sounds exactly as Alysandra does! And Dante is with her now, not aware of the ruse. Furthermore, there seems to be two other men who are also not what they seem to be, one of which is named William. This is the same man who beguiled Alysandra and then imprisoned her in the well, leaving her for dead. That is where Henry and I found her, barely alive, fighting for her life, trying to get to Dante!" Phoebe concluded.

"Where is Alysandra now?"

"She left for The Jack's compound; she is young and in a terrible rage over this trick," said Phoebe. "August, I believe Henry had figured out who this Star woman really is, but never told us. He too was on his way to the compound to warn King Dante when he fell and hit his head."

"Come, we must hurry," said August.

"Where?" she asked.

"Everything is converging at the compound," answered August. "That is where I must be as well. I pray that I. . . that we are not too late."

With that, Phoebe and August placed Henry into the back of the wagon. Henry looked up and down at Phoebe, not speaking, only mouthing his thoughts. . .

"It's okay Fool, you can speak now," said Phoebe.

Henry burst out hard, as if he had been holding his breath the entire time. Then he inhaled deeply. . .

"Is this man taking us to my wallet!?" he asked, anxiously.

"Yes, my good man, I am," answered August, as he snapped the reigns to the wagon, driving onward. . .

39.

THE PASSIONS OF YOUTH

Alysandra rode defiantly into the courtyard of The Jack of Diamonds. At first, the outlaw soldiers thought her to be Star and paid her no mind. She jumped off of her horse and quickly walked right up to one of the soldiers—it was Lucian. . .

"Where is he! I demand to see him now!" she said.

"What do you mean, Star!" replied a confused Lucian.

"Dante! Take me to Dante!" ranted Alysandra, her outbursts driven by the passions of young love and human jealousy.

Lucian quickly realized that this was the woman Star had been impersonating. He forcibly grabbed her arm, dragging her toward the hideout. . .

"Put me down hooligan!" Alysandra demanded, kicking and screaming. The nearby soldiers laughed at the sight of Lucian trying to control this squirming woman in his arms.

"What's the matter Lucian, too much woman for you!?" mocked one of the soldiers.

Lucian planted Alysandra back on the ground and slapped her face so hard that she passed out. He caught her as she fell and again picked her up in his arms; carrying her inside the stronghold to The Ace of Spade's room. Boldly,

Lucian kicked the door open. Inside were The Ace, Star, Pride and Magus. . .

"Lucian, what is the meaning of this!?" demanded The Ace of Spades.

Lucian dropped Alysandra into a chair.

"Take a good look at her!" said Lucian, to The Ace.

"I can't believe it! She's alive!" exclaimed Pride, his eyes bulging.

"Is this really her?" asked The Ace, as he circled Alysandra, carefully observing her. He turned to Magus and said, "The powers of your magic truly go beyond those of this world. If I did not see her with my own eyes, I would not have believed it! The likeness is exact!" Magus nodded, acknowledging the compliment. "Revive her," ordered The Ace.

Magus took some water and splashed it on her face. Alysandra came to. Her eyes bugged wide upon seeing Star, looking exactly like she, as if staring into a mirror.

"You are Star!?" exclaimed Alysandra.

"Actually, right now. . . I am you!" answered Star, sarcastically. The group all laughed.

Alysandra noticed Pride standing in the corner and immediately lunged after her former captor. Lucian quickly held her arms in check.

"And you William, or whoever you are! How could you do this to me, I trusted you!" raved Alysandra.

"Well my Q-U-E-E-N. . . It seems as though all I had to do was push but a little in the right places . . Your vanity did the rest!" answered Pride.

"Where is King Dante!? Take me to him now! I demand it!" railed Alsyandra.

The Ace of Spades stood in front of Alysandra, as he looked to Lucian, "Take Star to Dante now."

"You know, Alysandra," said Star. "Your King Dante's lips taste like cherry wine. You should know that he could not keep his hands off of me," she taunted. "Ah, but a proper girl like you would not know of such womanly things now, would you?"

"You bitch!" screamed Alysandra.

"Actually child, if you would be more of one. . . maybe then you could hold onto your King!" mocked Star, as she and Lucian left the room. Alysandra was about to speak, when The Ace of Spades put a small dagger to her lips, silencing her. . .

"I will let you see Dante soon enough," said The Ace. "Tell me my dear, do you think he would know who is the imposter?" mused The Ace, lowering the dagger from her lips just a bit.

"Of course he would," replied a defiant Alysandra.

The Ace looked to Magus and Pride, questioning. . .

"Never!" said Pride, most assuredly.

"Well than, let's put your heart to the test," said The Ace to Alysandra. "I will put you and Star in the same room with Dante and make him choose. Whoever he picks, gets to stay with him this very evening. . . The other. . . shares my bed tonight!"

Alysandra's eyes widened in shock! Pride and Magus smiled, cruelly, savoring the thought. The Ace stared hard at Alysandra. . .

"Well Alysandra, still care to stand on the certainty of your heart, or should I say Dante's!?" challenged The Ace of Spades.

"Everything I have ever heard of you is true! You are a cold-hearted bastard! You are evil!" railed Alysandra. "Take me to Dante now!"

"Gentlemen, I believe our young love-sick child has just thrown down the challenge glove at my feet," The Ace said. "Let's give Star a little more time with her new man. . . Then we will go in and see who he chooses," concluded The Ace, laughing at the thought of the upcoming sight.

Quickly, I sought out Star and found her being led by Lucian down the maze of underground passageways that lined the hideout. . .

"Lucian, let's have some more fun," Star said.

"Fun?" asked Lucian.

"Yes Lucian! Before I go in to Dante, take me to Justice's room; I have something delightful in mind!" said Star, enjoying her thought.

Lucian smiled.

"Very well, but you best be quick about it," he ordered.

"Of course," she replied, slithering up next to him.

"This way!" said Lucian, now looking at Star with lust in his eyes.

#

Chariot and Kent both paced anxiously in the great hall of the castle. . .

"Why have we not heard anything from anyone!? I don't like this Chariot!" said Kent.

"I must admit, I too don't have a good feeling about whatever is going on at The Jack's compound," said Chariot.

"Should we ride to the hideout in full force?" offered Kent.

"Not yet. It's too risky to leave the castle unguarded," said Chariot, keeping his reason.

"But if The Ace of Spades has them. . . and we do nothing but sit here. . . it will be too late!" said Kent, now more impassioned. "I say we go now!"

"Kent, your loyalty is most admirable. . . But we wait!" replied Chariot, pressing his rank upon young Kent. "We stand firm here!"

"Very well Chariot," said Kent, reluctantly accepting the orders.

"Go and make sure The Captain of the archers has his men whittling new arrows! I will check on our supply of gun powder for the riflemen," said Chariot. "Let's stay sharp!"

Kent saluted Chariot, inwardly knowing his judgment to be sound.

#

The guards unlocked the door to Justice's room. Lucian took Star by her arms and threw her into the room. Star fell to the floor at Justice's feet.

"Be grateful wench that The Ace has allowed you this visit! Make the most of it! You only have ten minutes," said Lucian, as he walked out of the room, locking the door from the outside. A stunned Justice bent down and took Star into her arms. . .

"Alysandra! Are you all right child!?" exclaimed Justice.

Star wrapped her arms around Justice tightly, and then broke down into tears.

"My Lady! They have my Dante! The Ace of Spades has him, vowing to kill him! How can this be stopped!?" implored Star, quite effectively.

"Has The Ace hurt you!?" asked Justice.

Star held her head low, somewhat shamefully.

"He tore my blouse, but I would not submit!" said Star, expressing both embarrassment and defiance.

Justice again held her close.

"Bless you child! Have faith; soon my husband will be here. Somehow, he will get us out of this!" said Justice, with complete faith in her words.

Then Star broke away and began laughing out loud.

"You foolish woman!" scoffed Star.

"Alysandra!? What has come over you!?" exclaimed a befuddled Justice.

"Look!" demanded Star.

Then, before Justice's eyes, Star transformed herself back into her real image and voice. Justice was in total shock!

"S-T-A-R!?" exclaimed Justice.

"Yes, Justice! I am no longer foolish and meek!" proclaimed Star. "I am in league with Darkness! For that is where real power lies!"

"But Star, you were always faithful to the light, shining as a beacon in The Forest for all!" continued Justice.

"What does one gain following the Light!?" countered Star.

"Everything that truly matters, Star. . . Peace, joy, contentment. . . True love, gentleness, and kindness! You know that Star, I know you do!" said an impassioned Justice.

"Justice, that is for the weak! I want power! And as for love, Justice. . . Your son is quite a man. His touch and lips have already sent shivers up and down my spine! I will soon have all of him!" bragged Star.

"What!?" exclaimed a startled Justice.

"You heard me! I will have all of him soon! And the best part, he won't even know!" declared Star.

"No Star! I will not let that happen!" exclaimed Justice, about to restrain Star when Lucian came back into the room, pointing his gun at Justice. . .

"Not another step woman!" demanded Lucian.

"Oh really, Justice!? You think your Dante will not take his queen. . . ME!" offered Star.

"Certainly not!" scowled Justice.

"Did you not hear me? Already he has held me and kissed me. . . But watch closely Justice, for there is more," demanded Star.

Now before Justice's eyes, Star turned into an exact likeness of Justice; her voice and mannerisms duplicating Justice exactly!

"Oh my God!" exclaimed Justice.

"Yes my Queen of Hearts. . . Magus has granted me the powers to change! And after I'm done sleeping with Dante, I will seek out The Jack of Diamonds and bed him as well! I assure you, he will not be able to resist my passions. . . After all, he will be holding his wife now, won't he!?" concluded Star, laughing in Justice's face.

"You silly woman! You cannot fool him! You may be able to deceive Dante, for he is still quite young, but never my husband!" scowled Justice!

"Really Justice?" answered Star.

Star walked about the room mimicking Justice's every mannerism. Then she spoke, her voice sounding exactly like Justice, mocking, "I love you Jack! You are my life!"

Justice lost her temper and charged Star, ignoring the gun pointing at her; it was an advance born from earthly passions not birthed in spirit. Lucian forcibly restrained Justice, and then threw her back into her chair. . .

"I will shoot you!" warned Lucian.

Justice collected herself, her emotions seething inside.

"I see My Lady does harbor some doubt about the forthcoming actions of her husband!" said Star, taunting Justice.

"I have no doubts. . . None whatsoever, you harlot!" exclaimed Justice.

"Why Justice, that is not like you, stooping so low as to call one silly names! How human of you!"

As Justice was about to speak, Lucian cocked his gun.

"Not another word, or I will shoot!" he warned.

"Ah, but alas, first thing's first, Justice. . ." trifled Star. "I go to Dante now!"

Lucian pushed the gun into Justice's face, halting her forthcoming reply. Star transformed back into Alysandra, laughing capriciously, as she and Lucian left the room.

An overwrought Justice pounded on the locked door. . .

"Let me out of here! This very instant!" she screamed.

For the second time, I had seen Justice's spirit truly broken. I can still vividly remember the first time, some twenty Earth years past. Again, I wondered long and hard—not daring to speak nor write the thoughts running through my mind. My concentration broke as I felt water spraying onto me; or so it felt. I looked out again and now saw the waters of the half filled Pond erupting high into the air. . .

"Stand back!" The Hermit shouted. "He is returning!"

The Hermit smiled as Strength took Temperance's arm. Juno held her husband close. They all watched in amazement as Death, seated on his horse, leaped from the innards of the void, back through The Pond, landing squarely in front of the steadfast Hermit.

"Damn you Hermit!" screamed Death.

The Hermit stared at his nemesis.

"You think this trick of yours will work!?" railed Death. "You cannot stop what I have put into motion. . . You may have managed to impress your pathetic righteous friends, but know this Virtue. . . Dante's death, as well as that of his father, will happen soon, whether I am there or not!" proclaimed Death. "And then, Justice will be sent back here to The Forest. I'm sure all of us will enjoy watching her die a slow agonizing death; most especially you Hermit, for you will be powerless to stop it!"

Juno charged evil's surrogate, shouting, "You will never have her! NEVER!"

"And why is that Juno? Because of The Jack of Diamonds?" he offered, sarcastically.

"Yes!" answered a defiant Temperance.

Death looked to The Hermit laughing, and said, "Go on Hermit, look into your pond. Maybe you can tell them where The Jack is. . . Or better still, you might be able to tell them what fate has already befallen them all!"

"What I will see means nothing. . . What I know to be true, is that your Darkness, and the master that you serve as well as those aligned with you, will never overpower The Light!" The Hermit boldly countered. "For The Dark cannot cover The Light; instead being exposed by it for all to see!"

"Your will is strong and most admirable," said Death. "But they are all close to death now, and it is just a matter time, a little more to be exact. . . and you above all, Hermit, know this to be true!"

The Hermit stood silent. Death looked to the rest of the group, pointing his finger at The Hermit, declaring, "You see! He stands silent! For he knows I speak the truth!"

Strength walked up to Death, staring him down. . .

"You!? Speak the truth!? That word, and its meaning, are not to be found anywhere in your being!" chastised Strength. "Ride on Death!"

"Silence, you foolish woman!" Death chided, as he pointed to The Hermit. "He knows my words are true! Go on Strength, ask him!"

All eyes were on The Hermit.

"That death hovers close to those that are loved, is real. That they will surely die, is anything but!" answered The Hermit. "Ride on Death. . . and play your poisonous hand."

Death spurred his horse, riding off. Jupiter looked hard at The Hermit. . .

"Will he succeed, Hermit!? Is there truly too much force arrayed against them?" asked Jupiter.

"The answer lies in the heart of The Jack of Diamonds!" The Hermit replied. "Where it has always been, since his birth."

With that, The Hermit turned and went to The Pond. Everyone looked at each other, not sure exactly, the meaning of his words. . . He looked in and I saw as he did. . .

The Sun burning hot in the hills of No Man's Land, scorching all that its rays touched. I could see The Jack, on foot, running through the plains. He was in tremendous pain, his body broken and badly banged up from the tribulations of the last two days. From my vantage point, there were miles of territory still in front of him. Over and over, he sprinkled water onto his head from a canteen he held in his arms. "You and me, brother! Soon! You and me!" he shouted into the air, over and over as he ran; seemingly gaining strength from each and every repeated declaration. . .

#

Dante held Star in his arms, passionately kissing her.

"Oh, Dante! I love you! You are my King!" said a fervent Star.

"Don't worry, Alysandra. I will get us out of this! I just need some more time to think!" said Dante, as he broke away from the embrace.

"Maybe if I submit to The Ace of Spades, he would let you live!" offered Dante.

"My precious, Dante, you continually prove your love for me!" answered Star, deepening the rouse.

Star again went to him, embracing the young King. Dante could not help himself, again kissing her, passionately. At that very moment, the door to his room opened and in walked The Ace of Spades, followed by Lucian who held Alysandra by her arm and quickly threw her toward a shocked and befuddled Dante. As soon as Alysandra saw Star, she lunged at her, tearing her nails into her. . .

"You bitch! Get your hands off of my Dante!" screamed Alysandra "I will rip you to pieces. . . You harlot!"

"Stop them," ordered The Ace, to Lucian. Quickly, Lucian grabbed Alysandra, restraining her.

"Who is this woman!?" exclaimed Star.

"Dante! I am Alysandra!" said an impassioned Alysandra. "This pathetic thing is really Star! She is an imposter, sent to fool you; beguile you. I am your betrothed!"

"Dante! Do not listen to her.. It is a trick!" countered Star. "Another one of The Ace's sadistic tricks!"

Alysandra broke free from Lucian and ran into Dante's arms. She threw her arms around him. As she was about to kiss him, Star grabbed Alysandra from behind, pulling her off of Dante. The two women screamed incessantly at each other. The Ace and Lucian just sat back, laughing at the sight. Finally, The Ace took out his gun and fired it into the floor. Everyone stopped.

"What is the meaning of this!" demanded Dante, to The Ace of Spades.

"You tell me. . . . Y-O-U-R G-R-A-C-E," answered a sarcastic but amused Ace.

"Choose! Who is the real Alysandra DellaSalle!?" demanded The Ace of Spades.

Dante was totally befuddled. He looked at both women who talked, walked, and acted exactly alike.

"Dante! It's me! I am your Alysandra!" said an impassioned Alysandra.

"Dante, my King! Do not be fooled by this black magic! I am your betrothed!" said Star!

Dante stood there in silence, looking at both women, trying to see something that would tell him who was the imposter.

"Maybe I can help you, Dante" said The Ace of Spades. "You will kiss each one now, and then decide! However, mark me well, nephew. . . the other, shares my bed tonight!"

"No! I will not play your sadistic games!" answered a defiant Dante.

"Oh you will nephew! If you don't, I will shoot them both! Right now!" warned The Ace, as he took out his gun and pulled the hammer back, holding it to Alysandra's head. "Now, this one first, and then the other."

Dante knew he had no choice. He walked up to Star who threw herself into his arms. She kissed him long and passionately. Alysandra tried to break free, but could not. "That is enough woman!" ordered The Ace. "Back away!" Star did as she was told. Lucian held his gun on her. The Ace let go of Alysandra. "Now this one!" Dante walked up to Alysandra and held her. Curiously, at first she did not kiss him, instead, holding him in her arms. Then Dante pressed his lips onto hers, kissing her deeply. "That is enough!" ordered The Ace. "Choose!" he demanded.

Dante, looked at each of the women long and hard. He pointed to Star. "She is the real Alysandra!" he said.

"Dante! No! She is the imposter!" screamed Alysandra.

"Quiet woman!" warned The Ace of Spades.

"Are you sure?" asked The Ace.

"No! She is the real Alysandra!" answered Dante, now pointing to Alysandra.

"Maybe you'd like to kiss each one again?" interjected a sarcastic Lucian.

"Do not speak to me boy! I know my betrothed!" railed Dante.

Lucian went to attack him. The Ace ordered, "Hold!"

An enraged Lucian did as he was told, staring hatefully at Dante.

Then Star went up to Dante. . . "My love, do you not know me?" she said, softly.

This time Alysandra remained quiet. . .

"I do know my love. . ." answered Dante. Star looked triumphantly at Alysandra. "And you are not she!"

He pushed her away and took Alysandra's hand, staring defiantly at The Ace.

"What do you want with Alysandra?" said Dante. "She means nothing to you; let her go! Is there no honor in you at all!?"

333

"Do not lecture me nephew!" answered an insulted Ace of Spades. "Now, for your insolence, I will only let you have one hour with this woman, whoever she may be! Lucian! Take this Alysandra and bring her to my chambers."

With that, Lucian grabbed Star by the arms and followed The Ace of Spades out of the room. . .

"Dante! Oh Dante! Do not be beguiled by this woman! She is the imposter! I am your Alysandra!" said Star. The door closed and locked. Dante could still hear Star's muffled impassioned protestations from outside of the room. . . "I am the real Alysandra!"

Now Dante took his betrothed into his arms. . . "A-L-Y-S-A-N-D-R-A!" he sighed.

"Alysandra pushed him back, enraged, "How could you touch her and think it was me!?"

"Alysandra! How could I have possibly known!?" answered a righteously indignant Dante.

"You could not tell the lips of a Harlot! A Trollop!" railed a jealous Alysandra.

"My Love! This was no ordinary woman! She is a creation of the black arts! Please, you must be reasonable!" said an impassioned Dante!

"Are you sure I am she!? Your beloved!?" she asked, forcefully, yet sarcastically.

"Of course I am sure!" he said, trying to take her into his arms. Alysandra pushed him back yet again.

"Now you are certain, but yet you picked Star first and then reconsidered! Why!?" she insisted.

"Alysandra please! All that matters is that I chose you!" answered Dante. Now, are you going to kiss me or not!" he demanded.

"NO!" answered a defiant Alysandra.

Dante broke out in uncontrollable laughter.

"Oh, my love. . . it is so good to have you back. . . to touch you. . ." he said.

"What is so amusing, Dante!? I do not understand?" she said.

Only YOU would have said no! Now I am sure!" answered Dante, laughing.

You mean to tell me that Star was that good!?" she demanded.

Alysandra P-L-E-A-S-E... We're talking about the black arts! Of course she was that good! But there is only one you. .. and you are it!" he said. "Now, do you want me to change my choice yet again, and ask for Star!?" he warned.

"Dante! I will run you though myself if you ever put your hands on another woman ever again!" she warned.

"Alysandra... It was the black arts!" answered Dante, trying to hide his impish smile, but he could not.

An overwhelmed Alysandra relented and ran into his arms, kissing him as she had never done before. Then, she broke off the kiss with her arms still around him and her body pressed tightly up against his, and seductively said, "My King is certain, and does not need any further reconsideration?"

"Alysandra... the black arts. .!" he answered, sticking to his explanation.

"How convenient an excuse," she said, as she took charge of him, kissing him over and over. "How very convenient, indeed!"

Alysandra stared into Dante's eyes and then relented, smiling at him.

For a brief moment, the evil that surrounded them, and those that they loved, had been pushed aside by the passions of their deep and abiding love for each other.

I faithfully wrote all the events that had unfolded. When I had finished the record, my attention had been drawn to laughter; coming from the courtyard above. They were all there: The Ace of Spades, Star, Magus, and Pride, gathered outside in the courtyard of The Jack's compound, laughing...

"Oh Magus, you should have seen him," said Star, boasting. Dante did not know what to do or who to pick! Alysandra was totally beside herself when his lips pressed on mine."

"Yes, it was indeed only a lucky guess that he chose Alysandra," said Magus, with pride in his work.

"I must admit, it was quite a spectacle," said The Ace of Spades. "I rather enjoyed it immensely."

Star slithered up next to The Ace...

"Does my lord wish to share my bed tonight as you decreed..." said Star, seductively.

The Ace took her and kissed her lips.

"Not now Star, now I want you to go and find my brother," replied The Ace. "Turn into Justice, beguile him, and get him here to the castle. Save your pent up passions for him."

"Very well my lord, maybe when I come back?" mused Star. "But where will I find him?"

The Ace looked to Magus...

"I have burned a piece of Justice's tunic in the black fire, said Magus "I now know where he is."

"Pride will ride with you until you are near," said The Ace of Spades. "Then you will ride on alone and tell my brother how I let you go to find him, and that I have Dante and Alysandra captive, and that I will kill them both tomorrow if he does not come to me!"

Star smiled, her countenance evil. She looked to Magus who nodded back at her, and then turned into the exact likeness of Justice. The Ace of Spades gestured his approval.

"It's time," said Pride. "The horses are ready."

As Star and Pride turned to leave, The Ace interjected, "Star, make sure you tell him how I raped you! And that you fought as hard as you could, but could not prevail; being brutally overpowered and ultimately having to submit!"

"Yes my lord... nice touch!" said Star.

"Indeed!" reaffirmed Pride, smiling to Magus.

The Ace led the group back to the stronghold...

40.

THE BLOODLINE LENGTHENS

Lucian barged into Dante's room, his sword drawn, heading straight for Alysandra. Dante, blocked his path, protecting Alysandra with his body in front of hers. Lucian's sword was now up against Dante's chest. . .

"Out of my way, or I'll kill you now!" ordered Lucian.

"With that sword in your hand, and me unarmed, I can see how you think you're the better!" insulted Dante.

Lucian stared hard into Dante's eyes, doing all he could to control his temper.

"Your time with Alysandra is up," said Lucian. "Now, step aside or I'll kill you both right here!"

"Where are you taking her!?" demanded Dante.

"Not to worry my King," answered a sarcastic Lucian. "She is being put in her own room. . . for now! You will see her soon enough! Now stand aside!"

Dante turned to Alysandra and whispered into her ear, "Don't be afraid. Nothing will happen to you. This will all be over soon. I love you Alysandra, be brave."

"Enough talk! Move woman!" commanded Lucian.

Alysandra, with Lucian's sword in her back, reluctantly followed him out of the room. Dante waited but a few moments and then went to the far corner of the room and knelt down on the floor. He began tapping the wooden floorboards, listening intently. I could hear the muffled echoes of his knocks. And then the sound changed. . . He had found the hollow.

"I knew it would be here somewhere, Father!" mused Dante out loud.

Dante took the metal spoon from the table and carefully dug out the mortar holding the board, he lifted it off the floor. Quickly, he loosened the four short boards next to it, lifting them off the floor as well. Dante climbed into the hole. He disappeared into the dark.

Then I saw Justice, kneeling on the floor in her room, her hands folded, eyes closed, silently praying. The room was dark, save a lone candle burning near her bed. Her attention had been caught by a tapping sound seemingly coming from beneath the very floor she was kneeling on. Startled, she took the candle from the bed and knelt down, shining it as close to the floor as possible. From beneath the floor, Dante could see his mother through the tiny cracks between the floor boards.

"Mother!" whispered Dante. "Stand back."

"Oh my God! Dante!? Is that really you!?" she exclaimed.

"Quiet Mother! Yes, it's me," he said. "Now stand back."

Justice stepped back, Dante pushed from underneath and a few floorboards broke free. In a few seconds, Dante's head popped up through the floor. His hands came up next and quickly he put his finger to his mouth reminding his mother to be silent. Justice took her son's hands and helped him out of the hole into her room. Dante hugged his mother as Justice kissed her son, trying to hold back her tears of joy. . .

"Mother, it's alright, I'm okay," he reassured. "Where is Father?"

"I don't know Dante! I have been praying night and day for him," she replied. "How in the world did you get here!?"

"Father told me of these tunnels he had secretly dug for situations just like this!"

"Dante, where is Alysandra!? And do you know of the imposter? A woman called Star?" asked Justice. "She has been impersonating Alysandra. I saw her with my own eyes and could not believe the transformation. I was completely fooled by her!" she exclaimed.

"Yes! I have seen them both and been with them both! I too could not tell them apart. . . Even after kissing each of them!" answered Dante.

"What! You kissed this woman!?" said Justice, loudly.

Dante put his hand to his mother's mouth, quieting her.

"Mother, like you said, I could not tell them apart either," answered Dante.

"But son, surely after you kissed Star, you must have been able to tell. . ." she countered.

"No mother, I could not. But don't worry, I finally chose the real Alysandra.

"What do you mean chose!?" asked Justice.

"There is no time to explain," said Dante. "'Here, take this gun, you may need it," said Dante, handing Justice a small pistol. "Father has weapons stashed all over these hidden tunnels."

Justice took the gun and put it in her tunic pocket.

"Now, what can you tell me of The Ace's plans?" asked Dante.

"Oh my God!" mused Justice.

"What Mother? What is it?" asked Dante.

If you could not tell Star from Alysandra, your father may fall prey to that same ruse. For this Star can impersonate me exactly as well!" said Justice, shaking her head in disbelief.

"Mother, this is not the time to be thinking of that. Father will figure it out, I'm sure," said Dante. "Now, I have to get back to my room. Replace the boards after I'm gone. We have to play along for now. Nothing will happen to any of us until father gets here. But then we'll be ready. And mother. . . If you have to use that gun. . . DO IT!" he implored.

"Yes Dante," answered Justice, kissing her son one more time.

Dante jumped back down into the tunnel. Justice quickly put the boards back into place, standing on wood, pressing them back into the floor.

"Surely, she can't fool Jack! He would most certainly know. . . How could he not!" mused Justice out loud, anxiously.

I heard the sound of cold steel thrashing through the air. Curiously, the candle's flame blew out; I looked downward and now saw The Ace of Spades standing alone, sword in hand, in The Jack's underground room. He moved about the room practicing lunges and parries; his blade flew through the air, cutting it with a whooshing sound. Lucian, stood by the door, seemingly unnoticed, quietly observing The Ace's deftness with his blade. . .

"En garde boy!" shouted The Ace.

Immediately, The Ace of Spades charged Lucian, cutting a piece of cloth from his shirt. Lucian drew his sword, and without hesitation, lunged at The Ace. Spades parried the first attack of Lucian's steel, seemingly playing with the young man.

Lucian would not be deterred. He charged relentlessly, forcing The Ace back into a corner. As like The Ace, Lucian's blade also cut the wind with the sharpness of a razor. The Ace of Spades had all he could do to keep up with the younger man. Finally, The Ace charged hard, breaking through Lucian's series of parries; The Ace's blade was now at Lucian's neck. . .

"Do you yield!?" scowled The Ace of Spades.

"No! I do not!" answered a defiant Lucian.

"Then you shall die!" countered The Ace.

"Cut away if you can! I do not yield!" replied Lucian, with a coldness in his eyes.

Lucian deftly took out a small knife from his waistband and thrust it up against The Ace's stomach. The two men now stood face to face, each with steel against the other. The Ace stepped back and saluted Lucian. . .

"Very good son! Very good indeed. I salute you," said The Ace of Spades. "Not for your cunning, but for your unwillingness to give in!"

"Thank you Father. You forget, I learned that from you when I was but a boy," said Lucian.

The Ace of Spades nodded. His demeanor hardened. . .

"Why have you left your post?" he demanded.

"It's that miserable wretch, Dante," answered Lucian.

"What matter about your cousin troubles you?" asked The Ace of Spades.

"Everything! I want you to grant me a request. . . In fact, I demand it!" railed Lucian, almost out of control.

The Ace of Spades frowned on his son's emotional unsteadiness.

"Careful Lucian, no one talks to me that way. . . Now, what do you desire?" asked The Ace of Spades.

"When you deem the time. . . I want to kill Dante myself!" answered Lucian.

The Ace had been genuinely taken back by his son's request.

"Y-O-U?" asked The Ace. "Why do you want this?"

"It's only fitting," replied Lucian. "You kill your brother, and your son kills his son! Then you will be the legitimate King, and I will be your rightful heir. Both of us having earned our position by the boldness of our swords. . . our bloodline in tact."

The Ace silently considered his son's audacious request. . .

"Leave me now, back to your post. I will consider the matter," said The Ace of Spades.

"Yes my lord," replied Lucian, as he nodded to his Father, and turned to take his leave. As he did so, The Ace interjected, "Lucian, do you think you CAN kill Dante? Are you in fact the better?" asked The Ace.

"Father, are you not better than your half brother?" replied Lucian, with impudence.

"You speak boldly for a boy!" snapped The Ace. "Answer me this. . . If I grant you your request, and Dante gets the better of you. . . He will surely spare your life, for he lives by the code of chivalry. Then what shall I do with you?"

"Then you shall kill Dante and me after that!" snapped back a defiant Lucian.

The Ace of Spades looked into the cold eyes of his son; it was as if he was looking into a mirror seeing himself. . .

"Back to your post" ordered The Ace.

Dante again nodded to his father and took leave.

#

Pride and Star rode across the plains of No Man's Land. They had just approached the far end of the winding river. Pride held up his hand and they stopped alongside of the water. . .

"The Jack of Diamonds can be found not more than one league further. He is on foot, following the riverbank," said Pride.

Star, looking exactly as Justice, smiled broadly.

"See you back at The Jack's hideout in the morning. . ." said Star. "Let's see what the night brings." Star sighed, loudly. . . "Oh Jack, you are my life!"

Pride could not help but laugh.

"Enjoy yourself all you want Star, just get him to us by tomorrow!" said Pride, as he rode off, back to The Jack's compound.

Star fixed her hair and kicked her horse onward, following the riverbank. As she rode, I took notice of the great Falcon, Dyami, flying high overhead, as if he had been observing. When I fixed my gaze on the vision of Dyami's sight, my eyes beheld August, Phoebe, and Henry, still The Fool, as they boldly rode into The Jack's compound. Immediately, Krispen and Arcus stopped them. . .

"Old man, you best turn around and be on your way. . ." said Arcus, sternly.

Henry heard Arcus' voice and began to rant, "Is that the man!? Does he have my wallet!?"

"Who is this fool!?" demanded Arcus.

"Pay him no mind," answered August, now instinctively looking toward Krispen.

"It would be best for you to turn around; this is no place for you," said Krispen, with more respect for August's age.

"I'm afraid we can't sir. Please take me to my son!" said August, somewhat firmer.

"Your son. . . Here with us. . ? And who would that be?" asked a mocking Arcus.

"You give me my wallet, now!" exclaimed Henry.

Arcus took out his sword, about to run Henry through, who quickly cowered as he stared at the blade.

"NO!" screamed Phoebe.

Krispen grabbed Arcus by his arm, stopping him.

"Hold your sword!" ordered Krispen.

Arcus' face rippled with anger.

"Who is your son?" asked Krispen, to August.

"He is The Ace of Spades, my lord," answered August.

Both Krispen and Arcus were taken aback by August's response.

"You, are The King of Clubs!?" asked Acrus, not really believing.

"Yes, I was once he," answered August.

"And who are these two?" asked Krispen.

"I am Phoebe, Counselor to King Dante. This is my husband, Henry who also is Counselor to King Dante; he has suffered a terrible blow to his head."

Arcus snapped back, "The Ace of Spades is The King!"

"Get out of the wagon and follow me," ordered Krispen.

"Where are you taking us?" asked Phoebe.

"To a room where you will be guarded until I speak with The Ace," answered Krispen.

"Phoebe, are they taking us to my wallet?" asked Henry.

"Quiet now, Henry! Don't speak another word," insisted Phoebe.

Henry nodded to Phoebe and then, like a child, gave Arcus a scathing look. Again Arcus was about to react when Krispen ordered, "Forget about that fool! Go and tell The Ace who has arrived. I will put them in with Alysandra."

Arcus hurried off; August looked long and hard at Krispen.

"For now the woman has not been harmed," said Krispen, answering August's unspoken question.

"Is my other son here?" asked August.

"No, he is who everybody is waiting for," replied Krispen. "As I said, it would have been better for you three if you had never come."

"May I ask your name?" queried August.

"I am Krispen, Captain of all under The Ace of Spades," he answered.

"Krispen. . ?" mused August. "Are you not the son of Malcus?

Krispen quickly startled by August's statement. . .

"Yes! My father once served you," answered Krispen.

"I remember your father well. . . When I was King, I never trusted him," said August.

"And why was that?" asked Krispen.

"Because, he had a sense of integrity. He was principled. . . And mostly, because he would always show kindness to the villagers," said August. "A soldier of that character—did not belong under my rule. And dare I say Krispen, you do not belong here with my son, The Ace of Spades."

Krispen pondered August's words, and stoically replied, "As I said before, it would have been better for you if you had never come. . . This way. . ."

The Great Falcon's vision changed. Once again he looked to the dry plains. My eyes followed his. Now I could see Star riding rounding the bend along the river's edge. Up ahead she saw him, running steadily in her direction. Star kicked her horse and galloped at full speed over to him. The Jack of Diamonds could not believe his eyes. At first he thought he was seeing a mirage; he stopped to breathe deeply and clear his eyes. It was Justice—or so he thought. Star abruptly stopped her horse and jumped down into his arms. . .

"Oh my God, Jack! I thought I would never seer you again! Thank God you're alive!" said Star, throwing her arms around him, kissing him as she spoke.

The Jack held her tightly.

"Justice, are you alright? Did he hurt you, and how did you escape!?" asked The Jack. "Did you see Dante? Does my brother have him?"

Star hugged him tighter; The Jack grimaced in pain.

"Jack! You're hurt!" exclaimed Star.

"Justice, answer me!" insisted The Jack.

"Yes, Jack, your brother has Dante! He let me go to find you. . . to bring you back to our compound!" said an impassioned Star.

"Dante is there!?" asked The Jack.

"Yes, my love. And he has Alysandra as well!" continued Star. " He swore he would kill them both if I did not return with you by noon tomorrow. The Ace of Spades has Magus, the Magician; and Pride, The Hanged Man with him!"

The Jack's eyebrows tightened.

"They are from The Forest of Cards. . . Jack, they are in league with Darkness and are very powerful, each with their own strengths!" continued Star. "It was Magus who saw, in a vision, exactly where you were. That's how I knew how to find you!" Then Star let her head hang low, her demeanor changing. . .

"Answer me Justice, did he hurt you?" asked The Jack of Diamonds, with ire in his voice.

"Yes," answered Star, reluctantly "But I would not submit! I managed to fight him off! He would have had to kill me before I would let him take me!"

Jack held Star close to him. . .

"I'm going to kill him!" said The Jack, with a strange calmness about him.

"Oh, Jack, what are we gong to do!?" exclaimed Star.

"We're going to give him what he wants for now. . . ME!" answered The Jack of Diamonds, now showing some uncharacteristic outward emotion. "Let's go!"

"Jack! No! You need to rest! You're badly hurt. We can spend the night right here and leave in the morning," said Star. "The Ace of Spades said we have till noon tomorrow to return. I think it's best if you rest here tonight, gain some strength back."

The Jack pondered Star's words.

"You're right Justice," said The Jack. "Besides, my brother would never hurt Dante without you or me there to see it! I'll make a fire."

"Good. I'll find us some wood," said Star.

"Don't worry, Justice, nothing will happen to Dante or Alysandra. This all ends tomorrow!" said The Jack, again with a quiet certainty.

Star threw herself into his arms, pressing her lips on his. She kissed him, passionately. The Jack held her tightly, returning her fervor.

"I'm not so sure we even need the firewood my love," said Star, her passions inflamed.

"Justice, we will freeze to death out here overnight, please. . . find us some wood. I'll start a fire with some kindling," said The Jack of Diamonds, undressing Star with his eyes; a look that motivated Star to hurry.

She walked off as The Jack bent down, gathering small twigs strewn about the ground. He ripped a tiny piece of cloth from his shirt and placed the loose twigs on top of it. Then he took out his gun and removed one bullet from the chamber. He opened up the projectile and emptied the powder onto the cloth.

The Jack stood and fired his gun directly into the kindling. The sprinkled gunpowder ignited, the cloth lit, and the twigs caught fire. Star walked back dragging two long pieces of deadwood with her. Jack stepped on the dried wood, breaking each branch in half. Carefully, he placed the four pieces into the fire: the wood caught the flame. . .

"This will keep us warm for now," said The Jack of Diamonds.

Star went to her horse and removed a blanket from her saddlebag. She spread it out next to the fire and laid down. . .

"Come my love. . ." said Star.

The Jack sat down next to her. Star placed her head on The Jack's chest. He put his arm around her. She looked up at his face. Her heart was pounding. Star's eyes expressed her wanting—her physical hunger. The Jack looked deeply into her eyes, staring intently, and then kissed her passion-

347

ately, keeping his mouth on her lips. Finally, he broke it off, smiling at Star. . .

"Come on Justice, we better get some sleep," said The Jack, to a disappointed Star.

The Jack laid down flat, pulling Star to him. She rested her head on his shoulders.

"I love you Jack," said Star.

"I know you do. . . And I love my Lady Justice," replied The Jack.

Star began kissing his chest. The Jack wickedly smiled.

"J-u-s-t-i-c-e," he said.

Breathlessly, Star replied, "I want you Jack!"

Star loosened the top of her tunic and unfastened the cinch around her waist. She removed her tunic, pulling it up and over her head. Star's beautiful body glistened against the embers of the glowing fire and the full moon's light over head. The Jack of Diamonds looked hard at Star, taking in her essence. . .

41.

LUCIAN

The Forest of Cards shook. I could clearly see The Tower: its number XVI. Lightning flashed across The Forest sky, repeatedly striking the magnificent edifice at the top. The electric bolts bored deeply into the mortared bricks. One by one, the rectangular stones, once precisely fit, now fell to the ground.

In a single jot in time. . . The Tower, and all its meaning, was gone: reduced to a pile of rubble and scattered across the mount. Only a small remnant remained, standing no more than the height of a man.

The shaking stopped. The lightning ceased. Curiously, an eerie quiet came over The Forest. The only sounds to be heard were those of the whistling wind that blew across the mound of ruins—spreading a fine cloud of mortared dust across the knoll; dust that once bound The Tower together.

Not knowing who or what was the cause, I looked to The Pond. There I saw him staring into the half filled pool; He too saw what I had seen, a vision of the decimated Tower. As the image reflected back at The Hermit's alarmed eyes, I reasoned from his shocked expression that The Hermit had not been the cause of this event; so my gaze tuned to The Hill of Death. As before, I saw Death sitting on his horse.

From his vantage point, he too could see The Tower off in the distance, now destroyed. . .

"Damn you, Hermit!" exclaimed Death, quite incorrectly.

For what had happened, and by whose hand, and just as importantly, why; I inwardly considered as I recorded the events. I struggled to find the meaning in what I had just observed, but try as I might. . . I could not.

Then I saw the arrow, flaming, flying high into the air, seemingly reaching the clouds. As the fiery dart reached the apex of its arc, it turned and descended back down to the earth, hitting its unsuspecting mark inside the court-yard of King Dante's castle—a wooden barrel containing gunpowder.

The dart landed unnoticed, boring deep into the wood. The fire quickly moved down the arrow's shaft, igniting the aged wood. In a matter of minutes, the fire burned through the wood barrel, igniting the powder inside. The barrel exploded, violently, shaking the ground and the castle. The sound could be heard for many a stadia.

The soldiers standing in the courtyard were knocked to the ground by the force of the blast. Two, who stood near the barrel, were killed instantly. Confusion and chaos ensued as the sky above the courtyard now had filled with a multitude of darts of fire, all landing at will, igniting most of what they hit.

The lookouts on the front wall searched the near grounds but could not see anyone. The arrows seemed to come from nowhere. Chariot and Kent ran out from the castle into the courtyard. Chariot sized up the situation immediately. . .

"Riflemen! To the rear tower! The arrows are from our rear! Shoot at will into the trees! Into the trees!" commanded Chariot.

Kent ran to the ladder leading to the rear tower and climbed. As he did so, he turned back to Chariot, acknowl-edging his expertise. At that very moment, a flaming dart of death struck him in the chest. Instantly, he fell from the ladder to the ground. Horrified, Chariot ran over to him, bending down and grabbing the fiery dart with his bare hands, pulling it out of young Kent!

"Hold on Kent! The doctors will bandage you!" said an impassioned Chariot.

"Protect the castle, Chariot! Protect King Dante!" said Kent, fighting to speak, taking his last breath. "It was an honor to know you!" dying in his arms.

Chariot closed Kent's eyes and climbed the ladder. He walked back and forth, defying the incoming arrows as he gave orders to the men. The castle had caught fire in many sections; the flames rising high into the air.

"You four! Let the front wall burn! Keep throwing water on anything smoldering under us here!" ordered Chariot.

Remaining calm and assured, he turned to a platoon of rifleman, ordering, "Put down your rifles. Man the catapults and launch the jars of oil up and over our heads. They want to play with fire?! We will burn down the trees and shoot them all on the ground!"

The rifleman hurried down the ladders, pulling the catapults into position. The soldiers quickly filled the baskets with glass jars containing a thick, dark oil. The soldiers took up torches and lit all the jars.

Chariot instructed the archers on the wall, ordering, "Shoot at the tree-tops!" Then he turned and shouted to the soldiers below, "Launch them now!"

The first of the three catapults' rope was cut, sending glass bottles filled with flaming oil into the air right over everyone on the rear tower. As the oil flew overhead, some spilled out, nearly hitting Chariot and his soldiers.

"Keep shooting your arrows! Do not leave your post!" commanded Chariot.

The soldiers, inspired by Chariot's bravery, held their positions, firing arrows relentlessly into the tops of the trees.

The sky was a sea of wooden darts, some landing back into the courtyard as well as those flying out.

The oil jars from the catapults flew up and over the castle wall, hitting the trees. The glass bottles shattered on impact, dripping hot scolding oil over everything. I could hear The Ace's men screaming as the scorching liquid burned their skin. In only a few minutes, the trees were all aflame. The Ace's archers jumped out of the trees to the ground, their clothes aflame. They all dropped their bows and desperately tried to put themselves out with their hands.

"Finish them now!" ordered Chariot.

King Dante's archers let loose their final volley of arrows, easily hitting The Ace's archers below. As fast as it had started, this secret attack was over.

Chariot turned to all his men, commanding, "Everyone, grab buckets and put out these fires!"

The soldiers did exactly as ordered, filling standing buckets from the many rain barrels arrayed around the courtyard, dashing the flames at their base. Soon, they had the fires under control. The air was heavy with the smell of burnt sulfur and charred wood. A thick plume of black smoke billowed high into the sky. The massive column could be seen as far as the eye could see, seemingly reaching the far horizon.

For now, the castle was secure on three sides. However, the gates of the front wall had burned to the ground. . . Chariot stood there alone, in the open. . . No one said a word, instead, all looking to Chariot, waiting to hear what he would say next. . .

#

The Ace of Spades sat at The Jack's table in the inner room. He heard a knock at his door and before he could answer, Krispen entered with August. The Ace could not believe his eyes. . .

"He rode into our camp with two of Dante's Counselors, said Krispen. "I have put them in with Alysandra. I assumed you would want me to bring your father here, immediately!"

"Wait outside," said The Ace of Spades. Krispen nodded and looked strangely in August's eyes as he walked out of the room, closing the door.

"I left you for dead! Yet, you are here. . . How!?" The Ace demanded.

"Your brother saved my life," answered August.

"And this is supposed to impress me!?" said The Ace of Spades, sarcastically. "Did you tell him how you murdered his mother and ordered the capture of his wife?!"

"I have asked for his forgiveness and denied nothing of my past sins," replied August.

"And the mighty Jack of Diamonds did not kill you right then and there!?" asked The Ace, incredulously.

"I stood ready to accept whatever punishment would come, including my death," said August.

"It seems as though my brother has grown weak of heart. . . no doubt from years of marriage to Justice and her repulsive virtues!" said The Ace of Spades.

August stood silent.

"Well old man, I have them all. . . all except my brother and rest assured, I will have him shortly! And then my revenge will be complete!" said The Ace, boldly.

"No son. . . I will not let you harm any of them. Only me, if that is your choice," said August, firmly.

The Ace walked up to his father and slapped him brutally across his face. . .

"You are pathetic!" he railed.

"Yes son, now you indeed speak truth. . . for I have been," answered August. "Can you too forgive me for what I have done to you?"

"Forgive you!? You have made me what I am! Powerful, strong, ruthless, cunning, fearless, and second to no one in all military skills! I very much like who I am, father!" said The Ace of Spades. "It is this ridiculous priestly transformation you have undergone that I despise!"

"What must I do to stop this vengeance?" asked August.

The question reached into a place deep within The Ace of Spades. It was a dark place. . . a sadistic place. . . born of his youth, taught by the former being of his father. Suddenly, The Ace's eyes lit up. . .

"Very well father, consider the following question carefully," said The Ace of Spades. "Is it better for one to die, unjustly, to save the lives of many?"

"I do not understand?" replied August.

"Oh, don't be coy with me, father. . . You may now be pious, but you know very well what I am asking!" scowled The Ace of Spades.

August considered his son's words but did not speak. . .

"Alright, if you insist, I will be quite clear father. . ." said The Ace. "Know this, I will kill Dante, his precious Alysandra, Counselor Henry, and his wife Counselor Phoebe. And then I will kill my brother in front of you and Justice. After all of that, I will send that vile woman back through the portal to The Forest of Cards where Death will see to her death, as she is now mortal!"

"No you will not!" exclaimed August.

"Old man, you are powerless to stop me!" said The Ace. "Now, consider carefully. . . I will let all but one live, if YOU kill just one of them; any one of your choosing! If you kill the one. . . then you will have saved the rest!"

August stood speechless, mortified. Without warning, he charged his son and managed to grab his gun. The two men struggled and the gun discharged. The bullet flew into the wall. Krispen came running into the room. He grabbed August, pulling him backwards from The Ace. . .

"Hold him right there!" ordered The Ace of Spades. "Well, well, father, I see some of the old King of Clubs is still in you! How did it feel, letting your pent up guilt and rage unleash your lust for blood!?"

"I have no bloodlust. . . only a certainty to stop you at all costs!" answered August, breathing deeply.

"Take him away! Put him in with Justice for now! That should prove very interesting!" said The Ace.

"August. . ." said The Ace, sarcastically. "Make sure to tell Justice of my proposition. . . If you kill one, the others live! I'm sure she will see the practicality in it!"

Krispen took August out of the room. The Ace sat down at the table.

"Star! Where are you!?" said the impatient Ace of Spades, into the air.

#

Dante crawled in the dark, feeling his way through the underground secret tunnel leading to his mother's room. As he was about to push up on the floorboards, he heard a knock on his mother's door from above. He waited, and listened—not making a sound. The door opened and Krispen led August into her room. Justice was flabbergasted. She embraced August. . .

"Oh, August, you too?" she exclaimed.

Then Justice turned to Krispen, demanding, and said, "If there is any honor in you, you will let him go. What pleasure can you possibly derive from harming one of such venerable years?"

Krispen stood silent. August stared hard at Krispen, seemingly searching his memory. . .

"You have your father's countenance Krispen?" said August to Krispen.

"Yes," replied Krispen.

"You know this man August?" asked Justice, befuddled.

"Yes, Justice," answered August. "His father, Malcus, was once chief of my archers. I remember this man as a child playing at court."

"Then you may remember how my father died as well?" interjected Krispen.

"He was killed in a skirmish with my son," answered August.

"Ah, but which one?" said Krispen.

"The Jack of Diamonds, of course," answered August, confused by the question.

Curiously, Krispen did not reply. He turned and walked out the door. No sooner had he left, than Dante knocked on the floorboards. . .

"Dante!" exclaimed Justice.

"What about him?" asked August.

"He is here!" said Justice, as she bent down, removing the floorboards. August stood dumfounded as his grandson emerged from beneath the floor. He embraced his mother, deeply. Then turned to August.

"Who else has been taken prisoner with you?" asked Dante.

"Counselor Phoebe and Counselor Henry, whose mind is now impaired. I believe they are being held captive with Alysandra," answered August.

"Any news of my father?" asked Dante.

"None that I know of," replied August.

Justice quickly interjected, "Star has gone after him! Transformed into the likeness of me!"

"What!?" asked August.

"There is another here from The Forest; her name is Star. She was once aligned of the Light, but now has embraced the Darkness; in league with Death, Magus, and Pride. She came to my room to boast how she had deceived Dante, and would also take in Jack!"

"Justice, surely she in not capable of fooling him?" asked August.

"Why don't we ask your grandson how good she is!" answered Justice, with both condemnation and jealousy in her voice.

"Mother, in the end, I chose correctly," answered a defensive Dante.

August sensed the growing contention between mother and son. . .

"The Ace of Spades will stop at nothing. . . nothing at all to taste of his revenge," said August, halting their mounting discourse. "Dante, do you think your mother and I could crawl through the tunnel?"

"I'm not sure. It's long and very narrow. I can barely fit through," answered Dante. "If we had more time, I might be able to dig it out a bit wider. . . but for now. . ."

As they spoke, soldier's voices, coming from the hallway, interrupted their conversation. Dante jumped back into the tunnel. . .

"Don't worry, I'll be back!" he said, disappearing beneath the floor.

Justice and August quickly put the boards back. The door opened; The Ace of Spades entered the room. . .

"Ah, the lovely Lady Justice and her pious father-in-law," said The Ace of Spades, mocking as he bowed. "So what do you think of my stunning proposal to August? Has he chosen who shall die?"

Justice looked to August, confused.

"I see he has not. Then I shall tell you of my offer, maybe you can choose for him. . ." said The Ace, sadistically gloating "You can be most convincing my dear. . ."

"Enough son! I will not kill anyone! And neither will you!" snapped August. My attention had been caught by Lucian, who raged to Pride, both standing outside in the courtyard, near the well. . .

"What is he waiting for!" raged Lucian, as he lowered the bucket into the shaft.

"Who, Lucian?" asked Pride.

"My father. Why doesn't he kill them all now and be done with it!?" ranted Lucian.

"He is waiting for your uncle, then all will be in place," answered Pride.

"Pride, my father is losing his edge. He stands too much on theater, and pomp, wanting a grand plan of revenge. . . Who cares if The Jack of Diamonds is not here to see it. What does it matter as long as they are all dead?" said Lucian. "There is plenty of time to kill The Jack when the right opportunity presents itself."

"Lucian, you would be wise to learn from your father. Tact and style do have their place," said Pride. "One day, you will be King, but first, King Dante must die so the throne falls legitimately to your father, and then to you."

"Dante! I'm sick of hearing is name!" ranted Lucian, as he ripped the rope of the bucket back up. "He is no King! He is a love sick puppy!"

"Do not be so foolish as to underestimate your cousin's skill," said Pride, deviously. "Your father once made the same mistake about his brother, The Jack of Diamonds."

"Do you actually think Dante is better than me!?" said Lucian, with his arrogance mounting.

"That I do not know. . . What I am sure of. . . is that Dante will not live long enough for anyone to actually know who is the better. . . Your father will kill him first," answered Pride, smiling. . .

In anger, Lucian threw the bucket at Pride's feet and stormed off. . .

For but a brief moment I gazed to the dry lake, anxiously looking for The Jack. I saw him riding on Star's horse, riding back to his stronghold. The imposter sat behind him, her hands tightly wrapped around his waist. . .

"Justice, you're sure that's the room Dante's being held prisoner in?" asked The Jack of Diamonds.

"Yes, Jack!" answered Star.

"Good! Then we'll enter by main escape tunnel. . . This should be easy!" he said.

Star pressed her body against his. . .

#

Arcus came running up to Justice's door, pounding on it from the outside. The Ace of Spades opened it, scowling, "What is the meaning of this!?"

"My lord! Lucian has locked the door to Dante's room! We can't get in!" said Arcus. "He's vowed to kill Dante!"

"Then break it down!" railed The Ace of Spades. "Stop him!"

"Oh my God!" exclaimed Justice, as August held her.

Arcus ran off. . . The Ace turned to Justice and August. . .

"It seems the cousins hate each other as much as the brothers do!" said The Ace of Spades.

"Cousins!?" said August.

"Yes father, you have two grandsons!" answered The Ace. "Dante and my son Lucian! And you Justice, are his aunt. Someday Lucian will take the throne. But for now, I will let him teach Dante some humility, before I stop him. It seems my nephew thinks his skills are superior to Lucian's."

With that, The Ace walked out of the room.

"Oh my God August! I have seen Lucian. . . Hate runs through him!" said an extremely distraught Justice.

"Where is The Jack!?" said August, still comforting Justice.

I followed The Ace Of Spades down to Dante's room. There, outside of the door, Krispen, Arcus and a gathering of soldiers stood listening to a would be brawl going on inside. . .

"Don't just stand there, break it down!" shouted The Ace.

The two soldiers took a battering ram and began pummeling the door. The door burst open and all observed Dante and Lucian fist fighting. They were both badly bruised and bloodied. The cousins rolled across the floor, pummeling each other at will, picking up any loose objects to slam the other with. At first, The Ace of Spades stood there admiring the skills of his son.

"I will be King!" ranted Lucian.

"Of a dung heap maybe! But never a real throne! You fight like a woman, Lucian!" insulted Dante, who now had Lucian finally doubled over from a severe blow to his stomach. . .

"Do you yield!?" said Dante, with a regal demeanor.

"Never, maggot!" fired back Lucian.

Dante smashed him in his face. Lucian passed out. Dante turned to a disgusted Ace of Spades, and said, "Take this boy out of here!"

The soldiers in the hallway laughed out loud, and then quickly silenced, seeing the anger in The Ace of Spade's eyes.

Krispen quickly interjected, "You two, take Lucian to his room."

The soldiers went in and picked up an unconscious Lucian, about to carry him out of the room.

The Ace of Spades commanded, "Wait! Sit him down and revive him!"

The soldiers placed Lucian into a chair and threw water on him. Lucian came around. . . His father stood in front of him.

"Stand up!" he shouted.

A weak Lucian stood defiantly in front of his father. The Ace of Spades turned to face Dante. . .

"Nephew," said The Ace of Spades. "Well done. . . You deserve to see this!" With that, The Ace of Spades, his eyes inflamed, raged, "You have humiliated me!"

Without any hesitation, The Ace of Spades hauled back and violently backhand slapped Lucian across his face. His son's knees immediately buckled; again he passed out, his body falling to the floor. The Ace of Spades turned to the soldiers. . .

"Now drag him to his room!"

The stunned soldiers went to pick Lucian up. The Ace commanded, "I said drag him!" The soldiers put Lucian's body down and dragged him by his hands out of the room. The Ace of Spades turned to Dante. . .

"It won't be long now," he said.

"I'll be waiting," answered Dante, without any fear.

The Ace stormed out of the room, followed closely by Arcus. Krispen remained behind. He stared at Dante, smiled, and said, "Lucian was never any good with his fists; But, he is exceedingly skilled with the blade. . . You would be wise to remember that."

With that, Krispen locked the door. . .

I wrote all the events I had observed. And as I considered further, I could not help but take careful measure of a side of King Dante's spirit I had never seen until his capture. It lay hidden deep within him; a will of cast iron and steel. A force that seemingly he had mastered well for a young man; one that he called upon—only in the most dire of circumstances.

42.

THE APEX

Arcus opened the door to Justice's room; standing in the hall with him were two 7's and a 9. . .

"It's time!" said Arcus, with a taste of blood in his eye. "Bring them!" he commanded, to the soldiers.

"Where is my son!" demanded Justice.

"Don't worry My Lady," replied Arcus, with glee. "He's outside, tied to the post!"

"Take heart Justice; he is still alive!" comforted August.

"Yes, old man. . . but not for long," interjected Arcus, quite sarcastically. "Although I must admit, he beat the hell out of Lucian. . ."

"Yes, Arcus, and so did his father!" added The 9, laughing.

With that, Arcus and his men led Justice and August down the hall and out into the courtyard. All of The Ace of Spades men were arrayed outside in the noonday sun—all except Lucian. Dante was tied to the Prisoner's Post. The Ace of Spades stood nearby, Krispen at his side. As Arcus led Justice and August closer, I saw four 10's emerge from the underground stronghold door. They were leading Alysandra, Phoebe and Henry to the Post. As soon as Alysandra laid eyes on Dante, she broke free and ran up to him, throwing her arms around her bound fiancée!

"Dante!" she exclaimed.

"Don't worry Alysandra! Be strong!" he said, as the soldiers pulled her off of him, putting her back with the others.

Arcus arrived with Justice and August. . .

"Keep them together!" instructed The Ace of Spades.

Alysandra now ran into Justice's arms. . .

"Oh my Lady!" she said, crying.

Justice looked to her son tied to the post. Her heart ached as she saw the multiple bruises on his face. Curiously, she stood silent. August tried to go up to his son.

"Stop this madness! I implore you!" said an impassioned August.

"Restrain him!" scowled The Ace of Spades, to one of The 9's. "Not another word old man, or I shoot Dante now!"

August held his tongue. An eerie hush came over the courtyard. The Ace of Spades walked over to his prey, looking directly at Justice. . .

"Where is your husband my dear. . .? Why is he not here to rescue you and the others?" he said, smiling. "Maybe he thought the better of it. . ."

"He will come. . . and when he does, your days on this earth will be over," answered Justice, with a serene calmness.

"My Queen, I stand reproved. You are indeed correct. He will come shortly, for my brother's delay was caused by the irresistible beauty and pleasures of your body," countered The Ace of Spades. "I believe you have already met Star. . . and I know our young King here has already partaken of her feminine pleasures," he countered, mocking her as he laughed. "She is quite magnificent. . . Don't you agree my dear Justice. . . Or maybe we should ask Alysandra?"

"Stop your cruelty this instant!" demanded August.

"My, my, father. . . with each passing hour, you seem more like your old self. . . giving orders at will!" said The Ace of Spades, sarcastically.

"Son, take me, do what you will. . . let them go. Save your soul!" said an impassioned August.

Before The Ace could answer, Henry, still The Fool, interjected, and said, "Who is that man Phoebe? Does he know where my wallet is!?"

All the soldiers burst out laughing, including The Ace of Spades. Phoebe quickly put her hand over Henry's mouth, silencing him.

"You know, I may just keep this fool alive; he provides me the most charming amusement," said The Ace, with a carefree air.

Henry forced Phoebe's hand off of his mouth and ran up to The Ace of Spades, demanding, "You give me my wallet now!"

The Ace motioned to Arcus who came up to Henry from behind and took out his gun. Holding it by the barrel, he smacked Henry on his head.

"H-e-n-r-y!" screamed Phoebe as he passed out, falling to the ground.

Arcus dragged him back to the prisoners. Phoebe knelt down taking her unconscious husband into her arms. Arcus warned her, and said, "You best keep him quiet, or I'll soot him!"

Then The Ace of Spades turned and walked up to Dante, and said, "How would you like to die. . . by the blade or the gun?"

"Uncle. . ." said Dante, a term he had never used before when speaking to The Ace.

"Yes, nephew," said The Ace of Spades, surprised by Dante's term of respect.

"I will willingly give up the throne and serve you. . . if you will let the others live," said Dante.

"Why, how noble of you Dante. . . But alas, my rule would thus be illegitimate, as **you** would still be alive. . . No, I'm afraid you must die," said The Ace of Spades, somewhat whimsical. Then The Ace's anger rose to the surface, his venom suddenly unleashed, declaring, "You have taken what is rightfully mine! You will die, Dante! Your father will die! Your fiancé will die! All of you! And. . . I will especially enjoy knowing your mother will die from where she came! Then my revenge will be complete!"

Before Dante could answer, Lucian appeared. He stood defiantly in his father's face. . .

"I will kill him! I demand it!" said Lucian, with eyes that reflected a lost soul.

The Ace hauled back his arm, about to slap him, yet again. With the quickness of a bullet, Lucian withdrew his sword, putting it to his father's neck. . .

"If you dare move your arm, I will kill you right here!" said Lucian, with a steely resolve.

The Ace of Spades certainly had been caught off his guard. I could tell he was outraged and yet, pleased by what Lucian had just done.

"Lucian, are you ready to die by my hand?" said his father.

"No! I am not. . . And it is you who will die by my hand, father! Make no mistake, it is more skillful than yours!" countered Lucian, still with is sword at his father's throat.

"No boy! Faster it may be, but not more skillful!" snapped back The Ace of Spades. "Step back and see!"

Lucian stepped back two paces, giving his father time to draw his blade. Everyone was stunned beyond belief!

"Boy! You have already made your first mistake. . . you let me draw my blade! Now feel its edge!" scowled The Ace of Spades, who lunged unexpectedly at his son. Lucian parried his advance, barely. Quickly, August ran in between the two men. . .

"This is madness!" he shouted at The Ace. You would kill your own son for your unbridled vanity!"

"NO grandfather!" said Lucian, sarcastically. "It is I who will kill him! I will be King!"

August went to Lucian, standing directly before him. . .

"Lucian, stop this nonsense!" said August.

"Out of my way!" replied an inflamed Lucian.

"You will have to go through me first!" said August.

Without hesitation, Lucian thrust his blade right into August's arm. Justice, Alysandra, and Phoebe gasped. Dante cringed at the sight. Justice ran to August's side. He was bleeding, badly.

"However, I am feeling generous today. . ." railed Lucian. "I have let you live to see me take the throne!" He arrogantly turned to his father. . . "En garde!"

Curiously, The Ace of Spades did not raise his blade.

"Put your sword down Lucian. . . You will die by my hand if you persist!" said The Ace of Spades.

Before Lucian could reply, The Ace turned to Krispen, pointing to Dante, and said, "Untie him!" Then he turned back to his son, and said, "Go on Lucian, today you have earned back the right! Kill him!"

Lucian smiled at his father. He watched as Krispen went over to Dante. The Ace shouted to a nearby 8, instructing, "Give him your sword."

As Krispen untied Dante, he whispered into his ear, "Just keep him at bay! Buy time for The Jack of Diamonds to return! It won't be long."

Dante was shocked by his words. Krispen moved back. The 8 threw his sword to Dante. The two cousins circled. Dante looked to Alysandra and his mother. Remarkably, both women's facial expressions were of firm resolve.

Lucian made the first lunge. The steel blades clashed. Dante parried successfully. Lucian charged again, wielding his sword like the wind. Blow after blow landed hard on

Dante's steel. The young King did not miss a single parry. Over and over they circled each other. Dante continued to defend rather than attack.

"This is the extent of your skill!" mocked Lucian.

"Cousin. . . why should I do anything else?" said Dante, goading him "You have not landed one blow yet, with all your so called skills of the blade."

The insult seemed to enrage Lucian even more, but this time, he remained focused. He charged relentlessly, over and over. Finally, Dante lulled him into thinking he would never lunge, only defend. From out of nowhere, Dante turned his next parry into a lunge; his blade pierced Lucian's left shoulder.

With boldness I have never seen before, Lucian grabbed the edge of Dante's blade with his right hand, and pulled it out of him while thrusting his blade into Dante's side. Both Alysandra and Justice winced at the sight. When The Ace of Spades saw this, he smiled broadly.

"Yes Lucian!" The Ace mused to himself.

Both cousins took a step back, neither yielding. Lucian again began his relentless lunges. Dante continued to stretch out time, skillfully parrying at will.

"Brother!" shouted The Jack of Diamonds. Approaching the crowd, unnoticed, from behind, Star at his side.

The Ace cold not believe his eyes; his brother boldly walking up to him, alone.

"Seize him!" shouted The Ace of Spades. Quickly, several soldiers surrounded The Jack of Diamonds, swords and guns drawn. None of the soldiers dared come up next to him. They all stood a few paces off. The Ace turned to Lucian, and ordered, "Halt!"

Lucian backed off, wanting to get a better look at his infamous uncle. The Jack forcefully grabbed Star by her hand. She was totally taken aback. He walked up to his brother, ignoring Justice and the others, and matter-of-factly said, " I believe this is yours!"

With that, The Jack threw Star toward his brother!

"She was quite convincing, I must admit!" said The Jack of Diamonds.

Star interjected passionately, "But you said you loved me. . . You said I was the only woman you ever loved! You said it to me, I know it was to me! You kissed my lips! I know what I felt! I know what you said!"

The Jack looked to Justice as he replied to Star, "I said, I loved Justice! That she was the only women I have ever loved! And I meant it!"

The Jack of Diamonds turned to his brother and said, "Did you really think she could fool me?"

"What does that matter. . . Only that her deception was sufficient to bring you back here. . . That is all that matters!" said The Ace of Spades. "And before you, she beguiled Dante, a most convincing Alysandra, wouldn't you say, nephew!"

Alysandra lunged after Star.

"You bitch!" she screamed out. Alysandra jumped on Star's back, clawing at her. She ripped her nails across her face. Everyone was stunned. All stood there mesmerized, watching the spectacle.

"How dare you touch my man!" screamed Alysandra.

Star was totally overwhelmed. Alysandra slapped her, punched her, and then pulled her hair out in clumps. She ripped at her clothes and repeatedly smacked Star's face. Alysandra tore the fallen Virtue apart.

"You harlot! I'm going to rip your eyes out! I'll kill you with my bare hands!" ranted an unrelenting Alysandra!

Alysandra threw Star onto the ground and kicked dirt up in her face. Next, she sat on her stomach and held Star's face with her left hand as she hauled back with her right, punching Star in her jaw. She passed out.

The Ace of Spades motioned to his soldiers. Quickly, they pulled an enraged Alysandra off of Star.

"I must say Dante. . . your betrothed is quite a handful!" Dante could not believe his eyes; he stood with his sword at the ready, only a few cubits from Lucian who had his sword pointing at Dante.

"Now that our amusement is over," said The Ace of Spades to The Jack of Diamonds. "You can watch your son die! Just as I planned! And after him, your precious Justice I will rape!"

The Jack of Diamonds laughed hysterically out loud. . .

"What is so amusing brother?" asked The Ace of Spades.

"But you only have eleven men and this passed out shape changing woman!" answered The Jack of Diamonds. "I'm afraid you're going to need a little more than that if you plan to challenge me and my son!"

The Jack of Diamonds looked at his brother long and hard, musing, "I do believe I have said these exact same words to you once before, Brother. It seems you are determined to keep on making the same mistake—over and over!"

With that, Krispen walked right up to The Jack of Diamonds with his sword sheathed. He looked into The Jack's eyes and then turned to The Ace of Spades, and said, "When I was but a boy, you killed my father because The Jack had let him live! You told everyone, including your father The King of Clubs, that The Jack had murdered him in cold blood. But it was your blade doing the bidding of your sick vanity that killed him, wanting to teach a lesson to the rest of your soldiers, who dared not speak a word!"

Krispen turned to his men. . . I have waited for just the right time to exact my revenge, and this is it. . . I stand with The Jack of Diamonds and Dante, the rightful King! Now, who stands with me!?"

None of the soldiers joined in. Arcus seized the moment, challenging Krispen. . . "You were always soft, Krispen! I'm going to enjoy running you through!"

"We shall see about who enjoys what!" answered Krispen.

The Ace of Spades stood calmly. He turned to his father. . .

"Well father. . . if you want to save them?" said The Ace of Spades. "Speak up now, and choose who you shall kill!"

August, weak from the loss of blood, walked up to his son and knelt before him.

"Please son, search you soul. You can end this hatred now. . . repent of your ways! I beg you!" said August, with his head hung low. Then, without looking up, August said, "If I choose to kill myself. . . will you keep your word and end this madness?"

"You would truly do this. . . to save Dante?" asked the shocked Ace of Spades.

August raised his head up to The Ace, and answered, "No son. . . to save you and Lucian! Your very souls!"

"And somehow you're certain that if you sacrifice your life, I and my son will repent, and begin a new heart?" asked The Ace of Spades.

"Yes, if that is what it will take to purge the poison I have sown in you," answered August.

"What do you think Lucian. . ?"

"Lets see, father. Put him to the test. . . Give him your dagger!" answered a brazen Lucian.

The Ace of Spades smiled broadly at his son, admiring his demeanor. He took out a small dagger from his waist belt and carefully handed it to his father. August looked back to Justice and then to The Jack, and then turned to Dante.

"No grandfather, don't!" implored Dante.

"I'm afraid, it is the only way!" answered a contrite August.

All stood by mesmerized, as August took the dagger and plunged it into his chest. Immediately, he fell forward onto the leg of his son who just stood there. The Ace of Spades bent down, staring into the face of his dying father, and callously said, "Your death is for naught, old man! Unfortunately for you, I feel no differently!" The Ace looked up at Justice and then to the others. . .

"You see! His life ends as an old fool!" said The Ace of Spades. "No different than this bumpkin," pointing to a semiconscious Henry.

With that, a resigned but determined August, near death, summoned strength from his spirit. He pulled the dagger out from his chest and quickly, with his last ounce of life, jammed it into his son's heart. The blade dug into The Ace's chest. He reeled back in pain; but the depth of the blow was not enough to kill. August looked up at The Ace of Spades, and said, "Forgive me my son!"

August fell to the ground, his arms outstretched.

"Kill them all now!" screamed The Ace of Spades, as he pulled out the dagger from his chest.

The soldiers advanced on The Jack and Krispen. They were outnumbered eleven to two, yet The Ace's soldiers were being killed, one by one. Dante and Lucian resumed their duel. Steel flew in every direction. Justice went over to August who lay dying on the ground. She held his head in her hands. The Ace grabbed Justice by the hair and held the dagger to her throat. . .

"Stop! Or I'll kill her now!" shouted The Ace of Spades.

The Jack, seeing Justice at the mercy of his brother, held his sword. The others followed. The Ace managed to get up, still with the dagger at Justice's throat, and ordered, "Dante! Over here now!"

Dante looked at the dagger on his mother's throat and immediately came over to The Ace of Spades. Quickly, The

Ace of Spades pushed Justice away and grabbed Dante as he had his mother; the dagger now at his throat. . .

"Now this is good, very good indeed!" said The Ace, pressing the dagger ever so harder on King Dante's throat.

A small blood trail began to flow down his nephew's neck.

"Lucian! You and Arcus join our third garrison. They are held up in the valley behind our camp!' said The Ace of Spades. "Marshall our forces and attack this peasant's castle! Re-take it at all costs! If I do not return, you are King! Be strong, ruthless! Do not be weak like these fools! Raise my castle to its former glory!"

Lucian, Arcus, and the remaining soldiers started to walk off. As Lucian passed Alysandra, he shouted to Arcus, "Bring her! I like her spirit! She will be my woman!"

Arcus grabbed Alysandra. She fought Arcus with all her might, kicking and screaming, clawing at his eyes, but to no avail.

Alysandra shouted, "Dante!"

Dante pleaded with his uncle, "Leave her, you have me! Isn't that what you wanted!?"

"Yes, nephew, but it is not I who takes her. . . It seems your cousin fancies her for himself!" mocked The Ace of Spades. "How fitting an end!"

Justice implored her husband, "Jack, save Alysandra. . . I'll take care of your brother!"

Justice removed the small gun hidden in her tunic. She held her arms outstretched, pointing the weapon directly at The Ace of Spades; her hands were steady. Immediately, The Jack ran in front of Lucian, drawing his sword on his nephew. At the same time, Krispen broke for Arcus, who had both his hands around Alysandra. The few remaining soldiers stood back, watching, as Krispen drew his sword on Arcus who pushed Alysandra away and drew his blade on Krispen. Nobody moved.

"It seems we have a bit of an impasse, brother. . !" said The Jack of Diamonds.

"Really brother? I do not think that is the case," said The Ace of Spades. "Consider carefully. . . I am prepared to die if need be; my son Lucian is as well. . . And most certainly, you, brother. . . have demonstrated over and over your willingness to give up your life for those you love. . . And then there is the virtuous Lady Justice, willing to do anything and prepared to die herself, if need be, to save her son. . . But, you both will yield to me, to save Dante's life. . . Of this I am sure."

The Jack of Diamonds knew his brother's words were true. He looked to Justice, still with her steady arms outstretched, gun in hand. He turned back to his brother. . .

"What do you want?" asked The Jack of Diamonds.

"Shut up!" scowled The Ace of Spades.

"Lucian, this is your chance to be King!" said The Ace of Spades. "Kill your uncle, and I will make you King now!"

"I will not duel with him brother. . . He is but a boy! And there is no need for his death!" The Jack said.

"Then your death will be swift, uncle. . . En garde!" said Lucian, stepping back and raising his sword.

"You will duel brother!" said The Ace of Spades, pressing the dagger a little harder into Dante's neck. Dante winced in pain. "Shall I plunge the blade all the way in!?" warned The Ace of Spades.

The Jack's eyes grew cold. . . "Very well, brother, but his death is on your head, not mine!"

Lucian seized an unfair advantage and charged The Jack of Diamonds as he was still talking to his father. Immediately, his blade cut The Jack's left arm. The Jack moved like a cat, lashing out at Lucian at will. In a matter of seconds, Lucian had all he could do to defend the lunges from The Jack. The Jack's blade sliced threw the air, barely making a sound. He cut Lucian on his right arm, lunged, and quickly pierced him in his left leg. Lucian dropped his sword, falling back to the ground. The Jack of Diamonds stood over him, holding the tip of his sword inches from his chest. . .

"Do you yield?" demanded The Jack of Diamonds.

"Never!" scowled Lucian.

"Very well" said The Jack, stepping back so Lucian could stand. Lucian picked up his sword and circled The Jack. The Jack lunged again and Lucian purposely dropped to the floor, rolling his body into The Jack's legs. The surprised Jack fell to the ground, and now, Lucian stood over him, with his sword pointing at The Jack. . .

"I learned that tactic from you uncle. . . The very same you used to best my father!" said Lucian, arrogantly. "It is quite legendary!"

"Well done boy, now strike!" said The Jack of Diamonds, curiously egging him on.

With darkness in his eyes, Lucian thrust his sword at the heart of The Jack of Diamonds. The Jack moved but a cubit, making sure the tip of Lucian's sword entered his upper shoulder. Lucian's blade went right through The Jack's skin, impaling into the ground. Lucian tried to remove his sword to strike again, but could not. The Jack raised both his legs up and kicked Lucian in his chest, knocking him backwards, still holding onto his sword. As Lucian fell back, the force of his bodyweight pulled the sword out of the ground and out of The Jack of Diamonds' shoulder. Quickly, The Jack rose, picking up his sword, and advanced on Lucian. They stood face to face, neither moving back. The steel from their blades relentlessly clashed with each simultaneous lunge. Blood from both of their swords spattered into the air.

The Jack picked up the pace of his lunges, masterfully snapping his sword from his wrist. Then, it was over. Lucian's sword flew out of his hand onto the ground. The Jack of Diamonds stood with the tip of his blade touching Lucian's heart.

Krispen momentarily took his eyes off of Arcus, looking to the duel. Arcus seized the moment and thrust his sword into Krispen's side; he dropped his sword and fell to the ground. Arcus raised his blade to finish Krispen, but then gasped out loud, blood running out from his side! Henry stood there, with a bloodied sword in his hand. Everyone was stunned. Henry stood in front of Phoebe and Alysandra; his sword at the ready, carefully watching the few remaining soldiers, who seeing the deteriorating situation, ran off. Henry then held his sword over Arcus.

"Help Krispen first, Phoebe!" said Henry, no longer The Fool. "Then attend to this one," pointing to Arcus.

An astonished Phoebe went to Krispen's aid. No one had seen Henry rise from the ground, let alone take a sword from the body of one of the dead soldiers.

Boldly, Henry shouted out to The Ace of Spades, "There is no need for further bloodshed! Release Dante and your son shall live!"

"Bumpkin! You do not give me orders!"

The Ace of Spades shouted to The Jack, "Release Lucian now, or I'll stick this knife into Dante's neck this instant!"

"Father, do not yield to him!" demanded Dante.

The Jack looked to his wife, still with her hands outstretched, then back to The Ace of Spades. . .

"Brother, let Dante go, and I shall let Lucian live. Then you and I can duel to the death," said The Jack of Diamonds.

"Very well brother. . . One of us will certainly die by the other's hand, today, here and now. . . It truly is better that way" replied The Ace of Spades. "Now, you first, let Lucian go!"

"Do I have your word. . ." demanded The Jack of Diamonds.

"Yes!" replied The Ace.

Slowly, The Jack of Diamonds raised his sword off of Lucian's chest. Quickly, Lucian backed away and picked up his sword, about to come to his father.

"No Lucian! Get Arcus and join the others. Take back my castle!"

"Father!" protested Lucian.

"Do as I say!" demanded The Ace of Spades.

Lucian went over to Arcus. Henry looked to The Jack who nodded back to him. Henry stepped back from Arcus. Lucian helped him up; his side now bandaged. The two quickly left, heading into the underground stronghold.

The Jack of Diamonds slowly moved toward The Ace of Spades.

"Now, release Dante," said The Jack.

"Yes brother, now Dante," answered The Ace of Spades, as his demeanor waxed more ruthless. "It's now Dante's time to die. . . before I kill you!"

Justice saw The Ace's hand start to press the knife into Dante's neck. Dante couldn't move and looked to his mother, nodding. Justice fired her gun. The bullet ripped into and out of Dante's fleshy neck muscle, and into the upper chest of The Ace of Spades. Dante dropped to the ground. Alysandra screamed out in horror, running over to him. The Ace's eyes bugged wide, barely standing, still not letting go of his knife.

The Ace stumbled forward toward Justice, bleeding from his upper chest. He raised his dagger hand and lunged toward her. Justice could not bring herself to shoot again. As The Ace of Spades was but a few cubits from Justice, who stood frozen, The Jack of Diamonds came up from behind Justice. He looked his brother directly in the eyes, and ran his sword right into his heart, the blade coming out of his back.

The horrified Ace grabbed the sword with both his hands. The Jack lifted up his foot and kicked him backwards. The Ace of Spade's body fell to the ground alongside that of August's dead body. The outstretched hand of August, once the mighty King of Clubs, now touched his son's hand; as if even in death, still trying to change The Ace's cruel heart. With his last dying breath, The Ace of Spades decreed, "Lucian will avenge me! He will kill Dante! For He is me, brother!"

The Jack took Justice into his arms. She was trembling, uncontrollably. Phoebe ran over to Dante. Henry helped Krispen up. In all the ensuing commotion, no one saw Star regain her consciousness, let alone leave, unnoticed.

Justice and The Jack went over to their son. Alysandra held him tightly; Father and mother smiled at the sight. Alysandra got up and threw her arms around Justice. . .

"You saved his life! You save our Dante, My Lady," said and impassioned Alysandra.

Dante looked up at his mother and then to his father. . .

"I didn't think she'd do it!" said Dante, now with his impish spirit back.

"Neither did I son!" said The Jack of Diamonds, also chiding her. "For once, she didn't flinch!"

Justice and the group smiled for the first time.

"You saved his life, Justice!" said Henry, with great admiration.

"I must admit my lady. . . That was one hell of a shot! It had to be perfect, or," Krispen said, pausing, not wanting to speak the alternative. "Where did you learn to shoot like that!?"

"Don't ask, Krispen! Father and I still have the scars from all her errant practice shots!" said Dante, playfully.

As Alysandra helped Dante up, he kissed her deeply.

"Young love! How wonderful," said a blushing Henry.

Phoebe, now more herself, challenged her husband, and said, "And where did you learn to wield a sword like that, husband?"

"Why from Kent," he answered, chuckling. "He would often teach me basic moves. I think he enjoyed the amusement; I often stumbled to the ground with each practice lunge."

Krispen went up to The Jack of Diamonds and shook his hand, boldly. Then he turned to Dante and kneeled. . .

"I pledge my loyalty to you, my King!" he said.

"Krispen, please, there is no need to kneel!" replied Dante, extending his arm out to him, gesturing for him to stand.

"Krispen, my brother spoke of a reserve garrison held up near his camp; how many men?" asked The Jack of Diamonds.

"More than one hundred strong; The Ace held back his largest force, in case the first two garrisons should be defeated.

"What news can you tell us of the castle?" asked Dante.

"Scouts have come back and reported that Kent and his unknown military commander. . ." said Krispen.

"Ah, that would be Chariot!" interjected Henry.

"Kent and this Chariot have successfully defended the first two waves of attack," continued Krispen. "I am told that the military maneuvers of this Chariot were extraordinary!"

"Excellent!" replied Dante.

The Jack of Diamonds smiled and said, "He is good! I've never seen anyone better."

"I knew Kent and Chariot would hold them off until we got back!" exclaimed Henry.

"Krispen, how long before this third wave attacks? And who leads them?" asked Dante.

"The Captain of this brigade is a soldier named Drake; he has the heart of a lion!"

"Have no fear Krispen. . . You haven't met Kent! He may be young like me, but his heart has no weakness!" exclaimed Dante, proudly.

Krispen's demeanor changed, his countenance fell, and said, "There is something I must tell you. . ."

Everyone could tell the forthcoming news would be bad.
"It's Kent. . . is it not so, Krispen?" said Justice.

"Yes, my Lady. During the second wave of our Archers,
one of their fire arrows struck him. Our scouts reported he
died within minutes. . ." said a reluctant Krispen.

Henry began to tear. Phoebe and Justice consoled him.
Alysandra put her arms around Dante; she too welled up,
tearing.

"He was like a son to Phoebe and me. We helped raise
him after Myra's death," said Henry.

"There is one more thing," said Krispen, to Dante and
The Jack.

Drake is brother to Lucian. . . Purportedly, The Ace was
father to both!" said Krispen. "Now that The Ace of Spades
is dead. . . Drake will not yield to Lucian; he will challenge
him for leadership and the throne. . . For he is the elder by
three years," said Krispen.

"Good!" said Dante. "Maybe that will keep them busy
for awhile while we regroup."

"Does this Drake have a hot head like his brother?" asked
The Jack of Diamonds.

"No, Jack. . . he is very well reasoned. But make no mistake, inside of him beats a firebrand's heart! If you ask me,
as much as they hated each other. . . their contempt for their
father was even greater!" answered Krispen. "The Ace of
Spades always favored Lucian. . . why, I don't know."

"Who is the mother of Lucian and Drake?" asked Justice.

"The Lady Arabella of Saxon," answered Krispen.

Alysandra's eyes bugged wide.

"Who did you say?!" exclaimed Alysandra.

"The Lady Arabella. . . of Saxon. . . My Lady," repeated
Krispen.

"Dante! The Lady Arabella is my cousin! She is the
daughter of my mother's sister, The Lady Cristiana, who
was lady at The Court of The King of Clubs! I never knew

her for she disappeared right before I was born! No one in my family has seen her in all that time. . . It was rumored that my aunt Cristiana gave birth to a girl named Arabella. I am told that no one knows if Arabella is alive or dead!"

Everyone expressed shock. . . All but The Jack of Diamonds. . .

"Arabella is alive! But where she is now, I do not know!" said The Jack of Diamonds.

All were befuddled by The Jack's cryptic declaration.

"Wait! Now, I remember her," interjected Phoebe "She is, or was, a most beautiful woman. Rumor had it that Arabella was the secret mistress of The Ace of Spades!"

"Jack, how do you know this woman?" asked Justice, instinctively inquisitive.

"She came to me once, and hired my gun" answered The Jack. "Before you and I met Justice."

"Why father?" asked Dante.

"At that time, she was with child, her second. Arabella was sure that a rumored secret was compromised and that The Ace of Spades had found out that her first born, Drake, was not truly fathered by The Ace. . . Her young hand maiden, Beatrix, betrayed her: also a mistress of my brother. . . When Arabella found out about The Ace's affair with Beatrix, she put a knife to the maiden's throat, and she quickly confessed of a plot by my brother to kill Drake, who was only two years old then. It seems my brother had been enraged by Arabella's deception," exclaimed The Jack of Diamonds, somewhat sarcastically. "Although, Arabella insisted that Beatrix's accusation was false: conjured up by Beatrix so she could have The Ace for herself!"

The Jack paused for all to take in what he had just said. . .

"I took the job, and shot the would be child killer. Then it was told: Arabella took a dagger and stood in front of her lover, my brother, and swore to kill herself, and The Ace's unborn child growing inside of her, if he ever dared to hurt her first born, Drake, again!

"Oh my God!" said an incredulous Justice.

"The fact that his dalliance with Beatrix was now known, coupled with Arabella's murder of Beatrix for betraying her, seemed to quell The Ace's wrath," continued The Jack of Diamonds. "But, if you ask me, he always wondered what the real truth was as to the father of Drake. . . himself, or someone else. . ."

The Jack shook his head and said, "Not really knowing for sure. . . He let Drake live! All of this took place before I even knew The Ace to be my half brother and The King of Clubs, my real father. . . Then Arabella simply disappeared. . ."

"This truly complicates things," said Henry.

"That may be so, but we need to get back to the castle and defend it!" said Dante, as he grabbed his head, still feeling faint.

Alysandra held him up, and said, "No Dante! You are too weak. . . You must rest!"

"Alysandra, I am King! Our soldiers expect me back to lead them!"

"Dante! Listen to your wife to be!" interjected Justice.

"Son, you are banged up pretty bad," said The Jack of Diamonds.

"Father. . . You look worse than me!" replied Dante.

"If I may," said Krispen. "My wounds are less severe than yours. I will ride to the castle and inform Chariot of all that has happened. There is no way that Lucian or Drake will attack immediately. We have a fortnight at the very least, maybe more; I'm sure of it."

"Dante, I agree with Krispen," said Henry. "Both of you need to rest here for a day or two. I will go with Krispen to confirm all he will say, and help make ready the next defense."

Dante looked to his father who nodded back. . .

"Very well. Krispen, you will guard Henry and Phoebe with your life. . .

"Yes my King," answered Krispen.

"Swear your oath before all now," said Dante, as King.

Krispen quickly kneeled on one foot and beat his chest, and said, "I swear my King! With my life if need be!"

Krispen rose and waited for Henry and Phoebe to embrace those remaining behind. As they walked off. . . Dante shouted, "Wait! Come back, Henry!"

The threesome stopped, puzzled by Dante's order.

"Henry, as Counselor, do you not have the legal authority to marry?

"Well. . . Yes. . . I believe I do, but I have never done so before, always a bishop," said Henry.

"Counselor Henry. . . Do you or don't you?" asked Dante.

Yes! I do," replied Henry, now with certainty of his authority.

Dante turned to Alysandra. . .

"Alysandra, over these past few days, repeatedly, you and I came close to losing each other, forever," said an impassioned Dante. "I declare before God, my mother and father, and these good people, my undying love for you! I do not want to spend yet not another minute on this Earth without you as my wife!"

Alysandra's heart leaped.

"I know this is not the wedding you've planned. . . But will you Alysandra DellaSalle marry me here and now!" asked an impassioned Dante.

Justice's eyes, along with Phoebe and Henry's, filled with joyous tears. Alysandra threw her arms around her King, holding him tightly. Then she knelt before him, solemnly, looking up at him. . .

"Yes, my King. And I too swear before God and this company, to love you forever and stand by your side always!

No matter what may come upon us. . . I am yours and yours alone! I love you Dante. . . with all my heart and soul!" she proclaimed.

Alysandra rose and stood next to Dante, holding his hand as much in love as in helping The King stand firm from his wounds. Phoebe poked Henry in his side, urging him to speak. . .

"By the authority granted me as Chief Counselor to the legal and rightful King," said Henry, with full weight. . . "I ask you the following: Do you Dante of Diamonds take this woman, Alysandra DellaSalle, to be your lawful wife and Queen forever, forsaking all and everything before her, as long as you both shall live on this Earth?"

"I do!" replied The King.

"And do you Alysandra DellaSalle, take this man, Dante of Diamonds, to be your lawful husband and King forever, forsaking all and everything before him, as long as you both shall live on this Earth?" asked Henry.

"I do!" replied Alysandra.

"Then, by the authority granted to me by The King's charter and by God's blessing, I now pronounce you Husband and Wife. . . King and Queen! Till death do you both part! You may now kiss the bride. . . although I think we've already covered that part!" said Henry, beaming from ear to ear!

The two lovers kissed passionately! Then Krispen raised his sword and shouted, "To Dante and Alysandra! King and Queen!"

Everyone raised their arms and shouted likewise, "To The King and Queen!"

Justice and The Jack came up to the loving couple and embraced them deeply. Alysandra put her arms around Justice and whispered in her ear, "Mother, I love him more than my own life."

"I know Daughter, you have had my blessing from the moment I saw the two of you together!" replied Justice, with great fondness. "Grow in each other's love. Care for each other, be kind to each other, respect one another." Then Justice's demeanor changed, and she fervently said, "And love him with the blazing fire and burning passions of the woman within you!"

With that Justice softly winked at Alysandra, who smiled and blushed in response to her unexpected provocative words. Henry and Phoebe, followed by Krispen, came up to Alysandra and Dante congratulating them. . .

Justice rested her head on The Jack's shoulder. The Jack put his arm around Justice's waist. . .

"Justice, I believe Dante has found a woman as worthy as his mother!" said The Jack of Diamonds.

Justice kissed his lips and said, "From the way she kicked the living tar out of Star, maybe even better" she answered, playfully.

"Justice. . I hope Dante's up to the task at hand! That's a lot of woman!" chuckled The Jack. "Better him than me!" as he took Justice passionately in his arms.

"J-A-C-K, you're terrible!" answered Justice, smiling.

"That I am Justice. . . That I am!" answered The Jack of Diamonds, grinning.

"Jack, now confess. . . Star really never fooled you did she?" asked Justice, with a tiny bit of uncertainty in her voice.

"Justice, as soon as she kissed me I knew!" Jack calmly replied.

"Then it's true, you did kiss her!?" asked Justice, accusingly.

"Yes, Justice! She looked exactly like you. Remember, she is a product of the black arts! But like I said, as soon as she kissed me, I knew," answered The Jack, with great care.

"Yes, it seems the black arts are a most convenient excuse. . . Now tell me this, how did you know!? Tell me how, Jack!?" demanded Justice, now a bit jealous.

"J-U-S-T-I-C-E. . . There is no other woman does that certain thing when they kiss—but you!" said The Jack of Diamonds, trying to hold off an innocent but guilty smile, as his wife scrutinized his facial expression. . .

"JACK! If you don't get that grin off of your face. . . I will make Alysandra's tirade on Star look pale compared to what I'll do to you!"

The Jack took her in his arms, devouring her lips and neck. Justice's tinge of jealousy disappeared. She fervently kissed her husband, at home in his arms where she belonged; overwhelmed with her love for him.

In all the years that I have observed The Jack of Diamonds, never have I seen such a profound sense of peace as that which now enveloped him. At that very moment, it was as if all the issues of his life had finally resolved.

As Henry, Phoebe, and Krispen departed, I saw The Jack of Diamonds look backwards to the bodies of his dead brother and that of his father, still with his hand touching The Ace of Spades. Tears began to run down his face. . .

He thought of The 3 and Cassie who raised him as father and mother. And then Lena who willingly gave up her life for him, though she never truly had his heart. He thought of Kellin, who he grew to love and respect for his courage and integrity; he missed him dearly. Then he fondly grabbed the red diamond around his neck and thought of his mother, the beautiful and virtuous Queen of Diamonds that he never knew, but who gave him the heart that he has.

The Jack wiped the tears from his face and looked again at his father's dead body. The love of his father that he had surely missed all of his life, now was his. And even though he had him only for a very short time, I was certain The Jack would carry August, not The King of Clubs, in his heart for the rest of his days.

The Jack turned and looked into Justice's eyes and knelt before her. He took her hand into his and kissed it. He knew full well that she saved his life, healing his heart. He rose, not saying a word and held her hand, walking slowly toward the house. The Lady Justice, known as The Queen of Hearts, cried tears of joy, humbled by The Jack's profound declaration of his love. Each of them put an arm around the other, saying not a word.

Theirs was a love destined before time, conceived of the spirit, together as one; fueled by fires of unbridled passion for each other. Their love was legendary; the tale of such would be passed down through the ages—until the end of time

43.

EPILOGUE - THE CREATOR'S GIFT

I finished the last scroll of the second book, not knowing what to do. Then, I heard the voice of my Creator. . .

"You have done well, Acellus. . . I am truly pleased," he said.

"But Lord, what is the meaning of all that I have seen? And who will read the words?" I asked, wanting to say more, but daring not to ask.

"All of Creation will read the scrolls. . . In these two books and the third yet to come," said the Creator.

"Will there be another scribe after me?" I asked.

"No, Acellus. . . You are my scribe. . . That is your purpose," he said. "You will write the last book."

I considered carefully his words. And now, I could see nothing but the void. My countenance sank. I realized how much I loved those of the Earth.

"Do not be troubled, Acellus. Ask me what you will," he said, knowing my innermost thoughts.

"Why Lord? Why have you allowed so much evil to attack those that are good!? I do not understand!" I asked, with reverence.

"Acellus, it is because of Divine love. . . My perfect love for all things I have Created!" he answered.

"Lord, I do not understand?" I replied, most humbly.

"My child, I give all of creation—free will. . . There can be no higher demonstration of my love. . ." he answered.

I paused to consider in the beautiful warmth and glow of God.

"But what will happen to those I have observed?" I asked.

"Life, my child. . . precious life. . . to be lived as one chooses" he said.

"But surely there are consequences for the evil that some of the Earth do?" I asked.

"That is so Acellus," he answered. "All actions have consequences, seen and unseen; some now. . . others later; this cannot be escaped. . . It is one of my universal laws of Creation."

I further thought to myself, again, not daring to speak my desire. . .

"Yes, Acellus, I will grant your request. . . You have but to ask in faith" said The Creator.

"You will Lord!?" I answered, in shock.

"Yes Acellus. .

"Thank you My Lord!" I said, certain of his truthfulness.

"Now sleep my child. And when your eyes awake, you will be one of the Earth—you will be human. . . as you have so desired to be."

"Will I still be able to see you and talk with you as I do now?" asked I.

"You will see me in all that you observe. You will talk with me, but not as you do now," answered The Creator. "Trouble not your heart, Acellus."

As I considered The Creator's words, I began to doubt—not sure if I wanted what I had hoped for.

The Creator smiled, knowing my thoughts, and said, "There will come a time when you will again see me as you do now, Acellus."

A sense of peace came over me. . .

My eyes grew heavy. . . In a flash, I was asleep. I remembered dreaming of all that I had seen. Everything contained in the scrolls of the two books I had written flashed in my mind. Yet, I knew there would be more, very much more. . . for evil was not done, only set back for a short time—certain that it would strike yet again. . .

My eyes opened. . . awake from my sleep. I was on the Earth—I am Human!

And then I saw her. . . Arabella of Saxon.

More cunning than The Queen of Spades. . .

More dangerous. . .

The Daughter of Darkness.

I could already feel her tentacles reaching!

I must protect Eleanor!

ACKNOWLEDGEMENTS

I want to acknowledge my youngest son and superb editor, Zack Hemsey whose eyes and heart locked up with my vision and narrative. Zack's creative insights consistently enhanced this work. There is none better.

To my beloved fiancé Toni, who believed in this book, page by page, as I wrote. She lights up my life each and every day. *I love you.*

To Arthur and Anne O'Brien, who when I first conceived of the project many years ago, when it was just in song form, immediately got it. To my wonderful sisters Jean Marie and Angela, who immediately felt the spiritual underpinnings, always encouraging. To my beloved daughter Tara, who when just a young girl of six, would often sing the title song I composed for this work; I can still hear her. To my beloved oldest son Louis Michael, who continually urges me forward. To Leona Bloom, whose final editing pass was outstanding.

And most importantly, to God Almighty, the Creator of all things.

CPSIA information can be obtained at www.ICGtesting.com
Printed in the USA
BVOW071306281011

274732BV00001B/1/P